# OTHER TITLES BY AMY HARMON:

*SLOW DANCE IN PURGATORY*
*PROM NIGHT IN PURGATORY*
*A DIFFERENT BLUE*
*MAKING FACES*

# Running Barefoot

## AMY HARMON

Copyright © 2012 by Amy Harmon
First Paperback Edition: April 2012
Second Paperback Edition: March 2014
Formatting by JT Formatting

Printed in the United States of America
Library of Congress Cataloging-in-Publication Data

Harmon, Amy, 1974-
   *Running Barefoot*: a novel / by Amy Harmon.—2nd edition
   ISBN-10: 1475043740
   ISBN-13: 978-1475043747

   1. Fiction—YA   2. Fiction—Coming-of-Age
   3. Fiction—Contemporary Women   4. Fiction—Christian Romance

http://www.authoramyharmon.com/

*For Shauna,*
*The first to read and love my book*
*And because she loves Levan.*

# 1. Prelude

I'VE LIVED ALL my life in a small town in Utah called Levan. Levan is located right in the center of the state, and people from the town like to joke about how Levan is navel spelled backwards. "We're the belly button of Utah," they say. Not very distinguished, I know, but it seems to help people remember the name. Generations of my family have lived in Levan, all the way back to the first settlers in the late 1860s, when the settlement had the nickname Little Denmark. Those first few families that settled the town were Mormons, trying to find a place to finally call home and be left alone, to raise their families and worship in peace.

Most of the people in the town were descendants of the fair-haired Danes. My Jensen ancestors were among those early settlers from Denmark, and my hair is still a pale blonde all these many generations later. My mom, with her rich brown hair, was the only non-blonde in the family, and she had no chance against a very stubborn Danish gene. My dad, my three brothers and I all share the same fair hair and sky blue eyes as my great, great Grandpa Jensen who crossed the plains as a very young man, settled in early Levan, built a house, and built a life.

Many years ago, Levan was a thriving little town, or so my dad said. Along Main Street there was Shepherd's Mercantile Store and an ice cream parlor where the ice cream was homemade from the blocks of ice cut and stored during the summer months in a big ice pit covered with earth, salt and straw. There was a healthy elementary school and a town hall. Then the new freeway was built, and it bypassed Levan by a few miles. The town had never been built to draw attention, but it began a slow death as the trickle of new blood slowed to a stop. The ice cream parlor was long gone by the time I was born, and then the mercantile had to close its doors.

The grade school fell into disrepair, shrinking to a one-room schoolhouse as the younger generation grew up and left without anyone to fill the desks they vacated. The older kids rode a bus for half an hour to a neighboring town called Nephi for junior and senior high school, and by the time I was old enough for elementary school there was one teacher for the kindergarten through 2nd grades and another for the third through sixth grades. Some people moved away, but most of the families that had been there for generations hung on and stayed.

All that remained along Main Street was a small general store where the townsfolk could purchase anything from milk to fertilizer. It boasted the name Country Mall. I have no idea why—it was the furthest thing from a mall there ever was. Long ago, the owner added a room on each end of the store and rented out the space for some locals to set up shop.

On one end it had a few tables and a little kitchen that served as a diner where the old men sat and drank their coffee in the morning. "Sweaty Betty" Johnson (we called her Mrs. Johnson to her face) ran the diner and has for longer than I can remember. She's a one-woman operation. She cooks, waitresses, and manages it all on her own. She makes fluffy homemade donuts and the best greasy french fries on the planet. Everything she makes is deep-fried, and her face has a permanent sheen from the grease and the heat, which is how she got the nickname Sweaty Betty. Even cleaned up for church on Sundays, her face glows, and sadly, it isn't from the Holy Spirit.

On the other end, my Aunt Louise provided cuts, color, and good company for most of the women in Levan. Her last name is spelled Ballow, but it's pronounced Ba LOO with the accent on Loo. So she called her shop Ballow's 'Do, but most people just called it Louise's.

Out in front of the "mall" there were a couple of gas pumps and a snow cone shack called Skinny's that Louise's kids (my cousins) run in the summer. Louise's husband Bob was a truck driver and was gone a lot, and Louise had five kids she needed to keep busy while she cut hair. Louise decided it was time for a family business. Skinny's Snow Cone Shack was born. Bob built a simple wooden shop that ended up looking a little like a tall skinny outhouse, hence the name Skinny's. The general store sold blocks of ice so they had a convenient source for their snow. Louise bought an ice shaver and some syrup from the Cola distributor in Nephi, along with some straws, napkins, and some Styrofoam cups in 2 sizes. It was a pretty simple business model with a very low overhead. Louise paid the kid on duty $5 a day, plus as many snow cones as they wanted. My cousin Tara, who is the same age as me, ate so many snow cones one summer that she made herself sick. She can't stand them to this day; even the smell of snow cones makes her gag.

There was a tiny brick post office down the street and a bar called Pete's right next to the church—interesting location, I know— and that was Levan. Everybody knew which skills each person possessed, and we had a blacksmith, a baker, even a candlestick maker. My dad could shoe a horse better than anyone; Jens Stephenson was a great mechanic, Paul Aagard, a handy carpenter, and so on. We had talented seamstresses, cooks, and decorators. Elena Rosquist was a mid-wife and had delivered several babies who had come without much warning, leaving no time to make the drive to the hospital in Nephi. We made do by trading on our skills, whether we had an actual sign out front or not.

Eventually, a few new families moved to Levan, deciding it wasn't all that far to commute to the bigger cities. It was a good place to settle in and a good place to have and create roots. In very small towns the whole town helps raise the kids. Everybody knows who everybody is, and if something or someone is up to no good, it gets back to the parents before a kid can get home to tell his side of it. The town wasn't much bigger than a square mile, not counting the outer-lying farms, but as a child it was my whole world.

Perhaps the smallness of that world made my early loss more bearable, simply because I was looked after and loved by so many. It made my later loss harder to recover from, however, because it was a collective loss, a very young life snuffed out on the brink, a shock to the sleepy community. No one expected me to move on. Like a shoe that has lost its mate is never worn again, I had lost my matching part and didn't know how to run barefoot.

The early loss I refer to was the death of my mother. I was just shy of nine years when Janelle Jensen, wife and mother, succumbed to breast cancer. I remember clearly how terrified I was when her beautiful hair fell out and she wore a little pink stocking cap to cover her baby smooth head. She laughed and said she would get a blonde wig to finally match the rest of the family. She never did; she was gone too soon. She had been diagnosed with cancer just after Christmas. The cancer had already spread to her lungs and was inoperable. By the 4th of July she'd already been dead for two weeks. I remember hearing the first sounds of celebration commemorating our country's independence, hating the independence that had been suddenly forced upon me. The jarring crack, boom, and whiz of neighborhood fireworks had my dad's lips tightening and his hands clenching.

He had looked at us, his four somber tow-heads, and tried to smile.

"Whaddaya say, J-Crew?" His voice had cracked on my mother's favorite family nickname. "You wanna drive into Nephi and see the big fireworks?"

My dad's name is Jim, and my mother thought their names starting with the same letter was just further proof that they belonged together. So she named each of her babies a J name to fit the mold. She wasn't terribly original, because in Levan you'll find families

4

with all K names, all B names, and all Q names. You name the letter, we've got it. People even have themes for their children's names, giving them monikers like Rodeo and Justa Cowgirl. I'm not kidding.

So in my family we were all J's—Jim, Janelle, Jacob, Jared, Johnny, and Josie Jo Jensen. The "J Crew." The only problem with that was that whenever my mom needed one of us she had to run through the litany of J names before she stumbled on the right one. I don't know why I remember this, small as it was, but in the days and weeks before my mom died, I don't ever remember her tripping over any of our names. Perhaps the distracting details of daily life that had once made her tongue-tied dissolved in their insignificance, and she gave her rapt attention to our every word, our every expression, our every move.

We didn't go see the big fireworks that year. My brothers and I wandered out to watch the neighbors set off bottle rockets and spinners, and my dad spent the night in the barn trying to escape the mocking sounds of revelry. Hard work became my dad's anecdote to depression; he worked endlessly and let alcohol blur the cracks in between.

We had a small farm with chickens and cows and horses, but farming didn't pay well, and my dad worked at the power plant in Nephi to make a living. With three brothers who were much older than I, my duties on our little farm were minimal. My dad did need a housekeeper and a cook though, and I expected myself to fill my mother's shoes. Jacob, Jared, and Johnny were 7, 6, and 5 years older than I was. My mom always said I was a beautiful surprise, and when she was alive I had relished the fact that I was the baby girl, doted upon by the whole family. But with Mom gone everything changed, and nobody wanted a baby anymore.

Initially, we had more help than we knew what to do with. Levan is the only town I know where no assignments are ever made to feed a family after a funeral. Traditionally, we have our viewings the day before the funeral and then again for an hour right before the service. After the funeral and the burial, the family and friends come back to the church for a huge meal served up by the good women of the town. No one ever says "I'll bring a cake," or "I'll supply the potatoes." The food just arrives—a plethora of meats, salads, and side dishes, cakes, pastries and pies. The women of Levan can make a spread unlike anything you've ever seen. I remember walking along the tables laden with food after my mother's funeral, looking at the beautiful assortment and not having any desire to eat a single bite. I was too young to understand the concept of comfort food.

The bounty continued for days on end after the funeral. Someone different brought dinner every night for three weeks. Nettie Yates, an older woman from down the road, came over almost every other evening and organized the food, putting most of it in containers and freezing it for later. No family could possibly eat the amount of food we received, even a family with three teenaged boys. But eventually, the food trickled to a stop, and the people of Levan moved on to other tragedies.

My dad wasn't very accomplished in the kitchen, and after months of peanut butter sandwiches and cereal, I asked my Aunt Louise to show me how to make a couple of things. She came over on a Saturday and showed me the basics. I made her outline in minute detail how to boil water (Keep the lid on 'til it boils, pull it off once it does!) how to fry eggs (You gotta keep the burner on low to cook eggs!) how to fry hamburger (Keep turnin' it 'til there's no more pink). I wrote everything down very carefully, making Louise describe each step. I wrote out recipes for pancakes (Turn them over when they get big moon craters in them), spaghetti (A touch of brown sugar in the sauce was Louise's secret), and chocolate chip cookies (It's the shortening that makes them soft and puffy). Louise was frazzled at the end of the day, but I had lists and lists of very detailed instructions, written in my childish hand, taped to the fridge.

After a month everyone was sick of pancakes and spaghetti— my brothers never get sick of chocolate chip cookies, and Louise said her head would explode if she "ever had to do that again," so I started asking women from church if I could come over and watch them make dinner. I did this every time I needed a new recipe. The women were always kind and patient, taking me through the process, describing the ingredients and where to find them in the store or in the garden. I even drew myself pictures of the cans and the cartons so I wouldn't forget what everything was. I made myself a vegetable chart with colorful depictions of what the TOP of the vegetable looked like (ie.carrots, radishes, potatoes) so I would know what to pull out of the ground. We didn't have our own garden the first couple of years after Mom died, but Nettie Yates let me raid her garden whenever I wanted. Eventually, she helped me plant my own little vegetable patch that expanded every year. By the time I was in high school, I had a good sized garden that I planted, tended, and harvested by myself.

I learned how to do the wash, separating out the whites from the darks, the grease-stained work pants from the regularly soiled clothing. I kept the house straight, imagining I was Snow White mothering the seven messy dwarfs. I even pedaled down to the old post office and picked up the mail every day. We didn't have mailboxes in front of our houses in Levan. Instead, everything was delivered to the post office, and each person in the town had a box and a key. Dad would lay out the things that needed to be sent, and I would make sure they had stamps and were taken to the post office. By the time I was twelve, I knew how to balance a checkbook, and my dad opened a household account for me. From that point on, I handled the utilities and the groceries from my account. Dad took care of the farm, and I took care of the house.

The only thing I did not want to do was look after the chickens. My mother had always taken care of the chickens, feeding them, gathering their eggs, and cleaning up after them. I had always been deathly afraid of the chickens. My mom told me once, when I was just a toddler, the boys had gotten distracted when they were supposed to be watching me. I wandered out to the barnyard and a particularly ornery red hen cornered me, and I was frozen in terror by

7

the time Mom found me. Mom said I wasn't crying, but when she picked me up I was as stiff as a board, and I had nightmares for weeks afterwards.

Chickens are hard to form attachments to. They are aggressive and ill-tempered and quick to peck and squabble. The first time I gathered eggs after Mom died, I almost hyperventilated I was so terrified. Little by little, the conquering of my fear made me feel powerful, and I began to take pride in caring for the unlovable birds. I named each one and talked to them as if they were my naughty children. With every task I mastered, the more in control I felt, and I became very adept at trudging along in my mother's footprints.

# 2. Maestro

I LIKED HAVING a purpose, I liked being needed, and I found that serving my dad and my brothers made me love them more. Loving them more made it easier to live without my mom. I had been a serious child before, more content to be alone than with playmates, but my mother's death made my solitary nature more solitary still. The more independent I got, the harder it became to act my age; I didn't climb up in my dad's lap or demand to be hugged and kissed. I didn't throw fits when I had been ignored too long. I suppose I acted like a very small grown-up. Loneliness wasn't something I minded all that much. It was better than other people's sympathy pressing at me all the time.

There were times, especially the year after my mom's death, when the grief in our house felt like putting a heavy quilt over your head and trying to breathe. The weight of our combined sadness was claustrophobic, and I found myself grieving away from home as much as I could. When I wasn't busy with chores, I would get on my blue bike and pump my legs as hard as I could until I reached the little cemetery at the bottom of Tuckaway Hill, about a mile from my house. I would sit by my mom's grave and let the silence loose the blanket of unshed tears until breathing became easier. I would bring my books and read with my back pressed up against the stone that bore her name. My books were my friends, and I devoured everything I could get my hands on. All my favorite characters became my heroes. *Anne of Green Gables* became my best friend, *A Little Princess,* and *Heidi,* sources of strength and example. I relished happy endings where kids like me triumphed in spite of hardship. There was always hardship in the stories, and this realization comforted me. I was inspired by sacrifice in *The Summer of the Monkeys,* and planted a red fern at my mother's grave for Dan and Ann after reading *Where the Red Fern Grows.*

It was on one of these days, reading alone in the cemetery, a little more than a year after Mom died, when a long, white Cadillac slowly slid its way down the dirt road that ran along the west side of the cemetery. There were no white Cadillacs in Levan; actually, there were no Cadillacs at all in Levan, white or otherwise. I watched as it made its way towards me, kicking up dust and drawing my attention from *The Lion, the Witch, and the Wardrobe,* which I had read twice before. It purred by and climbed the lane that led to the Brockbank summer homes on Tuckaway Hill. Maybe a new family had moved in. I was suddenly, overwhelmingly, curious to see where that car was going. I figured I could be sneaky, using the sagebrush as cover if I felt exposed when I got close. The lane was steep, and my skin was itchy with sweat and dust as my bike leveled out on the top of the hill.

Three beautiful homes had been built on Tuckaway Hill, all owned by a wealthy family named Brockbank. Apparently, the Brockbank sons, who dabbled in contracting and development, had had the idea that the hill would make an ideal summer retreat for the wealthy family and had built an impressive little compound. The Brockbanks and their grown children had visited the different homes at various times, but the houses had been empty now for several years. They had named the hill Tuckaway, but apparently it was too tucked away, because none of them ever came for very long.

The door to the garage of the largest home stood wide open, and the white Cadillac was parked demurely inside. I couldn't see anyone around—no boxes or moving van, no children's toys abandoned haphazardly on the walk.

I didn't dare knock, and peeking through windows when some-one was home was far too brazen for my cautious nature. I turned to go when a violent noise startled me into dropping my bike and yelp-ing in surprise. Belatedly, I realized someone was playing the piano with serious gusto. I didn't recognize the song, but it wasn't pretty. It was crashing and intense and reminded me of the kind of music that would be in a scary movie—a scary movie where the little girl who is snooping on someone else's property gets murdered by the crazy owner. I was seriously spooked and picked up my bike, only to dis-cover that the chain had come off when I dropped it. I squatted down and quickly began trying to force the greasy chain back around the sprocket. This had happened to me before, and I knew how to get it back on.

As I worked, I listened nervously to the powerful music pouring out of the house. All at once, the music changed and morphed into something equally powerful, but infused with joy in every note. The music swelled in my heart and had tears filling my eyes and over-flowing onto my cheeks. I wiped at them in amazement, leaving a streak of grease down the side of my face.

Music had never made me cry before. And these weren't sad tears. The music I was hearing made me feel the way I sometimes felt in church when I sang songs about God or Jesus. But it made me feel that way without any words. I loved words. I was surprised that the music could talk to me without speaking. I listened as long as I dared, and when the song seemed to near its soaring conclusion, I picked up my bike and sped away, pedaling in time with the music that now filled my head.

"It's a retired doctor and his wife," my dad told me at dinner that night when I relayed the story of the white Cadillac. "Name's Grimwald, or something or other."

"Grimaldi," Jacob corrected with his mouth full of mashed potatoes. "Rachel and her mom helped clean the house before they moved in."

Rachel was Jacob's girlfriend. Rachel's mom was the president of the women's organization at our little church, and duty made her a busy woman. It also provided an opportunity for firsthand knowledge of all the town's goings-on, although she wasn't the type to abuse her position.

"Rachel said the doc's wife insisted on paying them," Jacob continued. "She got kinda feisty when they refused. Rachel said her mom kept saying they were glad to help and wanted to serve. The doc's wife finally gave in, but said that if Rachel wanted to come back she would pay her to clean once a week." Jacob settled back with a satisfied burp.

"Why did they move to Levan?" I questioned. "Are they related to somebody?" Levan was a far cry from St. George three hours south, where retirees commonly moved to soak up sun and enjoy easy winters.

"Rachel says the old man is writing a book and he wants peace and quiet," Jacob said matter-of-factly. "The doc's wife said they are old friends of the Brockbanks, and Levan seemed like a good place to find it."

I thought of the loud and passionate music of earlier that day. It definitely hadn't been quiet then. I resolved to wheedle Rachel into taking me along when she went to clean again. And that was how I met Sonja Grimaldi.

Rachel was a tiny, pretty redhead who was good-natured and very hardworking. She was always moving and doing. She referred to everything as a thingy or a dilly, and she would probably never gain a pound, as she worked as fast as she talked and never seemed to tire. I loved her, but too much time in her presence made me long to sit down and drown in a deep book. She was a perfect complement to my laid-back, slow talking oldest brother, and I was grateful that someday she would probably be a Jensen, and I would have a sister.

That Saturday she was happy to let me tag along to the Grimaldis, and I found myself looking forward to hearing more music, hoping that whoever had played before might do so again. The Grimaldis were nowhere to be found when we arrived, though Rachel didn't seem concerned and immediately got to work. I tried to help her clean, but she shooed me away good-naturedly, saying she didn't want to share her profits. I tip-toed through the kitchen and into the room where I thought the piano must be. The piano was an enormous, black, shiny showpiece, the lid raised high, the seat a long smooth slash of ebony. I desperately wanted to sit down and run my hands across the keys. So I did. I slid onto the bench and rested my hands gently on the glistening whites. I played each one very, very softly, enjoying the individual sounds, the clear tones.

"Do you play?" a voice said behind me.

My heart jumped out of my chest and tumbled to the floor as I sat frozen, my hands still on the keys.

"You touch the keys so reverently, I thought you must play," the voice continued.

My heart returned to my chest, pounding loudly to let me know I was still alive. I stood and turned guiltily. A bird-like woman, not much taller than me, stood just behind me. Her silver hair was fashioned in an up-do, all swooped the way Jane Seymour had worn hers in *Somewhere in Time*. She wore black horn-rimmed glasses on her very long nose and a deep purple pantsuit with matching purple gems that I later learned were called garnets at her ears, hands, and throat.

"I'm Josie," I stammered. "Josie Jensen. I came with Rachel. I don't play...but I wish I could."

She glided past me and sat herself regally on the black bench I had vacated.

"Who is your favorite composer?" Her glasses slid down her nose as she tipped her face forward, peering at me above the rims.

"I don't know any of the composers," I confessed sheepishly. "Most of the music I know I hear at church or on the radio. I do love to hear the organ play the hymns." Thoughts of Jane Seymour moments before brought a memory to mind. "There was this music in a movie I saw once. It was my mom's favorite, and she cried whenever she watched it. The movie was called *Somewhere in Time* ... do you know it?" I rushed on when she didn't respond. "There was this beautiful song that kept playing."

"Ahhh, yes," she sighed. "That is one of Rachmaninoff's creations. Was it this?" She started to play the romantic strains of the music I remembered. I sank to a nearby chair and listened to the soul-stirring piece. I felt my heart swell to bursting and the tears rise in my eyes just like before.

She turned toward me as she finished and must have seen something in my face, must have seen how the music touched me.

"How old are you, child?" she asked quietly.

"My birthday is September 1st. I'll be ten on Tuesday," I answered shyly. I knew I looked older, and I always felt funny when I confessed my age.

"How does the music make you feel?"

"Alive," I responded immediately and without thought, and I blushed a little at my answer.

She seemed oddly satisfied.

"Would you like to learn to play?"

"I would love to!" I exclaimed, exuberant. "I'll have to ask my dad...but I'm sure he'll let me!" A thought clouded my happy musings. "How much does it cost?" I worried.

"The only cost is the pleasure of your company and the solemn promise that you will practice very hard." She shook her finger at me sternly. "The child who does not practice does not proceed with further lessons."

"I will practice harder than anyone has practiced before!" I promised sincerely.

"Has school started?"

"Yes, ma'am. It started last week."

"Then I will see you Monday after school, Josie." She held out her bony hands and clasped mine gently, sealing our deal. It was the best birthday gift I ever received.

Sonja Grimaldi had been a professor of music for thirty years. She had met and married her husband Leo, aka Doc, later on in life, and though Doc had a son from an earlier marriage, they had never had any children together. It had been a series of strange events and coincidences that had brought them to Levan. Doc had been a friend to the senior Mr. Brockbank since they'd gone to school together as young men. Doc had been the family physician since he had graduated from med school. Both Sonja and Doc were in their seventies but still spry and ambitious. Doc had always wanted to write, but while he practiced medicine he had never found the time. Sonja had the notion that she might like to compose a little as well, and Tuckaway Hill had seemed the perfect writer's retreat.

I combed the Penny Pincher classified ads for a few weeks until I found a piano for sale. It proved to be old and ugly, but it had a rich, lovely sound. I contributed all the money I had been saving from selling my chicken's eggs at the weekly farmer's market and paid for it outright. My dad grumbled a little when it cost $75 to have someone come all the way to Levan to have it tuned, but he paid for it, warning me that I had better practice.

Practicing wasn't my problem. I couldn't tear myself away from the keys. Sonja was an unconventional teacher, and I was a gifted student. Instead of lessons once a week, like most students, I had a lesson every afternoon. I flew through the rudimentary lessons,

quickly grasping musical concepts and theory, graduating to inter-
mediate books and songs after only a month. For a while I even
stopped reading, pushing everything aside for my music. I practiced
every spare moment. Luckily for my dad and my brothers, they were
outside more than they were in the house, and I rarely disturbed anyone with my obsession. Sonja said I was not exactly a child prodigy,
but close. I had deep passion and appreciation for the music, and I
quickly absorbed everything she taught me.

I learned that the music that had so frightened me the day I had
followed her white Cadillac home was a piece by Wagner. She pronounced it Vah gner. I didn't care much for Wagner, but Sonja said
it got her blood boiling, and she used it to give voice to her "savage
beast." She smiled when she said this, and I smiled with her. I didn't
think Sonja was ever "beastly." Sonja said we all had a little of the
beast in us.

If Wagner spoke to the beast, then Beethoven gave voice to the
beauty. Beethoven's ninth symphony became my lifeblood. I made
Sonja play it each day at the end of our lessons, and each day I
would leave full of hope, the beast vanquished.

Ten-year-old girls without mothers should not have to bear the
burden of early puberty, but be that as it may, I started my period not
long after I met Sonja Grimaldi. I believed myself stricken with
some sort of terrible malady when I discovered the blood in my un-
derpants. Overwhelmed, I had cried out my fear of certain death to
Sonja. She had been playing Beethoven's *Moonlight Sonata*, and the
beauty and melancholy of the music had me drowning in self-pity.

"I think I'm dying, Mrs. Grimaldi," I had wept. She had gathered me to her wispy self and coaxed further confession from me.
When she realized what was actually happening to me, she sighed

and put me away from her, tears glittering in her eyes.

"Josie! This is not death! It is a rebirth!" she exclaimed dramatically.

I stared at her with a dumbfounded frown.

"It is not surprising, you know. You are beyond your years in every other way. You have earned this rite of passage much sooner than most girls. Josie, womanhood is an incredible gift! It is God-given. It is bestowed upon us. Womanhood is incredibly powerful, and you have been entrusted with it years before your peers. This means you are very special in His sight. We must celebrate!" She clapped her hands and rose with a swoosh of her long red kimono.

So we did. We lit candles and had sparkling cider in crystal goblets. She read the story of Queen Esther with great passion, telling how her beauty, grace, and courage had saved her people. How her power had influenced nations. She read to me the story of the Virgin Mary from the New Testament, a girl only a few years older than I was, and mother to the Savior of the World.

Days later, Sonja and I drove to the city, and she bought me new underwear and bras in pretty pastels with matching undershirts to wear until the bras were absolutely necessary. We got our nails done, and she purchased enough feminine supplies to stock my bathroom drawer for several years. I felt my mother's presence that day and knew she had been instrumental in bringing Sonja Grimaldi into my life. After all, hadn't I been at her grave the day I first saw the white Cadillac? After that, I was much more secure in God's love for me, and I did not curse my rapid ascent into womanhood again.

One afternoon in early spring, I arrived for my lesson to find Sonja lying on the sofa with a book lying on her chest, her eyes closed.

"Sonja?" I whispered, not wanting to wake her, but not wanting to leave if she was in need of something. I was a little scared. She looked small and tired, and it made me think of my mom before she died, shrunken and pale.

"Sonja?" My voice quavered, and I put my hand on her arm.

She opened her eyes sleepily, her brown eyes huge beneath the thick Coke bottle lenses of her horn rims.

"Oh, Josie! Is it that time already? I was trying to read, and my eyes just get so tired when I read lately. I'm afraid I'm going to have to give up my books." She said the last part a little mournfully. Sonja was not a mournful individual in the slightest, and I looked closer at the book that she had been reading.

"*Wuthering Heights*," I read aloud. "What if I read to you while you rest your eyes? I'm an excellent reader."

Sonja smiled at this serious declaration of my ability and handed me the book. "All right then, you read for a while, and then we'll practice."

I hated *Wuthering Heights*. Each day I would come for my piano lessons, and I would read to Sonja for a half an hour before we began. After one week of *Wuthering Heights,* I threw the hated book down in disgust. Though I was young, I was sensitive and thoughtful, and with Sonja's explanation of different words and phrases, I had grasped most of what I had been reading and had comfortably followed the story line.

"These people are horrible! I hate them! I can't read this anymore!" I surprised myself by bursting into violent tears, and gulped desperately to rein in the embarrassing display.

"They are, aren't they?" Sonja agreed quietly. "Too much ugliness for a tender spirit. Maybe someday you will read it with different eyes...but maybe not. No more Heathcliffe for now. Off to the piano with you, child!" she said briskly, and I followed her meekly, scrubbing my eyes and feeling relieved that I would not have to spend any more time wandering the moors with ghosts.

The next day a new book was waiting for me. I noticed the author was also named Bronte, and cringed inwardly. But Jane Eyre was nothing like Catherine Earnshaw Linton. I adored *Jane Eyre* and begged Sonja to let me take it home to read between our visits. She acquiesced graciously, but made me promise to write down every word I didn't understand and look it up, so that I would truly grasp what I was reading. When Sonja found out I didn't have a dictionary of my own at home, she gave me a copy of Noah Webster's 1828 Dictionary. She said it was the second most important book in the English language, next to the Bible.

I kept my promise and, reading late into the night, would pencil words I couldn't define onto the wall above my bed. The next day I would delve into my heavy dictionary and look up all the words I had written the night before. With every book my "Wall of Words" grew, as did my hunger for more words. One day many months later, my dad climbed into the loft that served as my bedroom—which he rarely had reason to do—looking for something. I was downstairs whipping up a new recipe in the kitchen, and I dropped the mixing bowl when he bellowed my name.

I came running, fearing some disaster had occurred and found him staring at my wall in outrage.

"Josie Jo Jensen! What in the world is this?" He threw his hand toward the wall behind my bed, which was now partially covered in words.

"It's my Wall of Words, Dad," I supplied meekly. When he glowered at me and folded his arms across his chest, I decided I'd better explain myself further.

"See, at night when I'm reading I don't like to stop in the middle of the story and look up words I don't know…so I write them on my wall and look them up in the morning. It's very educational!" I said brightly, smiling at him hopefully.

My dad shook his head, but I saw a flicker of a smile across his lips. He walked over to the wall and read some of my words.

"Ameliorate?" he read doubtfully. "Now that's one I've never heard before."

"Ameliorate means to make better. My 'Wall of Words' *ameliorates* my vocabulary," I said cheekily.

My dad laughed out loud. "It does, does it?" He shook his head and looked at me fondly, all traces of anger gone. "All right, Josie Jo. You can keep your wall. But keep it up here, okay? I don't want words written all over the kitchen when you run out of room."

"Maybe I should start writing smaller," I said, suddenly concerned at my limited wall space.

I heard my dad laughing as he descended the narrow stairs.

# 3. Overture

SONJA HAD MADE the difficult shift into maturity easier than it would otherwise have been, but I still had to endure the scrutiny that my changing body encouraged. By the time I entered the seventh grade, I was fully grown. Though I was slender, I was taller than average and had breasts and curves when boys my age were still wetting the bed. Tara thought I was the luckiest girl alive and pestered me with personal questions and even asked me once if she could wear my bra "just to see how it feels to be a woman."

Being the only girl in a family of boys made my wardrobe choices pretty limited. I wore my brothers' old T-shirts and hand-me-down Wranglers because that's what we had. My dad had never thought to do anything different, and I'd never thought it important enough to ask. I had outgrown Sonja's underwear purchases the first year, and if it wasn't for my Aunt Louise making sure I had a sturdy bra I don't know what I would've done. The boyish clothing mostly disguised my figure, although I hunched my shoulders to hide my height and my breasts and was constantly self-conscious and awkward.

Sonja had insisted I get my eyes checked when I persisted in putting my face too close to the sheet music, "ruining my playing posture." I needed glasses to read or play the piano and since my nose was constantly in a book, I wore them most of the time. I used big words and blurted out deep thoughts, and I think my peers considered me extremely strange when they considered me at all.

The seventh grade was part of the junior high, and I was relieved to be leaving elementary school behind, hoping it would be easier to blend in with the older kids. But junior high was just a different kind of torture. The junior high was made up of grades 7-9, the high school consisted of grades 10-12, and we all rode the same bus into Nephi for school. I hated riding the bus. Johnny was a senior the year I started seventh grade. He drove Old Brown, our ancient farm truck, into school most days because he played several sports and practices were after school. Sometimes he gave me a ride, but more often than not, he took his friends, leaving no room for his little sister. The bus was loud and slow with kids crawling all over the place. I hated the elbows in my sides, the fighting, and worst of all, finding a seat.

The bus stop by my house was one of the very last, and every day I would dread walking down the aisle of the full bus, looking for a place to sit down. I drew unwanted attention from the high school boys, snickers from the younger boys, and confusing animosity from most of the girls. Tara, loyal cousin and friend, usually tried to save me a seat, but I almost preferred not to sit by her. At thirteen she was about as big as a nine-year-old, and our size difference made my discomfort all the more severe. Not only was she little, she was loud, and where I would prefer to shrink into the background, she would call attention to herself every chance she got.

There was an 11th grade boy named Joby Jenkins who sometimes hung around with my brother Johnny. He liked being the class clown and thought he was the funniest kid on God's green earth. I didn't like him very much. His humor was usually mean-spirited and always at the expense of someone weaker. The younger kids on the bus were his targets. My dad said he was a smart ass, but mostly he was just an obnoxious bully. Above all, I couldn't stand him because he stared at my chest whenever he saw me. Johnny seemed oblivious to this, as usual, and he thought Joby was hilarious and fun to be with. Because Joby didn't play sports he always rode the bus, holding court way in the back, making many kids' lives miserable.

One particular morning in early fall, I climbed on the bus, nervous and desperate for a seat, as usual. Tara waved at me and pointed excitedly to the nametags stuck on each seat. Mr. Walker, the bus driver, had made seat assignments. I felt a rush of relief and started looking for my name. Assigned seating meant never having to find a place to sit, and I was ridiculously grateful as I searched for mine. I began to notice that most of the younger, smaller, kids had been seated with older kids, making the three to a seat rule a little more comfortable. As I neared the back of the bus, red heat crawled up my face as an all too familiar voice rang out.

"Josie Jensen! Come to papa!" Joby Jenkins called out in a singsong voice. Everyone around him burst into laughter. "Hey, we can play Cowboys and Indians! Don't worry, Jos. I won't let Sammy here make you his squaw."

I had found my assigned seat. My name was on the seat just across the aisle from Joby. Joby was sitting with his legs in the aisle so his knobby knees and big feet in unlaced Reeboks made it impossible for anyone to get by without confrontation. He patted the green plastic across from him. Sitting inside the seat beside him was Samuel Yates.

Samuel Yates was the grandson of Don and Nettie Yates who lived just down the road from me. Don and Nettie's son, Michael, had served a Mormon mission on a Navajo Indian reservation twenty plus years ago. After his mission, he ended up going back to Arizona for some job. He had married a Navajo girl and they had Samuel. A few years later, Michael Yates was killed when he was thrown from a horse. I don't remember the details. It all happened when I was little, but in small towns everyone's story becomes known eventually.

I had heard about Samuel when several women, including Nettie Yates, had gathered in our kitchen to do some canning. Every year since my mom died, my neighbors would bring fruit and vegetables from their own gardens and can all day, filling our shelves with their

23

labors. That day in August, the kitchen was uncomfortably warm and smelled of stewed tomatoes. I listened to the women visit as I wished for freedom from the endless canning, although my gratitude would not allow me to leave. I found myself drawn into the conversation out of sheer boredom. Nettie Yates was venting her concerns to the other women:

"He's gotten so his mother can't handle him. She remarried, ya know. Seems Samuel doesn't get along too well with his step dad and his step siblings. My opinion is there is some alcohol involved. The step dad drinks too much, I think. Samuel's gotten in several fights this year, and he was kicked out of the school on the reservation. He's an angry boy, and I'm a little worried about having him come live here." Nettie Yates paused for breath and then continued. "I just hope people are good to him. It's what Michael would have wanted. We'd have taken him when Michael died, but his mother wouldn't hear of it. We told her to bring Samuel and come live with us, but she ended up going back to the reservation to live with her mother. Can't say I blame her. It's what she knew, and there is comfort in that, especially when you lose someone you love.

"We've barely seen the boy all these years. Don's looking forward to having Samuel help with the sheep. Them Navajos know about sheep, ya know. Samuel's helped his grandma tend sheep since he was six years old. Anyway, he'll attend school here for his senior year and hopefully graduate. Then he'll be old enough to decide what he wants to do." Nettie finished the telling with a long sigh as she continued to slice ripe tomatoes into her bowl, never breaking rhythm.

Samuel looked up at me as I tried to slide past Joby into my seat. Samuel's dark eyes and wide mouth were unsmiling, his eyebrows drawn together in an irritated slash against his warm brown skin. His shiny black hair skimmed his shoulders. I had never said two words to Samuel Yates. In fact, I'd never heard him speak at all. His face was filled with hostility, and his wide mouth turned down as he looked away. I inched past Joby, trying not to touch him as I sat down. Joby moved at the last minute, pulling me into his lap.

"Josie!" he said in mock surprise. "I didn't *really* mean come to papa!" Everyone laughed again as he pretended to push me off, all the while making it impossible for me to get free of his long arms and big feet.

I felt tears spring to my eyes as he continued to tickle me and jostle me around. Someone in front of me must have noticed my mortified expression, because a voice called out, "Uh oh, Joby! She's gonna cry!"

Joby whooped and looked down at me. "Don't cry, Josie! I'm just messin' with ya. Here, I'll kiss it better." Joby stuck out his lips comically and smacked a big kiss on my cheek.

"Stop it, Joby!" I sputtered and elbowed him as I fought my way out of his messy embrace. Suddenly, Joby pushed me onto Samuel. My head collided with the window, and my backpack slid down and pinned my arms behind me. I found myself face first in Samuel's lap and yelped as he jerked me upright. The kids around us howled with laughter.

Suddenly, Samuel's right arm lashed out and pushed Joby clean off the seat. Joby landed with a loud thump right in the aisle. Surprise whooshed out of his lungs in a startled grunt. Before I could register what was happening, Samuel maneuvered me across him and sat me down next to the window. He stood up slowly and leaned over Joby's stunned person. The laughter faded to nervous twitters, and then there was silence. The kids around us stared, their mouths and eyes wide. My face throbbed with humiliation. I felt faint, and I realized I was holding my breath. Samuel stared down at Joby, his arms braced on the seats on either side of the aisle. Joby stared back at him. His mouth was working but no words were coming out, as if he hadn't narrowed down what to say next.

"Don't cry, Joby! I'm just messing with you." Samuel's voice was deep and soft, his face completely expressionless. The kids who had been laughing started laughing again.

The bus had just pulled up to the last stop when the confrontation in the back of the bus drew the driver's attention. Samuel had pretty much ignored everyone since he started school two months ago. He hardly spoke, but he was tall enough and intimidating enough that everyone steered pretty well clear of him. Everyone, including Joby, stared at him incredulously.

"No fighting on my bus, boys!" Mr. Walker, the bus driver, yelled back as he threw the bus into park, engaging the brake and disengaging his seatbelt in a huff. He rushed down the aisle towards Samuel. Without acknowledging Mr. Walker's approach, Samuel slowly bent down, extended his hand, and pulled Joby to his feet. Then, like he had all the time in the world, he turned and looked down at poor Mr. Walker. He reached over and pulled Joby's name-tag off the seat where I was now sitting. I flinched and ducked my head as all eyes flew to me.

"Joby needs a new seat," Samuel said softly. He pressed the curling white label against Joby's forehead, all the while staring at the bus driver calmly. Mr. Walker looked confused, and Joby was, for once, at a loss for words.

"Can't he sit there?" Mr. Walker questioned, pointing to the seat I was now occupying. I noticed how Mr. Walker's voice had immediately softened to match the volume of Samuel's quiet declaration.

"Somewhere else," Samuel enunciated slowly, his voice still smooth. His eyes stayed on Mr. Walker's face for a moment, and then he moved out of the aisle and sat down next to me, turning his attention out the window. He didn't say anything else.

Mr. Walker quietly pulled my nametag from the seat across the aisle, put it on the seat where I was now sitting next to Samuel, and directed Joby to sit down in my place. Joby pulled the sticker from his forehead, the tables having been completely turned. He stuck his nametag in some kid's hair and laughed uproariously. He then slapped another in the back of the head, trying to downplay what had just happened. If I hadn't seen it myself I wouldn't have believed Joby had been knocked down and not responded with a fist and a few foul words. The only thing he said was "Damn! I guess Sammy doesn't like me!" The kids around him giggled nervously, and Joby shot a look at Samuel again. Samuel just stared over my head out the window and didn't respond or even appear to be aware of him at all.

Winter came early, and by the end of October, Levanites had their kids bundled in moon boots, hats, and puffy coats that made movement awkward. I had turned thirteen September 1, and in anticipation of the upcoming cold season, my Aunt Louise bought me a new coat in a bright, periwinkle blue. It was the nicest thing I had ever owned. My dad told her we didn't need her charity when she had brought it over. Aunt Louise was my mom's younger sister, and she proceeded to rip him up one side and down the other. It had been a couple of years since I'd had a new coat. I had worn Johnny's old jean jacket and layered flannel shirts all winter last year, and this year she wasn't having any of it. Dad seemed stunned by her accusations, and looked at me like he was seeing me for the first time. I just patted his hand and said, "I liked Johnny's jacket, Daddy. That's why I wore it." Lately, I had caught my dad watching me with a strange yearning on his face. I asked him about it once, asked him why he looked so sad. He'd smiled a little and shook his head.

"I'm not so sad, Josie Jo. I was just thinking about how fast you had to grow up. You weren't a little girl for very long. Not nearly long enough." He had patted my back and made a quick exit out the back door, retreating to the horse corral and safer pastures.

That particular Monday morning there was new 'Sunday snow' on the ground. Sunday snow was the snow that fell on Sunday, but hadn't yet been played or walked in. It was a beautiful white blanket when I tromped through it in my old tennis shoes. Samuel Yates was already at the bus stop when I arrived, and he climbed on before me, walking straight back to our seat and sliding in against the window.

He wore no hat over his glossy hair, and his quilted jacked was lined with that fuzzy sheep skin. He wore moccasins on his feet. I wondered if they were cold, but the moccasins seemed relatively dry, much dryer than my sneakers, so I didn't worry about him too much.

Samuel hadn't paid any attention to me at all—ignoring me and everyone else—since the day he had knocked Joby into the aisle. We hadn't been assigned a third person to our seat. Mr. Walker was probably a little apprehensive; maybe he had decided to leave well enough alone. So for the last week I had ridden back and forth from school sitting beside Samuel, not saying one word. I was not a person uncomfortable with silence, so I usually just read the whole time. I had started reading all of Jane Austen's books and was now working my way through *Persuasion.*

I was enmeshed in Anne's longsuffering when Samuel spoke.

"You read a lot." It sounded a bit like an accusation, his words clipped and soft.

"Yes." I didn't know what to say exactly, but to agree with him.

"Why?"

"I like books. Don't you read?"

"Yes, I can read!" His soft voice was angry, and his eyes flashed. "You think because I'm Navajo that I'm stupid?"

I stammered in my defense, my cheeks flushing at his perception of my words. "That's not what I meant! I don't think that! I just meant don't you *like* to read?"

When he didn't answer and resumed looking out the window, I tried to read again. But my thoughts swam wildly in my head, and I stared blankly at the page. I felt despondent that I had wounded someone who had so recently come to my rescue. I tried again.

"I'm sorry Samuel," I said awkwardly. "I didn't mean to hurt your feelings."

He snorted and looked at me, raising one eyebrow. "I'm not a little girl. I don't get my *feelings* hurt." His voice was slightly mocking. He took the book from my hands and began to read from the page.

*"I can listen no longer in silence. I must speak to you by such means as are within my reach. You pierce my soul. I am half agony, half hope. Tell me not that I am too late, that such precious feelings are gone forever."*

Samuel's intent had been to prove his reading skill, but he stopped suddenly, embarrassed by the deeply romantic missive from Captain Wentworth to Anne.

We both sat unmoving, staring down at the book. I couldn't help myself. I started to laugh.

Samuel scowled for a minute. Then his lips twitched and he seemed to exhale his discomfort.

"How old are you?" he questioned, his eyebrows slightly raised.

"Thirteen," I replied defensively. I always felt defensive about my age. I didn't feel thirteen, and I didn't look thirteen, so I hated *being* thirteen.

Samuel's eyes widened in surprise. "Thirteen?" It didn't sound like a question, but more like a doubtful exclamation. "So you're what, in seventh grade?" He said this in the same flat, yet incredulous, voice.

I pushed my glasses up on my nose and sighed. "That's right." I took my book out of his hands and prepared to tune him out.

"Isn't that book a little...grown-up for a seventh grader?" he argued. He pulled the book out of my hands again and read on, this time silently. "I don't even understand what most of these words mean. It's like a different language!"

"That's why I read with a dictionary...although I don't bring it to school with me. It's way too heavy." I looked down at the book again, feeling shy. "In some ways it is a different language. My teacher, Mrs. Grimaldi, says our language is disintegrating."

Samuel just looked at me, his expression incredulous.

"I'm sure it's not as different as Navajo is from English, though," I continued, trying to draw him into further conversation, surprised he was speaking to me at all, especially now that he knew I was just a lowly seventh grader.

"Yeah, Navajo is very different." Something shuttered over his eyes, and he turned away from me, looking out the window again, ending our very brief exchange.

It was several more bus rides before Samuel spoke to me once more. I had been shut down on our last conversation, and was unwilling to try again.

"I hate to read." His tone was argumentative, and he glared at me. As usual, I was tucked into my book, my knees drawn up to support its weight. I looked at him, wondering what he wanted me to say.

"Okay...?"

He drew a book out of his backpack and tossed it on top of the copy of *Pride and Prejudice* that was opened on my lap. The book was *Wuthering Heights*. I almost groaned in sympathy. I hadn't tried to finish it after Sonja had relieved me from it the first time. I had no desire to spend any more time with it. With school work, piano lessons, and piano practice, along with all the chores that came from living with two men—Jared and Jacob were up and mostly out of the house by then—my reading mostly took place on the bus and at bedtime, when I faithfully looked up all my undefined words. I still read a couple books a month, but I didn't plow through them as I had in the summer. *Wuthering Heights* was NOT on my list of Books-To-Read...and yes, I did have an actual list.

"I've read parts of this book," I said cautiously, not understanding why he had tossed the book in my lap.

"I was sure you were going to say you had," he said wryly. "It's as confusing as that book you were reading the other day."

"Why are you reading it then?" I asked, certain he must be, or he wouldn't have it in his possession.

He didn't answer for several seconds, and I waited, wondering if he would take the book and turn away again. "I am failing English. I have Ms. Whitmer, and she told me if I read that book and write a report on it, she'll pass me. So, I am trying to read that book. I have to read it and have the report on her desk in two weeks. I could see by the page he had dog-eared that he was in trouble.

Ms. Whitmer was a tough old bird who had taught at the high school for 25 years. She had a bit of a reputation, sometimes drove a Harley to school, and commonly wore combat boots. She was very intimidating, knew her stuff, and wouldn't take any crap. My older brothers had liked her, but had groaned about the workload. Johnny was barely squeezing by in her class as well.

"Why this book? Did she tell you why?"

"She told me she doesn't usually give extra credit. I told her I would do anything. She slapped this book down and said 'If you can get through this one I'll know how bad you want it.' So here I am. Now I know why she had that look on her face," Samuel said morosely.

"Why do you care?" My question just popped out.

Samuel glowered at me. "I want to graduate," he enunciated through clenched teeth. "I promised my grandmother I would graduate," he said this reluctantly. "I'm going into the Marines in May, and I want my diploma. My recruiter said I'll have a lot more opportunities if I graduate first."

We sat quietly for a minute. Samuel stared out the window as he was prone to do, and I fingered his book, still in my lap. I thought about how proud he seemed, and how hard it must have been to go to Ms. Whitmer and ask for the extra credit.

He reached over to take the book, but I held onto it tightly and moved it away from his outstretched hand.

"I'll read it with you," I blurted out, surprising both of us. He stared at me suspiciously. I shrugged my shoulders. "I told you I had read parts of it. I want to read the rest." I cringed at my lie. "We'll read it together. We spend an hour, sometimes more, on this bus eve-

ry day. I don't mind reading out loud if you don't." I couldn't believe I had been so forward. My neck got very hot underneath my
hair. I hoped I wasn't getting hives, which sometimes happened
when I got really upset or nervous.

"You read, I'll listen," he said stiffly.

"Now?" I questioned. He just raised his eyebrows.

I opened the book, swallowed my discomfort, and began at the
beginning.

# 4. Progression

I DECIDED OUR little book club was incomplete without the 1828 Webster's Dictionary, so every day I lugged the monstrous book to and from school for use on the bus. Samuel rolled his eyes when I pulled it out of my oversized bag the following morning. Every time he forgot himself and said in frustration "What does that mean?" I would nod my head toward the big green book lying between us. He would sigh and look up the word in question while I spelled it out for him. There were also words I wasn't sure of, and would make him look those up as well, though I was pretty certain if I didn't know what they meant, neither did he.

A week went by, and I read morning and afternoon as he sat quietly and listened. One afternoon as I was reading, I became engrossed in the story, and forgot to read out loud.

Samuel's brown, long-fingered hand suddenly covered the page my attention had been captured by. I realized I had been reading silently for at least several seconds.

"Whoops!" I giggled. "Sorry about that."

He reached over and took the book from my hands. "My turn," he said without rancor. He found the place where my imagination had quelled my voice and began reading in his deep baritone. I had always been the one to read, so I was startled by his sudden willingness to be the reader.

He spoke English perfectly, but his voice had a different cadence—the words delivered almost in a rhythm—and his tone stayed constant and unvaried, without the rise and fall that a storyteller adopts to convey emotion. I found myself listening to his voice, being pulled into it as I had, just moments before, been pulled into the story.

"Josie? Are you going to look up that word?"

I shook myself out of my reverie, not wanting to admit I hadn't the faintest idea which word I needed to look up.

"Spelling?" I said evasively to cover my ignorance.

"Where are you today?" he said. "Your mind is everywhere."

"I was listening to your voice." I flushed at my confession and inwardly cursed the constant blushing that gave me no privacy.

"No you weren't. You haven't heard anything I've read," he countered mildly.

"I was listening to your *voice*," I insisted again. He lowered his eyebrows in a scowl, not understanding me.

I tried to explain to him how his voice didn't seem to rise and fall in the same patterns as mine did. When he didn't respond, I thought perhaps I had made him angry. Samuel was very sensitive about being different, flaunting his Navajo heritage one moment with his long hair and moccasins, growing angry if someone took notice of it in the next.

He seemed thoughtful as he spoke. He chose his words carefully, as if he had never considered them before. "The Navajo language is one of the most complex languages on Earth. From ancient times, it was only a spoken language, not a written language. If you don't learn it as a child, it is almost impossible to master. Every syllable means something different. We use four tones when we speak: high, low, rising, and falling. When the voice rises or falls in Navajo, it can mean a completely different word. For instance, the words *mouth* and *medicine* are pronounced the same, but they are said with different tones. The same word, but...not the same word at all. Do you understand? Maybe that is why, when a Navajo speaks English, he says each syllable with the same intonation, because no intonation is stressed." He thought about what he had said for a moment. Then he asked me, almost as if knowing the answer would cause him pain, "Do I sound strange to you when I speak?"

My heart twisted a little at his vulnerability. I shook my head emphatically. "It's very slight…I don't think most people would notice it at all. I guess I have an ear for music, and the rhythm of your voice sounds like music to me, that's all."

I smiled up at him, and for the first time, he smiled back.

There was a big crowd gathered after school on the wide open field that separated the junior high from the high school. I ignored the excited shouts and the kids rushing to get in on the action. I couldn't see who the crowd had gathered around, but the bus had not arrived, so I found a spot next to the bus stop to wait, setting my backpack down on the patchy grass and sitting on it so I wouldn't get my rear-end cold and wet. The early snowfall had melted during a stretch of warmer days, and tufts of grass stuck up here and there between icy patches. It was cold enough to be unpleasant, the wind was always worst at the mouth of the canyon where the two schools sat. Utah weather is the most sporadic, unpredictable weather in the country. Folks complain about how you can plant your crops in late spring, only to have to replant twice more because it keeps freezing and killing everything off. We've had snow in June and none in December in the same year. It was November now, and Mother Nature had teased us with snow in October, only to have November be sunny and dry, with icy winds shaking the bare trees and mocking the winter sun.

I had no desire to go wading into the manic fray and sat shivering, wishing the bus would come. Tara, on the other hand, had wiggled her tiny self into the middle of the action, witnessing the fist fight firsthand.

"Mr. Bracken is coming!" a frantic shout went up across the field. Mr. Bracken was the principal of the high school and was a pretty genial and likeable sort, but no one doubted that anyone found fighting would be expelled upon discovery. The kids scattered immediately, not wanting to be questioned or reprimanded, and descended upon the bus stop in droves. The bus lumbered to a stop and a hasty line formed, kids shoving and jostling for position. I was not aggressive enough to maintain my place in the line and fell back to wait until the writhing mass thinned.

Tara came running towards me, backpack bobbing, hands hanging onto her thick shoulder straps to keep it in place.

"Oh, my gosh!" Tara gushed when she was still several feet away. "That Indian kid was fighting three different boys. Joby Jenkins and a couple of his friends were calling him half-breed, and he went crazy. Joby's friends tried to hold his arms but he just let loose, swinging at all of them. One guy has a chipped tooth and Joby has a bloody nose. The Indian kid must have caught his hand on the kid's tooth because his hand was all bloody!"

Tara was using too many pronouns, so I wasn't sure which injury belonged to whom and which guy had done most of the swinging, but my stomach lurched at the mention of "the Indian kid." That could only be Samuel.

"Where are they now?" My eyes scanned the area where the circle around the fighters had formed, not seeing Samuel, Joby, or Mr. Bracken, for that matter.

"When someone yelled that the principal was coming, Joby and his friends took off toward the junior high. The Indian kid picked up his backpack and headed this way with everybody that was running towards the bus. I don't know where he went." She looked around, jumping up and down to gain enough height to see over the swarm of kids. "I don't know if Mr. Bracken was actually even coming.

Somebody might have yelled that just to stop the fight."

"So you never saw Mr. Bracken?" I hoped Samuel wouldn't end up expelled. Word usually made its way around, and news of the fight would fill the halls tomorrow. But maybe if he made it home without being caught, the principal might not get wind of it until after the fact, making expulsion less likely.

The bus had quickly inhaled her anxious passengers, and Tara and I climbed up the steep steps, Tara chattering all the way.

"There was so much blood! The Indian kid…"

"Samuel! His name is Samuel," I interrupted her.

"Whatever!" Tara gestured impatiently, obviously not caring what his name was.

When I climbed to the highest stair and was able to see down the aisle, my eyes rushed to my seat. Samuel was there, eyes glued out the window, probably watching to see if he would make it home free. Tara continued talking, but I was no longer listening. I wondered how he had gotten past the bus driver without detection. I teetered down the aisle and swung in next to Samuel, my heavy pack sliding to the floor.

"Are you okay?" I asked breathlessly. I could see blood on his pants, and as I tried to get a good look at his face, I realized his lip was swollen and split as well.

"I'm fine," Samuel said tersely, keeping his face averted.

"If you don't stop the bleeding you're going to give yourself away," I insisted.

Samuel sighed in exasperation and, with one hand, unbuttoned his jean jacket. He'd wrapped his hand in the bottom of his t-shirt, baring his toned brown stomach. The light blue cotton was completely soaked through with blood.

"Oh, my gosh!" I sounded like Tara, but I couldn't help it. He must have split his knuckles open. "I'll be right back!" I headed back up the aisle. The bus was now in motion and Mr. Walker barked at me to sit down. I ignored him, walking purposefully, holding onto the seats to stay upright on the swaying bus.

"Mr. Walker, the kid sitting next to me has a bloody nose. Do you have a first aid kit or some paper towels?"

"Why is his nose bleeding?" Mr. Walker looked at me suspiciously.

"I don't know. It just started bleeding," I said nonchalantly and felt ridiculously obvious. I was a pretty pathetic liar. Acting was definitely not in my future.

"Harrumph," Mr. Walker grumbled, pointing to where a small tin box with a red cross emblazoned across the front was Velcroed above the big front windows.

I unstrapped the box and made my way back to Samuel. He had pulled the jacket back up over his hand, hiding the bloody state of his T-shirt from the nosy kids around him. All it would take was one kid seeing the blood, shouting out to Mr. Walker, and Samuel would be ousted.

I slid down next to him, pulling the little first aid kit open and rifling through the contents. There were several good sized bandages and antibacterial wipes, as well as some gauze and some white surgical tape. I pulled my backpack up onto the seat behind me, scooting forward until I was barely sitting on the seat. I turned sideways and effectively blocked Samuel from view. I stacked his backpack on top of mine and made a little wall that would be useless if someone in front of us or behind us stood up and looked over the seat. But it was the best I could do.

"Let me see your hand," I insisted softly.

Samuel unwound his right hand from the bloody T-shirt and held it out to me. Fresh blood immediately rose from the deep slice across his knuckles and spilled onto his fingers. I slapped a thick white gauze pad over it, pushing it down into the cut to stop the flow.

"Hold that!" I ordered him, grabbing some little butterfly sutures that I had seen Johnny use when he'd split the bridge of his nose during football practice. I pulled the tabs off and at my command, Samuel lifted the gauze pad and I swooped in, pulling the side of the gash together with the butterfly band aid. I put another one on, and the blood slowed to an ooze at the slit. I put the gauze pad over the top and again asked Samuel to hold it there.

"What happened?" I questioned lightly as I wrapped some stretchy gauze around the pad.

"Joby Jenkins needed a fist in his face," Samuel replied shortly.

"Why?" My eyes flickered up to his.

"I got tired of his half-breed jokes." Samuel's well-shaped mouth was drawn into a tight hard line. "What is it with some people?"

I yanked off a piece of surgical tape with my teeth and proceeded to secure the gauze. I wasn't very good at this, but at least he wouldn't bleed all over himself.

"What do you mean?"

"Some people just can't keep their mouths shut. Joby is constantly shooting his mouth off." Samuel watched as I cleaned the blood off the fingers poking out from my makeshift mound of gauze and tape.

I completely agreed with him about Joby. "Joby picks on whoever he thinks is weak," I replied, absentmindedly wiping.

"If he thinks I'm so weak, why did he come at me with two other guys?" Samuel retorted angrily, misunderstanding my words. "Why didn't he fight me one on one?"

"I didn't mean physically weak," I protested. "You're different, so you're an easy target. Other kids don't know you, so it's easier for him to talk trash and turn them on you. He was embarrassed when you pushed him off the seat. I think he's just been biding his time, don't you?"

"Probably. I broke his nose. I'm going to be expelled. It'll be just like the reservation school. I got the half-breed comments there too. Only at the reservation I was too white." His voice was bitter, his mouth drawn down at the corners.

"Didn't you grow up with all the kids you went to school with on the reservation?"

He dipped his head in a slight nod.

"So what was the big deal with being half white…I mean, was your skin color really an issue after all that time?"

"For most kids it wasn't," he admitted then, somewhat begrudgingly. "I had friends, a girlfriend." His eyes shifted to me briefly.

"I think most people aren't really so biased if you let them get to know you," I volunteered.

"It's not my job to make sure people know me or like me," Samuel said proudly.

"Well that's silly," I huffed.

Samuel's eyes flashed, and he clenched his jaw.

"I'm not exactly what you would call outgoing," I continued. "I kind of prefer being by myself, but I can't expect anyone to want to get to know me if I purposely keep myself separated." I paused as his face remained stony. "Mrs. Grimaldi says you can't build walls and then be mad when no one wants to climb over them."

"That's easy for you to say," Samuel sneered as his eyes flew over my blond hair and then met my blue eyes with a black glower.

"Oh, please Samuel!" I protested. "I may not have brown skin, but I am plenty peculiar," I rebutted. "And don't pretend you haven't noticed it."

Samuel shook his head in disgust and pulled his hand from mine. I was finished anyway. I gathered the bloody towelettes and wrapped them in several paper towels.

"How many other kids have you talked to since you came here?" I asked Samuel quietly. "Besides me?"

Samuel didn't respond, and I didn't really expect him to.

"People can be jerks. Joby is a creep, and he probably had that broken nose coming to him," I soothed. "But don't just assume that people don't like you because you look different. I, for one, like the way you look."

I blushed furiously and grabbed the first aid box and escaped to the front of the bus to return it to the Velcro straps, throwing the bloody wipes away while I was at it.

"Everything under control?" Mr. Walker questioned me as I stuck the box back where it belonged.

"Huh?"

"The bloody nose?" Mr. Walker prodded.

"Oh, yeah. All done. It stopped," I stammered.

Samuel had his arm back in his sleeve when I returned, his jacket buttoned back up to cover the stained shirt underneath. He had *Wuthering Heights* opened on his lap. I sat down and he began reading without preamble. I pulled out the big green dictionary, and that was the end of our discussion, for the time being.

"What kind of name is Heathcliff anyway?" Samuel grumbled as we labored through another day of reading. We had less than five pages left, and it had been tough.

"I think his name is one of the nicest things about him," I said sincerely. "At least it isn't something boring like Ed or Harry. It's kind of a romantic name."

"But that's his only name…no last name, no middle name, just Heathcliff. Like Madonna or Cher."

I was a little surprised that Samuel knew who Madonna and Cher were. It didn't seem like his type of music, though I had no idea what his type was.

"I think the fact that he didn't have a last name made him seem more alone in the world," I mused thoughtfully. "Everybody had these full English names, and Heathcliff was a gypsy without roots, without family, without even a name of his own."

"Yeah, maybe." Samuel nodded his head in agreement. "Names are a big deal to the Navajo. Every Navajo child is given a secret Navajo name when they are born. It is known only by the child, the family, and God. You don't share it with anyone else."

"Really?" I asked in awe. "So what's yours?"

He looked at me with exasperation. "You. Don't. Share. It. With. Anyone. Else," he repeated sarcastically.

I blushed and looked down at the book. "Why?"

"My grandma says if you do your legs will turn hard...but I think it's more a tie that binds the people together, keeps tradition alive, that kind of thing. My mom told me it's sacred."

"Wow. I wish I had a secret name. I've never really liked Josie Jo very much. It's kind of silly and babyish," I said wistfully.

"What name would you rather have?" Samuel actually looked interested in my response.

"Well...my mom really wanted us to all have 'J' names. I guess it was her way of binding us together, kind of like your family. So maybe I could just pretend it's Josephine and everyone can still call me Josie for short. Josephine is so much more dramatic and lady-like."

"All right. From now on, I will refer to you as Lady Josephine," Samuel said with the faintest of smiles.

"No. How about I just make it my secret Navajo name and only you and I will know it," I said, conspiratorially.

"You are the furthest thing from a Navajo," Samuel scoffed.

"Well, what if a beautiful Navajo woman had adopted me when I was just a baby? Would she have given me a Navajo name? Even if I had blonde hair and blue eyes?"

Samuel stared at me for a minute, frowning. "I really don't know," he confessed. "I've never known a Navajo who adopted a white baby. I'm the closest thing most Navajo get to a white baby." Samuel's countenance darkened. "Luckily, every Navajo child that is born belongs to his mother's clan, so I am a Navajo, no matter who my father was."

"Did you ever know your father?" I asked quietly, not liking that I might make him angry, but not fearing it either.

"I was six years old when he died. I remember things about him. He called me Sam Sam, and he was tall and kind of quiet. I remember my life before he died and then after he died when we lived on the reservation. I hadn't lived on the reservation before. It was very different than the little apartment we had been living in. I spoke Navajo because my mother had spoken it to me exclusively. I spoke English too, which made school easier when I started school on the reservation. My mother never talked much about my father after he died."

"Do you think it made her sad?" I ventured, thinking about my own mother's death and how hard it had been for my dad to say her name for the longest time.

"Maybe. But it was more about tradition than anything. The Navajo believe that the only thing that is left behind when a person dies is the bad or the negative parts of their spirit. They call it *chįįdii* and when you talk about the dead it invites the *chįįdii.* So…we never talked about him much. I know she loved him and missed him. When I was really young, she read to me from the Bible that my dad had given her. I think it made her feel close to him without talking about him. She became a Christian when she married my dad, but within a year or so after his death she rejected it. She has become very angry and bitter. She didn't know how to live off the reservation without my dad, and when he died, she went back, re-married, and I'm sure she'll never leave."

"I don't know what I would do if I could never talk about my mother," I whispered. "Talking about her helps me remember her. It makes me feel close to her."

"Your mother died?" Samuel's voice rose in surprise.

"Yes." I was a little stunned that he didn't know. I had just assumed that he knew what his grandparents knew. "She died the summer before third grade. I was almost nine years old." I shrugged a little, "I guess I'm just lucky I had her for that long. I remember lots of things about her. Like the way she smelled, the way she covered her mouth when she laughed, the way she said 'Josie Jo, to and fro' when she pushed me on the swing."

"Why are you lucky you had her that long? I think that makes you unlucky. She died and you don't have a mother." Samuel's face was stormy, and his lips tightened a little as he waited for me to respond.

"But I did have her for those nine years, and she loved me, and I loved her. Look at people like Heathcliff. He had no mother *and* no father."

"Yeah, I guess he had a right to be a jerk."

"I guess he had reason to be, at least in the beginning, but that doesn't make me like him any better. He was hateful and angry all the time. The first time I read the book, I kept waiting for him to change, to develop some character…but he never did. I just despised him for it. I wanted him to be lovable, even just a little bit, so that I could like him."

"People didn't *like* him because he had darker skin and he looked different than they did!" Samuel was angry again.

"Maybe that was true to a point, in the beginning. But the father, Mr. Earnshaw, loved him best of all…better than his own children. Heathcliff never did one thing with that love. Catherine loved him, too. What did he do?"

"He went off and joined the military or something, right? He made something of himself, improved how he dressed and how he looked!" Samuel defended Heathcliff like he *was* Heathcliff.

"But he never changed WHO he was!" I cried back passionately. "I wanted him to inspire me! I just ended up feeling sorry for him and thinking 'What a waste!'"

"Maybe he couldn't change who he was!" Samuel's face was tight and his hands were clenched.

"Samuel! I'm talking about him changing on the *inside*! Nobody that loved him cared that he was a gypsy! Don't you get it?"

"Catherine loved him despite of what he was on the inside!" He fought back still.

"Their version of love damned them both in the end! They were two miserable people because they never figured out what true love is!"

"Why don't you tell me what TRUE LOVE is then, Lady Jose-phine, since you are so wise at thirteen years old?" Samuel sneered at me, and his arms were folded across his chest.

My cheeks were flaming, and my finger poked him in the chest with every syllable I recited. "'True love suffereth long, and is kind; true love envieth not. True love vaunteth not itself, is not puffed up. True love does not behave itself unseemly, seeketh not her own, is not easily provoked, thinketh no evil. True love rejoiceth not in iniq-uity, but rejoiceth in the truth. True love beareth all things, believeth all things, hopeth all things, endureth all things!'" I stopped for a breath and one emphatic push against Samuel's chest. "1st Corinthi-ans, Chapter 13. Check it out."

And with that I picked up my big green dictionary and my over-flowing book bag and staggered up the aisle. The bus wasn't at my stop yet, but I was out of there.

Samuel didn't say much the morning following our heated Heathcliff discussion. I asked him if he wanted to read the final five pages. He said he already had and left it at that. He looked out the window the whole way into school, and I sat uncomfortably without anything to read. I wound up going ahead in my math book and do-ing the next day's lesson. The ride home was much the same. Lucki-ly, it was Friday.

Monday morning I arrived at our seat first. I wasn't carrying the dictionary anymore, having no reason to lug it with me if we were done. Samuel wasn't far behind and he said "scoot" when I sat down. I shifted over against the window, and he sat down next to me. Scoot was the only thing he said the whole way into Nephi. This time I was prepared, and I buried my nose in *Jane Eyre*. *Jane Eyre* was like comfort food to me, and I was feeling a little rejected.

After school, I climbed on the bus, dreading the half hour I would sit next to Samuel in silence. I missed the reading and the discussion. I even missed him a little.

Samuel was already seated, and he watched me come toward him down the aisle. There was a strange look on his face when my eyes met his. He looked almost triumphant. I sat down, and he held out a thin plastic folder.

"I guess you know something about true love after all. At least Ms. Whitmer thinks so," he said vaguely.

My eyes quickly scanned the cover page. It was Samuel's report on *Wuthering Heights*. He had titled it 'True Love or Obsession?' Ms. Whitmer had written the words "Brilliant!" across the page in bold red print. I yanked the cover page over, my eyes flying down the page. Samuel had taken 1 Corinthians Chapter 13, replacing the word 'charity' with 'true love' as I had done, and basically written a paper on the difference between true love and obsession, using examples from the book. His final sentence was wonderful, and it was all his own. He said "Where true love would have redeemed them, obsession condemned them forever."

I whooped loudly, only to have kids turn and stare at me curiously.

"Samuel! This is so cool! Did she say anything to you?" My smile felt like it was going to split my face in half, but I couldn't help it.

My excitement must have been contagious, because he grinned at me briefly, his smile a quick flash of white teeth.

"She said it was so impressive that she's not just going to pass me, she's going to give me a B."

I whooped again, and threw my fisted hands skyward in victory. This time half the bus turned and stared. Tara even stopped mid-sentence, eight seats up, and gave me a "What the heck?" look. I ducked my head and stifled a giggle. Samuel shook his head and rolled his eyes, but he was laughing too.

"Lady Josephine, you are something else," he said softly and reached over and took my hand in his. His hand was big and warm, his beautiful skin golden brown against my own. My hand felt very small as it lay in his, and my heart felt like a tiny hummingbird fluttering in my chest. Samuel held my hand for a second more and then gently slid his hand away.

It got dark quickly now that winter had gripped the valley. Getting up the hill to the Grimaldi's house had become more difficult with the snow, but I never complained, and whenever Sonja raised the issue of being concerned over the weather or the dwindling daylight, I just smoothed it over. My panic at missing a lesson must have been evident, because she never pressed me to postpone lessons until spring thaws made my way a little more hospitable. I had stopped riding my bike up the hill. The hill was so icy the tires couldn't get any traction. I would just ride to the base of the hill and then trudge to the top along the side of the road where the snow was piled and I wouldn't slip.

Sonja had begun teaching me how to conduct music as if I were conducting a live orchestra. She would put a record on, put the score in front of me, and I would conduct, keeping time with my waving arms, bringing in the imaginary instruments and cueing the dynamics as if I were the one in control.

I left my lesson that day with my head full of music. Sonja had been in a flamboyant mood, and the music still poured out of the house behind me as I made my way down the hill. She had turned on Ravel's "Bolero" and I had conducted it joyfully. It had a wonderfully insistent, repetitive melody, and it was perfect for a novice conductor like me to practice "bringing in" the instruments, as they were continually added, sections at a time.

It was times like these when the music felt like a thrumming,

47

pulsing power inside of me. I was practically levitating as I spread my arms and spun in dizzy circles down the snowy hill. The speed of my descent made me laugh as I recklessly conducted the internal orchestra swelling my heart to near bursting.

Unfortunately, I wasn't actually levitating, and I began to stumble, heavy boots tangling and arms flailing. The fog of musical euphoria abandoned me mid-flight. I cart-wheeled down the remainder of the hill, landing in a deep snow bank two-thirds of the way down. I acted like a child so rarely that it was strangely ironic that when I truly lost myself in child-like wonder, I ended up hurt and alone. My ankle screamed with a sickening, stomach-churning agony that had me whimpering and crawling on my hands and knees trying to escape the pain.

My piano books were scattered down the hill, marking my flight path. There was no way I was leaving them behind. I started crawling up the hill to collect them, realizing as my hands sunk into the snow that I had also managed to lose my gloves and my glasses. Without the assistance of my boots, I kept sliding down when I tried to inch upwards. I tried valiantly not to cry as I reprimanded myself on my idiotic behavior, talking myself through the ordeal of gathering up the books closest to me and praying for the books I couldn't get to. Going back up the hill to Sonja's was out of the question. I slid down the rest of the way on my butt, clutching my few books to my chest and slowing my descent with my good leg.

Once I arrived at the bottom, I faced the puzzle of how I would get home. Riding my waiting bike was completely out of the question; my ankle wouldn't bear any pressure at all. I didn't trust my balance most of the time *without* an injury, forget hopping and pushing the bike home. Looping my piano bag around my shoulders and pulling my coat sleeves down over my hands I began to crawl home. The darkness was settling around me, and I knew I was in trouble. I wasn't going to be able to go two miles on my hands and knees. Thoughts of my family finding me frozen solid at the side of the road had me crying in self-pity. I wondered if Samuel would miss me. I wished I could see him again before I died. Maybe he would cut his arm like the Comanche Indians used to do when someone died, so their arm would show a scar for each loved one lost.

I had asked him how he knew about the Comanche tradition when he was a Navajo. He had told me many of the tribes had many stories and legends in common, and his grandmother had told him it was the Comanche way of reminding yourself of a loved one without speaking their name.

I was startled out of my morbid thoughts by the sound of a sheep baaing from somewhere to my left. He sounded as lost and unhappy as I was. The sheep bellowed mournfully again, and I could make out his black nose and feet against the snow where he was huddled beside a scrubby enclosure of brush and juniper trees. I crawled toward it, thinking maybe I could huddle there with it. Wool was warm, wasn't it?

The sheep had other ideas. My approach made him complain even louder, throwing his head back and demanding that I stay away. "BAAAAAAACK," he seemed to say, and I half giggled, half sobbed at the futility of it all. "BAAAAAAAA!" he cried again.

Somewhere in the distance a dog barked. The sheep bellowed in response. The dog barked again. Maybe someone was looking for the sheep. I didn't have much hope that anybody would be looking for me. My dad and brothers loved me, but I had no real hope that they would think much of my absence until it was marked by many hours. The dog seemed to be getting closer. An occasional yelp indicated his progress in our direction. The sheep would bleat back when he heard the dog, and I waited hopefully for a canine rescue. I was very cold and a little wet from my tumble in the snow, and my hands were aching almost as much as my ankle. I huddled inside my beautiful blue coat and prayed for deliverance.

The darkness was complete as Don Yates' black and white collie mix, Gus, trotted up to the lost sheep. Not far behind him, Samuel trudged, bundled against the snow in a black ski cap and his sheepskin coat, having traded his moccasins in for a pair of laced work boots. I cried out to him in gratitude, and he stopped in surprise.

"Josie?"

"Samuel! I've sprained my ankle, and I can't ride my bike home. I tried to crawl," I stuttered out, my teeth chattering, "But my gloves are missing and it was just too far."

Samuel hunched down next to me and pulled his hat from his head and pulled it down on mine. The sudden warmth and my relief at his presence made the tears I had been trying to control stream down my face. Samuel grabbed my hands in his and started rubbing them briskly.

"Why are you out here?" He sounded angry and his hands rubbed harder in concert to his harsh words. My tears flowed faster.

"I take piano lessons every afternoon from Mrs. Grimaldi. She lives at the top of Tuckaway Hill." I didn't tell him how I had gotten carried away in the music and rolled down the hill.

"How did you end up on your hands and knees half frozen to death?" he barked out incredulously.

"I slipped," I said defiantly, pulling my hands from his and wiping the tears from my icy cheeks. Samuel yanked his gloves off and grabbed my hands back insistently. Forcing my hands into the gloves, he rose to his feet and reached down for me, lifting me to my feet.

"Can you walk at all if I help you?" His voice was a little less confrontational now, and I tried to take a step forward. It was like someone took an ice pick and rammed it into my ankle. I fell in a heap at Samuel's feet. The pain made me nauseous and the contents of my stomach rose up in rebellion. I retched just to the right of Samuels's work boots. Luckily, I'd had only an apple and half of a sandwich for lunch many hours ago, and there wasn't much left to throw up. But puking with an audience was worse than the pain in my ankle, by far. I moaned in mortification as Samuel kicked snow over the steaming remains of my lunch and squatted down beside me again. He handed me a handful of snow to clean my mouth, and I thankfully wiped and "rinsed" my mouth, my hands shaking.

"Did you say you rode your bike here?" Samuel's voice was gentle.

"It's at the base of the hill, back there." My voice wobbled dangerously, and I stopped speaking abruptly, not wanting to disgrace myself any further.

Samuel stood and walked away from me, in the direction that I had come. A few minutes later he was back, pushing my bike beside him.

"I'm going to help you get on…"

"I can't push the pedals, Samuel," I interrupted, my voice cracking again as the swell of tears clogged my throat.

"I know," Samuel replied calmly. "But the seat is long. I can ride behind you and pedal."

The bike was fine for me, but Samuel was over 6'0. This was going to be interesting. Samuel held the bike with one hand and pulled me to my feet with the other. Moving the bike close to where I was teetering, he straddled the bike and helped me climb on in front of him.

"Can you put your feet up in front of you?"

The bars made a big U shape providing a good spot for my feet when I wanted to coast. Samuel helped me raise my hurt leg, and I gingerly scooted as far forward on the seat as I could as he braced the bike with me on it. With a little shove, grunt, and a wobble we were off. The bike wove precariously, snow and gravel making it extremely treacherous. I squeezed my eyes shut and bit down on the yelp that escaped. Samuel used his legs to propel us forward until we established enough forward motion for an attempt at pedaling.

"What about the sheep?" I said suddenly, having forgotten about my partner in peril.

"Gus will get him home. At this rate, they might get there before we do." I looked behind us, peering carefully over Samuel's shoulder as to not disturb the equilibrium of the bike. Sure enough, the sheep was waddling down the road, Gus nipping at his heels.

I relaxed as well as I could, my head resting in the curve of

Samuel's shoulder as his arms and legs braced me from falling off the narrow seat. I couldn't comfortably reach the handlebars with my legs out in front of me, so I loosely held onto his arms just above the elbow. The silly song about a bicycle meant for two jumped into my head. *We won't have a stylish marriage; I can't afford a carriage . . .*

When the gravel road finally joined the black top, I felt Samuel relax a little. The ride was suddenly much smoother. Still, he couldn't be comfortable. I imagined how we must look riding down the moonlit road, not a soul in sight, like a creature with eight legs and two heads. I giggled a little despite my throbbing ankle and my wounded pride.

I felt a responding rumble in Samuel's chest and swiveled my head to look up at him in amazement. I had never heard Samuel laugh.

"Hold still!!!" Samuel's voice raised in alarm as the bike took a dangerous lurch. I had forgotten to move slowly.

"Sorry!" I squeaked, clinging to his arms as he expertly restored balance.

"Hold still," Samuel repeated again firmly.

We rode in silence for several minutes until I decided gratitude was in order.

"You saved me," I said simply. "I don't know what I would have done if you hadn't come along. You might have even saved my life. My dad and Johnny might not have noticed I was gone for hours. They aren't very aware of me."

"I'm not sure I want to be responsible for saving your life."

"Why? Don't you like me at all?" My voice sounded as hurt as I felt.

Samuel sighed. "That's not what I meant. And yes, I like you." He sounded a bit uncomfortable at the admission. "It's just that in many Native cultures, when you save someone's life you are responsible for them from that time forward. It's like you are their keeper or something."

That didn't sound bad to me. I kind of liked the idea of having

Samuel as my life-long guardian.

"I can't think of anyone I'd rather have looking out for me," I confessed. Somehow honesty was much easier when it was dark. Still, I tensed a little, awaiting his response.

No response came. We rode in silence for the remainder of the ride, gliding past the homes of our neighbors until Samuel slowed to a stop in front of my house. Old Brown, Johnny's truck, was parked carelessly in the gravel in front of the house, and my dad's work truck was parked in the drive. Samuel helped me alight and set the bike down as he pulled me up onto his back, piggy-back style. I wished he would sweep me up into his arms like a bride. I felt heavy and awkward sprawled across his long back, and I clung to his shoulders, holding my breath as he climbed the stairs and slid me down his back to knock on the door.

"It's my house! Just go in," I said, reaching past him and opening the front door. The sounds of Jazz basketball blared from the TV, and the warmth from the wood burning stove poured over us. Samuel swung me up and carried me unceremoniously to the couch, setting me down as swiftly as he could and backing away as if he thought he would be in trouble for touching me.

My dad sat in his recliner and gaped at us for a minute before he collected his wits. I counted two empty beer cans on his TV stand and another in his hand. I sighed inwardly. Dad was a sweet drunk. He didn't get mean and ugly, just drowsy and cheerful, as he drowned his loneliness in a nightly ritual of Budweiser and ball—football, basketball, baseball, whatever. He didn't drink at all when mom was alive. We Mormons aren't big drinkers. In fact, Mormons didn't drink at all if we were living true to the tenets of our faith. Maybe that's why Dad never went to church or cared if we went. Mom wouldn't be too happy about that, I was sure.

"What happened?" My dad's words weren't slurred; the night was still young.

I proceeded to tell him my abbreviated story involving the sheep, Gus, and including Samuel somewhere in there, too.

"No more piano lessons for you!" Dad grumbled. "It ain't safe. I knew somethin' was wrong. I was just about to come lookin' for you."

"Oh no, Dad!" I cried out hastily, sitting up and swinging my good leg to the floor. "I'll be more careful. I'm getting ready for the Christmas program. I can't miss my lessons. Besides, Sonja...I mean Mrs. Grimaldi...is going to have me practice at the church for the next few weeks so that she can start teaching me how to play the organ."

I didn't believe my dad had even noticed I was gone, nor had he been on the brink of starting out on a search and rescue mission, but I could tell he felt bad that I had been in trouble and he hadn't had a clue.

Samuel shook Dad's hand and made a hasty retreat, claiming he needed to go make sure Gus made it back to the corral with the wayward sheep.

# 5. Virtuoso

THE ONLY CHURCH in Levan was built in 1904. It was a beautiful, light-colored brick building with a tall graceful steeple and steps leading up to the double oak doors. Not everybody went to church services in Levan, but everybody went to church. That church had been the town gathering place for almost one hundred years. It had provided walls for worship, seen the townsfolk marry in its hallowed halls, and absorbed the grief of many a funeral. The beautiful chapel had high arching windows that were two stories tall. The heavy oak pews possessed the patina of time and tender care.

Sonja taught me to play the organ in that lovely little chapel. On the day of my first lesson, I had shown up in blue jeans, only to have Sonja send me home to change into a dress.

"This is a place of reverence and worship," she had said sternly. "We do not wear casual clothes when we enter the chapel!" .

Christmas was coming, and I was going to be performing "Oh Holy Night" on the piano for the annual Christmas Eve service. Everyone in town came to the Christmas Eve service, whether they came regularly to church or not. It was the spiritual highlight of the Christmas season for townsfolk. The choir would perform sacred Christmas songs, Sonja would accompany them on the organ, and the bells would be rung. The story of the Christ Child would be read at the pulpit by Lawrence Mangelson, who possessed a rich, deep, orator's voice. It was my favorite tradition, and my musician's heart was overflowing with thoughts of debuting at such an event. I had taken piano lessons, Monday through Friday, for three years and had yet to play for anyone but Doc, Sonja, and my family.

Originally, the church choir director, married to the aforementioned Lawrence Mangelson, had denied Sonja's request to let me play in the special worship service. She was kind, but she worried that my ability at thirteen would not be worthy of the occasion. Sonja had taken me to Mrs. Mangelson's home and insisted that she listen.

I played a powerfully moving and difficult rendition of "Oh Holy Night" on the piano in her little sitting room, and when I finished, the sweet old lady humbly asked for my forgiveness, begging me to take part in the program. Mr. Mangelson said it would be the best Christmas Eve Service ever and suggested we keep my piano solo a secret.

Christmas Eve fell on a Sunday that year, and I attended the 9:00 a.m. church services without my family. Because the congregation would be returning that evening for the Christmas Eve service, the morning services were shortened. I had let my Aunt Louise and Tara in on my little secret, so later that afternoon, Aunt Louise came over and styled my hair, smoothing my natural curl into shining waves and applying light makeup on my eyes, cheeks, and lips. Sonja said musicians often perform in classic black but thought white might be more age appropriate. She had driven to Provo, a city about an hour north of Levan, and found a simple yet elegant, long-sleeved, white, velvet dress. When I thumped down from my attic room, coiffed and wearing my new dress, my one foot in a heel and the other in a walking cast, thanks to my tumble down Tuckaway Hill, my dad's weathered face softened, and his lower lip trembled.

"You look like an angel, honey. I'd hug you but I don't want to muss ya up."

The night was cold and still, snow running in deep drifts along the edge of the poorly plowed roads. We made our way to the church which was lit up and welcoming in the moonlight. Sonja sat at the organ and played magnificent prelude music, softening hearts and moistening eyes before the program had even begun. We sat in our regular pew, with Rachel coming to join us to sit with Jacob. They were engaged to be married in the spring, and with Jared home from college for the holidays, we were all together. Everyone was scrubbed and solemn in their holiday best, hair slicked and ties tied.

The program began, and my stomach was in knots as it neared the moment of my solo. I was seated at the end of our bench to provide easy access to the aisle, which was a straight shot up to the stand where the piano was waiting, lid opened, choir members seated on the dais around it. Lawrence Mangelson's voice soared with the spirit as he spoke of the angels that heralded the birth of the King. Suddenly, it was my turn to play, and I rose on shaking legs and walked to the piano. There was a murmur through the congregation. The service always stayed close to tradition with little variance in narration or music. This was a surprise, and again, no one really knew I played.

I sat down and closed my eyes in silent prayer, asking for the nerves to stay in my legs and not my hands. My knees could knock harmlessly without hurting my performance. Softly, I began to play, tuning into the beauty of the sound, the soaring reverence of the melody, the magnificence of the musical phrasing. The audience faded around me as I joyously submitted to the song, and when it was done I slowly descended back to earth. I rose from the piano on steady legs, having forgotten my nerves, and looked out over the silent congregation.

My dad's face was streaked with tears, and my brothers' faces shone with pride. Aunt Louise and Tara smiled broadly, and Tara even waved excitedly before her mother noticed and pulled her hand down. Sonja was dabbing her eyes with a lacy hanky, her glasses in one hand.

Then, from the back of the room, someone began to clap. Mormons don't clap in worship services. The chapel is a reverent place, and speakers end sermons with an amen, followed by an amen from the congregation. When someone sings or plays, even amens are not given. The choir or performer knows how well they have been received only by the level of silence and attention that is afforded them.

The clapping drew a little gasp from the churchgoers, and my eyes flew to see who was committing the faux pas. Toward the back of the church, standing next to the pew where his grandparents always sat, dressed in a white dress shirt and black pants, his hair pulled back off his face and secured in a low ponytail, was Samuel. He was clapping, his face serious and unashamed, and he kept clapping and clapping. His grandparents were seated beside him, their faces torn as to whether they should silence him or clap with him. Slowly, people began to join him, standing up around him as broad smiles broke out and the clapping became a roar.

I stood unmoving, not knowing quite what to do, until Sonja stole to my side and asked me to play Schubert's "Ave Maria" . I knew "Ave Maria" by heart only because I loved it. I had never intended to perform it, but the continued applause encouraged me, and I sat back down on the bench and began the unplanned encore, inviting my audience to be seated and listen. When I finished the intensely beautiful and sacred number, there was no clapping. The silence was total and complete, the room hushed, as the congregation wept openly.

Sonja told me later there wasn't a dry eye in the place. I found my eyes returning to where Samuel had stood. His eyes met mine, and he nodded once, solemnly. I slightly bowed and walked back to my pew where my father waited for me with open arms.

"You never told me you could play the piano like that."

Samuel and I were back on the bus again, the heat pouring out of the heaters under the seats, the smell of wet feet and rubber boots wafting up all around us. Christmas vacation was over, two weeks of freedom ended, and the kids were glum. I had not seen Samuel since the Christmas Eve service.

"When was I supposed to tell you?" I asked, stumped. "We've never discussed music. Do you play an instrument?"

"No. We have traditional songs—but I don't really know anyone that plays an instrument." Samuel looked at me in wonder. "But you... you play like...like no one I've ever heard."

"Thank you." Samuel's words washed me in pleasure. "And thank you for clapping," I said softly. "It was the most beautiful moment of my life." I realized I sounded a little overdramatic, and I felt my cheeks turn pink. But it was true. I had never experienced anything like it. The music, the applause, the beauty of the church, and the people I loved looking at me and *listening* to me. I had never in my life been the center of attention, and I knew now why people performed. I had learned to play simply for the love of music and for the joy it gave me. But performing definitely had its perks. Just thinking of Samuel, of the expression on his face as he stood and clapped for me! I would never forget it for as long as I lived.

"It was for me, too." Samuel's voice was gruff, and I could see he was embarrassed by his admission. "I have never heard music like that."

"Did you know you weren't supposed to clap?" I asked shyly, smiling at him.

"Yes. But I couldn't help myself."

"Someday, I'm going to travel the world, playing beautiful music, making people happy, hearing people clap," I said dreamily, and for a moment we sat together in companionable silence, contemplating my future.

"Would you like to hear something?" I asked him suddenly, reaching for my cassette player and my headphones. Sonja and Doc had given them to me for Christmas, and I had spent the remainder of the holidays making tapes from my favorite music in Sonja's collection.

I pulled out my Sony Walkman and popped it open, looking at the music inside. 'Beethoven' it read, in careful print. I pushed play and Beethoven's Ninth Symphony filled my ears. I rewound it to the beginning and placed the earphones on Samuel's ears. I listened to music loudly; you can't really appreciate classical music, the rises, the individual notes and trills, if you don't turn it up and give it your complete attention. I pushed play and held my breath.

I don't know why I cared so much. But I did. I felt like I was revealing something very private about myself, and Samuel's approval and appreciation of this music was paramount to me. I had come to care deeply about his opinion, and I wasn't quite sure how I would react if he rejected my music. It might feel like a rejection of me. If he said, "It's okay" or "Hmmm, interesting" it might also affect the way I felt about *him*. Realizing this, I regretted my spontaneous gesture and tried to remove the headphones from his head. I suddenly didn't want to know what he thought.

His hands flew up and covered mine, and his eyes met mine fiercely as he pulled his head away. My hands fell to my lap, and I looked out the window dejectedly, waiting until he was finished. Every once in a while I sneaked looks at him. His eyes were cast downward, and his hands were locked over the earphones where he had placed them after my attempt to take them. There was rigidity to his posture that I couldn't decipher. The music was loud enough that I could faintly hear when 'Ode to Joy' ended. I clicked the stop button, and Samuel slowly pulled the earphones from his head.

"What is it called?" he asked, and there was reverence in his voice.

"It's Beethoven's Ninth Symphony. It's also known as 'Ode to Joy.'" Samuel looked at me as if he wanted to hear more.

"Beethoven first heard the poem called "To Joy" more than 30 years before he set it to music with his Ninth Symphony. The ninth symphony was his last. By the time it was completed, Beethoven was deaf and sick. It had taken him ten years to complete it. He changed the 'Joy' theme over two hundred different times until he was satisfied with it." I stopped, not certain whether he wanted to hear more.

"He was deaf?" Samuel's voice lifted in astonishment.

"Yes. Sonja told me that he couldn't hear the audience applauding behind him when he conducted it for the first time in Vienna. A singer turned him around so that he could see the people cheering and clapping throughout the concert hall. He would lie on the floor during rehearsals so that he could feel the vibrations of the music."

"How did he know what it sounded like? I mean, in order to write music, don't you need to be able to hear it?" Samuel replied in wonder.

"It was inside him, I guess." I pursed my lips in contemplation. "It was in his head and in his heart. I guess he felt the music, so he didn't have to hear it with his physical ears." I paused. "Sonja told me once that many of the great composers, including Beethoven, have said that the music they compose is in the air. That's it's already there, and you just have to be able to hear it. Most of us can't. We can only appreciate that people like Beethoven seem to be able to, and then write down what they hear."

"Do you hear it?" Samuel asked, his eyes penetrating.

"I don't hear it...but I know it's there." I struggled to express something that I had never put into words. "Sometimes I think if I could just *see* without my eyes, the way I *feel* without my hands that I would be able to *hear* the music. I don't use my hands to feel love or joy or heartache, but I still feel them all the same. My eyes let me see incredibly beautiful things, but sometimes I think that what I *see* gets in the way of what's...what's just beyond the beauty. Almost like the beauty I can *see* is just a very lovely curtain, distracting me from what's on the other side...and if I just knew how to push that curtain aside, there the music would be." I threw up my hands in frustration. "I can't really explain it."

Samuel nodded his head slowly. "I found myself closing my eyes while you were playing that night in the church. Other people did the same thing. Maybe that's why. Our ears were trying to hear what our eyes keep hidden."

He understood. I felt a swelling in my heart and a sudden, fierce urge to hug him.

"It's in the air," Samuel mused softly. His eyes were unfocused and his brow creased in reflection. "Like *nítch'i*."

"What?" I didn't understand.

"It's like *nítch'i*. *Nítch'i* is the Navajo for air or the wind...but it is more than that. It is holy, and it has power. My grandmother says *nítch'i* means the Holy Wind Spirit. Everything in the living world communicates through *nítch'i*. Because of this, the Holy Wind Spirit, *nítch'i*, sits at the ears of the Diné, or the people, and whispers instructions—tells them right from wrong. People who constantly ignore the *nítch'i* are abandoned. The *ni'ch'i* will not remain with them." Samuel's eyes became focused again, drawing down on mine. "My grandmother believes that the nítch'i is breathed into a newborn baby as they take their first breath. The child then has the companionship of the *nítch'i* at all times. *Nítch'i* guides him as he grows.

"It sounds like the Holy Ghost. I learned about the Holy Ghost in church. It helps you to do what's right, guards you, warns you, leads you, but only if you are worthy of his company. It only speaks the truth. My Sunday School teacher says it is the way God talks to us."

"Maybe what Beethoven hears is *nítch'i* singing God's music.

"I think you might be right."

I rewound the cassette and extended the earphones to fit a head the size of Goliath's. Then I leaned close to Samuel and fit the whole thing over both of our heads, one earphone on my left ear, one earphone on his right and we listened to God's music with our heads pressed close together for the rest of bus ride.

Samuel never complained about my taste in music. In fact, he seemed to enjoy it immensely. He rigged my earphones so that we could turn the fuzzy ear pads outward, so that our heads weren't pressed together when we listened. I hadn't minded a bit...but I wasn't going to admit it. He seemed concerned that someone might misconstrue the intimate proximity of our heads. We each held one side of the headphones pressed to our ear. After about a week of non-stop Beethoven, I brought my tape of Rachmaninoff. We were listening intently to Prelude in C Sharp Minor, and Samuel's black eyes were wide and shining. He turned toward me as the movement came to a stunning finish.

His voice was awed. "This music makes me feel so powerful, like I could do anything...like nothing could stop me as long as I kept the music pounding into my head. And there's just that one small part where the music becomes triumphant, like the intensity is climbing and climbing and pushing and reaching and then those three chords play and it says 'I did it!!!' Kind of like Rocky raising his hands at the top of all those stairs. You know what I mean?" His voice was soft and sincere, and he looked at me then, smiling a little sheepishly at his enthusiastic review. "It's so powerful that...I almost believe if I kept on listening I would really become Super Sam!"

I laughed, delighted with his rare humor. Samuel didn't joke around a lot, and he was definitely not verbose.

"I know exactly what you mean. Remember when I fractured my ankle?" I confessed sheepishly. "I got a little carried away with the music in my head and for a minute I was convinced I could fly."

Samuel stared at me with a half smile on his face, shaking his head.

"Maybe I will have to make us matching capes and this can be our theme music." I struck a pose. "Super Sam and Bionic Josie here to save the day!" I sung out.

Samuel actually laughed out loud. The sound was even better than the music, and I smiled at him, happier than I could ever remember being.

Samuel sat silently for a moment, not putting the earphone back up to his ear. I pushed the stop button on my player.

"Do you think you could make me a copy of that tape?" Samuel asked stiffly. I wondered why it was so hard for him to ask such a simple thing when I was so obviously his friend.

"Sure. Definitely," I said brightly.

Samuel looked at me, his eyes troubled, and the joy of the music fading to a new concern. "I told you I wanted to go into the Marines, right?"

I nodded my head, waiting for him to continue.

"I'm scared to death." He held my gaze fiercely, daring me to speak. I stayed silent.

"A Marine has to know how to swim...and I have been in a pool exactly twice in my life. I grew up on an Indian reservation, Josie, herding sheep all summer long, not swimming. I can dog paddle...sort of." His voice trailed off.

"Why do you want to be a Marine, Samuel?" I was curious as to why, if he didn't know how to swim, he wanted to try in the first place.

Samuel was quiet for a minute. When he answered I wasn't sure he had understood my question.

"My shimasani, my Navajo grandmother, said that when I was born she hung my umbilical cord on her gun rack because she knew I was going to be a warrior. It is a Navajo tradition." He smiled briefly as my eyes widened.

"It's a tradition to hang the umbilical cord on the gun rack?" I blurted incredulously.

"It's tradition to save the umbilical cord and put it in a special place that will be important to the newborn child when they are grown. It can be buried in the corral if it is believed the child will

64

have an affinity for horses. It can be buried in the cornfield if the child will make his living from the land or under the loom if the child is thought to have the gift of weaving. My grandmother said she knew I would have to struggle to find my way in two worlds, and I would need a warrior's spirit. Originally, she buried it in her hogan so that I would always know where my home was. But she says it felt wrong and she prayed many days to decide where to place my umbilical cord. She said the hogan would not always be my home, and she dug it up and put it on the gun rack."

I met his gaze, intrigued. He continued, "She believed I would follow in my grandfather's footsteps."

"Who was your grandfather?"

"My Navajo grandfather was a Marine."

"I see. So you've always thought you would be a Marine because your grandmother believed that was your destiny?"

"I believe it is, too. I've dreamed about seeing other places, about belonging, about being a part of something that had nothing to do with being Navajo or being white, or any other culture. If you make it through twelve weeks of Marine training, you're a Marine, one of the few and the proud." Samuel's mouth twisted humorlessly as he quoted the slogan. "I don't have any siblings. My mom remarried to a man who already had five children, so I have three step-sisters and two step-brothers, all older than me. I don't know them very well, and I don't especially like them. They call me 'the white boy' when my mother isn't around. I want out, Josie. I don't want to go back home to the reservation. I'm proud of my heritage, but I don't want to go back. I do not want to herd sheep my whole life."

"So...this swimming thing. Is that the only problem?" I said tentatively.

He looked at me sharply. "I'd say it's a pretty major problem."

"The school has a pool, Samuel. Can't you learn? Isn't there someone who would teach you?"

"Who?" Samuel gazed at me angrily, "Who Josie? When? You are such a child! I ride this bus for forty minutes every morning and forty minutes every afternoon. I have no way of getting to school early or staying late. I have no driver's license, so even if Don would let me take the truck, I'm useless."

"I'm not a child, Samuel!" He had turned on me so suddenly, and his anger made me angry, too. "Maybe you need to ask for a little help. Don't be so stubborn! I'm sure someone at the school would be willing to teach you, especially if they knew why you needed to learn."

"Nobody wants to help me, and I'd rather drown than ask anyone." Samuel's face was grim and his fists were clenched. "I'm sorry I called you a child. Just…forget it, okay?"

We sat in silence the rest of the way into the school. I wondered why the music had made him think about being a Marine. Maybe because Rachmaninoff made him feel powerful when he felt so powerless.

# 6. Impromptu

P.E. WAS MANDATORY in junior high. I had lived in fear of undressing in the locker room the entire summer leading up to seventh grade. I had horrible visions of having to shower in those open stalls, all of my skinny, prepubescent classmates staring at my private parts. I had nightmares of running through the locker room, bare naked, looking for a towel while everyone else stood fully clothed, gaping at me. Music by Wagner screamed through the dream.

Luckily, showering was not mandatory, and I brought a huge towel from home, kept it in my locker, and huddled behind it while I changed into my gym clothes every day. I had long legs and enjoyed running, but that was as far as my athletic prowess went. Organized sports were beyond me. I was more than slightly spastic. During our unit on basketball, I attempted to make a basket, throwing it as hard as I could at the hoop, only to have it rebound sharply off the backboard and smack me in the face, bloodying my nose and blackening my eyes. I hated dodge ball even worse, and jumping rope was an absolute joke. I usually ended up volunteering to turn the rope for everyone else or shagging balls in order to avoid having to participate. I was consistently assigned to 'work with' the two mentally challenged girls that participated in gym class, not because I could actually help them athletically, but because I was nice. I have to say though, both of them could beat me hands down in dodge ball and basketball. They were better at jump rope, too.

That day in P.E. we were doing calisthenics—a fancy word for stretching—which was fairly safe for those less coordinated, like yours truly. Ms. Swenson, my P.E. coach, had a teacher's aide leading us in the stretches. Her aid was a high school cheerleader named Marla Painter, who was very beautiful and very…stretchy. Her kicks were so high she could hit herself in the side of the head with her kneecap. She was showing us all three splits as I unfolded myself and slunk over to where Ms. Swenson was sitting grading papers. I supposed they were from the health class she taught. I had never seen a single sheet of paper in P.E.

"Ms. Swenson?" I asked shyly. Ms. Swenson didn't care much for me. She didn't have a lot of patience for the Klutz club, of which I was president.

Ms. Swenson finished checking the paper she was on before lifting her eyes in exasperation from the page.

"Yes?" she answered impatiently.

"I have a friend who needs to learn how to swim. Uh, how exactly could he go about doing that here at the school, preferably during school hours?" I finished in a rush, hoping she wouldn't slap me down too quickly.

"What grade is he in?" she asked, her eyes back on her page, checking away.

"He's a senior. He's my neighbor in Levan, and transportation is a bit of a problem. He wants to join the Marines when he graduates, but he needs to learn to swim." Again I rushed through my explanation, daring to hope, but not hoping too fervently.

"Why are you asking for him?" she said suspiciously.

"He's new to the school, and a little shy—so I told his grandmother I would find out," I lied, feeling my cheeks burn.

"Hmm. Go with Marla back up to the high school when she finishes. I'll give you a note. You have lunch next, right?"

All seventh graders had first lunch, and I nodded my head eagerly.

"Ask Coach Judd or Coach Jasperson about it. Maybe they can work something out for him. I have a brother who's a Marine. You gotta know how to swim," she finished in an almost pleasant tone.

"Thank you very much, Ms. Swenson." I waited while she scribbled me a note and signed it like she was in the medical profession.

Marla took me to the high school gym and snagged a boy, who was heading into the locker room, to see if either Coach Judd or Coach Jasperson was in his office inside. She bounced off after that, leaving me waiting outside the boys' locker room for the messenger to return. I waited for a very long time. Either the coaches weren't in there, or the boy had gotten distracted. I was about ready to give up in despair when the last person I wanted to see came walking through the gymnasium toward the boys' locker room.

"Josie...what are you doing?" Samuel said, befuddled to see me lurking outside a place I had no business being.

"Ms. Swenson sent me up to speak with Coach Judd or Coach Jasperson. Marla Painter came with me, but she left and I can't go in there!" My voice sounded a little like a wail, and I embarrassed myself with the sudden urge to cry. I wasn't about to tell Samuel I was here for him.

"Just a minute," he offered helpfully. "I'll go see if there's someone in there."

At that moment, Coach Jasperson accompanied Marla's messenger out of his inner sanctum. Coach Jasperson was eating a huge tuna sandwich with potato chips smashed in between the bread. Apparently, he hadn't wanted to give up any of his lunch break to chat with me. I breathed a sigh of relief and then shuddered in dread. This was going to embarrass me and embarrass Samuel. I knew he might never forgive me, but I did it anyway. As the messenger sauntered away I began to speak.

"Coach Jasperson, Samuel here is my neighbor." I gestured toward Samuel, not daring to look at him. "He wants to join the Marines when he graduates. The problem is he doesn't know how to swim. He needs to be in a swim class or something here at the school, working with someone who can teach him." I was talking so fast Coach Jasperson had stopped chewing in order to keep up. "He can't come early to school, and he can't stay late for transportation reasons, so it would be a very good thing if you could make sure he gets the help he needs during school hours." I sounded like one of those wind-up dolls, prattling along cheerfully.

I sneaked a look at Samuel. His face was like a cold, hard mask. I knew he would never speak to me again. My heart broke a little.

"I'm sure Samuel would be glad to speak to a guidance counselor to rearrange his schedule to make it work." I had done what I could do, and my voice trailed off nervously.

"The Marines, huh?" Coach Jasperson was chewing again. "I'm sure we could figure something out...it was Samuel, right? You speak English?"

I cringed. I could see why Coach Jasperson thought he might not. After all, I had done all the talking for him.

"Yes I speak English." Samuel's reply was sharp, and I heard the outrage in his voice. He was furious with me. Still, I hoped Coach Jasperson didn't hear it and misunderstand.

"Good, good!" Coach Jasperson was too busy enjoying his sandwich, and he missed the darts shooting from Samuel's onyx eyes.

"Well, you and I will go see Mr. Whiting, the guidance counselor, and I will set you up with one of the guys from the swim team. I think Justin McPherson could help you during second period. He's my aid, and I never have much for him to do. If we can free your schedule up during second hour, you should be set."

Bless Coach Jasperson for being very helpful and a little oblivious at the same time. He put one arm around Samuel's shoulders, pulling him along, talking to him while he licked the last of the tuna salad from his fingers. Samuel turned and looked at me over Coach

Jasperson's beefy arm. I bit my lip to keep from tearing up as he glared at me. He turned his head dismissively, and I left the gymnasium as quickly as I could.

I missed the bus on purpose that night and waited until almost five o'clock that afternoon to get a ride home with Johnny after wrestling practice. I was tired and hungry and more than a little distraught. I had finished all my homework, including a book report not due for another two weeks. I'd tried to read but found myself too jittery to focus. I longed for my music books—at least I could have gone into the band room and practiced the piano. I had called Sonja from the school office to tell her I wouldn't be at my lesson that afternoon. When it was finally time to go, I had to sit crammed in between Johnny and another sweaty wrestler all the way home from Nephi. I should have just taken the bus, but I couldn't face Samuel yet.

The next day I faked sick. My dad didn't question me too hard. In fact, he didn't question me at all. I never faked sick, so when I said I didn't feel well and wasn't going, he just shrugged his shoulders, felt my head, and asked me if I needed him to stay home from work to be with me.

"Ugh! Please no!" I thought desperately. Then I would have to fake sick all day. I told him I would just sleep and that I would be fine all by myself. He didn't need much convincing. I spent the day playing the piano until my back and neck ached and my fingers kept playing even after I stopped.

At 3:30, the doorbell rang. I was back on the piano playing Fur Elise, my feet bare, wearing my favorite old jeans and the soft blue BYU sweatshirt Jared had given me for Christmas. I ran my fingers through my hair and walked to the door, expecting Tara.

Samuel stood on the porch, his hands pushed down into his pockets, his head uncovered, and his silky black hair blowing in the cold January wind. He didn't have his backpack, so I assumed he had gone home first. I wondered what excuse he had made in order to come see me. My heart was pounding so hard I was sure he could hear it.

"Can I talk to you for a minute?" His voice held no anger, but there was a tightness around his mouth that I hated.

I moved aside and opened the door wider, indicating that he should come inside. He seemed hesitant to enter but must have realized we couldn't sit out on the porch in the cold for very long. Plus, his grandpa or someone might drive by, and explaining would be weird. People in small towns saw things and talked. If someone saw Samuel sitting on my front porch with me, tongues would start wagging and that would not be good.

Samuel stepped inside, and I shut the door behind him. He didn't sit down but stood stiffly a few steps from the door. I resumed my perch on the piano bench. I curled one leg up under me and stared down at the black and white keys, waiting.

"Are you sick?" Samuel asked bluntly.

"No." My voice was a whisper.

"Why didn't you go to school today? And where were you yesterday after school?" His voice was flat.

I tried to speak around the giant lump in my throat and had to swallow a few times to get the words to come out. "I was afraid to see you." He seemed surprised that I would just come right out and admit it.

"What did you think I would do?" he asked sharply.

"It's not what you would *do*," I answered miserably, the lump in my throat growing, choking me. "It's how you would *act*. I can't stand it—you being so mad at me. You looked at me yesterday like you wished I was dead, and I just couldn't face you knowing how much you hated me!" I folded my arms around myself, willing the pain in my heart to subside.

"I was mad...but I could never hate you." His voice was soft, and I felt the tightness in my chest ease just enough to make breathing easier.

"I wish you hadn't done that, but a part of me was glad that you did. I think that makes me even more ticked off. I hate it that part of me is thankful for what you did. It's weak to need or want someone to speak for me." He paused for a minute, and I shifted on the piano bench so that I could face him. He glared down at me, his jaw set, his eyes wet. "You can't do that again, Josie. I don't want you to take care of me. I know you did it because you *do* care....but don't take my pride from me."

"Is pride more important than friendship?" I said sadly.

"Yes!" Samuel's voice was harsh and emphatic.

"That is so ridiculous!" I threw my arms wide in frustration.

"Josie! You are just a little girl! You don't know how helpless and weak and stupid it made me feel to stand there while you arranged my life like I was some kind of charity case!" Samuel fisted his hands in his hair and, growling, turned toward the door.

"I am not a little girl! I haven't been a little girl for years...for *ever*! I don't think like a little girl, and I don't act like a little girl. I don't LOOK like a little girl, do I? Don't you dare say I am a little girl!" I pounded down on the piano keys, playing a violent riff, reminiscent of Wagner himself. Now I knew what Sonja meant by letting out the beast! I wanted to throw something or smash something and scream at Samuel. He was so impossible! Such a stubborn, mule-headed jerk! I played hard for several minutes, and Samuel stood at the door, dumbfounded.

Suddenly, Samuel sat down beside me on the piano bench and put his hands over the top of mine, bringing the din to a halt.

"I'm sorry, Josie," Samuel said softly. I was crying, tears dripping down onto the keys, making them slippery. I was a terrible beast, not fierce at all—just a blubbering baby beast. Samuel seemed at a loss. He sat very still, his hands covering mine. Slowly, his hands rose to my face and gently wiped the tears from my cheeks.

73

"Will you play something else?" he requested softly, his voice remorseful. "Will you play something for me...please?"

I wiped my tears off of the piano keys with the bottom of my sweatshirt. He waited patiently beside me, letting me regain my composure. I was still hurt and frustrated, and I didn't understand him at all. But I had never been able to hold on to anger very long, and I forgave him immediately, giving in with a soggy sigh.

"You know I love 'Ode to Joy' but I don't really want to play that right now." My voice was a little gravely from crying, and I looked up at him. "Have you ever heard Mozart's Piano Concerto Number 23 in A Major?"

"Umm, I really wouldn't know if I had." He smiled ruefully as he looked down at me, shaking his head and wiping a stray tear from my cheek.

"It's my favorite song...today." I grinned a little. "I have different favorites on different days. But today is a Mozart day."

His hands fell to his lap as I began playing. I plucked out the lilting melody, trilling through the notes, fingers flying though the rolling chords, coaxing every last bit of aching sweetness from the wistful concerto. How I loved this music! How it healed me and filled me and soothed me.

The last musical phrases were so soft, so faint, that Samuel leaned in to hear the very last high, clear notes as my fingers grew still on the keys. I looked up at him then. He was staring down at my hands resting on the now silent keys.

"Play more," Samuel urged softly. "Play the one you played at Christmas...the second one."

I acquiesced immediately, my heart swelling at his response, his sincere enjoyment.

"Does it have a name?" he said reverently when I finished.

"*Ave Maria.*" I smiled. "It's beautiful, isn't it? It was written by Franz Schubert. He was only thirty-one years old when he died. He died completely broke, not knowing that his music would be treasured by people forever."

"And you know this because....?" Samuel raised his eyes to mine in question.

"My piano teacher, Mrs. Grimaldi, tells me all about the composers when I play their music. She says to be a great composer, I have to love the great composers, and if I don't know them, how can I love them?"

"Which one do you love the most?"

I giggled a little. "It's kind of like my favorite song. It changes all the time, depending on what kind of mood I'm in. Mrs. Grimaldi says I am a very mercurial musician."

"I think I'm going to have to go look that word up."

"The dictionary says it means active, sprightly, and full of vigor." I laughed. "I had to look it up as soon as she said it, but I think Mrs. Grimaldi meant always changing, unpredictable."

"So who is your favorite composer today?"

"Lately, I have been enamored with Frederick Chopin."

"Does enamored mean in love with?"

I giggled again. "More like captivated by."

"Why are you captivated by him?"

"He *was* handsome," I answered promptly and felt like a silly idiot when Samuel raised his eyebrows and smirked. "But mostly it was because he wrote mainly for the piano...more than any other composer in history. I am a pianist so...I like that. He was also very young when he died, only thirty-nine years old. He died of Tuberculosis. He also had a torrid love affair with a famous writer. He was filled with guilt because he never married her, and he was certain he was going to go to hell because of it. He ended their relationship before he died, trying to repent of his sinful behavior, but it's so romantic. He was such a tragic figure."

"So play something by Chopin," Samuel demanded.

I had the first portion of Chopin's *Nocturne in C Minor* memorized, and I loved the dramatic rhythm of the low—high, low—high pattern throughout the beginning. It was a moody piece, and it appealed to my romantic nature when suddenly it became sweet and melodic, full of nostalgia and tenderness. I had not memorized the incredible difficulty of the final movement that tied it all together in a triumphant and impressive finish, so I improvised a little to end it before I got there.

"I can see why you are enamored," Samuel teased. He was relaxed and his mouth was curved in pleasure. "Now play me something you've written."

I froze in discomfort. "I am not a composer, Samuel," I said stiffly.

"You mean you haven't made up any songs? Mozart was...how old did you say? Four or five? When he started making up...what are they called?"

"Minuets," I supplied.

"You haven't even tried to compose a little?" he prodded.

"A little," I admitted, embarrassed.

"So...let me hear something."

I remained unmoving, my hands in my lap.

"Josie...all I know about music, I've learned from you. You could play something by Beethoven, say it was yours, and I wouldn't know any better. I will think whatever you play is wonderful. You know that, right?" he urged me gently.

I had been working on something. A few months back, a melody had shivered its way into my subconscious, and I hadn't been able to place it. It had lurked, pestering me, until finally I had hummed it for Sonja, fingering it on the piano, creating chords out of the single notes and embellishing the melody line. She had listened silently and then asked me to play it again and again. Each time I played I added more, layering and building until she stopped me, touching my shoulder softly. When I looked up at her from the piano, there was awe in her face, almost a spiritual glow.

"This is yours, Josie," she said.

"What do you mean?" I asked, confused.

"I've never heard this music. This isn't something you heard. This is something you created." She beamed, joyfully.

I thought of the music now as Samuel sat next to me, waiting patiently, hoping I would give in. The music had come to me after we had quarreled about Heathcliff and the meaning of true love. When I thought of the music, I thought of Samuel.

I brought my hands to the keys and exhaled slowly, letting the music seep into my fingers. I played intently. There was a yearning in the melody that I recognized as my own loneliness. The music never became powerful but moved me in its simplicity and its clarity. I brushed the keys gently, coaxing the song from my timid soul. It was a humble offering, not nearly worthy yet of Mozart even at a young age, but it echoed with the passion of a sincere heart. When the last note faded and Samuel had still not spoken, I peered up at him apprehensively.

"What is it called?" he whispered, bringing his ebony eyes to hold mine.

"Samuel's Song," I whispered back, staring at him, suddenly brave and unapologetic.

He turned his face away from me abruptly, and he seemed unable to speak. He stood and walked to the door. He paused there, with his hand on the doorknob, his head bowed.

"I need to go now." Samuel looked at me then, and there was a battle being waged in his eyes, turmoil on his face. "Your song…that is the nicest thing anyone's ever done for me." His voice was filled with emotion. And with that, he opened the door and walked out into the icy stillness, shutting the door softly behind him.

# 7. Dissonance

THE LAST WEEK in February, Samuel didn't come to school. On Monday, I thought maybe he was sick or something, but after a few days I was worried about him. By Thursday, I couldn't stand it anymore, so I came up with a plan to see him. Nettie Yates had given me a recipe for chocolate chip zucchini bread when we were canning the summer before. She had shredded the zucchini into freezer bags and taped the laminated recipe to the pouches so that I could "just whip some up whenever I wanted to!" I had yet to make it. Zucchini and chocolate chips seemed like an odd combination.

I was grateful now for an excuse to go see her and hopefully find out what was up with Samuel. I pulled some shredded zucchini out of the freezer, made up a couple loaves of the chocolate chip zucchini bread, and headed out into the icy February evening, a loaf of the hot bread wrapped in a dish cloth and held against me, keeping my fingers warm.

Nettie Yates answered the door after a couple of knocks and seemed glad to see me.

"Josie," she exclaimed happily. "How nice to see you! Come in, come in! Oh, it's miserable out there! Did you walk?"

"It's not far, Mrs. Yates," I said trying to talk between my chattering teeth. "I made zucchini bread from that recipe you gave me and thought maybe you would like to try it and maybe give me some pointers," I lied smoothly.

"What a perfect day for warm zucchini bread! I'd love some! Come into the kitchen. You can put your coat and boots back in the mud room by the back door."

I handed her the loaf, bound tightly like a baby in a blanket, and pulled my coat and boots off. I didn't see any sign of Samuel. I padded through the kitchen on stocking feet, trying to search without looking obvious about it. Samuel's coat wasn't hanging on any of the hooks in the mudroom. I turned to hurry back in the warm kitchen when I heard someone coming up the back steps. The door whooshed open and Don Yates came tumbling in, nose and cheeks red, cowboy hat pulled low. I scurried out of the mudroom into the kitchen, not wanting to be standing there staring if Samuel was right behind him.

"Woo Wee! It is colder than a witch's kiss out there!" Don Yates slammed the door closed behind him. I heard him pulling off his boots and unzipping his coat. Samuel wasn't with him.

"Josie Jensen is here, Don!" Nettie called out from the kitchen. "She brought us some nice zucchini bread. Come on in and I'll get you some hot coffee to go with it."

Don came tottering in, still bundled in thermals and flannel, rubbing his hands together.

"Hello, Miss Josie." Don went to the sink and washed his hands and face while Nettie cut the zucchini bread and spread butter thickly over the top. I sat down, not sure how I was going to get the information I needed. Samuel obviously wasn't here…unless he was sick in his room.

"Josie, the bread looks wonderful!" Nettie exclaimed. I took a big bite of the slice Nettie set before me, chewing it slowly, trying to buy myself some time to plot. It was really good. Who knew zucchini would work with chocolate chips? You couldn't taste the zucchini—it just made the bread moist. The bread tasted like thick, spicy cake, the chocolate chips imbedded around the edges. I felt a surge of pride that it had turned out so well.

"It's gonna be ten below tonight," Don muttered to himself. "I've got the horses inside, but it's gonna be miserable for 'em all the same. I hate February…most miserable month of the year," Don grumbled under his breath.

"So…Mrs. Yates.…I noticed Samuel wasn't on the bus…is he sick?" I stunk at subterfuge.

"Oh, heavens no!" Mrs. Yates declared, covering her mouth as she tried to answer between bites. "Samuel went back to the reservation."

Time stopped, and I stared at Nettie Yates in horror.

"For good?" My voice rose with a squeak, and I stared down at my half-eaten slice of bread, my mind spinning. "He's not coming back?" I said in a more controlled tone, though my heart was constricting painfully in my chest.

"Well, we don't know exactly," Nettie said carefully, sharing a meaningful look with Don.

"What does that mean?" My fear was making me impertinent.

"Well," Nettie started every sentence with 'well', especially when she was trying to be discreet.

"Samuel's mom wants him back home." Don's gravelly voice was blunt as he wiped the back of his hand over his lips, checking his mustache for crumbs.

"But…" I tried to proceed gingerly, not wanting to give my feelings away. "Won't it be hard for Samuel to finish school if he leaves now?"

"His mom said he doesn't need to finish if he's just going to herd sheep. She says they need him there." I could tell Don was none too happy about the situation. "Samuel is eighteen years old. Legally, he's an adult, and nobody can make him finish."

"But I thought she was the one who wanted him to come here!" I was angry and confused, and my face probably showed it.

"She did!" I must have hit a nerve, because Don's voice rose emphatically. "She talked to him on the phone last week. She said he sounded good and decided he 'was cured'." Don lifted up his fingers

80

and waggled them, making quotations in the air as he repeated the words Samuel's mother had used.

"But...what about the Marines?" I was trying to keep my composure. I couldn't let them know how much this conversation was upsetting me. "He's worked so hard! He's even learning how to swim!"

Nettie set down her bread and looked at me in surprise. "How did you know about the Marines?"

"Samuel and I are assigned to the same seat on the bus, Mrs. Yates," I confessed. "I've talked to him a little bit. He's been trying so hard to get good grades, too! I can't believe he's just going to quit school."

"Samuel's bein' pulled in two directions, Josie." Don shook his head and rubbed his hand over the back of his neck. "I don't know that he feels like he has a lot of say in the matter."

I needed to get out of there. I was going to burst into tears, and there was no way I was going to do it in front of Don and Nettie. I bit my inner cheek hard, the sharp pain postponing my rising emotion.

"Well, I'd better get on home. Dad's going to be wanting something hot to eat on a night like this." I headed to the mudroom and grabbed my things, not letting myself breathe too deeply, not releasing my soft inner cheek from my teeth.

I yanked on my boots and zipped up my coat frantically, pulling the hood down over my messy curls. Don made a move to get up, maybe to see me home.

"Don't worry about me getting home, Mr. Yates. I can see our front porch light from here. It's only a block. I'll be fine."

"Well, thanks for comin' by, Josie." Nettie seemed a little stumped by my erratic behavior. I'm sure she thought my interest in Samuel was a little peculiar as well.

I took my dishtowel from her outstretched hand and turned to leave.

I stopped, torn between my concern for Samuel and my wish to vacate the kitchen before I dissolved into a howling puddle.

"If you talk to Samuel soon will you tell him I came by and asked about him? Please remind him about his umbilical cord."

Nettie and Don stared at me like I had lost my marbles. "Just tell him, okay? He'll understand."

I fled through the house and out into the frigid February evening.

Another week passed. March came, and Samuel didn't come back to school. I didn't return for updates from Don and Nettie. It would only raise questions, and I had raised enough already. I had started making him tapes of all the music we had been listening to. I had made him a collection of greatest hits from all the composers I loved. I had ten tapes of my favorites, everything from Beethoven to Gershwin. I had put my absolute favorites on one tape and entitled it Josie's Top 10. I had included Rachmaninoff's Prelude in C Sharp Minor that Samuel had loved. It had not been among my top ten before, but it always would be now. Each cassette case had the titles neatly labeled next to the composer. I didn't know how I was going to give him the gift now.

Then one morning, about two weeks after he left, I climbed on the bus, and he was sitting there waiting for me like he'd never been gone. I rushed to him and sat down, grabbing his hand in mine and holding on for all I was worth.

"You're here!" I was whispering, trying to be discreet, but I felt like laughing out loud and dancing. He turned his face toward me, and I saw that the left side of his face, from his eye to his chin, was covered with a mottled green and yellow bruise, most likely a few days old.

"What happened? Oh, Samuel, your face!"

Samuel let me hold his hand for a moment, clasping mine tightly in his as well. Then he gently extricated his fingers and folded his hands together, like he was afraid he might take my hand again.

"I'm here until I graduate, which is going to be harder than it would have been two weeks ago. I have to go to my teachers and beg them to help me. I missed mid-terms and big assignments in every class. I have to read Othello." He grimaced and looked at me. "I might need your help with that." I nodded my head willingly as he continued. "When I graduate, my grandparents are going to take me to San Diego for Marine boot camp. I don't think I'll be going back to the rez any time soon." Sorrow bracketed his mouth and his lips turned down slightly.

I reached up with my right hand and gently touched his bruised cheekbone. "What happened?" I asked again, hoping he wouldn't pull away.

"Complements of my mom's husband."

"He hit you?" I whispered, shocked.

"Yeah. I hit him, too. Don't look so alarmed. I gave as good as I got. In fact, I had to hold back a little because he was so drunk it really wasn't a fair fight." Samuel's voice and face were smooth and untroubled. I wasn't really buying it.

"Your mom lets him hit you?"

"Mom doesn't have much control over anything at this point. She drinks way too much too, and she's scared of him. But she's more scared that he'll leave and even more scared that I will be the reason he does. It's better for everyone if I go and stay gone."

"But...I thought your mom wanted you back home. That's what your grandparents said."

"My mom doesn't want me to be a Marine and get myself killed in some white man's war. My mom doesn't understand why I want to go. She says she never should have married my father. She says I am leaving her because I am ashamed I am half Navajo. The funny thing is, she wants me gone, but she doesn't want me to go."

I felt his helplessness and didn't know how to comfort him. I didn't understand the relationship he had with his mother, or the difficulty in being of mixed race, from mixed cultures, full of mixed emotions.

"What made you decide to come back?" I didn't think I would have had the courage to leave my family.

"I spent some time with my grandmother. During the winter the sheep are corralled close to home, and my grandmother works almost non-stop at her loom. She makes these amazing rugs and blankets. She says her ability to weave is a gift from Spider Woman." He looked at me, a faint smile lurking around his firm lips. "Spider Woman is not related to Super Sam or Bionic Josie." He quirked his eyebrows at me and then continued, serious again. "Spider Woman is considered one of the Holy People—kind of like the Gods of the Navajo people.

"My grandmother never went to school. Her parents were suspicious of the schools of the white man. They hid her in the cornfield when the social service people came to enforce the education laws on the reservation. There were boarding schools for the children then. The children were sent away, and they weren't allowed to speak Navajo. Her parents worried that school would change her. They told her the sheep would provide for her and give her everything she needed.

"The funny thing is, they were right. My grandmother is very independent. She cares for the sheep, and they provide for her. She knows how to shear, wash, card, and spin the wool into yarn. From the yarn she makes the rugs and blankets to sell. The Navajo name for sheep means 'that by which we live.' She says she is grateful for the gift of weaving from Spider Woman, and for her sheep, for her hogan, for her life…but she wishes she had been able to go to school.

"When I was there she told me to study hard, to be proud of my heritage and not be afraid of myself. She said I was Navajo, but I was my father's son as well. One heritage was not more important than the other."

Samuel grew quiet, and I sat next to him in contemplative silence.

"I'll help you, Samuel."

"I know you will Josie. And Josie?"

"Hmm?"

"Remember when I told you that you were the furthest thing from a Navajo?"

I laughed a little, remembering the derision with which he had made the statement. "Yep, I remember."

"I realized something when I was with my grandmother." He paused, smiling faintly. "You remind me of her. Funny, huh?"

I pondered that for a minute. Samuel continued, apparently not expecting me to answer.

"She sang me a healing song before I left. Usually the chants and the songs are sung by the old men, but she said the words are like a prayer, and prayer is for everyone." The words of the song are:

*There is beauty behind me as I walk*
*There is beauty before me as I walk*
*There is beauty below me as I walk.*
*There is beauty above me as I walk.*
*In beauty I must always walk.*

"You always walk in beauty, Josie. You are constantly looking for it. I think you are secretly a Navajo after all." Samuel took my hand in his this time.

"Can I have a secret name?" I teased, but I was touched by his sentiment.

"I'll think about it." Samuels's lips twitched and merriment flitted across his stern features. "By the way, Nettie and Don said you came looking for me. They said you were acting strange and talking about umbilical cords." Samuel's eyes danced with laughter.

I giggled and covered my mouth with my free hand.

"Samuel?" He looked at me in response. "I think I have a new code word for music."

His forehead creased "What?"

"Sheep."

"Why?"

"Because music is 'that by which I live.'"

"B ee iináanii át'é?"

"Wow. Is that how you say it? That's even better."

And we listened to Mozart's 'Requiem' in peaceful companion-ship.

# 8. Deceptive Cadence

I TOLD SAMUEL that I would help him read Othello, but it proved difficult for me. I was not a stranger to Shakespeare's language, but the themes of jealousy, racism, and betrayal were not ones I enjoyed. I found myself increasingly anxious for Othello, and frustrated by the ease in which he fell for Iago's machinations. I desperately wanted a happy ending, and I wasn't going to get one.

Samuel seemed to take the story in stride, enjoying the plot and the complex Shakespearean prose. The play was not overly long, and by the end of the week we were in Act V, Scene 2. Samuel was reading the scene intently, and I was listening to his fluid voice relay the intricate tale without a single stumble or trip. I would have enjoyed just listening to his melodic cadence if it weren't for poor Desdemona's impending doom. I tried to hold my tongue and listen patiently, but found myself continually interrupting.

"She is innocent! Why is it so easy to believe she would betray him?" I was truly appalled.

Samuel looked up at me calmly and replied, "Because it's always easier to believe the worst."

I looked at him in disbelief. "It is not!" I sputtered. "I can't believe you would say that! Wouldn't you give the benefit of the doubt to someone you claimed to love?" The ease in which Othello accepted her betrayal was completely foreign to me. "And why would Othello believe Iago over Desdemona? I don't care how honest they think Iago is! Emilia even told Othello she thought he was being manipulated and tricked!"

Samuel sighed and tried to read to the end of the scene. I jumped in again. I couldn't help it. My sense of outrage was on overdrive.

"But he said, 'I loved not wisely, but too well!'" I was dismayed. "He had it totally backwards! He *did* love wisely! She was worthy of his love! She was a wise choice! But he didn't love well *enough*! If he had loved Desdemona more, trusted her more, Iago wouldn't have been able to divide them." I longed once again for Jane Eyre, where righteousness and principle won out in the end. Jane got her man, and she did it with style. Desdemona got her man, and he smothered her.

Samuel closed the book, slid it into his backpack, and looked at me affectionately. "It's over and done Josie, you never have to read it again."

"But...I want to understand why...why would he kill her? The one he is supposed to honor, protect, and defend." I was honestly devastated by the whole play. I felt a lump rising in my throat. To make matters worse, Samuel seemed outrageously unperturbed. I dug through my bag, looking for my Walkman. I shoved my earphones on and pushed the play button savagely. Then I sat back, squeezed my eyes shut, and tried to concentrate on the music. Chopin's 'Berceuse in D-flat' floated out of the earphones. After a few moments, I groaned in despair as the lovely melody seemed to underline the horror of innocent Desdemona's fate.

Samuel plucked the earphones off of my head, causing my eyelids to flutter open, and I stared at him stonily.

"What?" I mumbled.

"You are taking this too seriously," he said simply.

I jumped right back in with both feet. "Othello was so proud, and he was so accomplished! Yet, he was so easy to manipulate!" I argued passionately.

Samuel deliberated for a minute. "Othello was a man who'd had to fight and scrape to get where he was. He probably felt like at any moment his ship could spring a leak, and if it did? He would be the first one thrown overboard, even though it was his ship."

"So Othello was an easy target?" I muttered. "Easy because his pride was really a front for his insecurity?"

"Insecurity...past experience... life, who knows? His pride demanded that he seek justice. He had worked too hard to be mocked by those closest to him."

"So he was destroyed by his pride. Not Desdemona!"

"Ahhh, irony." Samuel smirked at me then and cuffed me lightly on the chin.

He handed me back my earphones, twisting his side outward so we could share Chopin. I studied the strong lines of his face, his black eyes growing unfocused as he zoned into the music. He was so striking, and his face grew serene as he listened. I felt increasingly bereft as the music played on, and I continued to watch his face, a face that had become so precious to me.

The bus chugged violently and jerked to a stop. Being the last ones on in the morning meant we were the first ones off every afternoon, as Mr. Walker worked backwards through his route. Samuel pulled his earphone off, handed the headset to me, and picked up my bag so that I could shove them inside. We swayed on unsteady legs down the vibrating aisle and down the steep steps into the late March sun. It bounced blindingly off the melting snow, and as Samuel started on his way I called after him, squinting against its brightness. He turned, eyebrows raised, swinging his backpack over one shoulder.

"Is love really so complicated?" I asked desperately. "Is it really so hard to trust? I don't understand." My mind flickered back to 1 Corinthians, Chapter 13. "Did Othello even love Desdemona to begin with?"

Samuel looked at me then, and there was a wisdom and understanding in his gaze that made me feel incredibly naive.

He closed the few steps between us. "Othello loved Desdemona. He was crazy about her. That was never the problem. Othello's problem was that he never felt worthy of Desdemona in the first place. He was the 'black Moor' and she was the 'fair Desdemona.'" Samuel's tone was conversational, but there was a certain wistfulness in his face. "It was too good to be true, too sweet to be reality for too long, so when someone set out to destroy his belief in her, it made more sense to doubt her than to believe that she had truly loved him in the first place."

"But she did!"

Samuel shrugged his shoulders a little, dismissing this. He turned away again.

"Samuel!"

"What Josie?!" The other kids that got off at our stop were trudging home and out of earshot by now, but he seemed reluctant to continue the conversation.

"But she did!" I insisted again, enunciating each word.

Samuel's eyes rested on my face, and I realized I was clenching my jaw tightly, my chin jutting out, daring him to deny it.

"I believe you, Josie," he said at last. He turned then and walked away, his gait smooth and unhurried, his moccasins quiet on the hard packed snow.

I felt relieved that we seemed to understand one another. It wasn't until I read the play again, many years later, that I realized we hadn't been talking about Desdemona and Othello at all.

The school year was drawing to a close. Samuel grew distant and withdrawn again, much like he had been in the beginning. He had been in constant touch with his recruiter and was mentally almost gone. He was swimming well enough now. He'd attacked the sport with a vengeance and was certain he would be okay throughout training, even if he wasn't the strongest swimmer. He had been running every night as well, trying to be as ready as he could be for boot camp. He told me that he wanted to get a perfect score on the fitness test. He had gotten all his medical records when he'd left the reservation. He had needed a series of shots that he'd never gotten, as well as some tests that were required. He was grim and testy the last month of school, ready to graduate, ready to move on.

I didn't really understand why he was so anxious to leave. Boot camp sounded horrible to me...and wouldn't he miss me at all? I couldn't imagine not seeing him every day, listening to music, reading together. As he grew increasingly more agitated and short-tempered, I grew steadily more forlorn. I wanted to give him a gift for graduation. He had made the honor roll, which he seemed proud of. He was Ms. Whitmer's new favorite student. She was so impressed with him that she had given him the Outstanding Senior English student award. But all this didn't seem to assuage his restlessness.

One morning on the bus I offered my earphones to Samuel, only to have him push my hand away irritably. I stifled the girlish instinct to cry from my hurt feelings. Sonja said women have many emotions, but only one physical response. When we're angry we cry. When we're happy we cry. When we're sad we cry. When we're scared, you guessed it, we cry.

"What's wrong, Samuel?" I said after several moments of tense silence.

"I just don't want to listen, that's all," he said tersely.

"Okay. But why did you push my hand away? Am I bothering you?"

"Yes." Samuel lifted his chin as he said this, jutting it at me, like he said the word purposely to hurt me and make me angry.

"What am I doing that's bothering you?" I again fought the wet that threatened to undermine my dignity. I spoke each word distinctly, focusing on the shape and sound instead of the sentiment.

"You are so..." His smooth voice was layered with turbulence and frustration. Samuel rarely raised his voice, and didn't do so now, but the threat was there. "You are so... calm, and accepting, and NAIVE that sometimes...I just want to shake you!"

I wondered what in the world had brought on this vehement attack and sat in stunned silence for several heartbeats.

"I bother you because I'm calm...and accepting?" I said, my voice an incredulous squeak. "Do you want me to be hyper...and, well, intolerant?"

"It would be nice if you questioned something, sometime." Samuel was revving up to his argument. I could see the animation in his face. "You live in your own happy little world. You don't know how it feels to not belong anywhere! I don't belong anywhere!"

"Why do you think I created my own happy little world?" I shot back. "I fit in perfectly there!" I hated it when he tried to start a fight with me.

"Come on, Samuel. Everyone feels like they don't belong sometimes, don't they? Mrs. Grimaldi even told me that Franz Schubert, the composer, said that at times he didn't feel like he belonged in this world at all. He created amazing, beautiful music. He had this enormous gift, yet he often felt out of place, too.

"Franz Schubert? He was the guy that wrote the song you played at Christmas, right?"

"Yes!" I smiled at him like a proud teacher.

"It's not quite the same thing Josie. I don't think Franz and I have much in common."

"Well I hope not!" I said saucily. "Poor Franz Schubert never made any money from his music and was completely broke and mostly destitute when he died from Typhus at only thirty-one years old."

Samuel sighed and shook his head. "You always seem to have an answer for everything, huh? So tell me what to do, Josie. My mother keeps calling me. She calls me late at night, and she's so drunk all she can do is cry and swear. My grandparents are trying to stay out of it, but I know her calling like that, at all hours, is upsetting them. She says I will never find *hózhǫ* in the white man's world. Can you believe she is using the Navajo religion to make me feel guilty while she is a complete mess?"

I realized none of Samuel's angst had anything to do with me.

"What's *hózhǫ*?" I plied him gently.

"*Hózhǫ* is at the heart of the Navajo religion. It essentially means harmony. Harmony within your spirit, your life, with God. Some people compare it to karma too, the idea that what you put out comes back to you. It is a balance between your body, mind, and spirit."

"Have you found *hózhǫ* on the reservation?" I held my breath, hoping I hadn't overstepped my bounds.

"Ha!" Samuel mocked, throwing his head back, "I feel closest to it when I am with my grandmother, listening to her, learning from her; but, no...I have never found it there."

"It doesn't sound like your mom has it. How can she lecture you about something she doesn't possess herself?" I grew indignant on his behalf.

"My mom has not had any *hózhǫ* since my father died. She says she turned her back on her people when she married him, but I think she turns her back on me when she says things like that. I was six years old when he died. I remember being a family! We were happy! My dad was a good man!" Samuel's composure cracked, and he visibly shook himself.

"Grandma Yates gave me my dad's journals. He kept them all through high school and during his mission on the reservation. When he left home, he boxed his things up, but somehow the journals were left behind with my grandparents. I haven't read them all, but what I have read makes me want to be *more* like him, not less! I feel like I am being ripped in half. I don't want to see my mother anymore. I am disgusted by her. Do you know my father never drank alcohol? Ever! In his journal, he said one of his friends in high school raped a girl after drinking too much. He said his friend never would have done something like that without the alcohol. It ruined both the girl's life and his friend's life. He decided then and there he would never touch the stuff.

"On the reservation, alcohol is a huge problem. I've seen my step-dad hit my mom so many times it makes me sick. I have fought him off of her only to have her turn on me. She wasn't always like that. I have memories of her being gentle and happy. She has no excuse! She had my grandmother to raise her. My Grandmother Yazzie is the finest woman I know. My Grandfather Yazzie was much older than my grandmother, and he struggled with his health, putting a lot more responsibility on her shoulders, but they both loved my mother and they raised her right. My mother was their only child. My grandmother had a lot of miscarriages, and they considered my mother a miracle, a gift. They taught her the traditions and language of our people. I think she turns her back on the *dine'* when she hides in the bottle."

"What does your Grandmother Yazzie tell you?"

"I really haven't talked to her about any of this. She doesn't speak English very well, and although she has access to a phone, she's not comfortable using one. She has my mother make calls for her when it's necessary, but unfortunately, with my mother in the state she is in most of the time, my grandmother stays away. My grandmother lives out on the land she was born on in her hogan. My mother lives in tribal housing with her husband and whichever of his kids that happen to be living at home."

"But you said your grandmother told you that you would need to survive in both worlds, remember? That is why you needed a warrior spirit. Maybe for you, *hózhǫ* won't come from either place, but from a merging of both," I offered, trying to comfort him.

Samuel looked at me then, his eyes sad, his expression conflicted. "Maybe my father's God can help me find the answers I need. I have his Bible. My mother gave it to me a long time ago, before she re-married. I told you she would read it sometimes. She believed it was true when she married my father. I don't think she's found any balance in trying to straddle both worlds."

"But Samuel, you just said she was happy once, before your father died. Maybe the loss of balance came when she rejected your father's God. She's rejected both her traditions and her beliefs. She's not embracing the Navajo way and shunning the other. She's shunning them both. So she moved back to the reservation after your father died. So what? Living on a reservation doesn't make you a Navajo."

"What?" Samuel looked at me with something akin to shock widening his eyes and slackening his jaw. He grabbed my arm. "What did you just say? Say it again!"

"You don't have to live on a reservation to be a Navajo?" I stammered, confused.

"You didn't say it like that," Samuel was shaking his head. "You said 'living on a reservation doesn't make you a Navajo.'"

"Right...so...?"

"So what *does* make a Navajo? Is that what you're saying?" It sounded more like a statement than a question

"Yeah, I guess so. What makes someone a Navajo, Samuel? What is it that defines a Navajo? Is it really where you live, the color of your skin, your moccasins, the turquoise you wear around your neck? What?"

Samuel was momentarily stumped. I was anxious to hear what his answer would be. I was a descendant of the Danes, and if someone asked me I could tell them a little about my ancestry. But was I Danish? I'd never even been to Denmark. I didn't speak the language. I didn't know any Danish customs or traditions. It was just my lineage. I had a feeling being Navajo was a lot bigger than just heritage or ancestry.

Samuel struggled to answer. "Being Navajo is about blood..."

"Check," I said smartly making a checkmark in the air. Samuel smiled and shook his head in pretend exasperation.

"Being Navajo is about language..."

"Check!"

"Being Navajo is about culture."

"What about the culture? Can you still be a Navajo and not live in a hogan?"

"Some of the traditionalists might say no. The old medicine men don't like some of the younger generation of *hataalii* (medicine man) trying to modernize or change the old ways. But Grandma Yazzie says culture is teaching your children the customs, the traditions, and the stories that have been passed on through the generations. This goes back to language. If the younger generations are not taught the language, we lose the culture. There are no English translations for many of the Navajo words. They carry their own meaning. You lose the meaning, you might lose the lesson in the legend, and you lose your culture."

"Hmm, I would say a definite 'check,'" I reasoned. "You were taught by the best. So, what else?"

"Being Navajo is about preserving the tribal lands."

"You'll have to explain that one." My brow furrowed in concentration.

"You may not have to live on the reservation to be a Navajo, but can you imagine not having a land to go back to?"

"Well, doesn't America belong to all Americans, Levanites and Navajo alike?"

"It's not the same."

"Why?"

"That's why they call America a melting pot. The idea is that different people from different places come to America, and they become one people. This is a good thing. The difference for the Navajo is that the land from which they originate *is* the American continent itself. There is no Navajo nation across the water that, simply by its existence, helps preserve the culture of the original people, like an Italy or an Africa or an Ireland. When people from Ireland migrate to America, Ireland still exists, full of Irish people. Where are your ancestors from?"

I knew Denmark had a role in this somewhere, and I answered him, engrossed in his grasp of the issue.

"Okay, so imagine some bigger neighboring country comes along and takes Denmark and makes it into a National Park and says to the Danes, 'Take your wooden shoes and get out. You are welcome to move into our country. After all, we are all Scandinavians, and you can live in our country just as easily as you can live here.'"

"I don't think it was the Danes that wore wooden shoes," I chortled.

"You get my point though, right? If the Danish people don't have a Denmark, they cease to be Danish eventually. They just become Scandinavian, or whatever. If you take away the land from the people, the people cease to be a people. If you take away the tribal lands, the Navajo people will eventually cease to exist."

It was my turn to stare at Samuel in awe. "You are one smart Navajo, Samuel. I hereby give you an enormous checkmark."

Samuel rolled his eyes. But there was a peace that hadn't been there before. He sighed and reached for my headphones.

"What are we listening to anyway?" he said companionably, and 'hózhǫ́' was restored on our hard green seat on the rickety yellow school bus.

# 9. Coda

I HAD GIVEN Samuel all the tapes I made for him when he returned from the reservation in March. I had lined them up neatly in a shoe box and written down each song title along with its composer, making a reference card to fit into each cassette. He said he listened to a different one every night before he went to sleep. I did the same, and I often looked out my window and down the street, to where I could see his grandparents' house, wondering what composer was keeping Samuel company that night. He would be leaving soon, and I wanted to give him a graduation present—something to remember me by.

Sonja was the one who actually ended up giving me the idea. She was recording my lessons and playing them back to me so I could critique myself, my finger speed, my musical phrasing, my timing. I suddenly knew what Samuel would like better than anything else I could give to him.

For the next week, I perfected the piece I had written for him, making sure it was exactly right. The night before school got out, I asked Sonja if I could have a brand new tape. She acquiesced, and I told her that I wanted to record my composition. She was eager to comply and lifted the lid on the grand piano to its greatest height and held her little microphone in its gaping mouth to record my effort. I played with all the feeling I could muster, our imminent parting accentuating my emotions.

When I was done, Sonja was staring at me oddly. She turned to push stop on the recording before she spoke.

"My dear, if I didn't know better I would think you had fallen in love." There was amusement in her tone, but also a hint of apprehension. Her back was to me, and I was grateful for it, as I felt a flush crawl hotly up my neck. She rewound the cassette and slid it into the case.

"I made myself a copy as well, if you don't mind." Sonja changed the subject smoothly, and we didn't end up discussing falling in love for several more years. Regrettably, I never told Sonja about Samuel. He remained a very closely guarded secret until it was too late to tell her, until she no longer had the capacity to care.

Samuel didn't want to go his graduation ceremony. He said he had earned the diploma whether they handed it to him or not, but Nettie and Don insisted that he go. Johnny was graduating as well, so my family went to the ceremony. It was pretty boring, full of all the trite platitudes about success and making a difference. There were a few lame musical numbers, and the graduating class sang the school song, which frankly could have used a little zip. The Nephi High School colors are crimson and gold. The guys get to wear the crimson gowns, and the girls wear the gold. The gold was a little bit mustard in color, and the girls looked mostly washed out.

Samuel was on the back row due to his height and the alphabetical placement of his last name. The crimson looked vibrant next to his warm skin, and I watched him surreptitiously throughout. He showed little emotion when his name was called, and he took his diploma and shook hands with Principal Bracken. Samuel's big moment had come in the school awards ceremony earlier that week, when Ms. Whitmer had named him her 12th grade English 'Student of the Year.' She said he'd shown such marked improvement and desire to learn over the course of the year that he had truly earned the award. The student body probably didn't care, but Samuel was quietly proud when he told me about it after school.

After the ceremony, parents were snapping pictures and kids were posing with their classmates. Nettie and Don were wrapped in conversation, and my dad was busy wielding the camera. I found Samuel standing to the side, his cap and gown removed and turned back in to the senior class advisor. He wore the black slacks and white shirt he had worn at the Christmas Eve church service. His black hair was brushed back off his face. It wouldn't be long before his long hair would be buzzed military short. His recruiter had told him to cut it before he reported for boot camp, but so far Samuel had refused.

His grandparents were driving him to San Diego the following morning. Don and Nettie wanted to make a leisurely trip of it; neither had spent much time outside of Levan. They planned on taking the 'scenic route.' Samuel would report at the Marine processing station on Monday morning.

"I have something I want to give to you," I said awkwardly, trying not to be overheard or draw attention, but wanting to arrange a meeting. "Are you going home afterwards?" There was always a big school celebration after graduation, but I doubted Samuel would stick around for the festivities.

"Nettie and Don want to take me to Mickelson's Restaurant for an early dinner, but after that we'll be home." He gazed down at me for a moment. "I have something for you, too." His eyes shifted away, detaching himself from me with his body language. "Do you know the big tree that's split in two?"

I nodded my head. I called the tree and the others around it Sleepy Hollow. Sleepy Hollow was where three huge trees grew in a triangle about half a mile up the road from Samuel's grandparents' home, just before the turnoff to the cemetery and beyond that, Tuckaway Hill. Lightening had struck the tallest of the three trees, splitting it in two about half way down its trunk. Interestingly enough, the tree didn't die, but simply forked into two trees support- ed by one massive trunk—like nature's version of Siamese twins. The upper branches, now angled at forty-five degrees, had created boughs, curving into the two other trees across the clearing. The lower branches were twisted and deformed by the strike, causing them to grow sideways instead of up, like leafy arms stretched out in supplication. In the late fall when the trees lost their leaves, the thick gnarled branches appeared like skeletal arms with claw-like fingers curled menacingly, inspiring the name Sleepy Hollow. But in the spring, as the trees donned their leafy adornments, this branched oddity, combined with the other two trees in the gully, created a thick green hideaway, a natural enclosure completely hidden from the dusty lane that ran close by.

"Can you meet me there later, say 8:00?" Samuel seemed un- comfortable but determined, and I agreed immediately. The sun didn't go down until almost nine o'clock as the looming summer days stretched daylight later and later, and I would be free until dark.

I arrived before Samuel and stood in the shelter of the trees, holding my gifts. I had decided at the last minute to give Samuel one more treasure, something I hated to part with, something that had been a gift to me, but something I knew would be especially mean- ingful to him.

Samuel rode up on horseback, holding something in his arms. He slid off the horse and looped the reins over a convenient branch. The horse immediately commenced grazing, and Samuel came around her, revealing his furry bundle. A pure white face and a wet black nose wiggled into view under the concealment of his folded arms. I gasped.

"Samuel! Oh, my gosh!" I squealed, rushing to him. The puppy in his arms was fat with very white fur, like a little polar bear. "Where did you get him?"

"Hans Larsen said I could have a pup when he found out his dog, Bashee, was expecting. My grandpa and Hans help each other out with their herds. I've moved Hans' herd a time or two."

"Is it a Lab?" I guessed, looking at his handsome doggy face.

"Half," Samuel replied. "In his case, half-breed looks a lot like the original, huh?" His voice was light, and I let the half-breed comment go without censure.

"What's the other half?" I stroked the silky head and tickled the tiny chin.

"Hans Larsen says the dog's mother is an Akbash. That's where the name Bashee came from."

"Akbash? I've never even heard of that."

"That's because they are sheep dogs native to Turkey. Hans has used the Akbash to guard his sheep for years. He says they aren't as hyper as your average sheep dog. In fact, they really don't herd sheep at all. They are considered guardians. They are very calm, and it is their nature to simply lie with the flock. Hans has a sheepdog to help him move the herd, and the Akbash to keep watch and live with the flock. He says this pup's momma thinks the herd belongs to her."

"So how did the Lab half come into the mix?"

Samuel put the warm body in my arms, and I rubbed my cheek along its back.

"Hans had corralled the herd close to home during that week of bad storms in January. The Stephenson's big white Lab came over for a friendly visit, much to Hans's disappointment. Hans had arranged to breed his dog with another pure bred. The Lab just got there first."

I giggled a little and sank to the soft dirt and grass, folding my legs and letting the pup waddle around me. "She looks like a Lab to me…but she's so white!"

Samuel squatted down on his haunches, reaching out to the little dog, letting his fingers smooth his snowy fur. "The Akbash is very white, and it looks like the Lab through his snout and head, but its legs are longer and it has a feathery curved tail. This guy's got his daddy's tail." Samuel patted the tiny rump. "He'll be a big dog. In fact, full grown, he'll probably weigh more than you, but he'll look out for you when I'm gone." Samuel's voice was quiet and serious. "After all, when I saved your life, I became responsible for you, remember?" He smiled a little to lighten the seriousness of his words.

"He's for me?"

Samuel chuckled a little, "I can't take him with me, Josie."

"Oh, my gosh, Samuel!" I breathed again, looking with new appreciation at the adorable creature before me. I had never even thought about having my own dog. Between chickens and horses and the various scrawny cats that ended up on our back porch, we had always had plenty of animals to care for. Suddenly, the thought was incredibly appealing. I scooped my new friend into my arms, cuddling him like an infant, cooing as his wet nose brushed my cheek.

"Do you think your dad will let you keep him?"

His question gave me a moment's pause. And then I considered how little I truly asked for. My dad wouldn't hesitate for a minute. If I brought him home and told my dad I wanted him, he would be mine to keep. "My dad won't mind a bit."

We watched the little dog toddling around, sniffing at this and that.

"What are you going to call him?" Samuel questioned, sinking down from his haunches into the grass, spreading his long legs out in front of him.

"Hmmm," I pursed my lips thoughtfully. "I named all my chickens after literary characters, so maybe Heathcliffe? That would definitely remind me of you!" I laughed, shaking my head as I recalled all those days with Wuthering Heights on the bus. I immediately felt a rush of melancholy, reminded of Samuel's impending departure.

"Heathcliffe is that fat cat that likes lasagna in Grandpa Don's Sunday comics," Samuel argued. "He needs something more canine...plus, we both agreed we didn't especially like Heathcliffe." He studied my face, and I saw a flicker of my own melancholy mirrored back at me.

"You're right. Maybe I should call him Rochester for Jane's true love. I could call him Chester for short." I thought on it a moment and then rejected it out loud. "No." I shook my head. "I want to name him for you. But I don't want to name him Samuel—that would be weird." I thought for a moment, staring off. "I know." My eyes swung back to him. "Yazzie."

Samuel's lips quirked and he looked down fondly into my upturned face. "Yazzie is perfect. Grandma Yazzie would like it, too. One guardian named after another."

The newly-named Yazzie climbed into my lap and plopped down with a tired huff. He laid his head on his paws and immediately began to doze.

"I have something for you too." I retrieved one of the packages lying next to me. I handed him the cassette first. I had wrapped it in plain brown butcher paper. Samuel was not the ribbons and bows type.

He ripped off the paper easily, holding the cassette up in the fading light, made all the darker by the shadowy enclave. "Samuel's Song," he read out loud. "You recorded it?" His voice rose with excitement. "This is the song you played for me that day? Your song?"

"Your song," I replied shyly, pleased by his response.

"My song," he repeated, his voice just above a whisper.

"Here." I handed him the other present. He didn't have to open it to know what it was. He shook his head as he pulled the paper from the big green dictionary we had forged our friendship upon. He smoothed his hand over the cover and his eyes remained lowered as he protested my gift.

"This is yours, Josie. You don't want to give this away. You love this book."

"I want you to have it," I insisted, leaning across him to open the cover where I had written:

To my friend Samuel,

A Navajo bard and a person of character.

Love,

Josie

"A Navajo what?" His eyebrows rose in amusement.

"Bard. Look it up!" I bossed, laughing.

Samuel sighed mightily, playing his put-upon-student role once again. He flipped through the pages quickly. "Bard: the trappings of a horse," he intoned.

"What?" I cried, reaching for the book.

Samuel laughed freely, momentarily shedding his persistent gravity. He moved the book out of my reach. "Oh, maybe you mean the *other* definition. A bard is a poet," he reported, his eyebrows again climbing in question as he looked up from the dictionary.

"And that is what you are—a Navajo poet. Gifted with beautiful thoughts and the ability to share them," I pontificated seriously.

"You're good at that, you know," Samuel said quietly.

"Good at what?"

"Making me feel special instead of like an outcast, making me feel important."

"You are important, Samuel," I said sincerely.

"See, you're doing it now," he retorted. "Here," he said suddenly, reaching up and untying the thin leather strip he wore around his neck. "You gave me something that was yours. I want to give you something that is mine." The turquoise rock swung from the black leather cord, and he held his necklace out to me. I had never seen him without it. I shook my head in protest as he had done moments before.

"Lift up your hair," Samuel commanded. I obeyed, lifting my blonde curls off of my shoulders and leaning toward him. His hands were warm and gentle as he tied the leather ends together around my neck. Then, ever appropriate and respectful, he leaned away from me. The stone was warm from lying against his skin, and I was overcome with my desire to keep him near, to beg him not to leave in the morning.

My voice was choked as I confessed my dread. "I wish you didn't have to go." I felt the tears brimming and could not hold them back. I wiped at them furiously, willing them to stop, only to have them mount a new attack. "You are the best friend I've ever had."

"If I stayed, you and I couldn't remain friends." Samuel's voice was measured and he maintained his customary distance, but his back was rigid, attesting to his own inner tumult.

"Why?" I cried, scrubbing at my cheeks, my tears halted by his blunt reply.

"Because our age difference is a problem. I shouldn't be here with you now. I only wanted to say goodbye...because the truth is, you are the best friend I have ever had too, and best friends don't leave without saying goodbye."

Samuel rose to his feet and, leaning down, offered me his hand. I gathered Yazzie to my chest with one arm and put my other hand in his, letting him pull me to my feet beside him.

"Will you come back?" I asked woodenly, feeling the numbness of denial seeking to shield me from the finality of the moment.

"I hope so," Samuel said wistfully. "When I do, maybe things will be different."

I studied my feet, my mind frenzied, looking for a reason to delay him, to elongate the end of goodbye. I felt his sudden nearness, and I looked up into his face, which was now mere inches from my own. His eyes were very black in the twilight, and his breath was warm on my wet cheeks. He leaned down cautiously, his eyes never leaving mine, until our faces became so close that shape and color blurred. He tipped his face slightly to the right, and I lifted my mouth to his in the briefest hint of a kiss that never was. His lips fluttered lightly by and came to a firm standstill on my forehead. His kiss lingered there as my eyes swept closed and my sigh slipped out. And there we remained for several long seconds. And then he stood apart from me. He held my gifts in his arms and my heart in his hand.

"I won't ever forget you, Josie." His voice was low, his face devoid of emotion, and he turned and walked out of the little clearing. The horse whinnied in greeting, and Samuel swung into the saddle, gathering the reins. He prodded the horse with his heels and rode away, a black outline against the dying violet dusk. I followed slowly behind him, holding Yazzie against me, his head on my shoulder.

When I got home, I told my dad the truth about Yazzie. I told him that he had belonged to Don and Nettie's grandson who was going into the Marine Corps, and he had given him to me because he couldn't keep him. Truth without embellishment, although one could argue that it was slightly abbreviated. My dad didn't seem to care where I had gotten him.

"I've been thinking about getting a dog around here," my dad cooed as well as an old cowboy can. "He's a good boy, oh yes he is! He's a little beauty!"

What was it about babies and puppies that made everyone talk with their lips pushed out in that kissy-faced way? I left Yazzie in my dad's enthusiastic care and climbed up to my room. I untied Samuel's necklace from around my neck and held it in front of me, watching the turquoise stone sway gently from the thin leather strip.

My dad hadn't cared about the puppy, but he would eventually notice if I was wearing the big turquoise rock. The pup and the rock together might set off alarms, and I was wise enough, even at thirteen, to grasp how others might perceive the relationship.

I rubbed the stone against my face, closing my eyes and thinking of our 'almost' kiss. I found myself wishing Samuel weren't so careful and so honorable. I would have liked a real kiss from Samuel, for my very first kiss to belong to him. Almost immediately, I felt ashamed of my wistful criticism. If Jane Eyre could walk away from Mr. Rochester's kisses, despite her own feelings, even though nobody would be harmed, and no one would really care, and do it out of principle, then I should expect no less of myself. That is what Samuel had done tonight at Sleepy Hollow.

I tucked his necklace into the little jewelry box I kept on my desk. A bracelet strung with silver hearts that had been my mothers, a sunflower pin that Tara had given me one birthday, and a green CTR (choose the right) ring from Sunday School crowded around my newest treasure. I shut the lid gently and trudged down the stairs, back to my roly-poly guardian.

# 10. Obbligato

I COULDN'T WRITE to Samuel at first. He didn't have an address yet. He had promised to write me and let me know as soon as he could. It was about two weeks after he left that his first letter arrived.

June 7, 1997

Dear Josie,

The first couple of days here have been a blur. They loaded us on a bus, and it was pretty late around 1:00 in the morning. It was so dark we couldn't see anything out the bus windows as we were taken to what they called receiving. When we pulled up, this guy in full uniform came on the bus and started shouting for us to get our trash together and lineup out on the yellow footprints that were on the pavement. It was kind of foggy and it was hard to even see where the footprints were. This guy is shouting "Any day!" the whole time.

One guy started to cry, just like that. He got control of himself, but I think everyone felt a little sympathetic, except for the drill instructor who got right in his face and told him to dry it up.

We got a chance to make a 15 second call, and I called my mom. Nobody answered, and I don't think I'll call again. I wrote her to let her know I'm here and what my address is, but now it's up to her. I don't know if she'll write or not. My grandmother Yazzie would if she could  she doesn't expect letters because she can't read them and she can't write back. She knows I will come see her when I get boot leave at the end of the 12 weeks.

We didn't sleep at all the first night. After we made our calls we went to a room with desks in it and they started throwing information at us  like the floor isn't the floor, it's the 'deck,' and the door is a 'hatch.' A hat is called a cover and running shoes are called go-fasters. When I'm done here I'll speak three languages, English, Navajo, and Marine. Then they gave us our platoon number, and we had to write it on our left hand in black permanent marker. My platoon is 4044, 1st Battalion. After that they collected all of our civilian clothes, all jewelry, all knives, personal items, cigarettes, any food, gum  all of it. One kid tried stuffing a candy bar in his mouth so he didn't have to turn it over. The drill sergeant made him spit it out on top of his stuff.

We can't use I, me, or my. We have to say 'this recruit' when we are referring to ourselves. Everybody keeps slipping. I am now Recruit

Yates no first name. The sergeant said the Marines are not about the individual, but the team. We should be all about our unit. We are now four zero four four. The number four is sacred among the Navajo. There are four sacred mountains that frame the Navajo lands. So, I think the repeating four can only be good luck.

They immediately took us to get what they called "cranial amputations." The drill instructor made a big deal of it when it was my turn to get my hair cut. I easily had the longest hair of anyone there, and I knew it was going to get shaved off because my recruiter told me what to expect. They shave us almost completely bald. There's just stubble left. I want to keep rubbing my head, but I don't want to call attention to myself. I have a feeling the less attention I call to myself, the better off I'll be. Anyway, it was still hard to see all that hair fall to the floor. It made me think about Samson in my dad's Bible. He lost all his power when they cut his hair.

Then we got our gear for the 13 weeks we are going to be here. We even got a little towel that has all the M-16 parts diagrammed on it, so that we will know where to place them when we clean our weapons. By this time it had to be after 4:00 in the morning, though I'm not sure because none of us are allowed to have watches. I hadn't slept since I'd reported at dawn the day before, and I was feeling it. They took us into our barracks. The racks (that's the term for the bunks here) had naked mattresses on them. The same guy that stuffed his Snickers in his mouth headed straight over to lie down. The drill sergeant was in his face telling him to 'toe the line'- which means to line up next to the white line with your toes up to it. He taught us how to walk in formation and then we marched to the chow hall. We aren't allowed to talk while we are in the mess hall, which is fine with me   except the drill instructor shouts the entire time. We have to hold our trays at a certain angle, heels together, thumbs on the outside. It's so much to remember all the time, but you better believe someone will let you know right away if you're doing something wrong. We had about ten minutes to eat before they were marching us back out of there again.

We actually didn't get to sleep until 8:00 that night. We learned to march, how to lift our feet, how to stand in line, that stuff. After that we were brought back to the barracks and we had to learn how to make our beds, Marine style. We were woken up in the middle of the night to a drill instructor screaming, "Toe the line, toe the line." One guy stayed asleep through it all   and the drill instructor pulled his blanket off and screamed in his face until the kid literally rolled off onto the floor. Luckily, he was on a bottom bunk. Another kid laughed when he did, and the drill instructor turned on him saying "Give me an hour, and I promise you won't be smiling, Recruit!" We get dressed one piece of clothing at a time, forcing us to follow orders exactly. When we are told to hydrate we have to drink our whole canteen of water and turn it over above our heads to prove it's gone.

One high point. I got a perfect 300 on the initial strength test. That means I did 100 sit-ups, 20 dead-hang pull-ups, and I did the three mile run in 17:58 seconds. I've been working hard and I wanted to be the best. It's hard to know if they were impressed or if I just drew unwanted attention. I guess only time will tell. One D.I. kind of sneered at me and told me they were just going to have to work me harder than the others.

On the fourth day here they moved us into our new barracks. We were introduced to the drill instructors that are assigned to our platoon from now on. Staff Sergeant Meadows is the Senior D.I., Sergeant Blood (his name is perfect, trust me) and Sergeant Edgel are the other two over our platoon. Sergeant Blood is constantly bellowing (learned that word from you). I have never heard him speak quietly. He is everywhere at once, moving, screaming, moving. We aren't allowed to make eye contact, and it's probably a good thing because I would be dizzy trying to keep up. We have to stare straight ahead. We are constantly yelling, "Yes Sir!" which I hate. I don't mind the Yes Sir! part. It's the shouting that gets old, but I had Sergeant Blood get right in my face, spitting in my eyes the whole time, telling me he couldn't hear me. I wanted to shove him off so bad.

A few guys have cried already. I don't care what happens to me here, I will not cry. I can't imagine having any self-respect left if I did. I won't quit, I will be the best, and I will not bawl or whine like some of these guys. It's embarrassing. One kid started crying after we yelled "Kill. Kill. Marine Corps!" Which we do a lot. This kid just freaked. Senior D.I. Meadows pulled him out and talked to him for a while. I don't know if the guy is going to make it. This is the same kid that tried to eat his candy bar and laid on the bare mattress last night without permission. His name is Recruit Wheaton, but a couple of the other recruits are already calling him Recruit Weepin.

My bunkmate is a big white kid named Tyler Young. He's from Texas but he talks like he thinks he's black, which irritates the guys that actually are black. I kind of like him though. He's good-natured and always smiling. He talks too much, but I think everyone talks too much. He asked me if I was Mexican. I just said no. Another guy in our platoon who is Hispanic piped up and asked me what I was. I told him I was a recruit. Sergeant Blood overheard and he seemed to like that answer, but the guys seem suspicious of me now, like I'm holding something back. It's not that I'm ashamed that I'm Navajo   I'm just really tired of that being what everything is always about. You won't catch me talking about my ethnicity here   Navajo or White.

Staff Sgt. Blood says I am whispering when I should be yelling. He got right in my face and yelled "Why are you whispering Recruit?!!!" He said I must not have any heart. I don't have to scream to have heart. I let my actions speak for themselves. No one will outfight me, no one will outrun me, and no one will outshoot me. I guarantee it- but I won't be the loudest Marine in the platoon, that's for sure. So, because I wasn't loud enough, D.I Blood made me do twenty extra push-ups, one hundred extra crunches, and squat thrusts and mountain climbers until my legs were shaking. They call it quarter decking when one recruit is taken aside and made to do punishment exercises. The only other guys that have been quarter decked are the whiners and the guys that continually screw up or lag behind. I don't want that kind of attention.

I know this letter is long, but I needed to tell someone about this crazy place I'm in. I hope you are okay, playing the piano, writing more music. School's out, so you've probably got more time to practice and read. They let me keep my dictionary and my dad's Bible. I decided I'm going to try and read it while I'm here, using the dictionary for all the words I don't know...which is at least half of them. I've got one hour of free time every day. No music allowed, so I will just have to keep Rachmaninoff in my head.

I hope you write,

Samuel

Dear Samuel,

I was so excited when I got your letter. I'd been checking at the post office every day, and when it finally came in I felt like crying. So I did. You know me—a little emotional. I have to say I probably wouldn't last a day at boot camp. I don't do well with people screaming at me. Plus, I'm a major klutz. I'd be tripping over myself and everyone else the entire time. Yuck! It's a good thing God blesses people with different talents. The world would be in trouble if I were a Marine.

I added a little bridge section to your song. Maybe someday I can record it and send it to you. I don't think you said whether or not they will let you listen to music eventually, so I'll save it for when you graduate. I've been playing constantly since school got out. Sonja has been working with me on composing music and actually writing it out on composition paper. Up to this point I've only read and played music, but never written it down. It feels like school, but I don't mind. Sonja says I have the ability to make a living as a musician, perhaps play with an orchestra or a symphony, maybe tour Europe. Wouldn't that be amazing? I don't know how I would feel about leaving my dad, though.

I was thinking about your comments on Samson when you had your hair shaved. I went back and read the story. I don't think Samson's power was really in his hair. I've always thought what an idiot he was to trust Delilah with his secret. She'd proven herself completely untrustworthy. She used everything he told her against him. After reading the story, it occurred to me that Samson didn't trust her. He just didn't believe that he would really lose his strength if he cut his hair. He believed the strength was his and that it hadn't really been given to him from God with certain responsibilities and conditions, like his parents had taught him. He didn't keep his promise to God. God said that his long hair would be a symbol of that promise. Not the source of his power. So when Samson revealed the symbol of his promise to Delilah, he rejected God and essentially cut himself off from the source of his power. So, to make a long explanation short and sweet—Your individuality does not come from the way you wear your hair, Samuel. Your individual worth comes from keeping your promises and being a man of character. Easy for me to say, I know, here in my comfy room, listening to Mozart. But I think it's true, all the same.

Do you remember that little part I read you from Jane Eyre? Jane Eyre's worth came from her sterling character. I guess none of us really knows what kind of character we truly have until we are really tested. I think you'll find you have plenty of character in these next few weeks. I believe in you. Would it embarrass you to tell you that I really miss you? Because I do.

I'll listen to enough music for both of us, and try to send it to you telepathically. Wouldn't that be cool, to be able to transmit our thoughts like radio waves? I think there has to be a way.

Be safe and be happy,

Josie

July 1, 1997

Dear Josie,

I got your latest letter last night during platoon mail call. I've read it slowly, in sections, making it last. My Grandma Nettie keeps sending care packages full of stuff I can't have. She communicates her love through food rather than letters, although she sent a short one. Your letters are especially appreciated thank you. Some of the guys pass around their letters, especially if they're from girlfriends. Some of those girls have no class. The difference between you and them is mind boggling. They aren't fit to lick your shoes. This big black kid from Los Angeles named Antwon Carlton was passing around some filthy thing and everybody was laughing. I didn't want to read it and refused to take it when Tyler passed it to me. It made Carlton mad and he started saying "You too good white boy? Or do you just not like girls?" I told him I had no interest in touching his trash. I don't think he likes me much, but the feeling is mutual.

Tyler jumped in, saying I wasn't white, and the Hispanic kid, Mercado, said "Well we know he ain't Hispanic." They all stared at me. I just kept cleaning my weapon. Tyler jumped in again and said 'He's Green!'" Green is what the Marines call themselves. I used to think it would be nice if people were all one color   everybody the same. Not anymore   because then you wouldn't be you. Your hair wouldn't be all white and gold and your eyes wouldn't be so blue. But here the goal is to make us the same   green. It's strangely therapeutic after all these years of feeling so torn by my desire to know more about my father's culture and still be loyal to my mother's. There's a whole new culture here.

I should have known you would find a way to comfort me about my hair. Interesting take on the Samson story...did you come up with that yourself? Knowing you, yes. I found the story in the Bible and read it yesterday during my free time. Samson was a serious warrior. I think you're right about his strength not actually being in his hair. It's probably a good lesson for most of us here. Samson was this unbelievably powerful guy, but he lost everything when he thought he could do it alone.

History is a big deal here at boot camp. We've been in classes for hours on end. It's interesting and it builds a sense of pride in me, like I'm part of something important. They've been drilling dates and battles into us — Inchon, Belleau Wood, Saipan (my grandfather fought at Saipan) Peleliu, Okinawa, Chosin, and more. Iwo Jima in World War II is kind of the pinnacle for the Marines.

We're also learning about the Warriors, as the D.I.'s call them — Marine's who did great things. I found out today that a Native American named Jim Crowe was a Marine. I recognized his name. He has an interesting story. We also have to memorize the fourteen leadership traits, which are things like integrity, knowledge, unselfishness, courage (I thought you'd like that — you're kind of big on character) the eight principles of camouflage, the six battlefield disciplines, and on and on. They call this stuff 'knowledge' and we are tested on it constantly.

There's no time for debate or discussion, and I thought of you one day, as they were drilling us on facts and traits. It almost made me laugh (which wouldn't have been good) knowing how much you would hate that. You love to analyze everything and discussion is important to you   you would hate just memorizing whatever they told you was important. Other than that, I think you'd make a great Marine. You said the world would be in trouble if you were a Marine. Don't even think that. The physical stuff you could learn   although it might be a little harder for you. You're unselfish and loyal and courageous. I can't think of one of the traits that you don't have. The world would be a much better place if there were more people like you.

We were introduced to the pugil sticks this week. Pugil sticks are basically a four foot stick with thick pads on each end. The recruits wear helmets and protective padding. We battled guys from platoons 4043 and 4045. They had us lined up along this boardwalk, and we fought one on one. The goal is to deliver a blow to the head or chest, both considered kill shots. The first guy who lands two kill shots wins. When it was my turn, I went flying up the ramp yelling like my grandmother taught me to do when a coyote is trying to attack the sheep. I knocked the other guy off the platform with one big blow to the chest. D.I Meadows actually cheered. Sergeant Blood said "What was that, some kind of Indian War Cry?" He seemed to like it   at least he didn't complain that I wasn't loud enough. I think my opponent was more scared by my blood curdling scream than the actual blow to the chest. I'm starting to realize that's the whole point with the constant yelling. Our troop got beat by troop 4043, so they get to carry the flag. I was a little disgusted with the turn-out. I've got to give it to Carlton. He may be a street thug, but he knows how to fight. He said the same to me when we were done, just not the street thug part. I almost liked him today. Some of these guys have never been in a single fist fight. I've been fighting my whole life. Who knew it would give me an advantage at boot camp. Anyway, since we lost, we ended up doing extra drilling.

I knew it was coming, and I was dreading the pool. After a bunch of classes and instruction we put on our jackets, helmets, packs, and boots and had to jump in the pool in full gear. They told us how to stay afloat, but I could feel the panic setting in right away. My face went under the water, but if you lean back as far as you can against the pack and tilt your head up, your face will be just above the water. We had to kick back and forth the across the pool a few times. Then we had to jump off of the diving tower and swim 15 meters. It wasn't too bad. I can just imagine how terrifying the whole experience would have been if I didn't know how to swim. I wasn't the fastest, but I didn't draw any negative attention to myself, either. There actually were a couple guys that didn't know how to swim at all. That would have been me if wasn't for you.

I have a new nickname. A few of the guys have noticed that I am reading the Bible on my free time. I am now Preacher. Not very fitting, if you ask me. Don't preachers have to stand up and teach people? I guess it could be worse. Some of the guys were talking about their favorite kind of music. Nobody said classical. I wasn't surprised, and I didn't volunteer my preference. Later on, I was talking to Tyler Young, and he asked me what I liked to listen to, so I told him about Beethoven. He asked me what songs I liked. I told him I especially liked Air on a G String big mistake!! He thought I was talking about women's underwear. He's calling me 'G' now. I think I prefer Preacher. Tyler has a big mouth, especially when he thinks he's going to get laughs, and before I knew it, he'd told everyone about Air on a G String. Now I'm Preacher G.

I'm actually enjoying being here. The whole point of boot-camp is to make you into somebody better. I like that idea. I'm four weeks in now, and I'm confident I'll make it through. By the way, how is Yazzie? I miss you too.

Don't change,

Samuel

I wrote Samuel several letters, trying to think of every possible thing he might be interested in. I told him how Yazzie chewed everything he could get his little teeth into, and how he made the chickens miserable. If he weren't such a raggedy ball of cute fluff, my dad might have made me get rid of him. I kept most of his escapades a secret in order to protect him. He was almost house broken. He definitely made more work for me. I had to brush out his coat everyday so that he didn't leave hair everywhere, but he was worth it. I smothered him with affection and was lavished with doggy love in return. He made my heart a little lighter.

Other than Yazzie, life was pretty uneventful, and I struggled for material to include in my correspondence. I couldn't tell him that I had cried yesterday while I fed my chickens, thinking of how I was going to be gathering their stupid brown eggs for the next five years at least, while they clucked and pecked ungratefully around my legs. Meanwhile, Samuel would be off, fighting battles around the world, being a man, falling in love with WOMEN. I hated that I was almost fourteen, and that I was way too young for him. I was alone in my room too often, daydreaming about him coming back in the fall and riding the bus, sitting next to me in his Marine uniform, holding my hand and listening to classical music from the Romance period.

I would feel even worse when I caught myself in these ridiculous fantasies, realizing how truly juvenile I was. I missed him horribly, and I had a terrible, terrible fear that I would never see him again. In my letters, I found myself saying these things, only to rip the letter up into tiny pieces and send the appropriate missive, chattering about music and telling him the interesting facts and stories Sonja always seemed to provide during our sessions together.

I spent my free time with Sonja and Doc—as much as I felt I could without wearing out my welcome. My lessons were eclectic and covered more subjects than music. Doc even participated every once in a while, putting in his two-bits, sharing his vast knowledge and opinions. He wasn't musically talented, but he liked listening to me play, and more often than not would be asleep in his chair when I left. I don't know what ever became of Doc's desire to write a book. As far as I know he never finished one, but for whatever reason, he and Sonja loved Levan and stayed. Doc's son was grown and lived in Connecticut or somewhere else on the other side of the Earth—so they didn't see him much. Their little eccentricities were not so great that they felt stifled by our little town. People seemed to like them, and Sonja's musical abilities were utilized on the organ each week at church. Doc fell asleep every week in church too, but he always went, even though he kept his pipe stuck in his mouth throughout the service. He never lit it, so I guess the congregation just decided to let him be.

I often thought if it hadn't been for Sonja and Doc, my brain would have atrophied with nothing to occupy it but chicken feed and recipes and unchallenging school work. They were a balm and ballast to my yearning heart and a stimulant to my intellect.

That summer, I checked the mail every day but only received letters from Samuel sporadically. Two months after he had left town, I received another. Racing home, I threw the rest of the mail in the bill basket for later perusal, and ran up to my room, throwing myself onto my bed and ripping the letter open. I smelled the pages first, closing my eyes and trying to imagine him writing it. I felt like one of those girls who cried whenever they saw Elvis. I shook myself out of my silliness and unfolded the pages. The letter was long, and his precise handwriting slanted forward aggressively. I read it hungrily.

July 31, 1997

Dear Josie,

I hear the drill instructors in my sleep yelling "pivot, align to the right, cover, don't close up, and don't rush it!" We drill for hours on end it seems like. I feel like I am marching in my sleep. Antwon Carlton actually did march in his sleep. Tyler was on Firewatch duty night before last and Carlton came marching by in his sleep. Tyler called out," Pivot, back to the rack recruit!" It worked, and big bad Carlton marched back to his bunk. Tyler had everyone laughing about it- you know he didn't keep it to himself. Carlton got a little ugly, but a couple of the other black guys told him to relax. They all thought it was pretty funny, too.

Everybody seems to realize if we don't hang together, we all suffer. One day our squad leader, a tough red-head from Utah named Travis Fitz, had to do punishment exercises every time one of us swatted at a fly or missed a drill order. He paid for our screw ups. It was a pretty big lesson. About half way through, I ended up requesting permission to speak and volunteered to take his place. It bothered me that he was taking the abuse for all of us. Sergeant Blood said that's what a real leader does   he takes one for the team. He did let me step in for Fitz, but the point was made.

We've been spending the last few weeks on the rifle range. I learned how to shoot from my grandma. When we were out with the sheep she would send me off away from the sheep, and I would practice. She called this time 'loose time'- when the sheep were finished grazing, and they were full and drowsy, and we stayed in one place for a while to watch them. When my grandma was little she actually used a bow and arrow to run the coyotes off. I know how primitive that sounds   most people probably wouldn't believe it. My grandmother had her own herd at eight years old. If she lost a sheep she would be whipped, because it meant loss of food and livelihood. She wasn't as hard on me, but the care and well-being of her sheep was the most important thing to her. I've seen my grandma ride full out, shrieking at a coyote, shooting from the back of her horse. My grandma probably would have made a good Marine, too. I'll have to tell her that when I see her again. She'll get a kick out of that.

I haven't had any difficulty on the rifle range, and it's all due to her. Again, some of these recruits have never shot a gun before. It blows my mind even the boys in Levan all have BB guns and 22's don't they? What is America coming to? Our generation is unbelievably soft. Man, I'm starting to sound like my D.I.'s. Anyway, on qualification day I scored a 280 on the course, which puts me in the high end of the expert category. Sergeant Meadows said I should set my sights on sniper school after Marine Combat Training and infantry training. I'm not sure yet what I'll do. I used to think maybe I'd just go into the Reserves, but I'm thinking I'm going to go Active.

We're about half way through, and we just got our Marine pictures taken in full dress blues. I felt a little like crying. It's funny, I haven't had the urge to cry one time, not when I've been sore and tired and screamed at. But putting that uniform on made me get a big lump in my throat. Unbelievable. For the first time, I feel like I truly belong somewhere.

You know I'm going to have to give in and read Jane Eyre one of these days. But I can't read it during boot camp, so please don't send it to me. I would never live it down i can you imagine my D.I. during mail call ripping open my package and pulling out Jane Eyre? I'd be on the quarterdeck for a year.

I think I'm having Beethoven withdrawals. What have you done to me? Keep working on the telepathic thing.

Don't change,

Samuel

I immediately rushed to my little desk and wrote him back.

Dear Samuel,

I listened to some John Phillip Sousa today and imagined you marching in your dress blues. Will you send me a picture when you graduate? I can't wait to see you all serious in front of the flag. You do serious pretty well, so I don't think you will look too different to me.

It doesn't surprise me you are doing so well. I love the stories about your grandma. Someday I'd really like to meet her.

I feel like I am standing still why you are running forward. I feel a little anxious and antsy, maybe even jealous that you are living your dream. I guess I'll have my chance someday.

I went and helped your Grandma Nettie in her garden today. She talked about you a little. She said you sent her a letter. She told me a lot of the things I already knew, but of course I didn't tell her so. She's very proud of you. She's looking forward to your Marine picture, too. She showed me where she's going to hang it. She's picked out a spot next to a picture of Don in his Army uniform. She said he was in the National Guard. I'm sure you know which picture I'm talking about. I saw another picture in her hallway I hadn't noticed before. I've been in the house many times, but usually just in the kitchen or the sitting room. It was a picture of you with your mom and dad when you were about four years old. I know pictures can be misleading, but you all looked happy. You look like both of them—don't you think? Your dad was such a handsome man and your mom was so pretty.

Life can be kind of cruel. Sometimes I think of my mom, your dad, people we love that have left us. I wish I understood God's plan a little better. My mom's death has definitely made me more capable and independent, and probably made me a stronger, better person. I just miss her sometimes. I miss you, too.

Love,

Josie

I didn't receive another letter until Samuel graduated from boot camp, and I was getting ready to start eighth grade. He sounded so different already, so grown up and focused. He seemed so far away. I mourned the loss of the boy who had been my friend, even though the man he was becoming was impressive to me.

The best part of the letter was the little wallet sized picture he had included. My breath caught in my chest and my heart ached and sang simultaneously. He looked so handsome. His hair was gone, and his strong jaw and cheekbones were prominent in his lean brown face. His ears lay flat against his head, no pixie ears for Samuel. His dark eyes were solemn and staring just below the slim black brim of his white cap. His wide mouth was firm and unsmiling. His deep blue uniform was resplendent, with gold buttons marching down his chest. The flag stood behind him, and there was a look on his face that said 'Don't mess with me.' It made me giggle a little. The giggle caught on a sob, and I threw myself down on my bed and cried until my head ached and I was sick to my stomach.

In the following months, the letters came fewer and farther between. I wrote as faithfully as his location allowed. Then the letters stopped altogether. I didn't see Samuel again for two and a half years.

# 11. Intermezzo

NETTIE YATES BROUGHT over a plate of Christmas cookies and candies two days before Christmas. We had gotten very little snowfall so far, but the temperatures were frigid. I welcomed Nettie into the house with a whoosh of cold air and forced the door closed behind her as I "oohed" and "aahed" over her offering.

"Come into the kitchen with me, Nettie. I have something for you, too." She followed behind me into the kitchen where I had loaves of chocolate chip zucchini bread wrapped in tinfoil and tied with cheerful red bows. I had at least twenty loaves spread across the countertop. Christmas can be especially stressful in small towns. You don't always know where to start and stop in the exchanging of neighbor gifts. Everyone is a neighbor, and people get easily offended. The same goes for weddings. You have to practically invite the whole town and have an open house. That way you don't risk missing someone, starting a Hatfield and McCoy situation that could last for generations. People were generally more forgiving of me because I wasn't an adult, but I wasn't taking any chances.

"Zucchini bread? Is it my recipe?" Nettie smiled at me when I handed her a loaf.

"Yep, but I didn't give you any credit on the Christmas cards." I smiled back. Chocolate chip zucchini bread had become one of my favorites since I had used it as an excuse to ply information out of Don and Nettie a few years before.

Nettie laughed good-naturedly and pulled out a chair next to the kitchen table where I had been tying the bows on the loaves of foil wrapped bread. She obviously wanted to visit a little, and I couldn't blame her for not wanting to head back out into the cold night.

"Well, Samuel will be at the Christmas Eve Service with me and Don tomorrow," Nettie said without preamble. "He sure did enjoy your playing when he went with us before. Remember how he embarrassed us with all that clapping?" Nettie started to giggle girlishly. "I thought we might get kicked out of the church." Nettie's giggle turned into a chortle as she reminisced.

My heart had stopped several seconds back, and I stood frozen to the old linoleum floor in my kitchen, hands raised to cut another long section of red ribbon. *Samuel? Here?!!* I must have been staring dumbly at Nettie, because her laughter stuttered and stopped as she rose to touch my cheek.

"Are you all right, Josie?" she asked, startled.

I shook myself a little, drawing myself up as I did and smiling brightly down into Nettie's worried face.

"I was just a little surprised is all," I said briskly, proud of myself when my voice came out sounding almost normal. "Why is he back? Is he just visiting for the holidays?" Memories of Samuel rose unbidden and an ache settled in my chest as I thought of how desperately I had missed him.

"Well," Nettie sighed, and, satisfied that I was fine, sank back into the chair and resumed tying bows as she spoke.

"He gets leave every now and again, kind of like vacation time. But he's been so busy and all. They taught him to be a sniper, you know." Nettie's voice dropped conspiratorially, like she was delivering good gossip, and her eyes grew wide at the thought of her grandson's sniping skills. "He doesn't talk about it much, but Don seems to think he's had some dangerous assignments."

I smiled at the thrill that was evident in Nettie's face. Nettie was a sucker for Tom Clancy novels. I could only imagine what she was thinking.

"Anyway," Nettie continued more matter-of-factly. "We've been begging him to come back for years, but he never seemed to want to. I think Samuel loves us, but I don't know how many good memories he has of Levan and the months he spent here. It was a hard time for him."

The little fissure in my heart with Samuel's name on it cracked wide open. Nettie continued on, completely unaware of my distress.

"Anyway, he's going to spend a couple of days with us and then go on to the reservation in Arizona for a week or so. His Grand-mother Yazzie is gettin' on in years. She was in her forties when she had Samuel's mother. Goodness, she has to be nearing eighty now. Samuel says she still looks after her sheep. She herds them on horse-back! Lardy, I can't even imagine it!"

"Is Samuel here now?" I turned away from her and started un-loading dishes from the drying rack, trying to seem nonchalant.

"Oh he'll be rollin' in tomorrow sometime. We'll make sure to say hello after the church program tomorrow evening. I sure can't wait to hear you play, honey. My word, it's like we have our very own Liberace."

I smiled at her comparison. I didn't have much in common with the flamboyant Liberace, but Nettie was sincere in her praise, and I loved her for it.

"Well, I'll be gettin' on home now, love. Don will be wonderin' where I am."

I walked her to the door, chatting merrily, smiling brightly, all the while having a mild panic attack at the thought of seeing Samuel again. I closed the door behind Nettie and slid down it until I was propped weakly against it, my legs splayed out in front of me. I was sixteen years old now. Samuel was 21. Would he be the same?

Would he even talk to me? Would he laugh to himself as he remembered our friendship? Would he be embarrassed that he had been such good friends with someone so young? I suddenly wanted my mother desperately. I didn't know how I would even be able to play at the Christmas service, knowing he was there. My stomach roiled nervously, and I pulled myself up and slid onto the piano bench, determined that I would play better than I had ever played before.

I spent the next morning digging through my closet in steadily increasing panic. Finally, after I had tried on everything I had in every combination, I gave in and called Aunt Louise. Louise was good with hair and make-up. After all, she made a living with her scissors, but Aunt Louise and her entire brood tended to be a little obnoxious and aggressive and way too blunt. I had shied away from asking for help with my appearance simply because I knew if I gave Aunt Louise or Tara an inch, they would take the proverbial mile. I shuddered as I dialed the phone, knowing Louise would be thrilled to help, but I might really regret asking. She picked up on the first ring. I could hear chaos in the background and had to raise my voice as I identified myself. I quickly gave Louise the run-down on my needs: The Christmas program was tonight and I had nothing to wear, and could she possibly help me with my hair and make-up? Squeezing my eyes shut and crossing my fingers, I asked if she might be able to come to *my* house instead of me going there. The thought of being on display for my cousins and Uncle Bob was more than I could bear.

"I need an excuse to leave the house," Louise said matter-of-factly. "When do kids grow out of this Christmas Eve fever anyway? My kids are swinging from the rafters. I think I'm gonna shoot myself." I heard her shout out a few orders to Bob, a couple of ultimatums to the youngest two, and a demand for Tara to "pull everything out of our closets that might work for Josie."

"I'll be there at 3:30. That'll give us plenty of time to play." I could hear the grin in Louise's voice, but I was too grateful to be

136

afraid.

"I love you, Aunt Louise. What would I do without you?" I breathed thankfully.

"Oh, heck girl. You'd be in a world 'a hurt, that's what," Louise cackled. "It's about time you started caring about how you look. How you gonna ever get someone to notice you if you wear Johnny's hand-me-downs for the rest of your life? You've got a good little figure and a pretty face, but nobody knows it because you hide behind your glasses and your books. What about those contacts we got you a prescription for? You better be wearin' 'em when I get there..."

"Thanks, Aunt Louise!" I interrupted brightly, sensing that Louise was winding up for a good nag. "I'll see you at three!"

My dad didn't seem to like the way I looked when Louise marched me down the narrow stairs from my little attic bedroom and announced that we were ready to go to the church. I was pretty happy with the results, however, and slid self-consciously into the kitchen behind Louise, not wanting to meet my father's eyes.

"Ah, Louise! What'd you go and do that fer?" my dad grumbled. "She's just a kid, and you got her lookin' like she's twenty-five."

*Twenty-five? Yay!*

I giggled into my hand and decided it had definitely been the right move to call my aunt. She had brought over a V-necked black dress with long sleeves that hugged my curves and swished around my legs when I walked. It had little black buttons from chest to hip, and it fit me perfectly. I even had on black hose and high-heeled black pumps. Aunt Louise had pinned my blonde curls up on my head, blackened my eyelashes and lightly lined them, and stained my lips and cheekbones with a deep rosy pink. I felt very sophisticated and hoped I could pull it all off without tripping on the way up to the piano when it was time to perform. I knew for sure I would need to kick the heels off before I began to play. It would be just my luck to have my shoes get stuck on the piano pedals and ruin everything.

"She is not a child anymore, Jim!" Aunt Louise folded her arms crossly and jutted out her chin at my dad. "You can't ignore the fact that your girl is practically grown! You better be ready to hand over some cash after Christmas is over! That girl has nothing in her closet! Nothing! I am takin' her shopping, and we are gonna throw out all those old T-shirts of Johnny's and those old Wranglers and cruddy gym shoes and all the other crap she's been wearin' for the last eight years since my sister died, and she's gonna start lookin' like the young lady she is! It ain't right, Jim!"

"I like the way Josie looks!" my dad protested. Any mention of my mother usually was a bad move. I started herding the two of them out the door as the bickering continued.

"That's because the way she looks is comfortable and safe—just the way a daddy likes it. No siree, not on my watch! Not anymore!" Louise was really warming up now. "It's high time she got a little woman's help. I shoulda done it long ago!"

My dad climbed into the cab of the truck with a huff. I moved over next to him on the bench seat, and Louise jumped in behind me, yakking all the way. I looked over at my dad and mouthed a silent "sorry Dad." He just groaned and drove us down the road to the waiting church.

My stomach knotted up as we looked for the closest place to park. The lack of snowfall made parking easier. Usually, the drifts ran up and over the sidewalks and poured out into the poorly plowed roads. Tonight it was just cold and still, with plenty of room along the sides of the road for the assorted farm-trucks and family vans that usually lined the church during services.

"It's gonna snow tonight. Mark my words," my dad interrupted Louise, who was still chewing him up pretty good over my lack of feminine clothing. "If it does, I'm gonna be gettin' a call to go into the plant. It's just Murphy's Law. I'll get called in and Daisy will have her foal..." Dad was worried about his mare that was due to have her baby in the next few days. His pessimism seemed to momentarily silence Aunt Louise who saw Bob and her kids pull into the church parking lot from across the way.

"Oh, there's my gang. Gotta go, Josie. Don't lick your lips! You'll ruin your lipstick! And try not to slouch. That dress bunches up in the front when you do! You don't want to make the buttons pucker and give everyone a peek at what's underneath!" With that she hustled off, still talking, and my dad and I sighed in tandem.

"I really don't care much for that woman," my dad mumbled. "She's nothin' like yer mother. I don't see how they even came from the same family tree, let alone the same womb." He sighed again and then said gruffly, rushing his words to get them out, "You look real pretty, Josie. Louise is right about one thing. Yer all grown up. One of these days you're gonna move away and leave your old man. I'm not lookin' forward to it."

"Don't worry, Dad. I'll always take care of you." I grinned up at him and looped my arm through his as we walked into the church.

The pews were filling up quick and I tried not to look around for Don and Nettie. And Samuel. I wanted to see him almost as much as I didn't want to see him. I kept my head forward as I tried to spot him peripherally. Everyone always sat in the same place. It just kind of happens. We're creatures of habit. There were families who sat in the same pew, generation upon generation. If I didn't know better, I would think the people of Levan bequeathed their pews in their wills. From what I could see, the Yates's weren't there yet. I exhaled in relief and at the same time my heart sank in disappointment.

I kept telling myself not to look for him. I kept my eyes trained on the podium where Lawrence Mangelson was just beginning his opening narration. When it came time for me to play, I was more nervous than I had ever been. I didn't think my legs would hold me as I carefully walked up the trio of stairs to the piano. I slid across the smooth surface of the bench, straightened my back, and slipped my pumps off to the side. I had to look. I just couldn't help myself. I let my eyes slide to where Don and Nettie usually sat for service. Samuel was with them, sitting to the right of Nettie, close to the end of the pew. I looked away before my eyes had time to register details. He was here.

With a deep exhale I dug into my piece, allowing my trained hands to take over. It was like watching myself from a few feet away. I didn't make any mistakes and, as usual, before I had gotten too far into the piece, the music reached out and pulled me in, so that by the time I played the finishing notes, the me that observed and the me that played became one again.

When the evening was over and the last choir notes sung, the congregation gathered around, commending each other on the beautiful service, talking about kids, cows, and who was doing what. I stood next to my family, waiting, with my back toward the direction Samuel had been sitting. I knew eventually Nettie would make her way to us. After ten minutes or so of making polite small talk and graciously thanking those who came up to compliment my performance, I realized, of course, that she would have no idea that I was waiting on tenterhooks for her to appear with Samuel. Maybe she wouldn't even remember that she had promised to say hello. Maybe they had already gone. Cursing myself for standing there like a cow waiting to be milked, I turned to see if maybe they had left the church.

It took me only a minute to spot Nettie and Don standing at the back of the chapel, chatting with Lawrence Mangelson. There was no sign of Samuel. Nettie caught my eye and waved me over to her. I moved toward her, eyes roving swiftly around the room to see if someone had cornered Samuel in conversation. Maybe he had stepped outside.

"Oh, Josie! You were wonderful. I just cry every time you play." Nettie hugged me and patted my cheek as she drew away. "Wasn't she wonderful, Don?"

Don added his less effusive praise as Lawrence Mangelson reiterated what Nettie had said as well. No mention of Samuel. I cleared my throat hesitantly.

"I thought I saw Samuel sitting with you. I'd like to say hello," I blurted out and then tried to look bored in an effort to camouflage my feelings.

Nettie waved off the question. "He was here, but he slipped out right after the closing prayer. I think he's plumb tuckered out. He drove a long way today and got in just in time to shower and come with us tonight. The beef stew and biscuits I left on the stove are probably calling to him!"

*"Beef stew and biscuits?!"* I thought to myself, outraged. He couldn't even say hello? I looked down at my silky black dress and high heeled shoes and suddenly felt very foolish. I had been passed over for beef stew and biscuits.

Excusing myself with wishes for a Merry Christmas to Don, Nettie, and Lawrence Mangelson, I walked out the wooden double doors and down the steps into the silvery night. My breath made little white puffs in front of me, and I pictured them as desperate smoke signals rising into the sky. Unfortunately, the only Indian warrior who knew anything about smoke signals seemed pretty uninterested in any communication with me.

My brothers and their significant others—Jacob and Jared were married, and Johnny had a steady girl that he was getting pretty serious with—always came over for Christmas Eve dinner, and we exchanged gifts then. Christmas day had gotten pretty lackluster since we had all grown up and toys and Santa had become things of the past. Dad and I would go to Aunt Louise's for Christmas Dinner tomorrow afternoon.

After eating half a dozen different appetizers, a huge ham, mashed potatoes, and homemade rolls, we sat by the tree and opened gifts. With full bellies and a warm fire, no one seemed to be in a big hurry to be on their way, so we all sat around and talked about nothing in particular. I had yet to take off my black dress and let down my hair. In the back of my mind, I just kept thinking maybe I would get an opportunity to let Samuel see me up close looking twenty-five, sophisticated, and beautiful. I sat stiffly on the edge of the couch, my only concession to comfort was my kicked off high-heels by the door. My brothers seemed confused by my appearance and started teasing me, only to have Rachel shush them up with a wink and a quick reprimand.

"Sometimes it's so much fun getting dressed up that it's hard to take it off at the end of the night." I smiled gratefully at her, and my brothers shrugged and proceeded to ignore me.

True to Dad's prediction, fat white snowflakes began to fall as the hour grew later, and with sighs and groans, my brothers bundled up their ladies and headed out. Johnny was spending the night at Sheila's house so that they could spend Christmas with her family the next day. Jacob and Rachel had purchased a little home in Nephi the previous year, and Jared and Tonya were in student housing at Brigham Young University in Provo. Everybody was heading north across the ridge, and suddenly nobody wanted to wait around for more snow to fall.

The ridge is a ten mile stretch of old two-lane highway between Levan and Nephi. Levanites travel it countless times a week for countless reasons—back and forth from school and work, to the Thriftway for groceries, or to the library for books to hold them over until the Bookmobile traveled through Levan again. Every sixteen-year-old in Levan drove the ridge many times before they actually turned sixteen. It was a farming community, and that was just the way of things. We drove early, and we drove everything from tractors to beat up old farm trucks. I could drive a mean stick shift when I was ten years old, and do it smoothly enough for my older brothers to keep their feet planted in the truck bed as they threw bales of hay off for the cows. The ridge was straight and narrow and very dark at night. Folks flew across it, lulled into a sense of security simply by the sheer number of times we all made the drive. It was made all the worse by the deer that would come down from the mountains looking for grazing and run across the road. The deer were constantly getting hit or causing accidents as people swerved to avoid them. Of course, a good snowfall made it even more treacherous. Every year someone died on that strip of road between the two little towns.

I stood on the front porch in all of my grown-up finery and waved my brothers off. The lights were still on at the Yates place. I could see a truck out front that must belong to Samuel. What possible excuse could I come up with to stop by at eleven o'clock at night so I could see him? I stood there shivering, willing him to come out. Instead, as I watched and wished, the lights flicked out and the house was dark. Trying not to cry, I walked inside and flipped off our front porch light in dejected response.

My dad woke me up at 5:00 a.m. to tell me he had gotten called in to work at the plant. The supervisor on duty had been in a car accident the night before, and they needed someone to cover the early shift. I told him to be careful and rolled over and immediately started to go back to sleep. I heard him whisper that he would be home in time for Christmas dinner at Louise's and to make sure I fed the horses when I got up.

I woke up again at eight and considered lying in bed and feeling sorry for myself, all alone on Christmas morning. But the truth was, I didn't mind having the house to myself, and I figured I would just make myself a big plate of leftovers from last night's feast and listen to Handel's *Messiah* as loud as I could blast it. I pulled on my softest pair of blue jeans, my green and red striped Christmas socks, and a truly ugly sweater with a giant reindeer head on it that I had received last year as a white elephant gift. I'd pulled the pins out of my hair before I'd gone to bed, but I really hadn't wanted to part with my new make-up…so I'd slept in it. I laughed at my raccoon eyes when I saw my reflection, and decided my makeover had definitely run its course. I scrubbed my face clean, brushed my teeth, ran my fingers through my riotous curls, and called it good. I had just sat down with my plate of food and hit play on the new CD player I had received the night before, ready to hear the sounds of Handel's opening movement, when I remembered the horses.

"Ah, hell!" I cursed, sounding exactly like my dad. It was hard not to grow up swearing when you lived on a farm. We never took the Lord's name in vain or said the F-word, but pretty much damn, hell, and shit were part of the vernacular of most folks born and raised in Levan. To tell the truth, those words weren't really considered swear words. Last week in church, Gordon Aagard was giving a sermon on trials. He referred to horse shit right in the middle of his talk, and nobody really batted an eye.

Pulling on Johnny's old boots, I trudged out to the corral. Yazzie danced his happy dog dance around my legs as I walked. Yazzie loved to visit the horses. Dad had built a little lean-to adjacent to the corral, and Joe and Ben greeted me with nickers and bunted me with their noses as I mucked out the lean-to and re-filled the feed buckets. The water in the trough was iced over and I broke it with my shovel, spooning the ice out and topping it off.

Daisy, Dad's mare, was in the barn, separated from the other horses where it was a little warmer and drier, until she delivered her foal. I swung into the barn, eager to be done with my chores, when I saw that Daisy was lying down, her breathing heavy, her back slick. There was a little blood on the floor of the big stall, and I dropped the shovel I was carrying as I ran to her. I'd watched enough foals be born to know that Daisy was well on her way to being a new mama, and I was home alone.

"Dad said this was going to happen," I said out loud, rubbing my hand down Daisy's soft nose, "So now what do I do?"

I ran inside and dialed the number to the power plant. Usually there is always someone in the front office who relays messages to the guys on shift. Today was Christmas, and the staff was at the bare minimum. Nobody answered the phone. A recorded message came on with instructions to call back during regular operating hours. I growled in response and hung up the phone. I called Jacob and Rachel's house and got Rachel's cheerful voice on the answering machine telling me she and Jacob weren't home and to please leave a message. They were home; they were just lying in bed enjoying their Christmas morning. I left a slightly panicked message demanding that Jacob get his butt to the farm. Johnny was at Sheila's parents' home, and I called their number with the same results, only this time I asked a little more nicely. Jared was too far away to do me any good. I left him alone.

I ran back out to the barn and paced nervously. I couldn't see anything. I wasn't sure I knew what to look for exactly, but there were no little hooves or a head sticking out of Daisy's nether regions. Daisy groaned, and a watery gush swooshed out between her hind legs.

"Oh man! I cannot do this by myself," I shrieked. Running out of the barn I ran as fast as my muddy boots would allow toward the Yates's house. Don would know what to do. Out of breath and gasping, I reached the front walk and slipped and slid my way up to the front door, banging on the screen and yelling for Don. I had been so focused on Daisy and the impending birth that I had run right by the truck that I'd seen the night before without really noticing it. I heard a door open behind me and swung around to see Samuel step out of the truck with concern playing across his handsome face. And it was a very handsome face. I momentarily forgot all about poor Daisy. He wore a pair of Wrangler's and a Carhart jacket. One foot was planted on the ground in a Justin boot and a black cowboy hat sat low on his head. The other leg was still inside the cab of his truck.

"Josie? My grandpa's not here. He and Grandma headed over to my Aunt Tabrina's house earlier this morning. They wanted to see the kids open their gifts. I'm heading over there now...would you like me to give him a message?" Samuel was so polite and formal that for a minute I just stared at him, wondering if I had just imagined our past friendship. He stared back at me, one eyebrow cocked, waiting for a response.

"Daisy's having her baby. Dad got called into work at five this morning, I can't get a hold of any of my brothers, and I don't know what to do." I realized I was spilling words out every which way, and Samuel looked a little alarmed.

"Daisy?" he queried slowly.

"Our mare!" I shouted at him.

Samuel turned off the ignition, pulled his other leg out of the truck, slammed the door, and started walking down the road toward my house. I watched him blankly until I realized he was going to help me. I clumped along after him until I reached his side.

"Nice sweater." Samuel didn't even look at me as he spoke, and my eyes flew down to my chest. Antlers and a shiny red nose poked out of my unbuttoned jacket. I groaned inwardly. Where was Samuel Yates last night when I was ready to be seen up close and personal? God must really have a sense of humor, I thought morosely. He'd answered my Christmas prayer—just in his own time. Ha, ha, ha, very funny. And why did I have to display my Christmas spirit this morning? Why hadn't I thrown this stupid sweatshirt in the compost pile where it belonged? My hands flew to my hair. I could feel loose curls bouncing in sunny disarray.

"Thank you," I replied stiffly. I might have imagined it, but I think Samuel's lips twitched.

"Have you ever helped birth a foal?" I asked anxiously as we rounded the house and headed back to the barn.

"Lots of lambs, only one foal," Samuel replied shortly. "I don't think there's too much variation. But I guess we'll find out. Isn't there a vet we can call?"

"There's a vet that covers the county, and I called his pager number, but I don't know if he'll get back to me and I'm not going to wait by the phone. Dad says he doesn't know his ass from his head anyway." Realizing that the vocabulary that I had worked so hard to build and that I so prided myself on had completely abandoned me in my flustered state, I clamped my mouth shut and swore I wouldn't say another word until I was in better control of my tongue.

Samuel didn't respond to my dad's opinion of the vet, and I led the way into the barn. Daisy still lay quietly, her only movement in the rise and fall of her breathing. Quickly, Samuel shucked his coat and rolled up his sleeves as far as they would go. Samuel knelt above her, stroking her head with his right hand. He sat waiting as her big body suddenly tightened up, a contraction causing her flanks to quiver with strain. As the tightening began to visibly ease, Samuel, speaking quietly and soothing her with his right hand, snaked his left hand between her rear flanks. Daisy's legs stiffened and she tossed her head, but she didn't fight him as he inserted his arm inside her all the way up to his shoulder. Yuck. I was so glad Samuel was with me I felt lightheaded with relief. After a few moments of concentrated groping he spoke.

"I think I can feel the head and the forelegs, so that's good. The baby is facing the right direction. At this point, your mare will do all the work. If all is as it should be, there's not a whole lot we can do. Let's go inside, and I'll wash up and you see if you can reach your dad again. It won't be long now."

I hadn't turned Handel off when I went to feed the horses. The entire production of his *Messiah* had played out to an empty kitchen, and the "Hallelujah Chorus" was reverberating joyfully throughout the house as we entered through the back door. My boots were muddy and I didn't want to take the time away from Daisy to pull them off and back on, so walking though the house to turn the music off in the family room wasn't going to happen; it would just have to play to the end. I ran to the phone and tried the power plant again with no luck. I hung up with an impatient sigh.

"My dad is going to be fit to be tied when he gets home."

"Isn't this what you played last night?" Samuel questioned from the sink, his back to me. My mind jumped from the failed phone call back to Handel's music pouring out of the family room.

"Oh. Uh, yes. It's Handel's 'Hallelujah Chorus.' It's pretty wonderful with a full orchestra, isn't it?

"It was pretty wonderful last night with just the piano, too," Samuel replied seriously, and turned his head to look at me as he dried his hands and unrolled his sleeves. Pleasure washed over me at his words, and I tried to stop myself from beaming like an idiot as we left the kitchen and headed back out to the barn.

There seemed to be no change as Samuel and I squatted down next to the laboring mare. She huffed and groaned a little with the next contraction, but didn't seem unduly stressed. I prayed silently that Daisy would be all right and that the birth would go well.

The quiet in the barn became more pronounced as we held our vigil, and I searched my mind for something to say. Samuel certainly didn't seem to feel the need to talk.

"Handel composed all three parts of his *Messiah*, including the orchestration, in a little more than three weeks. Two hundred and sixty pages of music in just twenty-four days. No other composer has accomplished anything like that in the history of music. He described it as an out-of-body experience." I sounded like a tour guide, and my voice faded off uncertainly as Samuel failed to even lift his head. When he didn't respond after several long seconds, I bit my tongue to keep from trying to continue to fill the embarrassing lull. When he did speak several minutes later his voice made me jump.

"Why did everyone stand last night when you started to play?"

"Did they stand?" I was dumbfounded. I really hadn't noticed.

Samuel just raised that one eyebrow and looked at me.

I blushed and shrugged. "I really don't know…"

"Your teacher was the first to stand—Mrs. Grimaldi, right? Everyone just kind of followed her up."

I giggled, suddenly understanding what Sonja had done. "It's actually tradition to stand on the Hallelujah Chorus. You see, when the King of England first attended a performance of 'Messiah," he was so moved when the Hallelujah Chorus played that he stood up. Apparently, when the King of England stands, everyone stands. I guess Sonja thought Levan should carry on a tradition that's been in effect for two hundred and fifty years."

"You really didn't notice that everyone was standing almost the entire time you played?" Samuel's smooth baritone was slightly dis-believing.

His tone made me feel defensive, and I waved my hand as if to brush off his doubts. "You know me, Samuel—I lose myself in the music. By the time I came back to Earth, everyone had probably sat back down."

My insistence that he 'knew' me rang in my ears as he turned back toward Daisy, again without comment, and stroked her long neck. He was acting like we had never known each other at all. I thought of how often my thoughts had been filled with him over the last two plus years and felt a lump rise up in my throat.

I was distracted from my misery several moments later when Daisy convulsed strongly and a wet nose popped out between her hind quarters. I gasped, and the little nose disappeared again as the contraction abated.

"One more and that should do it." Samuel's voice was calm and reassuring, but my heart was pounding as I waited for the next con-traction to come. Samuel ran his hands down Daisy's damp flanks, talking softly to her, urging her on.

"One more, girl, one more. You're almost done," he soothed. "Here it comes, here we go."

Moments later, the horse shuddered and her flanks shook as a nose and two hooves came plainly into view, followed by a wet tan-gle of big ears and wobbly, knobby legs. Samuel helped pull the new colt free, wiping blood and slime off the little fellow with handfuls of straw. Daisy turned her head and butted her awkward offspring gently, prodding as she urged him to his feet, licking and nudging him all the while.

"Way to go, Daisy! Well done girl!" I cried, clapping softly. I realized I was on my feet and there were tears on my face. I wiped them off hastily as I knelt back down and placed a kiss between Daisy's sweat-slicked ears.

"You did it, Samuel!" I grinned at him, my unhappiness forgotten in light of the triumphant birth.

"I didn't do anything—it was all Daisy," he replied, but his tone was mild and I could tell he was pleased that it had gone without incident.

I was happily contemplating Christmas names for Daisy's baby when the sound of a slamming door and boots on gravel carried back to the barn.

"I hope that's my dad!" I cried out, rising and running for the entrance of the barn. Jacob and Dad had parked the truck around the house and were high-tailing it toward the barn when I intercepted them with the happy news. My dad was beside himself with worry and rushed ahead of me into the barn. I followed him in, sharing details of the morning's miracle, relating Samuel's role in the excitement as we approached him where he still perched, balanced on his haunches next to the new colt. He rose smoothly to his feet, wiping his blood-stained hands on his jeans before extending a hand apologetically to my dad.

"Congratulations, sir. Sorry about the hand."

My dad grabbed it, completely unconcerned about shaking the proffered hand. Clapping Samuel on the back, he thanked him for coming to my rescue.

They all talked for a few minutes, admiring the new colt, commenting on this and that, rubbing his floppy ears, and enjoying the Christmas surprise.

"Well Josie," my dad turned to me suddenly. "I think you and Samuel have earned the right to name the colt. Whaddaya think?"

I looked at Samuel expectantly, but he just shrugged, dipping his head in my direction as he deferred to me. "Go ahead, Josie."

"George Frederic Handel," I said impulsively.

Jacob and my dad groaned loudly in unison and hooted in laughing protest.

"What the hell kind of name is that, Josie?" my brother howled.

"He's a composer!" I cried out, embarrassed and wishing I had taken a minute to think before I blurted out the first thing that came to my head.

A smile played around Samuel's lips as he joined in the fray. "He wrote the music that Josie played last night at the church service."

"I just thought the colt should have a Christmas name, and Handel's Hallelujah Chorus is synonymous with Christmas!" I defended and then cringed as Jacob and my dad burst out laughing again.

My dad wiped tears of mirth from his eyes as he tried to get control of himself.

"We'll call him Handel," he choked out. "It's a very nice name, Josie." He patted my shoulder, still chuckling. I felt like I was ten years old.

"Well, my grandparents are going to be wondering where I am." Samuel extended his hand to my father again. "I'd better get cleaned up and be on my way."

"Thanks again, Samuel," my dad called after him. Samuel inclined his head politely to me and Jacob, turned, and strode out of the barn.

I followed him out, my dad and my brother completely unaware that I was leaving. Samuel had picked up his stride and was a good ways in front of me when I exited the barn. Obviously, he was done here. *That was it? He was leaving without more than a nod to me?* He would probably be gone the next day without giving me another thought. Suddenly, I was very angry and more than a little hurt. Impulsively, I bent down and scooped up a big handful of snow, punching it into a sloppy snowball. I launched it as hard as I could at Samuel's retreating form.

I am not athletic in the slightest, and I can't throw a ball to save my life, but for once my aim ran true, and the hard-packed snowball plowed right into the back of Samuel's head.

He turned, stunned, his hand rising to his head and brushing the snow from his short black hair. I picked up another snowball and chucked it at him, too. He ducked, but I had another one ready to go right on its heels. That one struck him in the chest, snow plastering the front of his shirt where his jacket lay opened, and dripping down his neck. Samuel stared at me as if I had lost my mind. I definitely wasn't laughing.

"Josie! What is wrong with you?" he stuttered in disbelief.

"What *is* wrong with me?!" I cried back. "Why don't you tell me what's wrong with me, since you're so eager to get away from me?" I shook the snow from my hands and shoved them under my armpits, trying to warm them, the cold ache in my fingers in accord with the sting of tears threatening my eyes. Samuel walked back toward me, closing the distance between us until we stood face to face.

"I thought you were my friend!" I sputtered angrily. "Last night you didn't even come say hello, today you've acted like we're almost strangers, and now you're just walking away without so much as a "hey Josie, how are you?" It's been two years and seven months since you left, and I've thought of you every day. I've written you dozens of letters." I shook my head in bewilderment. "We were friends Samuel! We were good friends!"

Samuel sighed heavily and shoved his hands fiercely into his coat pockets. He cocked his head and stared at me for a moment, his expression undecipherable. After what seemed like a lifetime he spoke, and his voice was gentle.

"I'm sorry Josie. You're right. We were friends. Good friends." He sighed and turned away slightly, kicking at the snow at his feet. "Do you know how old I am, Josie?" he asked me, looking back at me seriously.

"You're twenty-one," I shot back.

"Yep, and you are?"

I waited without answering, knowing what was coming.

"You are sixteen years old. It's inappropriate for me to be anywhere near you."

I groaned loudly and threw my hands in the air. My physical and intellectual maturity, along with my sensitive nature and my love for English literature should have made me a prime candidate for romantic daydreams and girlish drama. But though I had fallen unabashedly in love with Jane Eyre's Mr. Rochester and Jane Austen's Mr. Darcy, the boys I attended school with held little appeal. I felt decades older than my classmates, and I possessed a certain seriousness and reserve that must have made me seem unapproachable and snobbish. Sonja always said I had an old soul. I kept to myself for the most part, took care of my dad, read my books, played my piano, and spent time with the Grimaldis. When I was forced into the company of my classmates, I kept close to my cousin Tara, who liked me despite my peculiarities. But I had never felt like I belonged. Hearing Samuel tell me I was way too young to be his friend just made me want to scream.

"What does my age have to do with us being friends?" I repeated aloud. "You don't just come back after all this time and act like you never knew me. Last night... I couldn't wait to see you, to talk to you...and you just...left! That was cruel, Samuel. You may have outgrown me, but would it have hurt you to say hello, to talk to me for a minute?"

Samuel scrubbed his hands over his face in frustration. "Last night you didn't look sixteen," he said tersely.

"What does that have to do with anything?" I replied, aghast.

"I was looking forward to seeing you too, Josie. But...after seeing you play at the church, I thought it was wise to stay away from you because I care way more than I should," Samuel bit off reluctantly.

My heart stuttered in my chest, and I stared at him, uncertain how to respond. He stared back at me, hands in his pockets, feet spread wide, brow furrowed. The expression on his face was so precious and familiar that I laughed and reached up to smooth the deep groove between his scowling eyebrows. He jerked back as my hand touched his face, and his hand snaked out and wrapped around my wrist.

"I didn't lie when I told you I would never forget you, Josie. But it can't be like it was. I guess you're right. I've outgrown our old friendship." His mouth twisted wryly, and he dropped my wrist suddenly. "Take care of yourself, Josie. It's been really nice seeing you." He turned without further comment and crunched across the snow without looking back.

I watched him walk away and amazingly enough, this time it hurt even worse than when he left the first time. This time I had no illusions about the future. There would be no letters and no comfort in delusions. Samuel was as gone to me as my mother was. The next morning his truck was no longer parked in front of his grandparents' home. I took his letters from my desk drawer and his picture and the necklace he'd given me from my treasure box. I put everything in an old shoebox and put it on the highest shelf in my closet. I slid it to the very back and shut the door firmly.

I pretended I had outgrown him, too. One day I would be gone. I would be a famous concert pianist. I would travel the world, and I wouldn't think about Samuel ever again. Someday, I would be the one to leave.

# 12. Interlude

**August, 2000**

A WEEK BEFORE my junior year in high school, everything changed. Kasey Judd had lived in Levan all his life, just like me. His family had lived there for generations, just like mine. We'd been born a few days apart, in the same hospital, in the same year. We had attended the same church, rode the same bus, and were in the same classes. Up until ninth grade, he wore braces and glasses and I was taller than he was. His curly hair was always unruly, his shoes always untied, and he constantly challenged me for first chair in the school band, which I found slightly annoying because I regularly trounced him. He had been a fixture on the periphery of my life ALL of my life, just like the comfortable couch in the living room or the patterns on the walls. He was just another boy...until I fell in love with him.

Kasey's dad was the football coach at Nephi High School. I played trumpet in the school band, so I attended my share of football games and cheered for my share of football players. Tara had a thing for football players, but I really wasn't interested in hearing about every single player, their stats, the position they played, and the way they looked in uniform.

Tara knew everything about everyone, and I mostly listened with an uninterested ear. Her ability to talk non-stop without any encouragement from me made our relationship work. I never had much to say, and she couldn't shut up, so it was a win/win all the way around. She was the only person I knew who had business cards touting her gossiping skills. The cards said "If You Want to Know How or Who, Ask Tara Ballow" (Ba LOO). I suppose Tara's chatter filled a feminine need inside of me. By this time, all my brothers had graduated, married, or moved out, and I lived at home with my dad. He was almost as quiet as I was which meant girl talk—or any other kind of talk—was pretty scarce, and Tara happily filled the void.

My piano playing ability made band a no-brainer, and I was the first chair trumpet player. We didn't have orchestra at the school, so when I joined the band in seventh grade, I had wanted to learn to play a more classical instrument like the clarinet until Tara told me that trumpet players made the best kissers. I figured someone as awkward as I was needed all the help I could get, and I had played the trumpet ever since. Tara played the flute...quite badly. But the competition wasn't fierce in a small school, and she managed to keep her chair. She might have played better had she just stopped talking! The huge pink bubble she was always blowing didn't help much either. Mr. Hackett, our band teacher, had forbidden gum in band, but Tara was constantly cleaning cherry Hubba Bubba out of her mouthpiece.

We started band practice two weeks before the school year started to get ready for the upcoming football season. Practice was ridiculously early because it was "Hell Week" for the football team, which meant two-a-days. The band practiced early to allow members of the football team, who were also members of the band, to make it to morning football practice. At a small school it isn't unusual for a jock to be in the band or sing in the chorus or to be in the school play. In my opinion, that is the best thing about going to a small school; less competition sometimes means more opportunity. Tara had been telling me all about "that cute Kasey Judd" all summer long. She'd said his dad had all the boys in the weight room getting them ready for football season. Tara had been up at the football field during several practices with binoculars to check out their new muscles.

I dragged into that first early-morning practice with my curly blonde hair in a sloppy ponytail, wearing an old pair of cut-off jeans, a ratty Survivor T-shirt and flip flops, only to discover my chair was occupied. I sighed. When would Kasey Judd ever learn? I looked, and then I stared. Kasey Judd had grown up. His shoulders were broad and his legs were long and stretched out in front of him. No more glasses, and no more braces. His hair was curly, like my own, but where mine was a light wheat blonde just like my dad's (and his dad's, and his dad's), Kasey's was dark brown and was now cut short to tame the once unruly mop.

I sat down next to him and shyly said, "That's my seat." I hoped the freckles I always got across my nose in the summertime weren't too noticeable, and I cursed myself for not *at least* applying mascara to my happily long, but sadly very blonde, eyelashes. I had started wearing my contacts on a more regular basis and was thankful that I'd taken the time to put them in that morning, saving myself from total ugliness. He looked at me with a little grin and a quirked eyebrow and said, "We'll see."

His eyes were a hazel green, and his smile curled up at the ends. Dimples creased his sun-tanned cheeks. I almost fell right off my chair. I had never had a physical reaction to a smile before, but I felt Kasey's grin deep down in my gut like a sucker punch, and I was a total goner. Over the moon, gone. He challenged me for first chair in the trumpet section that day and for the first time in umpteen years, he won, though I challenged him the following week and never let him have it back.

Two weeks later, we shared our first kiss under the stars at Burraston's Pond, and despite our inexperience, it was not an awkward meeting of lips and teeth. That kiss was as natural as a prayer at bedtime. Simple, sweet, sustaining. I fell so hard I saw stars, and the funny thing is I naively thought that that was just how falling in love was for everyone. We became inseparable from then on, to the point that our names became an extension of the other. Kaseynjosie. You couldn't say one without the other. It was all so easy with him—easy to love him, easy to be loved.

I had many people in my life that loved me...and I was not necessarily lacking in love. What I craved was awareness—awareness of *me*. I could sit quietly in my chair and read the night away, never demanding attention, never seeking it. I could sit behind the piano and play and have people appreciate the beautiful music and never take notice of the one who played it. I was a steady, quiet presence in the lives of those around me. But sometimes in my reading I would discover new insights or have seemingly profound thoughts that would change my way of thinking. I would be hungry to share my inspiration with someone, so I would try to share my epiphanies with my dad or my brothers. They would remain politely quiet for a few seconds and then become distracted by something more interesting or urgent than my newly acquired knowledge, leaving me to talk to myself. I usually just stopped talking when I could see they really weren't interested or listening, and they never protested or urged me to continue.

If I tried to philosophize with Tara she would stare at me blankly for a few minutes and then slowly cross her eyes and say, "You're losin' me Jos!" I would laugh because I knew it was true, and I would tuck my thoughts away for another audience. My Aunt Louise was too literal, too real, and too down-to-earth to enjoy the profundity of the universe and warned me away whenever I "started gettin' deep." Sonja had filled that void in many ways, but her own insights were so precious to me that when I was with her I found myself more interested in listening and soaking up her wisdom than talking myself.

When Kasey became part of my life he had seemed to enjoy letting me elucidate on any subject that had sparked my interest. He would quietly listen and look at me now and again. Often he would agree with whatever I said and hug me saying, "You are so smart, Josie." He never had much to offer in the way of deeper discussion, but I so appreciated his interest in what I had to say that I didn't much care. I had needed someone to listen to me and to seek out my opinions. I had needed someone to value me, to give credence to my thoughts, to be awed by my abilities, and there was nobody more aware of a pretty teenage girl than an infatuated teenage boy. It had felt new and wonderful, and his attention had kept me on a constant, heady high that was completely foreign to me.

I had felt God's power and presence in beautiful music, I had been taught principles of goodness from classic literature, and I had always felt certain both were blessings from a loving Father in Heaven. I was just as certain that God had given me Kasey to assuage my deep-rooted loneliness, the loneliness that even music, words, and the love of my family had not been able to extinguish. I thought Kasey was God's atonement for taking my mother.

Among my peers I was considered quaint and old-fashioned, but Kasey never seemed to mind. He too was a believer in the principles taught by simple, God fearing, and hardworking parents. We had both been schooled in faith and in a belief in God and family responsibility. We understood what was expected of us and wanted to make our parents proud. I'm sure during those two years our parents worried that we were too close. And we were too close…but they never tried to keep us apart. There is an intensity to young love that is hard to deny, but we managed to hang on to our virtue and keep our hands to ourselves for the most part. We were planning to be married, ending the torture, as soon as we graduated. Kasey had asked me to marry him on Christmas Eve, placing a little tiny diamond on my finger. Our parents shrugged helplessly and gave us their blessing. My dad looked at me with tears in his eyes and said, "Josie, are you sure, honey?" I remember looking back at him in amazement thinking what a silly question that was. I had responded with a laugh and a fierce hug. I'd never doubted it for a moment. Not one frisson of doubt. My dad had squeezed me back and kissed the top of my head.

"Okay, honey, okay ..."

Before falling in love with Kasey, I had assumed I would go to college and get a degree in music with a minor in English Lit and play piano professionally, making a living doing the thing I loved most. After Kasey, I wasn't quite as desperate for that dream. It wasn't that I had lost my ambition, but I couldn't imagine any of those things giving me more joy than just being near Kasey and making a life with him. I had received a music scholarship to any school of my choice, and Kasey had a football scholarship to Brigham Young University. I figured I could teach piano lessons and make good money doing it; every Mormon kid takes piano lessons at some point in their childhood. I would get a little car so I could make house calls, which busy moms loved, and I could help support Kasey and myself while we both went to school. When we graduated, he would teach school and coach football just like his dad, and I would play piano professionally and compose, and we would be together forever. We had it all planned out.

Kasey was like air to me. No matter how much time we spent together, it was never enough. He didn't share my love of literature or my obsession with classical music, but he wasn't threatened by it either. Kasey was probably the kind of man many women could happily love and be loved by. He laughed easily and liked to tease but never at the expense of someone's feelings. He could be feisty and competitive but was quick to forgive and ask forgiveness. Unlike me, he never felt awkward giving and receiving affection; he hugged his dad, kissed his mom, and said I love you without me saying it first. He always made me feel like I was the best thing that ever happened to him. He was a very good son. He would have been a good man, a good husband, and a good father. He was the sun in my universe from our very first kiss.

Kasey asked me out of the blue one time if I had ever been in love before. We were curled up on the big couch in his parents' living room on a Saturday evening, homemade caramel popcorn between us and a couple of cold Cokes on little coasters on the coffee table in front of us. Things were being blown up and decimated on the big television screen and all was right with the world.

I laughed lightly, surprised at his question, and instantly replied "No!" as I grabbed his hand. He'd responded in kind and let the subject drop, almost as if he had expected my answer and mentally moved on before I'd even spoken. I sat in silence for a minute, holding his hand between mine, studying his palm, tracing his lifeline, and wondering what had inspired his question.

"Why?" I asked, suddenly unable to contain my curiosity.

Kasey glanced over at me distractedly, "Why what?"

"Why did you ask me if I'd ever been in love?" I prodded.

Kasey shrugged one shoulder, turning his attention back to the screen. "I don't know, I've just been thinking. You may not have noticed me until last year, but I noticed you a long time ago."

"Huh?"

Kasey sighed and picked up the remote, pausing the movie, making the guy who was being hurled through the air pause midflight. He looked at me then, his eyes running over my face.

"Josie you're beautiful, and you have been beautiful your whole life." I warmed at the praise and found myself smiling sheepishly, embarrassed but pleased. "The nice thing about you," he continued, "is you don't seem to know it. When we were in junior high, my friends and I would talk about you. Some of the guys thought that you were stuck up because you were so quiet and you weren't interested in any of us." My eyebrows shot up, and it was Kasey's turn to be slightly embarrassed.

"Well, you were so much more mature than everyone else, heck, you were practically from a different planet. You were nice enough, but you were really distant, kind of like you were just putting in your time, you know? A few of the guys thought maybe you had an older

161

boyfriend or something." Kasey searched my eyes like he was gauging the effect his words would have—maybe wondering if I would volunteer that I had, indeed, had a secret boyfriend no one knew about.

"You were taller than all of us and looked a lot older, and you were definitely smarter. I knew better though. I knew you were just really shy, not stuck up. You probably don't remember, but in 7th grade Science you sat right next to me. You were very sweet, never snotty or full of yourself. I looked forward to that class every day. That was when I decided that someday you were gonna be my girlfriend. I've liked other girls, but I always had my eye on you."

I leaned over and gently pressed my lips to his, and the conversation was suspended as he kissed me back. His mom's voice from the kitchen brought us tumbling back to reality, and we pulled apart and resumed a safer proximity. Kasey hit play on the remote and the unfortunate victim finished his trajectory into the side of an apartment building. Kasey slung his arm around my shoulders, and I leaned against him, pulling my feet in fuzzy pink socks up underneath me.

I spent the rest of that evening in contemplation, feeling almost guilty. I was glad for the Schwarzenegger video Kasey had picked to watch; it had allowed my mind to wander as he enjoyed the destruction on screen. It had been a while since I had actively thought of Samuel. He still tiptoed through my thoughts every now and then. When the Twin Towers and the Pentagon had been hit, I wondered where he was and if he would be one of the Marines on the front lines in the war in Afghanistan. I had even watched the news coverage with his face in my mind. But I had not physically missed him, not really, not for a long time. After all, I hadn't seen him in more than two years.

But as I sat there holding Kasey's hand, I had to acknowledge my lie. I might love only Kasey now, but I had been in love before. I had loved Samuel. It was not a crush or infatuation. It had been love. Innocent, out of the ordinary, before its time, but….love. Time had provided perspective, and though I had never admitted it to myself, I knew it was true. The thought left me shaky.

I hadn't ever told Kasey about Samuel. Not a single word. I wondered at my silence. I wasn't ashamed of what had been—but there weren't words. Some things can't be explained or shared; they tend to lose their luster when passed around. It reminded me of the 'pearls before swine' scripture. A pig will never have any appreciation for a pearl, no matter how precious. He doesn't have the experience or the capacity to comprehend its worth. My relationship with Samuel had been a glimmering pearl in my life, and even those closest to me, though certainly the furthest thing from swine, would be unable to grasp its intrinsic value. The saying "you had to be there" pretty much summed it up. Nothing could be gained by me trying to expound on the subject so I never had. Samuel was no longer a part of my life, and that night as I held hands with my future, I determined to keep him tucked away in my past.

The day of graduation, May 28, saw us lined up with our classmates, marching down the aisle and getting our diplomas. Alphabetical order put Jensen and Judd side by side, and Kasey and I threw our caps into the air together. I was in the top ten in my class; I would have been Valedictorian had I tried. I made sure I wasn't. Graduating number three meant I wouldn't have to say one word into the microphone, and I had no interest in giving a speech at graduation. I didn't shed any tears as people around me, including Kasey, hugged each other and cried nostalgically. High school had never been the pinnacle for me, and I was so ready for what came next…and what came next was Kasey and me in church, in front of the whole town, saying "I do." When I was a little girl, I had watched the musical *Seven Brides for Seven Brothers* eight million times, and I was going to be a June bride. We had the date set, the announcements printed, and my wedding dress, the dress my mother had worn when she married my dad, hanging in my closet where I could see it as I fell asleep each night.

The after-graduation tradition was an all-night party for the seniors at a water park in Provo, about 45 minutes north of Nephi. Kasey was sociable and loved to play, so I happily went along, though water parks and all-nighters that didn't involve books weren't really my thing. Afterwards, the graduates would load into a school bus and head back to the high school for a big pancake breakfast served up by some of the moms. Kasey had a job stocking shelves in the early morning hours at the Nephi grocery store. He had to work that morning, so my brother Johnny was going to swing by and grab me at the high school after his night shift at the power plant ended. Kasey planned to grab a shower and a quick nap in the employee break room before his shift began.

As usual, we tried to postpone our parting to the last possible minute. It was just before 5:00 in the morning, and Kasey didn't have to be to work until 6:30, so he decided he had plenty of time to run me home himself and still get a shower and a catnap. We called the power plant from the phone in the school office and Johnny was paged to a nearby phone.

"I don't mind, Johnny," Kasey had said earnestly. Johnny had laughed at him.

"I'm sure you don't Kasey, and I know Josie doesn't," he said wryly, "but you two have had no sleep, it's 5:00 in the morning, I'll be ready to leave in forty-five minutes, and there's no reason for you to make the extra trip."

Kasey reassured him and I cajoled, and before long we were on our way to Levan in Kasey's beat-up, green Ford. We liked the old car because it had a bench seat in front, and I could sit right next to him. I sat as close to him as I could while he drove. He kept his left hand on the wheel and the other hand in mine. We both smelled like chlorine from the water park, and our hair had dried in stiff ringlets.

I had twisted mine up into a clip, but his flopped into his eyes, and I smoothed the curls off of his forehead as we chatted non-stop all the way to my house.

The sun was just peeking up over the eastern mountains that shadowed the sleepy town when we rolled across the gravel in front of my house. I had spent many a day up Pidgeon and Chicken Creek Canyons in those mountains. That year we'd had a dry, cold winter and not nearly enough snowfall, and as farmers in the West usually do, we'd spent a lot of time fasting and praying for moisture. The canyon wouldn't see much run-off that year, which would be hard on the farms. But I was too content to worry overmuch, and that morning, with the sun behind them, those mountains just looked like home to me, all framed in pink hope with streaks of golden promise spilling over the tops. Kasey stepped out of the car and I slid out after him, closer to his door than to my own. He leaned back against the door and pulled me up against him, resting his cheek against my head. We watched the sun rise in silence. Teenagers ordinarily don't like to get up any earlier than they have to, and we were pretty normal in that regard. We had never watched the sunrise together, so that morning was a first for us, and I remember being completely filled to the brim with contentment. There is a silent music in joy, and the music of that morning still makes my heart ache when I allow myself to a revisit it. Kasey's muscled young arms were strong around my shoulders, and when he leaned down and rubbed his cheek against mine, his breath was sweet and smelled faintly of maple syrup.

"I love you so much, Josie Jensen," he whispered against my cheek, and I turned in his arms and cupped his face in my hands. I felt a lump rise in my throat as I looked at him, and I felt strangely like laughing with the sweetness of it all.

"I love you too, Kasey Judd, and if you don't kiss me right now, I'm going to shatter into a million pieces," I whispered back. He leaned toward me, but I closed the distance, standing on my tiptoes and pulling him down. I tasted the lingering sweetness on his lips and breathed him in. My heart stuttered in a now familiar two-step, and we sank into each other just like the first time. Breathlessly, I had to pull myself from him, for there was a little edge to his kiss and an urgency in the way he held me to him. I thrilled at his passion, but knew Johnny wouldn't be too far behind us, and I didn't want to embarrass him or initiate a brotherly lecture on "being careful."

Kasey's chin dropped to his chest, and his eyes closed in mock agony. "UGH," he groaned out. "Three weeks is too long! I'm going to be the one who shatters into a million pieces." He echoed my words of a moment before.

"We'll make it. It's not forever." I laughed up at him. Pulling me into his arms he kissed me again, hungry like before, and I reluctantly ended it once more, pulling away with my hands linked in his.

His lips turned down at the corners, and his eyebrows curved in his best hang-dog expression. He looked wistful as he sighed out his goodbye. I laughed again, delighted by his need for me.

"Maybe we should stay apart until the big day," I teased him with a helpful smile.

"It seems like forever," he said quietly as he climbed into the car.

I stepped back and watched him pull out of the gravel drive. I waved and blew silly kisses. "Call me, later!!" I shouted, and he waved his hand out his window, signaling he'd heard me. I didn't even watch him drive away. I turned and walked into the house, suddenly eager for a shower and my feather pillow. I had no premonition, no inkling that it really would be forever. It was the last time I saw him alive.

# 13. Requiem

KASEY MUST HAVE gotten drowsy on his way back into Nephi. The officers that arrived at the accident said they think he'd swerved into the wrong lane and started to go into the irrigation gully along the side of the road. He'd overcorrected, slammed on his brakes, and flipped his car. Kasey was thrown through the windshield and killed instantly. The car was facing the other direction and upside down when it came to a stop, and my brother was the first person to drive by and see Kasey's totaled car. Johnny said he thought we were both in the car because of the way the car was facing, thinking the accident had happened on the way to our house. He said he found Kasey not too far from the car and ran around trying to find me. He couldn't see into the upside down car because the top was completely caved in. The doors were damaged and he couldn't get them open. He thought I was inside. Johnny didn't have a cell phone, and there was nobody on the road at a quarter to six on a Saturday morning. Johnny says he hardly remembers jumping back in his truck and racing home. I had foregone the shower for my bed and awoke to him shouting into the phone. I stumbled down the stairs from the loft and into the kitchen. Johnny saw me and dropped the phone, causing it to swing wildly on its curling cord, and stumbled over to me.

"Josie! I thought you were with him! You're okay! Are you

okay? Kasey...his car! You're here? How?" He was looking at me and rubbing his hands up and down my arms with tears running down his face, then holding me and pushing me away again as he tried to explain about the accident and how he thought I was with Kasey.

You know how you feel in a really scary dream? How you sometimes wake up and you're almost paralyzed for a minute? You can't feel your legs or your arms and you are hot and cold all at once? I remember standing there looking at my brother, his face taking turns contorting with joy at my safety and despair at my loss. The blood slowed in my veins, and my fingers went numb. Meanwhile, Kasey lay along the side of the road as the birds chirped in the blue skies of a flawless May morning. Understanding suddenly dawned.

"You left him there? You left him there?" My voice rose in an uncharacteristic shriek that clanged in my head. I turned and ran from the house, still in my swimsuit and shorts, no shoes on my feet. I was a strong runner and I ran full-out down the road, my brother yelling "Josie! Josie! Wait!" behind me. And then yelling, "Dad!... Dad!...Help me!...Dad!" as he cried for my dad, who must have been out with the horses.

I ran and felt nothing but an all-consuming rage that Johnny had been standing in our kitchen talking while Kasey was somewhere hurt. I had run about a half mile before Dad and Johnny caught up to me. They'd jumped into Old Brown, because it was out by the corral where Johnny had found my dad and the keys were in the ignition. Johnny was behind the wheel, and it was probably a good thing because if he'd tried to stop me, I would have scratched out his eyes. My dad was strong and I'd inherited my long runner's legs from him. As Johnny slowed, my dad slid out the passenger door and matched his steps to mine. Wrapping his big arms around me, he brought me down like a rodeo calf in the tall weeds along the side of the road.

"Josie!" he'd said roughly. "Josie stop! Honey! I'll take you to him! Stop it now! You'll get there faster if you go in the truck!" I had been kicking and bucking, trying to cut loose of him.

As his words registered, I stopped fighting and looked up him, both of us breathing hard. My dad was one of those men with a craggy, sun-tanned, rancher's face. Mom used to say he was her very own John Wayne. His speaking voice was loud and rough, and he rode my brothers hard growing up, but he was a big marshmallow once you got past the bark. I'd seen his eyes tear up a thousand times, and we all teased him about it. But when I looked up into his face and saw the devastation in his eyes and the tears on his cheeks, my anger became a rush of terrible fear.

"Honey, I don't think he made it," his voice caught as he held back a sob. "Johnny said he was gone. He came home to call the ambulance. He thought you were trapped in the car, honey."

"No!" I started fighting in earnest, and my dad rose and pulled me up in his arms, holding me and crying and struggling to fold both of us into the truck. "I'll take you to him...I'll take you, honey, just hold on..."

They'd taken me to him but wouldn't let me out of the truck. A highway patrol officer had arrived at the accident, and he'd covered Kasey up with some kind of sheet or tarp. My dad wrapped his legs and arms around me to hold me back as Johnny brought Old Brown to a stop and jumped out, running to the officer. It was one of the Carter boys, all grown up and official in his police uniform, dark glasses and all. He was five or six years older than I, but he'd grown up in Levan, too. I had known him all my life, but at that moment I couldn't think of his name. He put his arm on Johnny's shaking shoulders as they walked to where Kasey was covered. He knelt and gently pulled back the sheet just a little bit and Johnny nodded in response to something he said. I caught the briefest glimpse of Kasey's curly head. I heard Johnny say Kasey's name, and I put my head down on my dad's lap and wept.

After his funeral, Kasey was buried in Levan Cemetery next to his Grandpa Judd who had passed away when Kasey was ten. Kasey had loved his grandpa and would have liked that, but I secretly wished he could be buried next to my mom, that in his death I could claim him, that he could be numbered with my family, as I would now never be numbered among his. The anger I felt toward God kept me distracted from my grief for a while. I had suffered my quota already! It wasn't fair that He should take *two* people from me. It was someone else's turn. I fumed at Him. Even when I tried to pray for strength and understanding, I found myself too angry to finish, and would leave my knees in fury.

Underneath the anger there was also a question. In sorrow, I found myself asking Him, "Why was Kasey given to me, God, if you were only going to take him away?" It seemed so cruel, and the God I knew was not that God. It was the first time in my life I questioned His love for me.

The date I was supposed to marry Kasey came, and Tara came and got me, keeping me busy for the day. But when night descended, I found myself in my room fingering my mother's wedding dress, the dress that would have become mine that very day had Kasey lived. It was simple in style, high-waisted and long sleeved. It looked very Jane Austen to me, and I had loved it all my life. My mother had stored it carefully, and it was almost as white as the day she wore it.

I had a picture of her in this dress, looking up at my dad with the most serene smile on her face. She held yellow roses in her bouquet and wore a flowered wreath in her hair. Her hair was a rich, heavy brown, and it hung down almost to her waist. I didn't have her coloring, but my wide eyes and my heart shaped face were hers, as well as my slightly fuller top lip, which gave my mouth a Betty Boop effect.

Dad had affectionately called us Boop and Boop Two when Mom was alive. She and my dad looked so young and happy. The photographer had caught my dad with his eyes closed, but somehow that just made me love the picture more, like he was counting his blessings at that moment, eyes closed in profound gratitude.

I wondered…if they had known that time would pass quickly and my mom's life cut short, would their eyes have lingered longer? Would their hands have gripped each other tighter? I was suddenly envious of my parents, of the time they did get. They had twenty years together. They would always belong to each other now. My mother would always be Janelle Wilson Jensen. I would never be Josie Judd.

When the house was quiet and Johnny and my dad were asleep, I put her wedding dress on, arranged my hair, and carefully applied my makeup. I played Beethoven's *Moonlight Sonata* very softly on my CD player. When I finished the comforting feminine rituals of many a bride, I stood in front of my full length mirror and stared at myself for a very long time. The words of *Jane Eyre* came to my mind, and I understood my literary friend as I never had before.

*"Where was the Jane Eyre of yesterday? Where was her life? Where were her prospects? Jane Eyre, who had been an ardent expectant woman—almost a bride—was a cold, solitary girl again: her life was pale; her prospects desolate."*

My dad found me asleep on the front porch swing the next morning, still fully dressed in my stiff white dress, wrapped in the long lace of my veil. I had come outside to sit in the pale light of the moon, unwilling to remove the dress and relinquish what remained of my wedding day. I had fallen asleep to the creak of the wooden swing. My dad spoke my name, waking me up to the dawn of the day after. He sat down beside me and pulled me into his lap, rubbing my back in slow circles, rocking gently, letting the sun rise and the horses wait while he sat with me and held me in his arms. My anger eventually unraveled as it was sucked into the black hole of my profound disappointment. The life I had envisioned would never be, and

I mourned for it almost as desperately as I mourned for Kasey.

The months after Kasey's death were like a strange play where I became the leading lady with a helpless supporting cast and where the props of daily life kept me functioning in a stilted parody of existence. No one knew what to do or say. My outrage at my loss would return randomly, causing me to keep my own company in order to not lash out at loved ones who only wanted to help. I played my music constantly, even as I slept. It wound its way around me and through me, and helped me retreat from my reality.

I would run through the hills around my house, down the long country roads that meandered around the familiar farms and homes of my neighbors. The distances became longer and longer, endless nocturnes, concertos and sonatas saving me from thought, the tempo of my breath whooshing in tandem with the percussion of my pounding feet. I'd decided to wait until January to start school, but I was actually looking forward to leaving for the university after Christmas. My life-long dream of musical renown now felt very empty, the loss of someone to share it with had made it seem as hollow as an abandoned shell. But I still wanted it. I needed it. I needed to reclaim it, to reshape it. And I craved the anonymity of a town where nobody knew about my pain. Hiding it would be so much easier.

My dad was relieved that I seemed to be moving forward, and I'm sure a cloud lifted whenever I left the house, though he never would have admitted it. How painful it must have been for him! How intimate his knowledge of my pain! Ten years before his anguish had mirrored my own. But his empathy provided him a seemingly endless patience, and he cared for me now as I had tried to care for him then.

And poor Johnny. I had been so irrationally angry with him.

He'd tiptoed around me for the first month, trying to communicate his love for me in little ways...making my bed, stocking the fridge with cold Diet Coke though he and my dad drank nothing but Pepsi. One day he'd even washed a load of my whites, folding each sock and lacy underthing neatly and placing them on my bed. I'd eventually started doing some of the same things for him ... asking his forgiveness and returning his love by gathering the clothes from his bedroom floor, putting Twinkies in the freezer so he could eat them frozen the way he liked them, cleaning the mud from his work boots and shining them up, leaving them sitting neatly on the back porch. Little acts of kindness were easier to perform than words were to speak. And we never did speak of that horrible day.

About a week before I planned to leave for school, my dad left work early because of a terrible headache. I was upstairs boxing up some of my things when I heard the kitchen door bang open, and I called down to him in question. I heard the cupboards slam and then a glass break and I sighed, wondering what he was up to.

"Dad?" I plodded down the stairs and into the kitchen to find him swaying at the sink with a bottle of aspirin in his hand and broken glass around his feet.

He turned to look at me and teetered, grabbing for the edge of the countertop. He lost hold of the opened aspirin bottle, sending little white pills scattering all over the floor.

He started to speak, but his words were slurred, kind of the way he sounded when he'd had too much to drink.

"Dad! It's 2:00 in the afternoon! Are you drunk?" I accused angrily, arms akimbo.

"No booze," my dad mumbled out, and he fell to the floor as if his legs would no longer support him.

Fear slammed through me like a freight train, and I rushed to him, seeing the shadow of death's long sickle pulling him from me as he tried to right himself, his eyes squeezed shut in a terrible grimace.

"No!" I shouted, momentarily crazed at death's all-too familiar and terrible visage. I put my arms around him and threw his left arm around my shoulders

"Dad, we've got to get you to the hospital!" I helped him to his feet, and we staggered like a pair in a three-legged-race out the kitchen door and down the back steps. Somehow we made it out to his truck, and I toppled him onto the passenger seat and wrapped the seat belt around him, trying to hold him upright. Calling 911 would mean waiting for an ambulance to come from Nephi, and we didn't have time for that. I didn't know what was happening, but something was very wrong.

My dad had had what his doctors called an ischemic stroke caused by a blood clot in his brain. When we got to the hospital, his speech was unintelligible and there was no way he could walk. I had run into the emergency room calling for help and within minutes he'd been wheeled in while I had shouted out exactly what had transpired in the kitchen. After a scan to make sure that the stroke wasn't caused by a brain hemorrhage, he was put on blood thinners to loosen and break up the clot. But a great deal of damage had already been done.

After a week in the hospital, my dad came home unable to walk and unable to speak clearly. The part of his brain that controls movement and speech had been damaged. His left side was particularly weak, and he was unable even to feed himself.

I drove him back and forth to the rehabilitation clinic in Provo every day, where he spent three to five hours relearning everything from tying his shoes to writing his name.

I learned how to care for him by watching the team of doctors and therapists that worked with him each day. My brothers and their wives assisted where they could. Jacob took most of the farm work on, and I gratefully left that in his capable hands. Often, one of my sister-in-laws would drive Dad to rehabilitation or bring him home, spelling me on one stretch or another, but for the most part I was the caregiver, and I took on his care with a ferocious determination that he would be whole again. I had lost too many, and my dad would not be numbered with them.

Within a couple months, he was walking with a walker and making considerable strides in other areas. His words were not nearly as slurred, although he'd lost some of his cognitive ability and would sometimes forget what we'd talked about only moments before. I'd asked him once what does 'two plus two equal?' After thinking for a moment he'd responded, "What's a two?"

Even his sense of touch was affected. He couldn't tell hot from cold. It was as if the signal triggering sensation was off somewhere in his brain. One day he washed his hands under scalding water, not knowing he was burning them.

During the week he spent in the hospital right after his stroke, I called the Dean of Admissions at Brigham Young University, as well as the director of the music department whom I'd met with upon accepting my scholarship. After briefing them on my situation, both had been truly kind and told me that the scholarship would be deferred until the following school year. As I hung up the phone I knew I wouldn't be using it.

I stopped playing the piano after my dad's stroke. The first weeks after he was able to come home I was too tired to do anything but see to his needs. I fed him, bathed him, and took him through the exercises I'd been shown that would help him to regain the strength and mobility he had lost. And of course, the long hours in rehabilitation took up the months that followed. Every once in a while I would finger the keys, waiting for that familiar pull in my veins, but the music that had once been forever dancing in my thoughts was strangely silent. I didn't let myself dwell on it. I don't know if it was exhaustion or just an unwillingness to face what was happening to me.

Then I stopped listening to classical music when I ran. Instead, I borrowed Tara's iPod and listened to Tim McGraw and Kenny Chesney—according to Tara they were 'real men in cowboy hats.' My dad had always loved George Strait and Johnny Cash. I found the music occupied my thoughts while I ran and left my heart untouched—which was just what I wanted.

When my dad was well enough for me to leave him for any length of time I started teaching piano lessons. Financially we were in trouble, and I needed to work. But the lessons were noisy, and our house was small and not conducive to a recovering stroke patient who needed a great deal of rest, so the bishop of our church gave me permission to use one of the rooms in the church to teach my students. By that time it was summer, and school was out. I could schedule my students around my dad's rehab schedule. But when school started, my students would not be able to accommodate me as easily, and I needed an additional source of income that still had some flexibility. I had to do something else.

Tara had gone to beauty school and graduated the year before with big dreams and blue hair. One evening she made an off-hand suggestion that I could take classes at the beauty college in the hours my dad was doing his rehabilitation. I decided that cutting hair would be as good a way as any for me to stay close to home and pay the bills. Jared lived in Provo, about ten minutes from the hospital, and when I wasn't out of class in time to pick my dad up, he would pick him up and take him to his house until I was finished with classes. Somehow we stumbled through that year and, unlike Tara, I graduated with my hair color mostly intact, and no dreams to speak of.

Tara had wanted out of Levan and had gotten grunt work in a pricey salon in Salt Lake City, hoping to learn from the best and work her way up. I'm sure Louise would have like her to come work with her at Ballow's 'Do, but she wasn't surprised at Tara's need to do her own thing. Tara's lack of interest in the family business helped me, because Louise let me work in her shop. I was able to cut hair in the day and teach piano students in the evenings, and my dad and I limped along, financially and otherwise.

Tara was the kind of stylist who experimented on everyone who knew her and with mixed results. My hair went through several different shades and cuts before Tara's mom pulled Tara aside and kindly but firmly told her she was to experiment on someone else. I was a perfect guinea pig as I had absolutely no interest in how I looked. In beauty school, I had practiced on her as well, with much more conservative results, and though I would never be as creative as Tara was, I was conscientious and precise. My loneliness made me a good listener, and I was able to give customers what they wanted, rather than what I thought would bring out their inner sex kitten, as Tara was prone to do.

Every once in a while, I would find myself contemplating how different my life was from the life I'd dreamed of. There was a time when I had dreamed of attending a Performing Arts High School. I never told my dad about that, although I'm sure he would have tried to make it a possibility. The tie that bound me to my home was much too tight, much too strong. Then there was Kasey, and all thoughts of leaving had fled. I remembered the days when Sonja had dreamed that I would perform with the Utah Symphony. But Sonja never made me feel guilty about my choices. She understood what held me. However, I knew she ached for me and worried that I would bury my talent in duty and then someday try to uncover it, only to find it had rusted with time and inattention.

Sonja had aged. The spry seventy-year-old of our first days together was suddenly eighty. She had started getting more forgetful, wandering off, not remembering where she was or how she got there. A year after Dad's stroke, Sonja was diagnosed with Alzheimer's disease. Doc called me and asked me to come see her. Sonja was devastated, and I was distraught but somehow unfazed. Life seemed to have become one tragedy after another, and I had gotten good at coping.

Sadly, Doc's health had deteriorated as well. His mind was sharp, but he was physically ailing. They hired a live-in nurse so they could remain in their home for as long as possible.

It was for Sonja that I started playing the piano again. I would ride my bike up the hill around sundown every day and play for her, just like I had for my daily lessons years before. I played music that demanded great skill but that didn't engage my soul. Sonja seemed to crave the cascading scales and the pounding chords and never complained that I spent too much time courting the 'beast.' The disease that was slowly robbing her of her personality and her very spirit would cower in the face of my musical onslaught. It was as if the neurological synapses and pathways in her mind that had once been forged by her intense musical study were regenerating and re-firing as the music reminded her confused brain of its intricate knowledge. My fingers would fly, and I would pour all my energy into a frenzy of furious music.

After I played, she would be almost normal, invigorated, without a quirk or slip. This was the only kind of playing I ever did. No beautiful Beethoven or dreamy Debussy, no heartbreaking concertos of love and loss. I played only the technical, only the difficult, only the demanding. She was my sole audience. For most of the next two years, she was coherent and healthy enough to remain at home.

Then one day, I rode my bike up the hill to the house, only to have her nurse tell me she was unwell and sleeping. I came back every day for a week. Sonja refused to see me. When I finally insisted on seeing her she seemed fearful, her lip quivering and her eyes filling with tears. She wailed at me to go home. I went to her piano and played desperately, trying to coax her back. For once it didn't seem to help. She locked her bedroom door, and I could hear her sobbing behind it when I knocked. Her nurse said arrangements needed to be made to put her in a home. Doc and Sonja had made some inquiries and crafted a detailed plan. When it became necessary for Sonja to go to a convalescent home, Doc went with her. Doc passed away in his sleep two months later. Sonja was physically quite healthy, but the spiritual Sonja, her *self*, was gone—hidden away somewhere, leaving me to grieve as her body lingered to unintentionally mock and remind.

I visited her often at her convalescent home, and she seemed to enjoy the CDs I brought. But she never woke up to the music again, although she seemed to favor the mellow and the melodious now, shunning the powerful pieces of the last two years for the sweeter nocturnes and serenades. I read to her, as I had done many times before as a young girl. She also enjoyed this, but liked *Nancy Drew* in lieu of *Pride and Prejudice*. I tried reading her beloved *Wuthering Heights* only to have her fling it across the room as I had done in her sitting room so many years earlier. The medication she was on made her less fearful, but I could tell she was always relieved when I left. After all, I was a stranger.

# 14. Reprise

**August, 2007**

IT HAD BEEN threatening rain all week, dark clouds rolling in, the sky grumbling, only to roll out again without relinquishing a single drop. The horses would stomp and whinny, the air would crackle with static, and then ...nothing. It was late August and the summer had been especially brutal. We'd had little moisture that summer, and we'd had a fairly mild winter as well. We needed the rain desperately. Still, a week had gone by, and the clouds remained stubbornly full.

That morning I woke up at dawn, pulled on my running shoes and walked out to find the skies thick with gray storm clouds. Again. I debated going back to bed, laying under my covers and listening to the rain. I scoffed a little. I knew it wouldn't rain if I went back to bed, and I would miss my run. The early morning was relatively cool, the darkness of last night having scared off the heat of yesterday. It was perfect running weather, and I wasn't going to waste it.

I was three miles into the run and just starting to swing back toward home when Mother Nature decided to have a little laugh at my expense. The air grew eerily still, and then there was a mighty crack.

Lightening pierced the sky and the thunder boomed. Rain gushed out of the heavy clouds, pounding the dirt road like an overzealous drummer. I squeaked and picked up my feet, flying toward home.

There is nothing like a summer downpour, and I didn't even mind being caught in it a mile from home. I flew down the road, arms pumping, hair streaming out behind me, shoes squishing. I might have blisters on my feet from the friction, but for now the squishing wasn't enough to slow me down or put a damper on my gratitude.

I was nearing the place where the dirt road meets the black top, and knew from experience that the blacktop could be slick. I was watching my feet as I rounded the corner, speeding down the homestretch. A sudden whinny and a Whoa! had me looking up in alarm, arms flailing and feet flying, trying to avoid running right into the rear-end of Don Yates' chestnut mare, Charlotte.

Charlotte did a skittish two-step, and I slid right by her prancing feet, belly down, hands sliding through the gathering puddles. I processed a few things as I slid. Charlotte didn't have a rider, and I wondered if she'd jumped the corral again. The horse was notorious for escaping. I had found her in my garden a few times, curling her horsy lips around my carrots. But I had distinctly heard a male voice say Whoa! and knew Charlotte had been apprehended before I almost ran face first into her ample rump. After coming to a complete stop and ascertaining that I was not seriously damaged, I pushed myself up to my hands and knees, palms stinging but otherwise unscathed. My lifelong klutziness had taught me a thing or two about falling.

"Josie?" There was astonishment in the deep voice above me. "Are you okay?" Strong arms reached down and gripped mine, pulling me to my feet.

A large hand smoothed my wet hair off of my face and out of my eyes as I wiped my muddy palms on my sopping shorts. The rain was starting to abate, and I tipped my face up against the slowing torrent to apologize to Don for my clumsiness. I found myself face to face with Samuel Yates.

I hadn't seen him in almost seven years. Stunned, I drank in his familiar face, so dear and yet so different. My old friend on the cusp of manhood was gone. In his place was a grown man, confidence in the set of his mouth, awareness in his observant black eyes. There was a greater resemblance to his father's family, or maybe he just wasn't as desperate to disguise it anymore. He was still lean, but definitely brawnier, his neck thicker, his shoulders wider. The long black hair that had once been a symbol of his individuality was short now, almost hidden under his cowboy hat. His hat kept the wet from dripping into his face, but I had no cover, and the water kept running into my eyes. I swiped at the rain impatiently, not quite believing he was there, standing right in front of me.

"Josie?" He'd started to smile, although his black eyebrows were drawn together in question. "Are you okay?"

I realized I'd been staring at him, smiling, but not saying anything.

"Samuel," I said softly but with great pleasure, and I felt a sweet nostalgia flood my soul with warmth. His lips quirked tenderly, making his eyes crease at the corners, and I saw that he shared my emotions.

I became aware all at once of my very wet behind and the hair that had fallen from my ponytail and was dripping down the sides of my face. I was completely drenched, and my T-shirt and knit running shorts were plastered to my skin. I shivered and pulled self-consciously at the clinging cotton. His eyes widened slightly as he took in my unintentional immodesty.

"You're soaking wet." He pulled off his sweatshirt and handed it to me—damp, but considerably better than what I was wearing. I turned slightly from him and pulled the sweatshirt over my head. It was mostly dry inside and hung down past the bottom of my shorts. It was deliciously warm from his skin. It smelled like aftershave and rain, the scent very male and, to me, wonderful. It smelled like safety and soap and my broken dreams. It smelled like coming home feels.

I was instantly swamped with a longing so powerful, a yearning to intense, that I gasped out loud and felt my eyes swim with tears.

"Josie? Are you hurt?" Samuel was worried now, and reached for me again, gripping my arms through the baggy sleeves of his sweatshirt. Something cracked around my heart. The crack reverberated through my chest. It felt the way I imagine ice would sound breaking under my feet on a frozen lake. My breath burned in my chest like I'd run 10 miles in subzero temperatures. The icy control I had demanded of myself since Kasey's death slipped, wobbled, and then lost its hold on me all together.

Without conscious thought, I stepped toward Samuel and laid my head against his broad chest, my hands splaying across his muscled shoulders, my fingers fisting handfuls of his T-shirt. I breathed him in, my inhale a ragged sob. I let go of his shirt and wrapped my arms tightly around his trim waist. I clung to him like my life depended on it. Maybe it did. I hadn't seen him for so many years, and so much had happened in my life since I had last seen his face, but at that moment I was thirteen again. Someone I had loved had returned, someone lost had come back to me, and I held him fiercely, with no intention of ever letting him go.

I couldn't see his face, but I imagine he was shocked at my behavior. I hadn't even spoken to him, other than to breathe his name, and I was suddenly wrapped around him in a rainstorm, in the middle of the road. Slowly, I felt his strong arms come up around me, holding me, enfolding me. I was enveloped in warmth. The pleasure of the embrace was so intense I shuddered with it. I felt his hand in my hair, and he made those soft shushing noises. I realized I was crying. We stood in the rain, and he held me up, letting me hold him in return. No comments, no questions, just comfort.

Eventually, he untangled me, slipped a loose lead rope over Charlotte's head, and with one arm wrapped tightly around my shoulders, led us both home. I gratefully walked beside him, ridiculously relieved that in this moment I was not alone.

He stopped outside my house, the horse nickering and nudging at his back to get out of the storm. His arm fell from my shoulders, and he looked down at me, his hat dripping with rain.

"Will you be all right?" He asked softly.

I nodded my head.

"Thank you Samuel. It's so good to see you again," I said sincerely, then turned and walked quickly up the walk and slid my soaked shoes off under the covered porch. He still stood in the rain, holding the horse steady, watching me. I stepped inside and gently closed the door.

I stood in the bathroom and pulled the sweatshirt over my head so it covered my face; I breathed in the smell. I didn't want to take it off, though I was cold and shivering and the heat rose deliciously out of the tub I was filling with water. I couldn't find it in myself to be embarrassed by my actions toward Samuel. Samuel! I marveled that he was here, back in Levan. So many years had gone by! Again, I considered my unusual behavior, and although I knew I would be mortified when I saw him again, for now the sweetness of the contact remained too acute for regret.

I had enjoyed effusive affection from Kasey for two years only to suffer a famine when he was gone. Afterwards, any sympathy or affection had sabotaged my efforts to control my despair, so I had effectively shunned both from anyone who offered them. For a long time I had stiffened at the lightest touch. If you push people away for long enough, isolation become a terrible habit. People start to believe you prefer it.

I felt suddenly ravenous for a gentle touch. Just like physical starvation, the hunger for contact was all-consuming. Human beings are not designed to be alone. Our creator gave us smooth, sensitive skin that craves the warmth of other skin. Our arms seek to hold. Our hands yearn to touch. We are drawn to companionship and affection out of an innate need.

I pulled off the sweatshirt with a jerk, shaking my head to dislodge my indulgent musings. I finished undressing and slid down into the tub until the very hot water covered me completely, submerging my head, my face, and my thoughts. Then I willed my long dormant neediness to retreat before I made a complete fool of myself.

I turned twenty-three on a Sunday that year. The family typically gathered for birthday parties, which was nice, but we always gathered at home, dad's home, which also happened to my home, which meant I did all the cooking, as usual. I was actually hoping that I could take a little walk up to the cemetery and visit Kasey's and Mom's graves. Maybe I could spend a little time reading against Mom's cool headstone like I did when I was young. Maybe I would make a chocolate cake for later. There was nothing better than chocolate cake, cold milk, and quiet. But with the family gathering there wouldn't be any quiet, not until much later.

I felt a little guilty for not wanting my family around on my birthday. I knew I was strange. I was always glad to see them, always glad to kiss their kids and cook for them. I just felt a little melancholy. Seeing Samuel had me thinking about Beethoven. I hadn't expelled music from my life completely. I taught piano lessons, and I played the organ in church, but my days of listening for the pure rapture of listening had become few and far between; I guarded my emotions very carefully, and the music just oozed its way around my walls. But maybe I could enjoy something that would lift my spirit without widening the cracks in my heart I thought I might listen to a little Hungarian Rhapsody with my chocolate cake.

I went to church that morning, and Dad came along with me, which he had begun to do more often as of late. I hadn't asked him why; I'd just enjoyed the fact that he would come and be with me. Except for a little persistent weakness on his right side he was completely recovered from his stroke. He looked handsome in his light blue dress shirt and navy slacks. His hair had gone white, as I am sure my hair would one day do. His skin was very brown from his life as a horseman. His vivid blue eyes were arresting, and I wondered why some lonely widow hadn't gobbled him up. I guess there weren't too many to choose from. There was always Sweaty Betty down at the diner. She thought my dad walked on water and had hot coffee in his hand before he could say "Please" whenever he found time to sit a while and shoot the bull with the old boys that gathered there every morning. The thought of my dad with Betty had me giggling into my hand, and my dad shot me a look under his furry white brows.

I had chosen to play the hymn 'The Lord is My Shepherd' from the 23rd Psalm for the closing number. I loved the 23rd Psalm. The words spoke of such simple faith and beauty; it was a prayer I had often uttered when I found myself teetering on the brink of depression. The congregation sang along with very little feeling ... hard pews, hungry bellies, and impatient kids eager to be free of their Sunday clothes, make sincere expression difficult. After the closing song, the prayer was given, and I stood from the organ, only to see Nettie and Don Yates a few rows back. My heart stuttered and my breath quickened. Samuel was with them, looking starched and pressed in a white shirt, dark slacks, and a red tie. I wondered what he looked like in his 'dress blues'. I hadn't seen him since I had literally run into him in the storm. I still had his sweatshirt sitting, washed and folded, on top of the dryer. I had been trying to work up the nerve to walk down to Don and Nettie's and give it back to him.

My dad was making his way toward them, extending his hand to Don who hadn't been to church, except for Christmas Eve service, in years. I wondered if Samuel being in town had something to do with their attendance. It seemed unlikely, but I couldn't come up with another possibility to explain his presence at church today. Samuel saw me walking toward them and something flickered across his handsome face. I was grateful I had worn my red that morning.

Another weakness of mine...red shoes. Tara had given them to me when I graduated from beauty school. She'd purchased them for her mom's birthday, kind of on a whim, thinking Aunt Louise would have a good laugh at the red, four-inch heels. Louise had laughed all right, and then told Tara to take them back. I can't explain why I couldn't let Tara return them, but I had wanted them. I had the same size feet as Louise, and the shoes made me feel happy when I looked at them. For me, happy had been kind of hard to come by. I'd offered to buy them from Tara, but she'd seen the look on my face and was thrilled to declare them a graduation gift.

I didn't have anything in my closet to wear with them, and ended up getting a bright red dress with little cap sleeves and a full skirt, just to have something to go with the shoes, but it was worth it. I worried that it was a little much for church. Fire engine red shoes, dress, and lipstick were a little conspicuous. I wore the outfit rarely because I felt a little silly in it, but every once in a while, I wore my red shoes while I did house work, just because they made me feel good. There's just something about red shoes. That morning as I'd dressed for church, I'd decided I should celebrate my birthday with my red dress and my red high heels. I wondered what Samuel thought of my outfit and felt a little flash of guilt that I cared.

"Come on by this afternoon," I heard my dad say. "We're having a little barbeque for Josie's birthday, and we'd love to have you."

"I'll bring lemon squares!" Nettie replied firmly. "Then you won't have to worry about dessert, Josie." I groaned inwardly. I hated lemon squares. And I wanted to worry about dessert. I wanted chocolate cake.

"That'll be fine," my dad said, walking out of the chapel's big double doors into the Sunday sunshine. I walked at Samuel's side, trying to think of some way to still make chocolate cake and not hurt Nettie's feelings.

"I like red," Samuel said softly. All thoughts of chocolate cake fled my silly head.

I glanced up at him quickly. He was looking down at me. "Happy Birthday, Josie."

"Thank you," I said a little too brightly.

"Do you really want us to come for your celebration?" he asked quietly. "Your dad didn't ask you before he invited us."

"We'd love to have you." It was just a little fib, having everything to do with dessert. "Then I can give you your sweatshirt back. I've been meaning to bring it by." I wished I would have kept quiet about the sweatshirt. It made me think of clinging to him in the rain. I looked down at my red shoes shyly.

"I wasn't worried about the sweatshirt," he said quietly. "I'll see you later then." He turned as his grandparents waved and walked with them to Nettie's grey sedan.

Jacob and Rachel had four little blond boys, ranging in ages from seven to two years, who were constantly underfoot. Jacob's only instructions were "don't kill yourselves," and Rachel was always busily doing this or that, setting out food, helping me in the kitchen, and she seemed unaffected by the antics of her wild brood. One time the older boys had tied four-year-old Matty up in the chicken coop. He had been hollering bloody murder for at least a half an hour before anyone realized he was gone. The chickens hadn't hurt him, but he'd been pecked a time or two and will probably never volunteer to help me gather eggs again.

Jared had married an "out-of-towner" when he went off to school. Her name was Tonya, and she came across a little uppity. She didn't mix very well, and Jacob's boys made her very nervous. She kept their two little girls close to her sides, and she spent many of the family get-togethers watching the boys in horror. She was very pretty with her glossy brown bob and perfect makeup, but she had a perpetually pinched look to her mouth, and she was constantly saying things like "Jared, don't you think you ought to…" and "Jared, you need to ..." Jared had the look of brow-beaten husband these days.

Johnny's wife Sheila was pregnant with twins and was so big she could hardly move. Her feet were swollen and her skinny arms stuck out to the sides like Popsicle sticks. She sat in a lawn chair and didn't move the entire time they were there. I kept her in cold root beer, and Tonya kept her bored with tales of her own deliveries, which we had all heard a trillion times.

I'd made rolls that morning before church, letting them rise while we went to the service. I had marinated chicken breasts for my dad to grill, and we'd added some hot dogs for the kids. I'd thrown a big green salad together from my garden and made my dad's favorite tangy potato salad. Chips, watermelon, and root beer rounded out the simple meal, and I was putting tablecloths over the picnic tables we had set up in the backyard when Don, Nettie, and Samuel arrived.

Every woman, including both the pregnant and the uppity, ogled Samuel when he walked into the backyard. He still wore his slacks and dress shirt from church, but he'd taken off his tie, undone the top two buttons, and rolled up his sleeves. He was brown and muscular and his coloring made a stark contrast to all the fair hair and freckles. He carried lemon squares. I sighed in defeat. I had all the ingredients for a double chocolate cake with butter cream frosting in my kitchen. I would just have to whip it up when everyone went home. The thought cheered me, and I went forward to graciously take the lemon squares from Samuel's hands.

The food was set out, the blessing given on the dinner, and people were digging in before I got a chance to sit down for a minute. The tables were filled with my siblings and their families, so I settled myself on the steps leading from the back door and picked at my plate. I was never very hungry when I cooked. It must be all the nibbling and testing along the way. Samuel's shadow soon hung over me.

"Can I sit?"

I scootched over and made ample room.

"This is good food." Samuel's voice was polite and formal, and I searched for something to say after the obvious 'thank you.'

"I remember Johnny from school. He was in a couple of my classes. The kids are nieces and nephews, obviously, but I don't recognize any of the women, and I don't know which of your older brothers is which."

I pointed people out, naming them, organizing them into family groups, telling a little something about everyone.

"Tonya seems tense." Samuel indicated with his head to where Ricky, Jacob's oldest, was chasing Matty around Tonya's chair. Tonya's four-year-old Bailey was sitting on her lap, shrieking with excitement.

"She isn't great with kids." I laughed a little as Tonya let out a panicked "Jaaaarrreeed!"

Just then we were interrupted by Ryan, Jacob's six-year-old, hollering from around the side of the house.

"Aunt Josie! Ya got company!" He came around the house, holding a bouquet of brightly colored helium balloons so large that he was in danger of being lifted into the air. Trailing behind him were Kasey's parents, Brett and Lorraine Judd. Lorraine, bless her pea-pickin' heart, was carrying a huge, triple-layer, chocolate cake.

"Happy birthday, Josie!" Lorraine sang out. I ran to greet them, putting my arms around Brett and getting a big bear hug in return.

"I know chocolate cake is your favorite. I hope you haven't eaten dessert already!" Lorraine said brightly.

"Oh, Lorraine, I love you," I breathed, euphoric. "I'm hiding this cake in the kitchen so it won't get devoured. I'm not sharing!" She laughed with me and looped her arm around my waist as I took the cake from her hands and passed it off to Rachel with explicit instructions to "keep it away from Johnny!"

"So how are you, Josie? I've been meaning to swing by the beauty shop, but just haven't had a minute."

"I'm okay..."

"Coach Judd!" Johnny came striding up, clasping Brett's hand in a guy handshake thing. Quick pats on the back in a half-hug completed the greeting.

Everyone called out their hellos, and soon Lorraine and Brett were being introduced to Samuel.

"I remember you," Coach Judd said, squinting up at Samuel. "I had you in my P.E. class your senior year. You were a good athlete, a heck of a runner. I was hoping we'd get you to sign up for track. Did you ever end up becoming a Marine like you planned?"

"Yes Sir," Samuel replied in answer, and Brett clapped him on the back. "Well done then. Good for you."

Lorraine was looking from Samuel to me with something akin to hurt in her eyes. I perceived the direction of her thoughts and felt a twinge of guilt. The guilt was followed by a flash of irritation. I hadn't dated even once since Kasey died; I hadn't wanted to. But Kasey had been gone for more than four years. I wondered if Lorraine thought I had a new boyfriend. The thought made me feel a little sick at heart.

When Kasey was killed, the shockwaves had echoed throughout the community with unparalleled intensity. He was very popular in school and well liked by everyone who knew him. The football team had his number retired, put his name on their helmets the following school year, and the football from the first win of the season had been given to Coach Judd in his name.

The Levan church was too small to seat the number of people expected at his funeral service. His family had to hold it at a much bigger church in Nephi where the chapel could be opened up into the gymnasium to accommodate huge numbers of people. There were no empty seats and many people had to stand throughout the two hour service. The line for his viewing extended all the way out and around the church, lasting for hours. I had stood in the line with the family, hugging sobbing friends and neighbors, enduring the endless ridiculous questions and comments of "How are you, Josie?" and "He's in a better place now." I spent the viewing wishing the non-stop stream of mourners and sympathizers both curious and sincere, would just, please, go away.

The shock and sorrow was enormous, the sensationalism of small town drama almost cloying. It had been truly awful. Afterwards, every day that I did not grieve for Kasey felt like a betrayal. Everyone wanted to keep him alive; Kasey's grave was always adorned with flowers, little notes from friends, photos, and stuffed animals. Even four years later, friends and loved ones visited his grave regularly. Kasey was still a priority in his mother's heart, the grief very fresh. I wondered if it would always be that way. I thought of all this as I studied Lorraine's pretty face. She was an attractive blonde in her late forties, but the strain of losing a child had aged her face prematurely, and she had a weariness around her eyes that had not been there before Kasey's death.

"We've just been up to Kasey's grave, Josie," Lorraine said a little too loudly. Brett's conversation with Samuel trailed off awkwardly. "We knew he'd want us to stop by and wish his girl a happy birthday." She patted my arm, but her eyes were on Samuel's face. Samuel looked at me, his face smooth and expressionless. He excused himself politely and wandered over to where his grandparents were visiting with Jacob and Rachel.

Lorraine prattled on for another half an hour, staying close to my side. Brett had eventually gone to talk football with my brothers, and I was alone with Lorraine, wishing I knew what to say to comfort her. She didn't ask me about Samuel. There was nothing to tell if she did, but I was grateful all the same. Eventually, she ran out of steam and gave me a quick hug, telling me she'd be sure and stop by the shop this week. I really hoped she wouldn't and felt guilty all over again.

After Brett and Lorraine left, my head was aching and it didn't look like my brothers and their families were going anywhere soon. Sheila had fallen asleep in the lawn chair in the shade of the huge maple. The kids were playing a relatively quiet game of duck, duck, goose. Tonya had roped Rachel into conversation about the latest book on child psychology and discipline techniques, and Rachel was holding her sleeping two-year-old son while still managing to cross stitch. Nettie fanned herself contentedly, and Samuel and Don were being included in the debate about the new football season.

I needed to get out. I crept around the house and out the front, snagging a book and my bicycle on the way out. I couldn't ride the baby blue bike of my childhood anymore, but I had a big goofy bike with large round wheels, handlebars like a Texas Longhorn, and a basket on the front. It made me laugh because it looked like something an English lady would ride through the countryside. It suited me. I breathed as I made my escape and pedaled quickly down the road, winding my way down and over to the cemetery. The sun was dipping low in the west, and the breeze was just light enough to be pleasant.

I went to my mom's grave first, pulling the long grass around the stone and brushing off the stray leaves and debris. I liked the feel of her name beneath my fingers. I talked to her a minute, told her how I was, that I missed her, and then made my way over to Kasey's headstone. His parents had purchased the biggest marker they could afford. It was glossy and ornate with 'Our Beloved Son' centered across the top. They'd had a picture of Kasey embossed in the stone, so that everyone who visited the grave could see the handsome youthfulness smiling from his happy face. You would have to be made of granite not to feel something when you saw him, not to feel the enormous tragedy of our loss. He had been so alive and bright and beautiful…and his picture only captured a tiny piece of his magic. It hurt to look at him, and I brushed my hand in regret over his image before walking to the other side where I wouldn't have to see his face as I read.

I had only been lost in Baroness Orczy's *The Elusive Pimpernel* for mere minutes when I saw him approaching. Samuel made his way respectfully through the headstones, never stepping over, walking around and down as he made his way to me. I remembered what his grandmother had taught him about anything associated with the dead being somewhat feared among the Navajo. I didn't know if that was true so much anymore, but wondered at Samuel coming here all the same.

He stopped when he was a few feet away. I sat on the east side of Kasey's marker, sheltered from the sun. Samuel was facing the setting sun and had to turn his face a little to look at me. He squatted down and found relief in the shade of the monument. I thought he would ask me if I were okay or one of those things that people usually say when nothing else seems appropriate. Instead he just sat with me, not speaking, looking around at the stones, embracing the quiet. It was I who finally spoke.

"That was a little strange back at the house." I struggled to find words to explain without assuming an interest he may not feel. "I was engaged to Lorraine and Brent's son Kasey. He was killed in a car accident three weeks before our wedding. It's been over four years, but for them, and sometimes for me, it seems like yesterday."

"My grandmother told me." He didn't expound further, and I wondered what exactly Nettie had told him and when. I decided it didn't matter.

"My father's buried here. Right over there." He pointed back in the direction he had come. "My grandparents brought me to see his grave when I first came here eleven years ago. I'd never seen it before. I've never been back until today." The silence was heavy around us.

"Does it make you feel better to come here?" he asked solemnly, his black eyes bottomless as they trained in on my own.

I started to answer in the affirmative, and then couldn't. I didn't know if I felt better when I came here. Often, I felt fresh pain and a sense of timelessness that kept me rooted in the past. My mother's grave had once been a quiet place for comfort and reflection. I didn't know if Kasey's resting place provided the same solace. Guilt had my stomach churning, and I wished Samuel had not come here.

"What do you mean?" My voice was a little sharp, and I bit my lower lip in censure.

Samuel stood and walked around Kasey's grave. He looked into

Kasey's smiling visage without reaction. "Do you feel better when you come here?" he questioned me again.

No. "Yes," I lied. "I like the quiet." That was true, at least.

"There is quiet, and then there is too much quiet," Samuel said cryptically.

I waited for him to continue, but he stood still, looking again at Kasey's picture.

I climbed to my feet, grumpily brushing the grass and twigs from the colorful skirt Tara had brought me back from her vacation to Mexico earlier in the summer.

"Did you love him very much?"

Okay, now I was irritated. Samuel regarded me openly, unmoving. The way he held himself was so still, so contained. He never seemed to breathe, his only movement was the blink of his ebony eyes. He had always had that stillness. I wondered if his training had made it even more pronounced. He definitely didn't have any scruples about asking very pointed questions. I don't think that had anything to do with the training. That was just Samuel.

I picked up my book and started making my way toward where I had left my bike. He followed me; I could see him peripherally. He moved so quietly that if I didn't know he was there, I never would have heard him. I wondered how he had gotten to the cemetery. I couldn't exactly give him a ride back home on my bike. Memories of him pedaling the two of us home all those years ago when I'd sprained my ankle rose unbidden to my mind. I quickly replaced the image with one of Samuel stuffed in my flowered bicycle basket. It made me feel a little better.

"Did you walk?" I questioned him now.

"I rode." He indicated with his head toward the grassy shoulder of the dirt road where a chestnut mare nibbled contentedly.

I realized belatedly that he'd changed into jeans and boots. How observant of me. I didn't want to just ride away, but bikes and horses make awkward riding partners. He didn't seem in a hurry to retrieve his horse.

"Did you follow me?" I didn't like my peevish tone, but I *was* peeved.

"It didn't take Navajo tracking skills or Marine recon to figure it out, Josie." His face was serious despite his sarcasm. "I just asked your dad where he thought you'd gone." He waited a few beats. "You didn't answer me." His tone was not accusing, but it was persistent.

"I really didn't think it was any of your business!" I flushed at my contentious words. I was not good at confrontation, and any time I was forced into one I usually stood my ground but cried later in my room. It was not something I willingly participated in, but Samuel raised my ire. Most people stayed away when someone went to a cemetery, ALONE. Not Samuel. He just walked right in and asked me if I had loved my dead fiancé.

"I'm trying to understand you." He said it point blank.

I just shook my head in wonder. "Yes. I loved him. I miss him." My breath huffed out in exasperation. "That's why I'm here, to visit him, you know?"

"But he's not here," Samuel was emphatic. "He's never been here. Not since his death, anyway."

I desperately needed chocolate cake. Now. Or I was going to scream and pull my hair out. Or scream and pull Samuel's hair out. The temptation to do just that had me gritting my teeth.

"Why are you here, Samuel?" I crossed my arms and thrust my chin at him defensively. "I mean…why did you come back to Levan after all this time? It's been seven years…and here you are. I'm sure you and I could probably be friends again, but…what's the point? You know? You'll be gone soon."

"My grandparents are getting old. I wanted to see them." Samuel cocked his head to the side and narrowed his eyes at me. "Didn't you think I'd ever come back?"

"Actually, yes. I just thought you would come back sooner. Where have you been? What have you been doing? I mean…you were gone so long!" Now where had that come from? I flushed and held my hands to my cheeks, mortified. Since the day I had seen Samuel in the rain I didn't know myself. This was the second time I had acted completely out of character, speaking without thinking, reacting totally on emotion.

"I still have the letters you sent me," Samuel offered softly.

"I wrote so many of them," I blurted out and winced again. I didn't seem to be able to curb my impulse to just tell him whatever came into my head. "But when you came back that Christmas and told me you had outgrown me…well, I thought it was time I stopped making a fool of myself." My voice faded off awkwardly, and I tucked my hair behind my ear nervously.

Samuel was looking off, almost as if he hadn't been listening. "Even at boot camp, I didn't feel right about writing to you, but I couldn't help it, not then. I needed you too much." His voice was low, and his eyes swung back to me, a brutal honesty in his expression. "But you were so young, and the feelings between us were too intense. I found myself thinking about you like you were my girl. Then I would remember how young you were, and I would be ashamed of myself. One of my buddies at sniper school asked me one day when I was going to show him a picture of you. I hadn't talked about you, but you were the only one I ever got letters from and the only one I ever wrote to. I felt like a scum bag, nineteen years old, writing letters to a fourteen-year-old girl. I knew it couldn't be good for you. You needed to grow up and so did I. I had things I had to do, and I did them." His gaze narrowed. "I thought maybe it was time to come back."

The way he said this made it sound like I was part of the reason he had returned, and my mouth grew dry. I cleared my throat.

"And when you leave? What then?" I wasn't sure what I wanted him to say, and I felt incredibly foolish all over again.

He looked at me wordlessly, considering, and I cursed myself silently. So what if he left? What was wrong with me? I felt like I was thirteen all over again and hated that he could make me feel so vulnerable. I picked up my bike, throwing my book in the basket. I climbed on the seat, twisting my skirt around my legs to keep it out of the spokes. He remained silent, watching me. I didn't look back as I rode away.

# 15. *Parody*

THE FOLLOWING MORNING I arose early as usual, pulling on my running shoes, slipping on my shorts and a T-shirt, and pulling my hair up in a ponytail. I took a forkful of chocolate cake, chugged down some milk, and walked out into the morning. Lying on the mat in front of the door was a thick manila envelope. Written across it in neat caps, someone had written *JOSIE*. I picked it up and turned it over. It was heavy, and I tested it in my hands curiously. I had ordered some piano books for some new students, but this wasn't addressed or postmarked. Someone had set it on the mat early this morning, or maybe even late last night.

Curiously, I peeled the seal and pulled out the contents. Inside were stacks of sealed legal sized white envelopes, all with my name written across them in the same handwriting as the writing on the front of the manila envelope. I sank down on the porch swing and pulled one out. Turning it over, I saw a date written across the back: 8-19-1999. I pulled out another one. Another date was scrawled across the back. Swiftly, I pulled out all the letters, finding them ordered according to their date. Suddenly, I knew what they were. The first date was June 5, 1999, about a year after Samuel left Levan.

My heart pounded, and my blood felt icy in my veins. Reverently, with shaking hands, I opened the one on the top of the pile. It picked up where his last letter, so long ago, had left off. He confessed his agony at not being able to respond to me, asking me over and over again to forgive him. Samuel had written me dozens of letters. Most of them were from the first year. Maybe that was when he had felt the most alone. But they continued on, through the following years. There was a letter written on 9-11-2001. I had thought of him when the towers were hit, wondering where he was, or if he would be sent somewhere. When the U.S. had invaded Iraq, I had watched the television, wondering if Samuel was among those first Marines sent in. Apparently he'd thought of me, too.

I read several of Samuel's letters, standing there on the front porch, and marveled at the places he'd been and the things he had seen and done. He told me about the books he'd read. I noticed many of them were ones I had read, and some of them were books I hadn't heard of. There was a definite loneliness in many of them, but a confidence and sense of purpose was present as well. I abandoned my run and went back upstairs to my room. Running could wait. I had some catching up to do.

I walked out into the front yard a few mornings later, the screen door banging behind me. It wouldn't wake Dad; he was already up looking after the horses. I sniffed hopefully, trying to smell fall in the air, but sadly got a whiff of summer leftovers instead. I leaned down and re-tied my running shoes, wiggling my toes.

I meandered out to the road and faced my mountains wreathed in sunrise. I breathed and raised my arms high above my head, stretching and arching and working out my morning kinks.

"You look like Changing Woman greeting the Sun." A voice spoke immediately to my left.

I was startled, and my arms dropped to my sides as I whirled around. "Oh! Samuel!" I cried out. "You scared me!"

"I'm a sneaky Indian, what can I say?"

I looked into his face. It was the kind of thing he would have said at eighteen, but it would have been laced with bitterness. This time he just smiled a little and shrugged. He had on a pair of faded Levis and his worn cowboy boots again. His black T-shirt, with *Semper Fi* written in white print across the front, fit snugly across his powerful chest and shoulders. His dark hair, military short and spiky, was still wet like he'd just climbed out of the shower. He looked like my Samuel, but not. For many months after he left the first time, I had quietly cried myself to sleep, unwilling to admit to anyone how my youthful heart had ached in his absence. I had missed him terribly. I'd had so few friends, and I knew how rare he was, this friend who was truly a kindred spirit. When he'd left the second time, I had been hurt and angry and had done all I could not to think about him. My heart twisted painfully at the memory, and I swiftly redirected my attention to the man who stood before me, in the present.

"Changing Woman and the Sun ... is that a Navajo story?" I resumed my stretching, trying to portray a casualness I did not feel.

"It's a Navajo legend. Changing Woman is thought to be the child of the Earth and the Sky. She is closely tied to the circle of life, the changing of the seasons, the order of the universe. She was created when First Man shook his medicine bag repeatedly at the holy mountain. Days later, Changing Woman was found on the top of the mountain. First Man and First Woman taught her and raised her.

"One day Changing Woman was out walking and she met a strange young man whose brilliance dazzled her so much she had to look away. When she turned back toward him he was gone. This happened two more times. She went home and told First Man and First Woman what had happened. They told her to make her bed outside that night with her head facing east. While she slept, the young man came and lay beside her. She awoke and asked him who he was.

He said, "Don't you know who I am? You see me every day. I am all around you. In my presence you were created." She realizes he is the sun's inner form. In order to see him each day, she went to live by the Pacific Ocean so that when the sun set on the water he could visit her."

We were quiet for a moment. The birds started warbling, and I wished they would be still. The silence was silky without them.

"She must have been lonely waiting for him to come see her." I hadn't meant to speak out loud, and wondered where my sentiment had sprung from.

"She was." Samuel eyed me quizzically. "According to legend, she was so lonely for companionship that she created the Navajo people from the flakes of her skin, rubbed off different parts of her body."

The story was strangely sensual, the beautiful young woman, waiting each day for the Sun to come to her. I gazed up at the rising orb and closed my eyes as I lifted my face to its warmth.

"What do you listen to while you run?" Samuel nodded toward the iPod strapped to my bicep.

The memories of sharing my precious symphonies with him on that bumpy bus bombarded me. I remembered our heartfelt and intimate discussions of "God's music," and I turned from him realizing I didn't want him to know what I listened to when I ran. I stretched back and pulled my right foot up behind me, stretching my quad, pretending I hadn't heard him. He reached over and took the earphones from my ears, stuck one in his own, and pushed play on the iPod. After a moment he grimaced.

"This is electronic music. The kind you'd hear at a club or an aerobics class! Boom, Boom, Boom, Boom." He pounded his foot for effect. "The same repeated phrases over and over again. Synthesizers!" he said in mock horror.

"I run with it to keep a steady pace," I defended myself, chagrined, yanking the earbud out of his ear.

He stared at me thoughtfully, his head tilted, considering. "You run with it so that you don't have to think," he answered finally.

I glared at him, stung that he had so easily guessed the truth—at least partially. I listened to the electronic music so I didn't have to *feel*. I didn't want to explain that to him. I resorted to walking away.

Samuel quickly caught up to me. I picked up my pace and started to jog. He started to jog with me. His cowboy boots clopped loudly as we ran. I sped up. So did he. I ran full out for a mile, stretching my legs, knowing he had to be dying in those boots. He didn't complain, but ran with me, stride for stride. I ran another mile. Then two more. My lungs burned. I had never run this fast. He didn't seem winded.

"What do you want, Samuel!" I turned on him suddenly, skidding to a halt. "You're going to hurt yourself running in those boots!" He stopped and looked down into my flushed face. He put his hands on his hips, and I was gratified to see his chest rising and falling, indicating some exertion.

"I'm a Marine, Josie AND I am Navajo, an Earth-walker. I am Samuel of the Bitter Water People." He grinned, his eyebrows wagging devilishly. He leaned into me and said slyly, "Therefore you can't outrun me even when I'm wearing shitkickers." He used the Levan slang for cowboy boots, and it made me laugh despite myself. My laughter seemed to please him.

"Where is 'Ode to Joy', Josie?" he said, ever-so-softly.

My eyes flew to his, startled. He remembered the music that had once so moved me that I could not go a day without its company.

Again, I felt at a loss for words. When I'd seen Samuel last I was a girl and he was a man. He had pretty much rejected me outright. I hadn't written to him again. I had occasionally asked his grandma about him, wanting news, wanting to hear how he fared. The problem was nobody but Samuel and I truly knew of the bond we had struck. It was encapsulated inside those trips back and forth across the ridge, day after day, with kids talking, laughing, and arguing all around us. Nobody was ever aware of our conversations, our discoveries, our shared moments.

His grandma had given me generalities, but never knew to share more with me, never knew how much I desperately wanted to know, and I had been unwilling and unable to explain my interest. Knowing how private and careful Samuel had been, I was pretty certain he hadn't asked about me. Yesterday, he said Nettie had told him what she knew about Kasey, but Nettie only knew what was on the surface, just details.

"The truth is Samuel, you and I don't know each other at all anymore." My voice came out a little more bitterly than I had intended, and the words stung my lips.

He studied me for a minute, but didn't reply. Wordlessly, we began walking back toward our neighboring houses. We had made a wide loop when we ran, and we weren't very far from home. I walked alongside him, feeling raw and wrung out.

The silence was strained, and I longed to escape. Nearing his grandparents' house he spoke again.

"You ran in the wrong direction."

"What?"

"You ran west this morning, away from the sun. The Navajo always run east, into the sun, greeting the sun. Lift up your face and let the Sky Father shine down a blessing upon you as you run toward him."

I didn't know how to respond. I had always had to twist Samuel's arm to tell me anything about his Navajo traditions. Now he was sharing legends and stories with absolute comfort. He had changed.

Samuel's eyes were grave. "Changing Woman is called Changing Woman because she grew up so fast. The legend claims she became a full grown woman in only twelve days. She wasn't a child for very long. I guess in that way you are just like her. You weren't a child very long either. At thirteen you were far wiser and more mature than anybody I knew, except for my Grandma Yazzie." Samuel paused, his eyes drilling down into mine. "Changing Woman is also called Changing Woman because she is responsible for the ever moving cycle of life…but in her heart, in her spirit, she is as steady and constant as the sun she loves."

I shook my head, bemused.

"The truth is, Josie," Samuel began his sentence just as I had several minutes before. "You're a full grown woman now. But I don't think you're really all that different here." Samuel lightly touched the smooth skin exposed by the open V of my T-shirt, laying his knuckles against my heart. "I think you're still you. And I'm still the Samuel you knew." His fingers were warm on my skin, and I fought myself not to reach up and cover his hand with my own.

Then he dropped his hand, and it was his turn to walk away.

Over the last few years I'd raised my prices and made a name for myself as a piano teacher. In the summer, I taught piano lessons almost exclusively and made decent money doing it. I'd never had to resort to house calls. I was by far the best pianist around, and I had no children, no husband, no other demands on my time and attention. I had students as far north as Provo, and as far south as Fillmore, almost an hour away in each direction, and they came to me. At home, my piano still stood faithfully in the exact same place it had since I purchased it through the Penny Pincher ad, but even after Dad had gone back to work after his stroke, I hadn't taught lessons on it. I still used the room in the church for that. I loved the old building; I'd even been entrusted with my very own key. Dad and I needed a quiet place to come home to, without the endless stream of students and the necessary noise that accompanied their learning.

When fall came and school started, schedules changed and my lessons filled the after school hours from 3:00- 6:00. From September to May, I spent my mornings down at Louise's shop listening to gossip and cutting hair. Louise had a steady clientele; being the only shop in town for twenty years has its advantages. Over the last couple of years she'd been more than happy to shoo a few folks my way, though more often than not, she kept her women clients, who had become attached to her as women are prone to do with their hairstylists. I mostly cut the children's hair, the men's hair, and had once even trimmed Iris Peterson's miniature poodle, Vivi.

September is typically a beautiful month throughout the West—the light is softer, the temperatures abate, the sky is often impossibly blue, and a hint of color starts to tempt the trees with autumn. August had left Levan with an angry huff, leaving heat in its wake, and I was ready for September's cooler head to prevail. Fall was my favorite season, and I was eager to smell it and feel it on my skin. Unfortunately, as I walked the mile to Louise's that morning I saw no sign of it. The yellow sundress I had put on that morning (because it reminded me of yellow autumn leaves) now mirrored a persistent summer sun, and I picked up my pace to escape its rays.

I slammed into the shop with a sigh, the screen door whooshing behind me, Louise's bell tinkling above me. The cool air that hit me felt like salvation, and I closed my eyes and lifted my damp blonde curls off my neck so the fan whirring by the door could blow directly on my skin.

"Good mornin', Sunshine," Louise drawled, with a smile in her voice.

"Good morning, Louise," I sighed again, my eyes still closed and my head still bowed in grateful worship to the humming fan.

"When yer done prayin' you can say hello to Nettie and Samuel, too."

My head jerked up, and my eyes flew open at the mention of Samuel's name. Nettie was sitting in Louise's pink swivel chair, patiently reading a magazine with Julia Roberts on the cover while Louise rolled her hair in little pink pin curlers.

"Good morning, Nettie," I said lightly, my eyes darting to see Samuel leaning against the wall next to the swinging doors that led into the general store.

"Good morning, Samuel," I said, striving again for lightness. Instead, my voice squeaked a little, and Louise looked at me quizzical-ly.

Samuel dipped his head slightly, and Nettie spoke up, never lift-ing her eyes from the glossy pages. "Samuel wants a trim, Josie, if you don't have anything scheduled right away."

"She doesn't," Louise supplied without hesitation, and she and Nettie looked over at me expectantly.

"Certainly, Samuel," I stammered. "Right this way."

I walked quickly to my station and pulled a black apron over my dress, tying it swiftly and trying to control the nervous heat that pooled in my stomach. I couldn't understand why I felt so off kilter when he was around me. I hadn't seen him since we'd ended up run-ning together yesterday morning. Part of me desperately wanted to avoid him, part of me was intensely happy to see him again.

I turned, expecting him to be behind me, and met his gaze across the room where he still leaned unmoving, watching me with an undecipherable expression on his face. In a fluid and easy manner he shifted his weight and walked toward me. Again, I felt the sensa-tion of butterflies dancing in my belly and wished I'd foregone breakfast.

He folded his length into the pink chair, and I levered the chair downward so I could lower his head back into the sink. I made my-self busy, not looking into his face. I tested the water temperature and slid a towel beneath his neck so the water wouldn't drip into his shirt when he sat up. I focused on his thick black hair and the decep-tive silkiness of its texture in my hands. The water was warm as it rushed through my fingers and I massaged the shampoo into his scalp. There is something about washing another person's hair that is very nurturing, and the caregiver in me normally enjoyed the simple act of service. I took pleasure in the sighs of contentment that were invariably expressed. Most people closed their eyes and relaxed un-der my gentle hands.

Samuel kept his eyes opened and trained on my face. I tried desperately to avoid his gaze. It made the act of molding my hands to his head incredibly intimate, and I longed to shut my own eyes to relieve the tension his perusal was creating between us. I tried to distract myself with thoughts of Kasey. I had never kissed Kasey with my eyes open…I'd never even thought about it. I'd always closed my eyes and enjoyed the sensation of his lips on my lips. I wondered if Samuel would kiss me with his gaze locked with mine. I grimaced inwardly and chastised myself, mortified at the direction of my thoughts. I didn't want him to kiss me! He was infuriating and inquisitive and exhausting, and I wished he would go away!

I rinsed his hair with fervor and shut off the water with a frustrated yank. Levering furiously, I sat him up and briskly rubbed the towel over his hair.

"You seem angry," he said smoothly. I wanted to slap him. I *was* angry. Ridiculously and desperately angry. Why did he have to come back? I didn't want to deal with old feelings that brought fresh pain. I was through loving people who would only leave. I met his eyes furiously in the mirror and saw a humbling compassion in their depths. My anger slipped off me like a soiled silk dress. My hands grew still in his hair, and my eyes held the gaze of my old friend.

"I'm sorry, Samuel. I have behaved very badly since you returned," I confessed in a whisper. "I can't seem to get my balance, and I'm not sure why." I fell quiet, trying to control my unruly emotions. "Will you please forgive me?"

He studied me for a moment before he spoke, which was his way. "Lady Josephine, there is nothing to forgive." I laughed a little as the memory of my childish wish resurfaced.

"Thank you, Sir Samuel." I curtsied deeply, and with clippers in hand, finished trimming his hair in silence. When I was done, he tipped me well, offered his grandmother his arm, and left without a word.

I walked wearily home from the church that evening after teaching piano lessons to some very uninspired and obstinate children. There was no joy in teaching unwilling students. I thought of the quiet house that would greet me. Dad would be on shutdown shift for one more week, and the evening ahead would be spent alone. I felt unusually melancholy at the prospect, and was cheered by thoughts of the leftover chocolate birthday cake from my party Sunday evening. I felt twenty-three going on fifty.

As I neared my house I saw Samuel sitting on my porch in the shadow of the overhang. He rocked slowly in the big wooden swing my dad had fashioned for my mom many years before. I tamped down the telltale flip of my traitorous heart as I approached him. I didn't have the energy for Samuel right now. Exhaustion descended on my soul, and I considered feigning sickness. But in light of my apology earlier that day, I did not want to seem hostile. I sat down next to him on the swing and greeted him with a tired smile.

"Why do you cut hair, Josie?" Samuel said without preamble.

"Why not?" I was immediately flustered. Couldn't he just say hello like a normal person?

"When I drove my grandmother to the beauty shop today I had no idea you would be there. Imagine my surprise when I saw you walk in. Then my grandma says to you "Samuel needs a haircut," as if you work there. I was completely floored. You walked back and put the apron on, and I almost thought the three of you were having a little fun at my expense. But then you looked back at me, and I could see you weren't kidding."

"Was it really so hard to believe?" I slipped off my sandals and stretched my arches, my toes with their pink toenails pointing and flexing in relief.

"Yes," he clipped, with no embellishment.

"Why?" I almost laughed in disbelief at the tightness in his eyes, the grim set to his mouth.

"Did you always want to work at Ballow's Do's?"

I was hurt by the mockery I heard in his voice and didn't answer him. He shook his head, and there was frustration in his expelled breath.

"Do you remember Ravel's 'Pavane for a Dead Princess'?"

I laughed in disbelief. "I can't keep up with you Samuel!" I cried. "One moment you are being snide about my work, and the next you're asking me about classical music!"

"Do you remember the piece?" he insisted.

"Yes! But I'm a little surprised that you do!" It was my turn to be snide, and I felt childish in my attempt. "It was a favorite of mine," I added in a more conciliatory tone. He glowered at me for a minute.

"Come here." Samuel grabbed my hand tightly, yanking me to my feet. Then he was striding across the grass, pulling me behind him.

"Samuel! My shoes!" I yelped as I tried to keep up with him. As we neared the gravel he swept me up into his arms, marching across the sharp rocks without a hitch in his step. I sputtered and squeaked, clinging to his neck. His truck was parked in front of his grandparents' house across the street about half a block down. I felt ridiculous being carried down the middle of the road. He opened the passenger door to his black Chevy truck, slid me in unceremoniously, and shut the door with a bang.

He climbed in and backed out, gravel spitting up behind us, and roared down the street toward the mountain that jutted up into the sky not a mile from town.

I stared at him in wonder. "Can I ask where we are going without my shoes?"

For once his eyes were not glued to my face, but were fixed intently before him as he began to ascend into the pretty little canyon with the unattractive name we called Chicken Crick.

He didn't answer me but drove until he found a little turnoff that looked out over the town. The teenagers in the valley regularly used it as a trysting spot. The ledge wasn't high, and the town lay just below us, surrounded by the patchwork quilt of farmland, softened by the burnished glow of the approaching twilight seeping over the mountains to the west. The big-wheeled sprinklers ran in long rows across the gold and green fields, the water from their spray creating little rainbows in the setting sun. Samuel rolled to a stop facing the breathtaking view, and silence flooded the cab of his truck. He sat for a minute, contemplating the rosy splendor before us. He reached over and pushed some of the buttons on his console. I recognized "Pavane for a Dead Princess," immediately. I should have known. The music spilled out of the speakers, tip-toeing up my arms and legs, raising gooseflesh on my arms. So beautiful, so melancholy, so... intrusive. I folded my arms across my stomach and held myself tightly. I was intensely grateful when Samuel spoke.

"I think I told you that my Navajo grandfather was a Marine in World War II. He was a code talker. He lied about his age when the recruiter came to the reservation. He had heard about the special program they were experimenting with, using the Navajo language to create a code that could not be cracked by the Japanese or the Germans. He was only sixteen years old when he signed up but spoke relatively good English, so he was a shoe-in. The Navajo code talkers actually created the code using Navajo words to describe military operations—like the word for bombs was *ayęęzhii,* which meant eggs in Navajo. The word they used for the United States was *ne-he-mah,* which means 'our mother.' They also created a code alphabet by taking an English letter, thinking of an English word that started with that letter, and then using the Navajo word that means the same thing. For instance, ant stood for the letter "A". The Navajo word for ant is *wóláchíí.* So the word *wóláchíí* meant "A" in the code. The word for "B" was *shash,* which meant bear in English. The language of the Navajo was so unique that it just sounded like gibberish to the code crackers."

"I never knew this!" I said in wonder. I had never heard of the Navajo code talkers.

"The Navajo code talkers were asked to keep quiet about the code, in case it was needed in future wars, so after the war the American population knew very little about their role in the battles throughout the Pacific."

"That is fascinating! Your language helped save our country! What an incredible honor!" I had forgotten the pain of the beautiful music, which had changed to "Traumerei" by Schumann.

His mouth turned up slightly as he looked at me, listening to my glowing response. "Yes, it was an honor. I didn't think so when I was an angry young half-breed. I thought the *bilagáana,* the white man, just used my grandfather and others like him. Used them, and then spit them back out when they were done. Out of sight, out of mind. I asked my grandpa why he was so proud of his service. He told me this country is the country of his forefathers. His ancestors lived here long before the white man so it is our country as much as any man's and we have to defend her. He also said he made many friends among the white Marines. He had a *bilagáana* body-guard...someone assigned to him to look out for him and keep him alive, because it was so critical that he not be killed or captured by the enemy. Without the code talkers, there wasn't a safe way to communicate, and the enemy would have loved to get their hands on one of them and torture them to reveal the code. He said this *bilagáana* Marine saved his life over and over again, risking his own in the process. That is why I was named Samuel. I was named after Samuel Francis Sutorius, a Marine from the Bronx, who my grandfather could not speak of without weeping."

Again we sat silent—moved by the story, lulled by the music.

"So...your middle name is Francis?" I snickered and pinched him affectionately.

"Yes, Josie *JO* Jensen, it is."

"Ahhhh," I moaned theatrically. "You would wound the small-town girl who longs for a classic name?"

Samuel smiled softly, but his voice was grave when he spoke. "You were never small-town, Josie." He shook his head to under-score his words. "You always had this light that made you seem like royalty...such an incredible mind, such beauty and humility. You took my breath away, time after time, day after day, on that smelly old school bus."

The lump in my throat made it impossible for me to speak, and I blinked away the wetness in my eyes. He continued:

"The day of the rainstorm, when you realized it was me, your big blue eyes lit up, and I wanted to swing you around and laugh. I couldn't wait to talk to you and listen to you, and see what you'd read, and finally hear you play again."

Samuel stopped talking, and his eyes locked on mine. "But you were so sad... and I felt the loneliness pouring off you when you put your arms around me. It was as wet as the rain, and I knew you were changed somehow. You were different. I was angry with you when I heard that silly music that you listen to while you run. I was angry that you seemed so resistant to the things that had once made you so radiant. And today! There you are, working in that little shop, cutting people's hair, ignoring your gift! Here in this small town that keeps you hidden…a princess acting like a pauper, and I just can't figure it out."

My face flushed, and I felt as if I'd been slapped. "Is that what this is about, Samuel? 'Pavane for a Dead Princess?' So, I'm the dead princess? Am I not good enough for you anymore? Where would you have me go, Samuel? What do you want me to do?" I cried out in wounded disbelief. "I loved music and books partly because I wanted to escape, to leave this town for bigger and better things. But I can't let my music to take me away from everything I love, everything I have left!"

"So what changed, Josie?!!" Samuel's voice was as impassioned as my own. "You've just turned off the music? You used to say that Beethoven made you feel alive, made the mysteries of God seem attainable. You said you could feel your mother when you listened to your music. Like you knew she was out there somewhere, living on. Has that changed? Don't you *want* to feel your mother anymore?"

"When I listen to beautiful music, I can't just feel *my mother* now. I feel other things, too," I groaned out the words and pressed my hands to my feverish cheeks.

"I don't understand!" Samuel pulled my hands from my face and pulled my chin up, forcing me to meet his glittering gaze. "Why is that a bad thing?"

"The music makes me feel too much! It makes me long for things I will never have! Don't you see? The music makes it so much harder to forget."

Samuel's hand dropped from my chin and understanding washed over his features. "What things? Tell me what things you can never have."

I didn't want to share anymore. I felt cornered. None of this was any of his business. I was suddenly very tired, and I closed my eyes, refusing to answer him.

Samuel lifted my chin again, waiting until I lifted my eyes to his once more. "So that's it, you're just done at twenty-three? What about school? I seem to remember you had big plans to travel the world, playing the piano."

I twisted my head away, pulling my chin from his hand. He was so…infuriating! I didn't remember that side of him. I tried for nonchalance.

"I was set to go. I had a full-ride music scholarship to Brigham Young University." I had won the Outstanding Musician Scholarship, allotted to one high school senior in the state of Utah each year. I remembered the thrill of winning, of seeing my career as a concert pianist, composing music in my spare time, stretched out before me. The dream was faded now and buried under layers of responsibility.

"And?" Samuel demanded.

"And Kasey died, and then my dad had a stroke." I started listing things, my voice rising with irritation, frustrated that I had to defend myself. "Then Sonja was diagnosed with Alzheimer's, and I was needed here! Okay?" I threw my hands up in frustration. "I was needed here, so I stayed."

"I've seen you with your family, Josie. You kind of take care of everyone. You're good at being needed, that's for sure."

214

"What is that supposed to mean?" I was very angry now. *How dare he?!* "My dad had a major stroke a week before I was supposed to leave for school. I decided to defer my scholarship for a while to take care of him. Dad couldn't work and someone had to. I did what I had to do. Dad started getting better, but the medical bills had piled up, and he still couldn't work full time, so I decided to wait a little longer. "Then Sonja was diagnosed with Alzheimer's and Doc Grimaldi passed away not long after we put her in a home, and I couldn't just leave her. Nobody else cared, Samuel. And by then the scholarship was long gone anyway!" I was babbling and I forced myself to stop talking. My breathing was haggard, and my throat felt raw with pent up emotion. Samuel was staring out the window, listening, so reminiscent of the boy I had once befriended.

There was nothing more to say. Samuel seemed at a loss, and I was drained. After a moment, he started the truck and we backed out, turning sharply onto the road, turning our backs on the grandeur of the gloaming.

When we pulled off onto the gravel outside my house, he slowed to a stop and came around to my door. I had opened it and put one bare foot down on the rocks, curling my toes under to protect my sensitive arch from the sharp gravel. Samuel gently swung me up in his arms again, cradling me like I was something precious. He walked easily to the grass and set me down carefully. His big hands came up and framed my face, his thumbs brushing my cheekbones in a brief caress. I shivered involuntarily. He searched my face for several heartbeats.

His voice was low as he spoke. "It's not too late, Josie." And with that, he withdrew his hands and left me. I remained standing, barefoot in the grass and buried in introspection, until the sky was cloaked in darkness and the stars blinked back to life.

# 16. *Modulation*

TARA BLEW INTO the shop like a hurricane one afternoon—pink hair, red lips, flashing smile, hugging everyone and squealing as if she had been gone for a century instead of three months. She showed up now and then, got her 'Mom' fix, and was gone again in a whirl. She threw herself into my swivel chair and proceeded to tell me everything, down to the last detail, that had happened to her since she'd last seen me. All at once her eyes narrowed on my face and she pursed her crimson lips in speculation.

"I like your hair." She said it with such surprise in her voice that I laughed out loud. "No! I do!" She insisted. "You're letting it grow out and the curls are all soft and flowy." I had had Louise cut my hair boy short after starting work with her in the shop. It had been so tortured and teased after living through a year of experimentation by Tara that I had just told Louise to "take it off." Louise had clucked her tongue the whole time she cut it. She kept asking me, "What were you thinkin' girl, lettin' Tara have her way with your hair?"

I touched the hair that hung past my shoulders self consciously. "I guess it's just longer. I haven't really styled it any special way."

"Are you dating anybody?" she queried, and then she laughed like she had just told a hilarious joke. "Who would you date? Everybody's either sixteen, married, or loooong gone!"

Louise spoke up from her station where she was cutting Penny

Worwood's hair. "Oh, I don't know 'bout that. A few days ago, Nettie Yates came in here with her grandson. Now that is one goodlookin' man!"

"Nettie's grandson? You mean Tabrina's son? That man is as homely as a mud fence! You're gettin' desperate in your old age, Mom!"

"Not Tabrina's son! You're right, you couldn't pick that boy out in a pen of pigs! No, I'm talking about Michael's son!" she said triumphantly.

"Who is Michael?" Tara was completely bewildered.

"Tabrina's older brother."

"I didn't even know Tabrina had an older brother!"

"Yep. He died when you were just a baby, which is why you probably never heard about him. Michael Yates was one tall drink of something yummy!" Louise sighed. "He was more religious than the rest of his family, and went on a two year mission for the church, though nobody else in his family had ever gone. He was kind of a quiet guy, but yum, yum, yum, he was something to look at! His poor little sister Tabrina got what was left over, bless her heart, and her kids 'er even uglier than she is!"

"Mom! Focus!" Tara laughed. "So this guy Michael? He had a son?"

"Yep. He lived here with his grandparents for a while when he was in high school. He's part Navajo or something. I can't believe you don't remember him. What's his name again, Josie?"

"Samuel." I turned and made myself busy cleaning my worktable, not wanting to look at Tara, fearing I would give something away that I was not yet ready to discuss.

"Samuel..." Tara scrunched up her face trying to remember. "Oh, yeah! Hey, Josie, wasn't he the kid you had to sit by all year long on the bus in seventh grade?" She shivered dramatically. "I thought for sure he was gonna kill his grandparents in their sleep!"

"Tara!" I turned and glared at her. "Why would you say something like that?"

"What?" she protested. "He was intimidating! He never said two words to anyone, and he always had a scowl on his face. He wore his hair long, and I swear he carried a tomahawk strapped to his leg. I don't know how you stood it. I would have peed my pants if Mr. Walker had assigned me to sit by him."

"I liked him," I said simply. "We actually became friends. He was quiet and kind of intense, but I've been accused of that myself." I looked at Tara pointedly.

"Wasn't he the guy that clapped in church that one time?" Penny Worwood piped in with her two cents.

Louise whirled around and pointed her comb at me, waving it wildly and dancing around like she had ants in her pants. "It *was* him! He stood up and clapped for you after you played your solo! At the time, I just thought maybe he was trying to stick it to his grandparents a little, embarrass them, be a smart ass, ya know? I didn't realize you two actually knew each other! Woo! Hoo! Man, that was really something when he did that! I still remember the look on your face, Josie Jo! You coulda died and gone straight to heaven right then."

"So…this Samuel guy…why's he back in town?" Tara interrupted her mom's giddy monologue.

"Well, Nettie told me he's come back to help her and Don get things in order," Louise responded. "They don't really have anybody else, ya know, and they're gettin' on in years. Tabrina and her husband are no help. Those two together are about as smart as a box of rocks."

"Louise!" I scolded

"Oh okay, Josie. A box of rocks is kinda harsh." She amended with, "Tabrina and her husband are about as smart as a box of frogs." She smirked at me over her right shoulder before she continued.

"Anyhow, this Samuel—and he is a fine specimen now, Tara, no matter what you thought when you were in seventh grade—he's come back to do some legal work for them, help them get their sheep sold, sell some land, stuff like that. Don's health isn't great, and it's just time to stop workin' so hard."

"You said he was doing some legal work for them. Is he some kind of lawyer?" Tara asked with interest. Lawyers meant money to Tara, and money was number one on the top of her marriage-must-haves.

"No, he's a Marine," I volunteered.

"He's a Marine, all right, but Nettie says the Marines helped pay for his college and then he went to officer's training, and now he's going to attend law school. He's on some kind of leave right now."

I gasped right out loud. Samuel, becoming a lawyer? I felt a little weak in the knees, and then I felt ridiculously like crying. I was suddenly, euphorically, proud of him. I hadn't read far enough in the letters obviously, and he'd said nothing about it. But when had he really had the opportunity? Each of our conversations had been riddled with emotional grenades and catching up had just not come up. I felt ashamed that I had asked him so little about himself.

"Earth to Josie!" Tara was waving her hands in my face. "You look like you're gonna cry, you okay?"

I brushed away her questions, smiled brightly, and wished the day were over. I needed to go find Samuel, regardless of whether or not he believed the princess was dead.

Samuel was not home when I knocked on Nettie Yates' screen door later that evening. I'd baked some cookies as an excuse for stopping by. I had also filled a basket of vegetables from my garden. Nettie had stopped planting a garden in recent years, complaining that she was just too "brittle to work in the dirt anymore." It was sweet irony that she had shared with me and my family from her garden for so many years and had shown me how to plant one and care for one, and now I could share my garden's bounty in return.

Nettie was crocheting something, and she invited me in to sit and chat a minute. "Samuel and Don went to bring the cows down from the mountain early this morning. I didn't want Don to go; I worry about him sittin' a saddle all day, but he wouldn't hear nothin' of it. I didn't fight 'im too hard. He's been bringing the cows home from Mt. Nebo every fall since he was old enough to tie his shoes, and this will probably be the last time. We're sellin' off the cattle and the sheep, ya know. Don's relieved, but it's hard for him, too. Samuel bein' here helps take the weight off his shoulders a little.

"When Samuel came to live with us all those years ago I didn't know what to think. He never talked to us much, and he seemed so angry at first. But then slowly he started changin'…don't really know why, but I'm grateful for it. He's grown up to be a real good man and a blessing to us now when we need him. He says he'll stay until we've got things buttoned up."

I was terrible at small talk and didn't quite know what to say to keep the conversation flowing. I decided I would just come out and ask for the information I sought.

"When will they be back?" I ventured casually.

"Oh they should be pullin' in any time." Nettie looked at me curiously.

I changed the subject quickly and asked her if I could do anything for her before I left. She hemmed and hawed, not wanting me to bother, but ended up confessing she needed help with the flower beds in the front yard. Before long, I was on my hands and knees in the dirt. I actually liked pulling weeds. Call me crazy, but there's something immensely therapeutic about yanking the noxious things from the cool brown soil. I got busy and made short work of the flower bed on one side of the front walk and was working my way down the other when I heard a truck crunching over gravel. I had hoped to be cool and composed when I saw Samuel again. Instead, I was on my knees with my rear in the air, pulling dandelions out from among the marigolds.

"Well hello, Miss Josie!" Don Yates stepped stiffly out of the pickup, approaching me with a slightly bow-legged gait. He'd been tall once but had become stooped and shrunken in his later years. He'd been a bull-rider in his younger days, and he'd been beaten up and put back together a time or two. Nettie said he'd broken every bone in his hands by the time his career was over. His fingers were as big around as sausages, his palms thick and muscular. Combine that with his muscular forearms, and he looked a little like Popeye. All arms, no butt, and bowed legs.

"Hello, Mr. Yates." I brushed my hair back from my face and wiped my hands on the skirt of my now dirty pink dress. "How was the cattle drive?"

Samuel was behind him and without a word he knelt beside me in the flower bed and started pulling weeds.

"It was long, Miss Josie! Woo Wee! I'm gonna go in and have mother make me a cup of coffee. If I don't keep walkin' I might fall right over. I'm way too old for cattle drivin' anymore. You want me to send some lemonade out for the two 'a ya, or somethin'?"

"Not for me, thanks." I glanced at Samuel in question.

"Go on in, Pop. I'll just help Josie finish up."

A minute later the screen door slammed behind Don Yates, and Samuel and I worked in silence. I figured it would be easier to talk if my hands were busy, so I took a deep breath and jumped right in.

"I'm proud of you, Samuel." I pulled weeds faster, my hands keeping pace with my galloping pulse.

Samuel looked up at me in surprise. I met his black gaze and quickly looked down to make sure I didn't start yanking out marigolds with nervous zeal.

"There was some talk today at the shop." I smiled sheepishly. "Well, there's always talk at the shop. But today I actually found it to be of interest to me."

Samuel had stopped pulling weeds, his head tilted to the side, regarding me quietly.

I looked back down, anxiously trying to find a weed within

arm's distance. "I heard you're going to law school," I paused, the pride I felt in him swelling in my heart, just like it had earlier. I looked up at him, swallowing to keep my emotions in check. "I can't tell you how I…I felt when I heard. I just wanted to cheer out loud…and...jump for joy all at once. I'm just so...so...well, I'm just so proud of what you've accomplished." I kept my eyes on his, and he seemed to be considering my words.

"Thank you, Josie. You have no idea with that means to me." His eyes remained on mine for a moment, and then he resumed pulling weeds until the last stubborn trespasser was removed from the flower beds.

"And Samuel…thank you for the letters…I haven't had a chance to read them all, but I will." I struggled to express myself honestly without getting too personal, but gave up when I realized I couldn't. "It almost made me feel like I was there with you. Most of all, it made me feel like maybe I wasn't alone all those nights I cried for you and missed you." My voice was choked, but I remained composed. I made a move to rise from the flower bed, but Samuel's hand shot out and curved around my bare arm, just above my elbow, detaining me.

"I'm sorry, Josie." Samuel's voice was husky and low. "I'm sorry for what I said that night. For making you feel like I was disappointed in you. There's nothing wrong with who you are and what you do." He reached up and ran the back of his fingers lightly along the side of my face. "I just hate to see you suffering. I handled it all wrong. Will you let me make it up to you? Will you let me do something for you?" His voice was almost pleading.

I wanted to close my eyes and press my face into the palm of his hand. His touch was feather light, but his eyes were heavy on mine. I nodded my consent, realizing that I didn't really care what the something was, just as long as I could be in his company a little while longer. He stood and reached down for me, pulling me to my feet.

"I've got a day's worth of sweat and horse ground into me, and I need to shower. I'll come by in about 30 minutes if that's okay?"

I nodded again and turned to walk away.

"Josie?" His voice stopped me. "Is your dad home?"

My heart lurched a little at the implied intimacy of his question.

I shook my head this time and found my voice. It came out smooth and easy, for which I was grateful. "He's on shut-downs for one more night."

"I'll be by." He turned and walked into the house. I tried hard not to run, but ended up sprinting down the middle of the street like a silly kid.

I was waiting for Samuel on the front porch swing when he came walking down the road half an hour later. I had slipped into the tub and washed the dirt from the flower beds off of my arms and legs. I'd traded my soiled pink summer dress for a skirt and a blue fitted t-shirt that I happened to know was the exact color of my eyes. The skirt was white eyelet, and it was comfortable and pretty. I didn't put any shoes on my feet. My calves and feet were brown from the recent summer days, and the lack of shoes made my preference for skirts a little less formal. I rarely wore pants and only wore shorts when I was running. I liked the feel of pretty, feminine clothes, and had stopped caring whether or not anyone thought I was old-fashioned. I hadn't had time to wash my hair, so I pinned it up, fixed my makeup, and put a little bit of lavender on my wrists. I felt silly waiting for him, but I waited all the same.

Samuel wore clean Wranglers and a soft chambray shirt rolled to his elbows, exposing his strong forearms. He wore moccasins on his feet, and his short black hair was brushed back from his smooth forehead and prominent cheekbones. He carried a big jug and an even bigger wooden pail. He stopped in front of me, and his eyes swept over my bare toes and upswept hair appreciatively.

"We need music," he said quietly. I could tell by the speculation in his eyes that he wasn't certain how I would respond to his request.

"All right," I replied evenly.

"Debussy."

"Debussy it is."

"I'll be out back." He turned and walked around the house, not waiting to see if I would do as he said. Samuel had changed in many ways, but he was still a little bossy. I was glad. I walked in the house to find Debussy.

He was sitting in the back yard on the long bench just beneath the kitchen windows when I opened the screen and set the CD player up on the ledge above him. The light from the kitchen spilled out into the rapidly darkening evening and onto his broad shoulders and bowed head. He was cutting into something with a sharp knife, pulling the outer bark-like shell away, exposing a white fibrous root that looked slick and soapy. Leaning forward, he pulled a big silver bowl from the large wooden pail he'd been carrying. He put the white root into the bowl, picked up the enormous pewter jug he'd been carrying, and poured steamy water over the root. Samuel rubbed the root as if it was a bar of soap, and little bubbles began to form. As the bubbles changed into suds he kept rubbing until the silver bowl was full of thick white lather. Setting the bowl down, he pulled a hand towel and a fat white bath towel out of the wooden pail. He stood from the bench, put the hand towel over his shoulder and laid the bath towel over the bench. Then he turned to me and patted the bench.

"Lie down."

I had been watching him in fascination, wondering what he was up to. I thought maybe he was going to soak my feet when I saw the big bowl of soapy stuff. I was curious, but I didn't question him. I arranged my skirt and lay back on the bench. He reached up then and pushed play on the music, flipping through the tracks until he found what he was looking for. He turned the wooden pail over, placed it near my head, and sat on it, using it for a stool. Then, pulling on the towel underneath me, he slid me toward him until my head hung over the edge of the bench and settled in his lap. One by one he pulled the pins out of my hair. His strong fingers ran through my curls, smoothing them over his hands. I belatedly realized that the music that was playing was Debussy's "Girl with the Flaxen Hair."

"How very appropriate," I said softly, the smile apparent in my voice.

"I like it," he answered easily. "I can't listen to it without thinking of you."

"Do you listen to it often?" I asked a little breathlessly.

"Almost every day for ten years," he replied evenly.

My heart stuttered and stopped, my breath shallow.

He continued quietly as if he hadn't just confessed something wondrous. "You washed my hair. Now I'm going to wash yours. My Navajo grandmother taught me how to do this. She makes soap from the root of the yucca plant. The root from a young yucca makes the best soap, but the yucca in my Grandma Nettie's yard was planted many years ago by my father. It's not indigenous to this area, but when he returned home from his two years on the reservation, he wanted to bring something back with him. I dug up a piece of the root. You have to peel off the outer shell. Then you kind of grind up the white part inside…that's the soap. I wasn't sure it would lather up, but it did."

Gently holding my head in the palm of one hand, he reached down and picked up the bowl, setting it in his lap that was now covered with the hand towel. He lowered my head into the soapy water, holding it all the while. His other hand smoothed the suds through my hair, the heat seeping into my scalp, his hand sliding back and forth, pulling my hair through his fist, sinking his fingers deep down to the base of my skull and sliding them back up again. My eyes drifted closed, and my nerve endings tightened. I pulled my knees upward, sliding the soles of my sensitive feet along the rough wooden bench, my toes curling in response to the sweet agony of his hands in my hair.

Samuel continued, the music of his voice as soothing as the warm water. "My grandmother uses the yucca soap to wash the sheep's wool after she shears it every spring. She says it works better than anything else. Your hair won't smell like lavender or roses when I'm done, but it'll be clean. My grandmother says it will give you new energy, too."

"Your wise grandmother. I think about her every time I feed my chickens."

"Why?" There was a smile in his voice.

"Well, you told me once how she had names for all her sheep, and she had so many! I named the chickens when I was a little girl, after my mother died. Somehow it made it easier to take care of them if I named them. I gave them names like Peter, Lucy, Edmund, and Susan after the characters in the *Chronicles of Narnia*. But your grandmother named her sheep names like 'Bushy Rump' and 'Face like a Fish,' and it always made me laugh when I thought about it."

"Hmm. The names do sound a little more poetic in Navajo," Samuel replied, chuckling softly. "Sadly, I think 'Bushy Rump' and 'Face like a Fish' have died, but she has a new one named 'Face like a Rump' in honor of both."

I let out a long peel of laughter, and Samuel's finger's tightened in my hair.

"Ah, Josie. That sound should be bottled and sold." He smiled down at me when I looked up at him in surprise.

He looked away and picked up the jug, sloshing the hot water over my hair and into the bowl of suds, starting the process over.

"My mother is the only other person who has ever washed my hair," I offered drowsily, the slip and slide of his fingers through my hair leaving me loose and relaxed. "It was so long ago. I took for granted how wonderful it feels."

"You were a child. Of course you took it for granted," Samuel answered quietly.

"I know why my mother washed my hair," I said, brave behind my closed lids, "but why are you washing my hair, Samuel? I've washed a lot of people's hair down at the shop. Not one of them has ever come back and offered to wash mine in return."

"I'm washing your hair for the same reason your mother probably did."

"Because my hair is dirty and tangled after playing in the barn?" I teased.

"Because it feels good to take care of you." His voice was both tender and truthful.

My soul sang. "I've taken care of myself for a long time," I replied quietly, incredibly moved by the sweetness of his answer.

"I know, and you're good at it. You've taken care of everybody else for a long time, too."

He let it go at that, and I didn't pursue the conversation. It took too much energy, and I felt myself lulled by the music, the spell of the night, and his firm hands.

The sound of Debussy's "Reverie" slid through the inky darkness as the light pooled just beyond us, leaving our faces in shadows. Samuel held my wet tresses in his hand, twisting the thick sections around his fingers tightly, pulling my head back, and arching my throat as he forced the excess water out of my hair. I heard him set the bowl down and felt him stand, still supporting my head in one hand. He drizzled hot water down the soapy lengths, rinsing them over and over, hands combing through my dripping hair until the water ran clear.

Again he wrapped his hands in my hair, twisting and wringing, and then he swathed my head in the towel he'd laid on his lap. Samuel left me momentarily and straddled the bench below my raised knees. Leaning forward, he grasped my hands and pulled me up toward him until I was sitting, my legs on either side of the bench, my forehead resting on his chest. He took the hand towel and lightly dried my damp curls, kneading my scalp in his hands, blotting the water from my hair. The hand towel fell to the ground as he lifted my face toward his. His hands smoothed my hair back, away from my forehead and cheekbones. My breath caught in anticipation of a kiss, but instead, he threaded his left hand into my hair once more. Lowering his head, he rubbed his slightly rough cheek back and forth against the silkiness of my own, the heat of his breath tickling my neck. The gesture was so loving, so gentle, and my eyes stayed closed under his simple caress. I held my breath as he ran his lips along my forehead, kissing my closed eyelids. I felt him pull back, and I opened my eyes. His eyes held mine in the dark. I wanted desperately for him to lean in and kiss my lips.

Samuel's hands framed my face, and he seemed not to breathe for an eternity. Then his palms and fingers traveled lightly down my arms and over my wrists until he held each of my hands in his. "Clair de Lune" whispered through the breeze and lightly trickled down my skin, creating little rivulets of desire where his hands had just been.

"Do you remember the first time I held your hand?" His voice was thick.

My thoughts were slow and heavy, my mind soft from his ministrations, but after a moment I responded thoughtfully. "It was after we argued about Heathcliff. You were mad at me. You didn't talk to me for days," I replied, remembering my hurt and confusion, wanting him to be my friend again. "I wished I hadn't said anything. You just made me so mad." I laughed a little, thinking about how Samuel had seemed intent on proving my every theory wrong.

"You were thirteen years old! A thirteen-year-old who was beautiful, wise, patient…and infuriating! I just kept thinking, 'How does she know these things?!' You quoted that scripture like you'd studied it just for the purpose of teaching me a lesson. Then you got up and walked off the bus! I was so blown away that I missed my stop. I was still sitting there when everyone else was gone. I ended up having to walk home from the bus driver's house. Mr. Walker got nervous and thought I was up to something. I guess I can't really blame him, I was acting pretty strange."

I looked down at our clasped hands, goose bumps skipping up my arms as his thumbs made slow patterns on my skin.

"1 Corinthians, Chapter 13…how did you know?" His voice contained a note of wonder. "I don't care how brilliant you were, thirteen-year-old girls don't quote scripture off the cuff like that."

I shook my head a little and smiled. "A few weeks before you and I had our discussion, I was sitting in church with my Aunt Louise and my cousins. My dad didn't go to church very often, but Aunt Louise dragged her bunch to church every week. She always said she needed all the help she could get…and I liked church."

Samuel groaned, interrupting me. "Of course you did."

"Shush!" I laughed, and proceeded to defend myself. "Church was quiet and peaceful, the music was soothing, and I always felt loved there. Anyway, that particular Sunday someone stood and read 1 Corinthians, Chapter 13. I thought it was the most beautiful thing I had ever heard. I was afraid that I wouldn't be able to find it again because, you're right, I wasn't very familiar with scripture. I told Aunt Louise I was sick and ran home, repeating 1 Corinthians, Chapter 13, 1 Corinthians, Chapter 13 all the way to my house so I wouldn't forget it. When I got home I pulled out my…"

"…big green dictionary?" Samuel finished for me, grinning.

"My big green dictionary," I repeated, smiling with him. "I also pulled out the Bible we kept in the bookcase. I read verses 4 through 9, over and over, looking up every word, even the ones I knew. I wanted to have a perfect understanding of every word. Those verses are like the most incredible poetry! To me it was even better than just a beautiful collection of words though, because it was the truth! I could feel the truth of it when I read it. When I was finished, I wrote verses 4-9 on my 'Wall of Words' and read it every night before I went to bed. I had it memorized pretty quickly."

"Your Wall of Words?" Samuel's eyebrows shot up.

"You don't know about my Wall of Words?!" I whispered in mock horror. "I can't believe I never told you about my Wall of Words!" I leaped off the bench and pulled him up, my hands still clasped in his. "Come on, I'll show you."

I went inside, Samuel trailing behind me, and climbed the little staircase to my attic room. Samuel's shoulders looked huge in the narrow passageway. At the top of the stairs, I stopped.

"Wait! I forgot Dad's rules! No boys allowed in my room. Darn! I guess I'll have to take a picture of my wall and show it to you later." My lips twitched, and my eyes widened with laughter. I acted like I was going to descend the stairs again.

Samuel's arm shot out and secured me around the waist. "I'll stand in the doorway."

I laughed, enjoying the flirtation, and walked into the little room that had been mine since I was old enough to traverse the stairs. Samuel followed behind me and, true to his word, leaned his shoulder against the doorframe. His eyes scanned my masterpiece.

I looked at my wall with new eyes, remembering the books where I had found each word. I pointed out the spot where I'd written 1 Corinthians, Chapter 13. "Here it is ...written before you and I ever discussed the definition of true love." I turned and looked at him. He moved from the door, walking toward the wall to read the small print. He ran his hands over the wall, like I had done many times before, feeling my words.

"So much knowledge...and it's all in here now," he said tenderly, reaching over to gently knock on my forehead. He walked to the window and looked out, pointing down the street to where the lights of his grandparent's house shone in the darkness.

"It's strange to think of you at thirteen, up here in this room reading, while I was just a few blocks away." He hesitated for a moment, carried away, remembering. "That year changed me. I thought about you all the time, had arguments with you in my head, and cursed you when I couldn't read anything without a damn dictionary." We both burst into laughter. After a few seconds he continued. "Sometimes I was angry with you because you made me question what I thought I knew. I started thinking maybe I didn't know anything at all. Half the time I wanted to shake you, the other half I just wanted to be with you, and that made me even angrier. When I left Levan, I swore I wouldn't come back until I could teach you a thing or two or I could prove you wrong, whichever came first."

I remembered what he said to me the night he had made me listen to "Pavane for a Dead Princess." Sadness and regret trickled down my throat and made my stomach turn over. "Now you're here. And here I am. Not quite what you remember." I tried to laugh, but it got caught and sounded more like a hiccup.

He turned from the window, his thumbs hooked in his front pockets, and slowly closed the few steps between us. He gazed down at me intently. I looked down at my hands and then tucked my hair behind my ears. My hair was mostly dry now and curling around my shoulders. I stifled the need to run my fingers through it, and held myself still under his scrutiny.

"No, you're right. You're not the same. Neither am I. You're not thirteen anymore, and I'm not eighteen. It's a damn good thing." He reached for me then, cradling my face in his hands, pulling me to him. Ever so softly, he brushed his lips across mine. Then again. And again. His breath was the barest caress across my sensitive mouth. He never increased the pressure, never stepped any closer. Deep inside my soul I felt something rumble and quake, and I ran my hands up his arms, wrapping them around his wrists where he held my face in his work-roughened palms.

"Will I see you tomorrow?" he whispered, lifting his mouth from mine.

I wanted to exclaim that he would see me more tonight, but bridled my pounding emotions. He seemed to know where he was going, and I had no idea.

"All right," I breathed, and I stepped back from him, trying to retain my dignity. "I'll walk you out."

Just before he descended the stairs, Samuel turned and looked again at my wall. "I remember a few of those words. Some of those words are our words." He looked at me with tenderness.

We walked down the stairs and through the back door. He gathered the big bucket, the bowl, and the towels, putting the now empty water jug inside with everything else. The music had long since ended. We walked around to the front of the house, silent. I wished he wouldn't go.

"Goodnight Josie," Samuel said quietly.

I didn't respond. I thought I might reveal my desperate disappointment that the night was ending. I tried to smile and then turned and began walking back towards the house. I heard a guttural groan behind me. I heard the pail and the silver bowl hit the ground with a jarring twang. When I turned, Samuel was striding towards me, and I gasped at the vehemence in his face. I was suddenly gripped tightly in his arms, the force of his embrace lifting me off my feet. Then Samuel's mouth was on mine, his hands buried in my hair. His lips were demanding, his hands holding my head firmly beneath the onslaught of his kiss. My hands gripped his head in return, fisting in his hair, pulling him into me, feeling his arms around me, holding me to him, breathing him in, triumphant. The kiss was endless and infinitesimal all at once. He pulled his reluctant mouth from my lips and rested his forehead against mine, our combined breath coming in harsh pants. He pulled away just as suddenly as he had embraced me, his hands steadying me. Then he let me go, his eyes on my swollen lips.

"Goodnight, Josie."

"Goodnight Samuel," I whispered. He backed away, black eyes on blue, and then turned and picked up the items he had thrown to the ground. Then he slowly walked home, turning every now and then to watch me watching him. Then I listened to his footsteps fade as he moved beyond where my eyes could follow.

That night I tried to lose myself in Shakespeare and ended up staring at my Wall of Words. The writing had changed over the years from the large, loopy letters with heart-dotted i's, to the neat script of a practiced hand. I quizzed myself absentmindedly, defining every word my eyes focused on.

**fractious**: *tending to be troublesome; hard to handle or control.*
**insipid**: *dull, uninteresting*
**docent**: *teacher, lecturer.*
**immanent:**

My eyes stopped on the word, as a memory resurfaced. I remembered the day, many years ago, that I had discovered its meaning.

Samuel and I had been attacking some of Shakespeare's sonnets for his English homework. I had been reading aloud and had come across the word *immanent*. I stopped, the usage not consistent with the word I thought I knew.

"You know...*imminent,* meaning it's about to happen ...it could happen any minute," Samuel had volunteered.

"I don't think that's it...or it's spelled wrong, if it is. Look up immanent, with an 'a' instead of an 'i' in the middle."

Samuel had sighed and opened up the dictionary, quickly skimming the pages until he found the word. He'd read it to himself and then looked up at me, shaking his head in wonder.

"You were right. It is a different word. You have a good eye...or maybe it's those elfin ears," he said dryly.

Completely aghast, my hands had flown to cover my ears. I had absentmindedly tucked my hair behind my ears as I read, and I anxiously pulled the hair down again so it shielded them. I hated my ears! They weren't big, and they didn't stick out from my head, but they were slightly pointed at the very tips. And to make matters worse, the tips turned out just a bit, giving me the look of one of Santa's holiday helpers. When I was little, my mother had told me they made me look like a wood sprite. My brothers, of course, said they made me look more like a troll, and I had been hiding them ever since.

Samuel must have seen the dismay his words had caused. The blood rushing to my cheeks had made my face pound in concert with my heartbeat. I gripped the book in my lap tightly and asked him what *immanent* meant, eager to distract him from my crimson countenance.

He was quiet for several seconds, holding the dictionary, his eyes cast down. Then he reached up and gently tucked my hair back behind the ear closest to him. I froze, wondering if he was teasing me or poking fun at me.

But when he spoke there was no mischief in his voice. He said, "I like your ears. They make you look like a wise little fairy. Your ears help give you an *immanent* beauty." His words were sincere, and I felt my curiosity peak. My expression must have conveyed my question, for he quickly supplied the answer.

"Immanent: dwelling in nature and the souls of men." His eyes met mine seriously.

After a moment, I slowly raised my hand and tucked back the hair on the other side, uncovering my other ear. I then continued on with the reading and nothing further was said on the topic.

When I got home from school that day, I wrote *immanent* on my wall and looked it up for myself. In addition to the definition Samuel had given me, *immanent* meant having existence only in the mind. I had laughed to myself and decided if the beauty of my ears existed only in Samuel's mind, it was good enough for me.

Smiling, I reached out and touched the word as I let the memory warm me. I was strangely soothed and suddenly very sleepy. I turned to my bed, climbed in, and fell instantly into a heavy and dreamless sleep.

# 17. *Rubato*

SAMUEL WAS WAITING for me in front of my house when I slipped out into the rising sun the next morning for my run. Somehow, I had known he would be. We hadn't arranged it, but there he was. Today he wore sneakers and mesh shorts, his long brown legs muscled and lightly furred with dark hair. He wore another USMC T-shirt in soft grey. It fit snugly, clinging to his V shaped back and narrow torso. Yum. I walked toward him, not quite knowing what to say. Last night's kiss was very fresh in my mind.

"Hi," I said lightly. "Are you coming with me?"

Samuel looked me over silently, his eyes lingering on mine. He was never in a hurry to reply. I had forgotten that about him. He always took his time when he talked, and I tamped down my urge to fill the silence. That was Samuel's way. He might not reply at all. After all, he was obviously coming with me. The question was pretty rhetorical.

"I'm really hoping you'll come with me," he finally said softly, his voice deep and a little rough from sleep, indicating these were probably the first words he had spoken out loud since we'd parted the night before.

It was my turn to study him in silence, not sure what to make of his comment. He met my perusal with steady black eyes. We were quite the pair, standing in the middle of the road, staring at each oth-

235

er for long stretches, not talking. I laughed suddenly at our owlish behavior.

I threw my hands toward the mountains. "Lead on, Super Sam," I said gallantly. "Wherever you want to go, I'll follow."

Samuel's expression lightened at the old nickname, but he didn't smile. "I'm going to hold you to that, Bionic Josie."

Samuel started off at a pretty brisk pace, and I wasn't naive enough to think he was trying to impress me. I knew better. The man was fit, and he knew how to run. I kept up pretty well, finding a rhythm and settling in. We didn't converse at all, just ran in quiet companionship, our feet drumming and our breath echoing the cadence. We ran east a couple of miles, climbing higher and higher as we neared the base of the canyon, until the fat orange sun had shoved off its mountain perch and hovered heavily just above us in the early morning sky. Then we turned, with its rays nudging at our backs, and ran back toward town. We picked up our feet as gravity pulled us forward, gaining speed as we hurtled back down into the valley.

Fall was in the air. The light changes in the autumn. Even at sunrise the angle is different, the intensity softened, muted, like looking through a painting under water. The air was just a few degrees cooler than it had been on previous mornings. I felt a sudden weightlessness, a burst of joy, and I looked at Samuel and let myself smile with it, let it pour out. I felt better than I had in a very long time. I felt whole, I realized. Complete. How was it possible that in two weeks I could undergo this radical shift? Like somehow I had discovered the key to the secret garden, a place that had been there all along, but had become overgrown with neglect. I had unlocked the door and stepped inside, and I was ready to pull weeds and plant roses.

Samuel must have felt it too, because his white teeth flashed back at me as his grin stretched wide in his strong golden face. My eyes lingered on his face appreciatively, and then I turned again to the dusty dirt road in front of me. I knew better than to look away from the road ahead for too long. I ran face first into horse butt when I did that.

As we neared the end of our run, my muscles protested the downshift in speed, having become accustomed to the flying sprint we had maintained for the last mile of the home stretch. I needed to run with Samuel every morning; he made me push myself, big time. No more lazy morning jog for this superhero.

Samuel continued on with me past his grandparents' house, and we slowed to a walk as we arrived at mine. My dad was sitting out on the front porch, feet up on the rail, a Diet Pepsi in his hand. My dad liked his caffeine cold. He called it cheap whiskey and claimed there was nothing better then the burn of that first long pull after he popped the tab. I was my father's daughter, and I couldn't agree more, though I favored Diet Coke.

"Looks like ya got yerself a runnin' partner, Josie Jo," my dad called out in greeting as we walked across the grass toward him. Like every girl does, I felt a flash of relief that my dad seemed fine with the fact that I had male company.

"Morning, Daddy." I leaned over the porch rail and grabbed his drink, stealing a swig of ice-cold fire.

"Sir." Samuel nodded toward my dad and stuck out his hand. My dad's boots fell heavily to the porch as he grasped Samuel's hand in his own.

"I'm glad you've got someone to run with, for the time being at least, huh, Josie? I always worry a little with you running all alone. Even in a little place like Levan, ya just never know."

I shrugged off my dad's worry. On my morning runs I had never seen anything but chipmunks, birds, livestock, and the neighbors I'd known all my life.

"Samuel, come on in and I'll get us something cold to drink, since I'm sure Dad doesn't really want to share." I smiled at my dad, and Samuel followed me, excusing himself with another polite "Sir" to my dad. I liked that.

"The manners, is that a Marine thing?" I said over my shoulder as we walked through the living room into my cheery kitchen. "Water, orange juice, milk, or caffeine?"

"Orange juice. And yeah. Definitely a Marine thing. I couldn't not say "yes ma'am" or "no sir" if my life depended on it. You live around it for ten years, and it becomes pretty ingrained."

I poured Samuel a tall glass of orange juice and handed it to him. Then I gulped down my requisite 8 oz of water before I let myself pop the tab on a cold can of caffeine. We leaned against the counter together, nursing our drinks in thirsty silence.

"So what comes next?" I propped my hip against the counter, turning to face him. "I mean, as far as the Marines?"

"I honestly don't know." Samuel's face was contemplative. "I just got back from Iraq three weeks ago."

"Three weeks?" I yelped, stunned that he had so recently returned. "How long were you there?"

"All told, except for some leave stateside, I've spent almost three years in Iraq. Two twelve month tours, with the last one being extended by six months. It was time to come home, whatever that means."

"Whatever that means?" I repeated, puzzled.

"I didn't really have a home to come home to," Samuel said matter-of-factly. "I have been in the Marine Corp since I was eighteen years old. I did two tours in Afghanistan after 9/11, and then did the two tours in Iraq. When I haven't been deployed, I've either been receiving specialized training, or stationed at Camp Pendleton, or on a ship. Anyway, once I was through debriefment, my platoon was given a month's paid leave. I've stored up more than that in the last ten years; I haven't taken much. I borrowed that truck from a member of my platoon. I don't own any wheels. No house, no wheels, all my possessions fit in a suitcase. Anyway, it's been two weeks since I got here, and I have about two weeks more."

"And then what?" I couldn't imagine going back to Iraq for round three. I was exhausted just listening to him.

"And then I have to decide." Samuel's eyes met mine.

"Decide?"

"Decide whether I want something else." Samuel was being cryptic again.

"You mean, something besides the Marine Corp?"

"Yeah." Samuel set his glass down and pushed away from the counter. "What are you doing today?"

He changed the subject abruptly, as if his future was not something he wanted to discuss, and my brain spun with thoughts of his last ten years, wondering at his experiences, his losses and triumphs, his friendships…his life. Somehow, because his letters had dwindled after boot camp, I had always imagined him in the context of that environment, in the relative safety of a military base with drill instructors watching his every move. In actuality, he had spent most of the last ten years in very hostile environments, in very dangerous places. I shuddered a little bit, and shook my head in wonder. Even when his Grandma Nettie had marveled at his sniper skills and his prowess as an 'assassin,' I had not processed the fact that he had most likely spent the majority of his time as a Marine in different war zones.

"Josie?" Samuel's voice prodded, and I realized he had asked me a question.

"Hmm?" Samuel was looking down at me with one eyebrow peaked, patiently waiting for my response.

"What are you doing today?" he repeated.

I glanced at the clock. "I go into the shop at 11:00, work until 2:30, and then I walk over to the church and teach piano lessons until 7:00ish. What about you?"

"Kick around with my grandpa until you're done at seven-ish." His eyes crinkled a little, hinting at a smile and softening his assumption that I would be at his disposal as soon as lessons were over. My heart skipped wildly, and I resisted the urge to glance down at my chest to see if the skipping was noticeable under my thin shirt.

The back door off the kitchen swung open, and I jumped guiltily, although Samuel stood several feet away. My dad stuck his white head around the door frame, standing a few steps down on the back stoop. "Hey, Jos?"

"Yeah, Dad?"

"I don't think I told you, me 'n Jacob are headin' out to the Book Cliffs this weekend. Jacob drew out a tag in the bow-hunt out there. We've got some days comin' now that shut-downs are done at the plant, so we're gonna take the trailer and the horses and go see if we can get us an elk."

The Book Cliffs were in Moab, about five hours southeast of Levan. They were named the Book Cliffs because that's what the mountains looked like, books lined up in a bookshelf. It was breathtaking country, and every hunting tag in that area was hard to come by and highly coveted. The only thing my dad liked as well as horses was hunting, and I knew he must be tickled pink about Jacob drawing out.

"Are Jared and Johnny going too?"

"Jared hasn't been given permission," my dad grumbled, referring to Tonya's position as head of the household. "Johnny's afraid to leave with the twins being so close to comin', so it's just Jake and me. I think Marv might come with us, though." Marv was Jacob's father-in-law. Marv didn't miss many hunts, either.

"When are you leaving?"

"I'm thinking we'll head out later on today and probably be gone til' next Thursdee or Fridee," my dad hemmed and hawed, as if I would complain about him being gone the six or seven days he was suggesting.

"Sounds fun." I shrugged.

"You can come," my dad offered insincerely.

"Ha, ha, ha, Daddy," I said sarcastically. "Now what if I said I wanted to, what would you do? Whose bed in the trailer would I take?" I laughed at his chagrined expression. I walked to him and kissed his scratchy cheek. "No thank you, but have a lovely time. And thank you for giving me the heads up. Actually, while you're

240

gone, I think I will play the piano until all hours of the night and eat chocolate cake for every meal," I teased.

My dad eyed me soberly for a moment. "That'd be real nice, Jos. It's been a while since I've heard you play. Maybe you could play a little somethin' for me when I get back; I sure do miss it." He said the words softly, searching my face as he spoke them. I flushed, realizing Samuel was hearing the exchange.

"It's a date, Dad," I said lightly, patting his cheek and turning from him.

I expected Samuel to comment on my dad's request, but he let it rest, kneeling to greet Yazzie as he lumbered into the kitchen from his bed in the washroom. Yazzie didn't sleep in my room anymore. He was ten years old, an old-timer in dog years, and he didn't like climbing stairs, although every once in a while I would wake with him sprawled across my feet. I think sometimes he missed the old days. I missed them too, although on his rare visits I awoke to no feeling in my legs and feet.

"Hey Samuel," my dad swung his gaze to where Samuel crouched. "You're welcome to come along. I wouldn't mind seein' some real shootin.' We got room for one more man." My dad glanced at me apologetically as he clarified "one more man." Apparently, my dad had learned a little something about Samuel's expertise at the barbeque on Sunday.

"No thank you, Sir," Samuel said politely. "I've done all the hunting I want to do for a while." A flicker of embarrassment crossed Samuel's face as if he had spoken without thinking.

My dad grinned as if Samuel had said something funny and ducked his head back around the corner without further comment, the screen door banging behind him.

"Hey, boy." Samuel didn't do the baby talk thing when he talked to Yazzie. His voice was mild and low, and he spent another minute scratching and stroking the big dog. Yazzie yawned widely, leaning into Samuel's big hands, his eyes rolling back in his noble head and his tongue hanging out in sheer delight.

Eventually, Samuel looked up at me and said simply, "I'll see you later."

Yazzie and I followed him to the front door. Samuel waved a hand and stepped outside, striding across the lawn and up the street toward his grandparents' house. Yazzie and I watched him forlornly, identical expressions on our mugs.

"Oh for goodness sake!" I laughed, looking down at Yazzie. Yazzie ruffed back at me, as if to say "look who's talking," before he shuffled away to find breakfast.

Samuel must have tested all the doors and found the one that was unlocked, because he was waiting outside the church's little side entrance when I walked my last student out to her bike. I was ridiculously glad that I didn't have to make friendly small talk with a waiting parent. Or introduce Samuel. I'd had some well-meaning friends try to fix me up in the last few years, and I had had to get downright obstinate with a few folks who just couldn't stop playing matchmaker. I had refused every date they had arranged. Imagine how the tongues would wag when I was seen with Samuel. All bets would be off, and I would have no excuse. I would be lined up with every cousin, brother, and sister's roommate's uncle from now 'til Christmas. I shuddered at the thought.

Samuel walked toward me as little Jessie Ann Wood pedaled away. I double-checked to make sure I had gotten the light and pulled the door closed, sliding the key into the lock.

"That's your bike, isn't it?" Samuel halted beside me, nodding his head toward my old-fashioned bike leaning up against the side of the church. I felt goose bumps dance up my arms. He didn't invade my space or reach out and touch me, and I wondered if the kisses last night had been a fluke, an impulse brought on by too much moonlight and sweet remember-whens.

"Yes. I rode this morning. It was easier than walking. My legs are shot from our run. I'm not used to running that fast. You've pushed me hard twice this week, and my legs are like jello." I smiled up at him wryly.

"In that case, I know just what you need."

Samuel picked up my bike and began walking toward his borrowed black pick-up, lifting it up and setting it in the bed of the truck.

"What do I need?"

"You'll see. Are you hungry?"

"Always," I admitted honestly, and Samuel looked at me and chuckled. "Well let's go put a little meat on those bones."

He opened the door, and I stepped up into the passenger side, smoothing my violet skirt around my legs as I sat. Samuel reached out and fingered the crinkly material gently. "You wear skirts a lot. I like that. You don't see a lot of women who enjoy being feminine. It's nice." His hand dropped from my skirt and shut the door before I could respond with more than a smile.

Samuel climbed in and turned the key. Immediately the sounds of Tchaikovsky's "Octobre—Chant D'Autumne" slid into the space around us. I forced myself to relax into the leather seat, hearing the music and letting it in. We drove for a few minutes, listening, before Samuel spoke.

"In Iraq it's hot more often than not, and the sand is this constant presence. I used to dream of Autumn, of the cool mornings with my grandmother herding sheep away from home, waking before the sun rose and actually being chilled, sitting by the campfire and eating jerky and cornmeal cakes and Navajo tea."

"Is that why you're listening to 'The Autumn Song'?" I smiled.

"Exactly."

"Tchaikovsky was paid to create a short piece for each month of the year. He named the entire work "The Seasons." He had to have an assistant remind him when it was time to write another 'month.'

He joked that there are two kinds of inspiration: one that comes from the heart, and one that comes from necessity and several hundred rubles."

"She's ba-ack," Samuel said under his breath in a sing-song voice, and I giggled like a little kid.

"I used to play 'Octobre', " I sighed dreamily. "It always made me think of fall, too." I shifted my attention back to Samuel, "I could feel it in the air this morning when we ran."

"Is that why your face lit up, and you smiled that great big smile? You looked like you were about ready to take flight. I thought I was going to have to hold onto you to keep you with me," Samuel teased, his eyes touching mine briefly.

"I'm always pretty eager for autumn to get here." I tried to be matter-of-fact as I confessed the reason why. "Both Kasey and my mom died when summer was just beginning…and I guess summer brings back bad memories. I'm always glad when it's over." I twiddled my thumbs uncomfortably in my lap. "Fall has always felt like a chance to start over. I know nature hasn't designed it that way, that it's actually the opposite. The leaves fall off the trees, the flowers die, and winter rolls in…but I love it all the same."

"What happened to Kasey?" Samuel was very still, his eyes moving from me to the road and back again.

"You don't mince words, do you?" I murmured, tucking a stray curl behind my ear.

"My Grandma Yazzie says it's the Navajo way not to hurry. We have all the time in the world. We move deliberately, take our time, and do things precisely. Life is all about harmony and balance. It's probably the reason I'm a good sniper. I can outwait anybody. But I don't feel like I have all the time in the world anymore, not now. I don't want to waste any of the time I have with you." Samuel's expression was unflinching, and I flushed at his bluntness.

"He rolled his car not too far from here," I pointed out my window, at the long narrow highway we were driving on, "He had just dropped me off. It was the morning after we graduated from high school."

Samuel remained silent, waiting for me to continue.

"I used to marvel at the irony that I had wanted him to spend an extra twenty minutes with me that morning, taking me home, instead of remaining in Nephi like he'd planned. I had another ride, you know. He never would have been driving back into Nephi at all if it weren't for me. I traded an extra twenty minutes with him for a life-time. Ironic, isn't it?"

"Have you ever thought that he might have rolled the car there in Nephi just as easily, and if he hadn't taken you home you wouldn't have had even those last twenty minutes? There are many ways to die, Josie. You didn't necessarily place him in death's only path." Samuel's voice and face were blank, like he was discussing the height of the wheat in the fields we drove past or the way the mountains in front of us looked purple beneath the sky.

"There was a guy I served with in Iraq. His mom didn't want him to go; she was scared to death of him going. Of course, he went anyway. He'd signed up for it, and he went. His younger brother, who still lived at home, was killed in a car accident while he was gone. My friend came home from Iraq without a scratch. That's iro-ny."

I didn't know how to respond, so I didn't respond at all. I knew the truth of what Samuel said, but sometimes a little guilt was a good distraction from sorrow. The sorrow had faded through the years, but somehow the guilt remained.

We rolled into Nephi, and I wondered if Samuel would pull into Mickelson's Family Restaurant. It had good food and it sat at the edge of town by the freeway off-ramp, making it accessible to thru-traffic and town's folk alike. I wondered if I would see anybody I knew inside, someone who would come up and get the scoop and an introduction on the pretense of giving two hoots about how I was doing. I hated making small talk and avoided people in the grocery store and other places just so that I wouldn't have to think of things to say. I liked people, I cared about them, and I wanted to be a good person, but don't make me chat idly on the telephone or make pleasant conversation just for the sake of being polite. We neared the restaurant and Samuel kept driving. I breathed a little easier and wondered aloud where he was taking me.

"My grandpa told me an interesting story about a pond in this area. I thought we'd have a picnic. Grandma Nettie packed it, so it should be full of good stuff."

"Burraston's Pond?"

"That's the one."

Thoughts of Kasey filled my head. He and his friends would swing out of a huge tree and into the pond. Some of the branches extended far out over the water. Some kids had built a rickety platform high up in the same tree to jump from. The platform was about two feet by two feet, and it was a wonder nobody had been killed. They had never been able to talk me up into the tree. I was way too sensible. So, with my heart in my throat, I had watched them climb high into the uppermost branches, steady themselves on the little platform, and then hurl themselves out and over the water, screaming with terror and delight.

We took the old Mona road, and at the turnoff to the pond, veered west on the dirt road pocked with deep grooves and tire tracks. Since school was back in session the campsite was empty, and the little lake was completely void of people and boats. There was no wind, and the setting sun shimmered on the still water, coloring the water a deep amber edged in ebony shadows. I hadn't been to Burraston's since before Kasey had died, but felt no overpowering melancholy at returning. This had been a hangout, a place to play, and except for sharing our first kiss here, it was not a spot I was especially nostalgic about.

Looking at it now, I realized how lovely it was. Quiet and abandoned, it seemed to bloom in its solitude. We bounced over the bumpy road and took the fork that took us up and around the pond.

"Where's the best spot?" Samuel looked to me for guidance.

Burraston's Pond was actually Burraston's Ponds, with a few

little water holes that broke off the biggest part.

"Keep going around until we're on the furthest side of the main pond." Trees were thick in some spots, sparse and others, and I directed him to the famous big tree overlooking the water. Samuel pulled off the dusty road and grabbed a coarse blanket and a little cooler from the back of the truck as I climbed out and gingerly made my way down to a little clearing at the water's edge where I thought we could picnic.

The silence was broken only by the crickets warming up for their evening symphony and an occasional buzz of a mosquito flitting over the water. I had never been to Burraston's when it was deserted. It was not surprising to me that I liked it much better this way. Samuel spread the blanket out, and we sat watching the water lap up against the rocks and twigs that littered the shore at the base of the big tree.

"So what's the story your grandpa told you?" I leaned back against the blanket, propping my head in one hand and looking up at him.

"It wasn't about the pond, I guess. It's more about the town. I didn't ever come to Mona when I lived here. I never had reason to. So when I asked my grandpa if there were any good fishing spots around here, and he mentioned this pond, I asked him about the town. He said Burl Ives, the singer, was once thrown in jail here in Mona. It was before his time, but he thought it was a funny story."

"I've never heard about that!"

"It was the 1940's, and Burl Ives traveled around singing. I guess the authorities didn't like one of his songs. They thought it was bawdy, so they put him in jail."

"What was the song?" I snickered.

"It was called 'Foggy, Foggy Dew.' My grandpa sang it for me."

"Let's hear it!" I challenged.

"It's far too lewd." Samuel pulled his mouth into a serious frown, but his eyes twinkled sardonically. "All right you've convinced me," he said without me begging at all, and we laughed together. He cleared his throat and began to sing, with a touch of an Irish lilt, about a bachelor living all alone whose only sin had been to try to protect a fair young maiden from the foggy, foggy dew.

> *One night she came to my bedside*
> *When I was fast asleep.*
> *She laid her head upon my bed*
> *And she began to weep*
> *She sighed, she cried, she damn near died*
> *She said what shall I do?*
> *So I hauled her into bed and covered up her head*
> *Just to keep her from the foggy, foggy dew.*

"Oh my!" I laughed, covering my mouth. "I don't think I would have stuck Burl Ives in jail for that, but it is pretty funny,"

"Marines are the lewdest, crudest, foulest talking bunch you'll ever find, and that song isn't lewd. I've sung much, much worse. I tried to remain chaste and virtuous, and I still have the nickname Preacher after all these years, but I have been somewhat corrupted." He waggled his eyebrows at his ribaldry.

"I kind of liked that song…" I mused, half kidding. "Sing something else but without the Irish."

"Without the Irish? That's the best part." Samuel smiled crookedly. "I had a member of my platoon whose mom was born and raised in Ireland. This guy could do an authentic Irish accent, and man, could he sing. When he sang 'Danny Boy' everybody cried. All these tough, lethal Marines, bawling like babies. He sang this one song called 'An Irish Lament' that I loved so much I memorized it. In fact, when I saw you in the rain a couple weeks ago, it was the first thing that came to my mind." The smile had gone out of Samuel's expression, and his eyes narrowed on my face. His moods were so mercurial, I found myself challenged to keep pace with him. There was now intensity in his gaze where moments before he'd been singing a bawdy tune in a borrowed brogue.

I stared back, trying to wait him out. After a few moments I caved.

"You aren't going to sing me "An Irish Lament," are you?"

"It depends," he countered.

"On what?"

"On whether you will play for me when I take you home to-night."

It was my turn to become moody. I was not blind to my feelings for Samuel. Where this would all lead, and whether either of us could or wanted to go there was what had me digging in my emotional heels. I knew the incredible power of music and the mood it could set. Exhibit A: the kisses we had shared the night before after Debussy wove his spell. I didn't trust myself with a large helping of Samuel sprinkled with symphonies. I didn't know if my heart could take another love lost.

"I think the 'Irish Lament' might scare you away." The sun had lowered itself discreetly behind the western hills. Samuel's voice was as smooth and quiet as the deepening shadows around us.

"Maybe so..." I avoided his gaze and reached for Nettie's basket, needing sustenance to keep my wits with Samuel.

Nettie had packed thick turkey sandwiches on homemade bread, chocolate chip cookies, and thankfully no lemon squares. She'd included a few peaches from her big tree, and Samuel had added a couple Diet Cokes and a bottle of water. We dug in without further discussion, except for an occasional moan from me.

"Everything okay?" Samuel smiled after a particularly gusty sigh.

"Food just tastes so much better when I didn't prepare it."

"You're a great cook."

"Yes I am," I agreed without artifice, "but there's something about having someone make you a sandwich. It just tastes better; I can't describe it."

"Being a Marine has given me a new appreciation for making

my own dinner. Chow hall isn't so bad when it's available, but boxed lunches, no thank you. At boot camp we used to call them boxed nasties. I prefer to know what's in my food, and the only way that happens is if I make it myself."

"Have you become a control freak, Samuel?" I teased, biting into my peach.

"Hmmm. Yeah, I guess I have." Samuel looked off across the inky water. "When you realize there's so much you can't control, you get pretty stingy with what you can."

We finished off our meal in silence as the shadows grew and grew and eventually touched, crowding out the light, until all traces of the sun were banished, and the stars began to glimmer overhead.

"I can't believe I'm here," Samuel sighed, his arms crossed beneath his head, his long frame stretched out on the scratchy army blanket.

"Why?"

"A month ago I was in Iraq. Suited up day in and day out, camo, boots, flak jacket, glasses, helmet. And I never, ever, went anywhere without my weapon and plenty of ammo strapped on me. This feels surreal." He paused for a few seconds. "Let's go swimming."

"What?" I laughed, and then choked as my laughter caused me to inhale some of the juice from the peach I had been enjoying.

"I want to swim. Look how the stars reflect on the water. It almost looks like we're looking down into space."

"You should see it from up in the tree," I said without thinking, and wished suddenly I hadn't suggested it.

"Really?" Samuel eyed the big tree speculatively. Instantly, he started shucking off his boots and undoing his pants.

"Samuel!" I felt heat flood me, and I wasn't sure if it was embarrassment or a genuine curiosity about what I was about to see.

"I'm going to climb the tree and jump off into the water."

I sighed. It must be a man thing. Why did every guy I knew feel compelled to climb that tree and jump?

"Come with me, Josie." Samuel narrowed his eyes at me, holding his shirt in his hands. His chest was broad and well-defined, his shoulders and arms corded with muscle, his abs rippled down into his boxer shorts. I looked down at my hands as I spoke so I wouldn't gawk.

"Uh-uh. The farthest I've ever gotten was a few branches up, just so I could see the effect of the stars reflecting on the water."

"This morning you said you would follow me wherever I went." His voice was cajoling and light. "Please?"

I was wearing a black tank, and I supposed my black panties combined with my tank top would be as modest as a swimsuit. I didn't let myself think about it too long. I had always been too practical, too sensible, too boring for my own good. I was going swimming. I slid my skirt down my thighs, stepping out of it and my sandals. I reminded myself to breathe. I looked at Samuel and squared my shoulders as if I did this sort of thing every day.

"If I fall and kill myself you're going to be very sad," I said, trying to be brave.

As if sensing my discomfort, Samuel's eyes didn't linger on my scantily clad form. He turned and hoisted himself up into the tree like it was as simple as climbing a few stairs. I cringed, thinking about how in the world I was going to get up there and retain any dignity. He stood in the broad base, where the branches spread and lifted away from the trunk. He leaned down toward me, extending a long brown arm.

"Grab my arm at the elbow and I'll pull you up."

I did just as he asked, wrapping both of my hands just below his bicep. He leaned down, wrapped his left hand around my upper arm and, holding onto a thick tree branch above him with his right arm, began pulling me easily up the tree. I marched my legs right up the trunk and was quickly standing balanced beside him, easy as you please. I felt like Shera, Queen of the Jungle, HeMan's female counterpart. "Wow," I breathed and then giggled like a little girl.

"There's a little platform up there, see it?"

"Oh yes," I groaned, "I know all about the platform. Please

don't make me jump from there."

"Let me check it out." Samuel was monkeying up the tree before I could protest.

"It seems pretty solid," he called down several moments later. It was solid. It had been there for at least a few generations of dare devils. I sighed dejectedly. I was going to have to climb up there and jump with him. It was too late to back out now.

"Come on, I'll guide you up."

I knew I was going to fall out of the tree. Girls as athletically challenged as I was should never climb trees. At the very least, I was going to snag my underwear on a branch and be stuck wearing only a tank top high up in the tree. I shuddered in horror. I was NOT that kind of girl. I had a decent rear end, but I don't think anyone's butt looks good climbing trees. At the very worst, I would impale myself on a sharp branch like a pig on a spit. Knowing me, both would happen, and I would soon be pantiless and impaled. I could just see the story in the local newspaper: "Local Woman Found Dead and Half Naked in Tree."

I focused intently on placing my feet and hands where Samuel instructed and amazingly, I eventually climbed close enough for him to reach down and loop his arm around my waist. He pulled me up next to him on the narrow section of plywood that was wedged and nailed into the wide reinforcement of crisscrossing branches. The view below was truly breathtaking…and terrifying. The black bottom of the pond created an illusion of endless sky below us. The glassy surface reflected the brilliant stars in the firmament above, and it seemed as if we stood on the precipice of a miniature galaxy.

"Oh, dear God," I whispered, panic flooding my heart with ice.

"It's beautiful," Samuel whispered too, only his voice was filled with awe.

I squeezed my eyes shut and clung to his arm, which he had kept braced around me.

"Are you ready? Here we go, on three…"

"No!" I yelped emphatically. "Not yet! I'm not ready!"

Samuel snickered softly, but I was too afraid to slap him.

My eyes were shut so tightly, I was giving myself a headache, my face scrunched up in denial of what I had gotten myself into.

I felt Samuel's arm pull me against him, and then I felt his breath against my mouth. He smelled like peaches and pine, and I breathed in, relaxing my face, tipping my chin toward him as his mouth came down over mine. And I completely forgot to be afraid. Tipsily, I wound my arms around his brawny shoulder, winding my fingers up into the silky pelt of his closely cut hair. He pulled me in even more tightly, lifting my feet off of the platform, and then, with no warning, Samuel pushed off the platform with a powerful thrust, and we were air born. I was falling….and screaming, and falling. Just before we hit the surface, Samuel released me, untangling himself from my limbs as we shot through the black, star-filled water.

Instinct took over as I kicked my legs wildly and swam upwards, or what I thought was upward. I felt Samuel beside me, and he reached for my flailing hand and dragged me up with him, our heads breaking the surface together. I gasped, spitting pond out of my mouth and sweeping my streaming hair out of my face as my legs tread water furiously to keep me afloat.

"Don't ever do that again!!"

"What? Kiss you, or kiss you while we're jumping out of a tree?" Samuel practically drawled the words, they were so slow and mild. He wasn't breathing hard at all; in fact, he laid his head back in the water and barely seemed to be working at keeping himself afloat.

"Ugh!" I huffed, completely disgusted. "I feel tricked! You didn't want to kiss me! You just wanted to get me out of the tree!"

"Oh, I wanted to kiss you." The drawl was even more pronounced. "I just killed two birds with one stone." He lifted his head up off the water and grinned at me, his teeth flashing, and I was dazzled. So much so, that I stopped kicking and my head sunk beneath the water like a stone. I splashed wildly and popped up, spitting and swiping at my hair again.

"Lean back, Josie," Samuel commanded, the words gentle and

coaxing as he slid up beside me. "Kick your legs out in front of you and float on your back. Quit fighting. Floating's easy."

"Ha!" I grumped. "I knew how to swim when you were still wearing floaties in the high school pool!" I wasn't done being mad at him.

"Very funny," he chuckled warmly.

I did as he instructed, spreading my arms and legs wide like I was making a snow angel, my head back and my face peeking just above the surface. The stars twinkled down at me sweetly.

"There you go." Samuel spread out beside me, his fingers brushing mine as we bobbed on the placid pond. My anger slipped away as I exhaled lightly, not wanting to upset my precarious relationship with the water.

"Do you see the Milky Way?" Samuel reached his arm up and pointed.

"Uh-huh."

"My grandmother says the Milky Way is a pathway for the spirits leaving the earth and ascending into heaven. Navajo legend says the Milky Way was created when Coyote, the trickster, got impatient as First Woman was trying to arrange the constellations in the sky. First Woman made a constellation for almost every bird, every animal, and even every insect. She made a constellation for *Atsá* the eagle, and *Ma'iitsoh*, the wolf. She created a lark, *Tsídiiłtsoí*, so he could sing a song to the sun every morning. She even made *Dahsání*, the porcupine, who was in charge of growing all the trees on the mountains. First woman laid each star in a pattern out on a blanket before she had Fire Man carry them to the sky and touch them with his fire torch to make them shine. Coyote wanted to help, but First Woman told him he would only make trouble. Finally, there were just small chips and star dust remaining on the blanket. Coyote was impatient, and he grabbed the blanket and swung it up into the air, spreading the star dust into the sky creating the *Yíkaisdahí*—the Milky Way."

"Is there a Navajo name for all the constellations?" I stared up, trying to pick out the few I knew.

"Yes. My grandmother could tell you the story of every one of them, why First Woman placed them where she did, and how they were named. Grandma says the laws of our people are written in the stars. She says First Woman put them there because, unlike the sands that blow away or the waters that flow and shift, the sky is constant. That's the great thing about the sky. It's the same in the waters off of the coast of Australia as it is right here at Burraston's pond. When I was stationed on the U.S.S. Peleliu the first couple years I was in the Marine Corp, I would often climb up to a little upper deck where I could see the sky, and I would name as many of the stars and constellations as I could. It made me feel like I was right there with my grandmother, sleeping under the stars, listening to the sheep."

We were slowly being rocked toward the shore, and I scissored my legs downward, finding that I could stand, the water reaching just below my shoulders. The water felt comparatively warm to the air, and I was in no hurry to get out. Samuel remained on his back, staring up into the heavens. I thought of him, in the middle of the ocean, searching the firmament, comforting himself with thoughts of the only home he'd really known. My heart ached for him.

"I like being alone, but I hate being lonely. That sounds pretty lonely. At times like those did you ever regret becoming a Marine?" I ventured, studying Samuel's chiseled profile.

"No. I never did." Samuel's voice was low and sincere. "I'd do it all again in a heartbeat. I had nowhere else to go. I found purpose, discovered I was of use, made some damn good friends, lost my self-pity. I did my best to be a man you could be proud of."

I forgot to breathe. Samuel never gave me time to shore up my defenses; he just said the darndest things right out of the blue.

"Me?" My tone reflected my own feelings of inadequacy. I didn't want to be the yardstick of righteousness; I was too lacking.

Samuel dropped his legs and stood, the water lapping around his torso.

"Yes you." Samuel's reply was contemplative, and he kept his face turned away from me. "You were the bar I measured everything by." Samuel paused, caught between what he'd said and what he was about to say. His voice was low and solemn when he spoke his next words. "I wasn't sure what you would think the first time I actually had to pull the trigger and take someone's life, and how you would feel if you knew about all the lives I've ended since."

His words were so unexpected that I gasped, and his eyes flew to mine, glittering with sudden intensity. He didn't speak for a moment, his jaw working, clenching, as if he were swallowing the words that he still needed to say.

He turned and waded to the shore, water sluicing off his powerful back and thighs as he climbed out. He shook himself violently, and then picked up his clothes, pulling his shirt over his head and shoving his legs into his jeans.

His back was to me, and I rose up out of the water behind him, uncertain of what he needed from me, but certain he needed something other than my censure, although censure was never what I had intended to communicate. He had just caught me by surprise.

I climbed out of the pond, dripping and shaking, and ran my hands down my legs, removing the excess water, wringing out my hair and my tank top as I pulled my skirt on over my shivering body. I wrapped my arms around myself, both for modesty and for warmth. Samuel picked up the abandoned picnic, stacking everything in the cooler and picking up the blanket. He handed the blanket to me and turned from me again as I wrapped it gratefully around my shoulders. He walked back toward the shore, squatting down beside the shallow pool, and trailing his hand across the silvery water.

My voice sounded uncertain as I spoke. "Samuel. It's war. I wouldn't condemn you for defending yourself." I didn't approach him, but waited.

He was silent for several seconds before he answered. "I've killed some men in firefights...but many of the men I've killed, Josie...they didn't even know I was there. That's when pulling the trigger is the hardest. I would watch them through my rifle scope, sometimes for days on end, and when the moment was right and I got the order...I would shoot." He made no excuses, and there wasn't sorrow or regret in his voice. But there was vulnerability. He wanted me to know.

I walked to the water's edge and knelt next to him, reaching my hand out as he had, feeling the cold silk of the water kiss my palms. I brushed the tips of my fingers against his hand, wondering if he would pull away. In the bruised darkness my skin shone pale against the starlit surface. I laid my hand on top of his, twining my fingers through his fingers, light on dark. I watched him as he turned his face toward me, his expression full of question. I leaned into him, my eyes on his, and answered in the only way I knew he would really hear me.

I brushed my lips gently across his, the way he had done after he had washed my hair the night before. Only this time, I stared into his eyes, black pools reflecting the water we knelt beside. I heard his swift intake of breath, but other than the clenching of his hand in mine, he held himself completely still as my lips played softly over his. Still, I didn't close my eyes but watched him, silently soothing him.

"Do you really believe what you do in the service of your country, for the men you fight beside, is something you need to explain to me?" My voice was just above a whisper, my face a breath from his. "You think you have to justify yourself to me? Me? Someone who's never had to march umpteen miles with one hundred and fifty pounds on her back, or been shot at, or gone days on no sleep? Someone who hasn't spent the last ten years in harsh conditions, with few comforts, someone who's never been asked to do incredibly difficult things to keep people safe?" I kissed him again, the tips of my wet fingers resting lightly on his jaw. "Where would we all be without people like you?"

Samuel's eyes shone down at me, emotion tightening the corners of his mouth. And still he made no move to kiss me in return.

"Do you remember what God told David? How He said David

had too much blood on his hands?" Samuel's voice was a hoarse whisper.

"No. Remind me." I remembered the story of David, of his lust for Bathsheba, his plot to murder her husband, and subsequently the death of their child. The Bible was full of such stories. Anyone who said it was boring hadn't read past Genesis.

"God told David he couldn't build the temple because he had too much blood on his hands. He allowed him to gather the materials for the temple, but God commanded David's son Solomon to actually build it."

"I don't understand what you are trying to say to me, Samuel. Do you think you have too much blood on your hands? That you've fallen from grace?"

Samuel simply stared down at me.

I floundered, not following his line of thinking at all. "David caused the death of Uriah, Bathsheba's husband, because Bathsheba was pregnant with David's child, and David wanted her for himself. Maybe *that* is the blood that is referred to, the blood God couldn't overlook. Not the blood of those that David had commanded in war, or killed in battle."

"Am I really so different?"

"Samuel! I don't understand how you can equate yourself with David. Even so, David died in God's good graces. We have the book of Psalms to prove he was favored by God." I was truly befuddled. Samuel's silence lasted several minutes this time. I was getting better at waiting him out. When he spoke, the subject had seemingly changed, and I mentally cart-wheeled to catch up.

"I got a letter from my Grandma Nettie when you got engaged, Josie. She thought I would remember you. She mentioned it kind of in passing." Samuel paused.

"I remember where I was when I read that letter, where I was sitting, what I had been doing in the moments leading up to it. I was completely leveled by the news, to say the least. I had been gone for almost five years; I hadn't seen you for more than two. You were still so young, and I thought I had time. You see, in my mind, I always kept track. I would mark time with your birthdays. Josie is sixteen—but I'm twenty-one. Josie is seventeen, still too young. Then out of the blue, this kid came in and snatched you up, and you were suddenly taken."

I stared at Samuel, my mouth hanging open, completely undone by what he had revealed. Samuel expelled a short, harsh laugh at my stunned reaction, and suddenly his wet hands gripped my shoulders, and he rose to his feet, pulling me with him.

"I didn't know who Kasey was. My grandma mentioned his name and said that he was a nice local kid. I just remember how angry I was and how much I wanted to hunt him down. I had another two years on my contract with the Marines, but all I wanted to do was come to Levan and kill him and plead my case to you. I wanted to beg you not to marry him. I even wrote a letter to you telling you to wait for me."

"I never got a letter." My lungs were burning. I realized I was holding my breath.

"I never sent it. I couldn't. I had absolutely no right."

Samuel suddenly held my face in his hands. They were cold and still a bit wet from the water. I shivered as his eyes burned holes down into mine. "A few months after that, my grandma sent me a letter telling me Kasey had been killed. I felt sick, because in my heart of hearts I had wished it. I had wanted him gone. So am I really so different than David?"

I couldn't answer immediately. My head was spinning with the passion in his voice and the intensity in his eyes. He interpreted my stunned silence as censure once more, and he dropped his hands from my face. "I'm sorry, Josie. I had no intention of telling you any of this. But I just couldn't let you kiss me and comfort me, and let you tell me what a good man I am, without telling you everything. And the worst part is…I'm *glad* he's gone. I'm not glad he's dead. I don't wish that. But yes, I'm glad he's gone. And I don't know what kind of man that makes me."

"I guess it makes you an honest one," I whispered, finally finding my voice, unsure of what to say beyond that. He stared at me intently, and I met his gaze without blinking. "I never would have guessed you would have reacted like that...that you even thought of me after you left. I didn't know you...you cared," I finished ineptly, unable to communicate the awe I was feeling at his confession.

"I did, and I do," Samuel responded flatly. His mouth was drawn into a tight line, his eyes on mine. I exhaled slowly, feeling faint. The water from my dripping hair found its way down my back, and I shivered violently. Samuel reached down and took my hand, and we walked back to the truck, the blanket trailing behind me. He stooped and picked up the cooler and set it in the back as he opened my door and helped me in.

With the heater on full blast, we drove back toward Levan. Music tinkled softly from the speakers, and I heard a hint of Rachmaninoff's "Elegie." I had always loved this piece. Rachmaninoff was considered one of the finest pianists of his day. Sonja had a live recording of him playing "Elegie", and it had brought me to tears when I had first heard it. It had been many years since I had enjoyed the expressive breadth and the rich lyricism in his piece. Hesitantly, I reached up and slid the volume louder, allowing the music to fill the cab and reverberate off the glass.

"This is my favorite piece of music, by my favorite composer." Samuel's voice broke through as the music slowed and sighed.

"You always did love Rachmaninoff." I remembered the first time he had heard Rachmaninoff on the bus and his reaction to the power and the intensity of "Prelude in C Sharp Minor."

"Rachmaninoff was the last of the great Romanticists in classical music," I mused. "He was often discouraged by the modernist music that was becoming popular. Once, in an interview, he said that the modern music of the new composers was written more in the head than the heart. Their music contained too much thought and no feeling. He said the modern composers 'think and reason and analyze and brood, but they do not exalt.'" I held up my fingers and wiggled them to indicate quotation marks.

"I looked up the word exalt in the dictionary when Sonja made me memorize his quote. The meaning I liked best was to 'make sublime, to magnify, to praise, to extol.' Rachmaninoff's music raises us up, it elevates."

"I love 'Elegie' because it is what yearning sounds like." Samuel stared ahead as he spoke.

I stared at Samuel for a moment, moved by the simplicity of his description. "I think 'Elegie' actually means lament. Some say Rachmaninoff was depressed when he wrote it, but there's such pronounced hope woven throughout the piece that I tend to think, in spite of his suggested moroseness, 'Elegie' wasn't an expression of defeat. He was just...yearning." I smiled at him slightly as I echoed his simple synopsis. "He considered quitting early on in his career. His philosophy was one rooted in spiritualism. He wanted to create beauty and truth in his music, and he felt like his music didn't belong. It's ironic that he gave his last major interview in 1941, when the world was at war. The world needed truth and beauty then more than ever."

We drove through Nephi and out onto the long ridge connecting the small towns. Soon, the lights of Levan twinkled before us, and we pulled into the sleepy little town, turning on to a pot-holed side street, driving past the bar and the old church before heading up the dimly lit street toward home.

We crunched over the gravel in front of my house. It was dark and empty, my dad long gone on his way to Moab and the beckoning Book Cliffs.

"Would you like to come in for a minute? You could check the house for bad guys, and I could make us something yummy to eat. I think I have ice cream in the freezer and I could make us some hot fudge topping to put on top?" I waggled my eyebrows at him in the dim interior of the truck, and he smiled a little.

"Bad guys?"

"Oh you know, I'm here all alone, the house is dark. Just look under the beds and make sure no one is hiding in my closet."

"Are you afraid to be alone at night?" His brows were lowered with concern over his black eyes.

"Nope. I just wanted to give you a reason to come inside."

His expression cleared, and his voice lowered even further. "Aren't you reason enough?"

I felt the heat rise in my face. "Um," was all I said.

"Josie."

"Yes?"

"I would love to come in."

We climbed out and walked inside. I flipped on the lights and excused myself for a minute. I ran upstairs to my little attic room and pulled off my wet clothes. I ran around looking for something to wear Sweats? No. Pajamas? No! I settled on a loose pink sundress and ran my fingers through my damp ringlets. My hair smelled a little like pond water…ugh! I spritzed myself with lavender and pulled my hair up into a clip, not wanting to look like I was trying too hard. I left my feet bare and ran back downstairs. My feet got a little tangled up, and I came hurtling off the last stair into the washroom like a bat out of hell. I steadied myself on the dryer and took a deep breath. "Geez! Calm down, woman!" I told myself sternly. When Samuel was around I seemed to be one frazzled bundle of gooseflesh and hormones. "That's just what we need, fall down the stairs and spend the rest of the time Samuel has in Levan on crutches," I muttered.

I walked into the kitchen where I'd left Samuel a few minutes before. I gathered the butter, evaporated milk, sugar, vanilla, and cocoa powder as we chatted about this and that. Soon the smell of hot fudge sauce wafted through the kitchen, and I sighed in contentment. Grabbing a couple bowls, I scooped up two large servings of cookie dough ice cream and drizzled generous amounts of hot chocolate over the top.

"Let's eat!" I declared, sitting down and scooping up a giant spoonful of ice cream.

Samuel laughed right out loud, a rich rumble that echoed in my heart.

"What?" I said, my mouth full of ice cream.

"You make me laugh."

"Why?"

"You're this beautiful girl, blonde curls, big blue eyes. You always wear dresses and paint your toenails and you're completely old fashioned—books, music, you name it…you're completely all girl. I just didn't expect you to dig in like that. You did the same thing earlier tonight at the pond. You like food. I thought for sure you would put a napkin on your lap and eat very small spoonfuls like a dainty little lady."

"Lady, schmady," I giggled. "I love to eat. That's why I run every morning. Otherwise, I might grow to be very voluptuous and rubenesque."

"I'm not sure what rubenesque means exactly, but I'm sure it would look good on you." Samuel dug into his bowl as well, and we enjoyed our ice cream in silence until the last of the hot fudge sauce was scraped away. I restrained myself from licking my bowl. Samuel didn't.

"That was unbelievable sauce," he said appreciatively.

"Yep! My mom's own recipe. It's an original."

I washed our bowls, and Samuel wandered in to the family room and sat on the piano bench, watching me through the narrow door opposite the kitchen sink.

"Will you come with me to see my grandma?"

"Nettie?" I questioned, confused.

"No. I want you to come to Arizona with me and meet my Grandma Yazzie."

My eyes flew to his face, and I could see from the firm set of his wide mouth that he was serious.

"When?"

"Tomorrow."

"But…I have to work at the shop tomorrow and…how long

would we be gone?"

"Your aunt wouldn't let you go?"

"Of course she would. I don't have anything scheduled. I would just be there for walk-ins."

"Dilcon is over 700 miles away. We'd need an entire day of driving each way, and I want to stay for three days in between. So five days. Tomorrow is Saturday. We'd be back late on Wednesday night. Could you arrange it?"

I bit my lip as I mulled it over. I was so tempted. The long hours of driving were incredibly enticing. Conversation with Samuel was always enlivening, and the thought of listening to music and talking for hours on end with him was more than I could pass up. My dad was gone. He wouldn't be calling home. Cell phone reception wasn't available where he was going. I would have to cancel my piano lessons, but the loss of revenue wouldn't hurt me. What did I have to spend my money on anyway? I guess I hesitated a moment too long.

"Please, Josie?" His voice was insistent. "I want you to meet her. I've told her about you. You'll love her."

I turned to face him. "All right. I'll go. I've always wanted to meet her. But…" I held up one finger as a stipulation, "I can't leave bright and early. I have to call my students and Louise…"

"Call them on the way, Josie. Bring your cell phone. I'll pick you up at 6:00 a.m."

So much for "please, Josie." Bossy Samuel was back. Bossy really wasn't the right word. He was more blunt and plain-spoken, but calling him bossy made me feel better when he started giving orders. He continued on:

"I want to get to the reservation before dark. It's hard enough to find Grandma's hogan in the daytime. And she could be anywhere. I called the trading post when I got back stateside and left a message for her. I told her to plan on me this weekend. I got word to her through the man that works at the trading post. I called him today, and he said she had been in with one of her rugs. He gave her the message for me."

"Is that how you communicate?" I said incredulously.

"It works. Grandma doesn't read or write, and she doesn't have a phone."

I felt a frisson of unease that this meeting might be very awkward. Talk about two different worlds. Samuel must have seen something in my face, because he stood and walked to where I still stood, leaning against the sink. He reached out and ran a hand lightly down my cheek.

"Don't worry. Grandma is easy to love. Just think of it as an adventure."

I smiled tremulously.

"I'll see you tomorrow," he said, his voice husky.

"I promise to pack some jeans and boots," I said with a grimace. I'd given up wearing my Wranglers and hand me down T-shirts long ago. I still had Wranglers and T-shirts (who doesn't in Levan?) but they weren't my preference.

"My grandma wears a skirt every day too....but, yeah. You might want to bring some jeans, unless you have a big long pioneer skirt you like riding a horse in," he teased. He said goodnight and slipped quietly out the door, and I heard the truck start up and drive away.

I sped up the stairs and started throwing stuff in my suitcase. It was almost ten o'clock. I would never be able to sleep. My heart thudded in anticipation.

# 18. Oratorio

I SLEPT RESTLESSLY, getting up to repack my bag several times. I had never been on an Indian reservation. I had no idea what I would need. I woke up before the alarm and laid there feeling tired and wishing I hadn't agreed to go, wondering what had initiated such a bone-headed move. Actually, I knew why I was going. If I was being honest with myself it was strictly to spend time with Samuel, which again was completely moronic. Samuel would leave again. Soon. And I would be back here again. Soon.

I threw off my covers and showered, trying to get the sleep-deprived, hairy eyeball feeling to retreat. I was ready before Samuel got there and sat on the front porch waiting with Yazzie. He laid his big head in my lap and looked at me with mournful eyes. He knew I was going and that he wasn't coming with me. Samuel had called after he left the night before and said Nettie would come and feed the chickens and look after Yazzie. It embarrassed me a little that she knew I was going with him, although I appreciated him making arrangements for Yazzie. I wonder what she thought of his invitation. I really didn't want to know. I hoped she would be quiet about it, but figured the entire town would know shortly. Maybe when I got back it would be old news. I sighed gustily, knowing that I was going to get curious looks for a long time for this little "adventure" Samuel had planned.

Samuel pulled up promptly at six, and my heart sped up like a silly girl when he shut off his truck and stepped out, a small smile playing around his lips.

"Ready?"

I gave Yazzie a hug and a nuzzle and stepped off the porch with my bag. I may not have known exactly what to pack, but I knew enough to realize that showing up at Stella Yazzie's hogan with a huge trunk full of clothes and toiletries would be all wrong. I'd packed as light as I possibly could.

Samuel looked at my duffle approvingly and took it from me as he eyed my worn Levi's. I'd dressed them up a little with a gauzy white tunic and hoop earrings. I just couldn't rough it completely. I had on a pair of sandals, too. I put my old boots behind the front seat of his truck, knowing I would need them once we got there.

"Yep, all girl," Samuel smirked.

"Hey, I can ride a horse, muck out the stalls, milk a cow and fight off ornery chickens, Mister," I said tartly. "I just like dressing like a girl. I spent too many years wearing my brothers' old clothes. Do you have a problem with that?"

"No ma'am. I definitely don't have a problem with the way you look," Samuel replied, all signs of teasing gone from his voice.

I swallowed hard and tried not to smile.

Samuel had gassed up the truck before he'd come for me, and there was a Diet Coke in the cup holder waiting for me, as well as a heavenly smell coming from a brown bag sitting on the seat.

"Sweaty Betty's cinnamon rolls!" I squeaked, recognizing the aroma.

"What did you just call her?" Samuel raised his eyebrows as he slammed his door and started up the truck.

I filled him in on Betty's unfortunate nickname as I happily munched on the warm, sticky piece of paradise.

"I wish I had known her nickname before I inhaled three of those rolls." Samuel shuddered in mock horror.

"If you've lost your appetite I still have room for this last one," I supplied, licking my fingers. "Say what you want about Levan, but it definitely has its perks. Sweaty Betty's cooking is one of them, sweat and all."

"Honestly, I have nothing but good things to say about Levan." Samuel rested his forearms against the steering wheel, settling in for the long drive.

"Really?" I was a little surprised. I remembered how his grandmother's words at my kitchen table so many years ago had left a different impression. "Do you think you would ever want to live here?" As soon as the words left my mouth I viciously regretted them, realizing how eager and desperate I must seem, like a woman who was already making wedding plans and looking at houses. I hadn't meant it like that.

Samuel stared out his window for a minute and then looked at me soberly, his eyebrows drawn down in a slight V.

"No Josie. I don't think I'd want to live here," Samuel said softly.

I considered opening the door and hurling myself out onto the highway. I bit down on the urge to explain myself, realizing that anything I said would just dig the hole deeper. I finished my cinnamon roll without enjoying it and gulped down half of my Diet Coke. The awkward silence between us remained for many miles as the morning sun climbed sluggishly above the hills and stretched its long arms across the sleepy valley to the left of the long stretch of I-15 we traveled along. We would be traveling on I-15 for ninety miles until we turned off onto I-70 and traveled east towards Moab, cutting down through Monument Valley and into Arizona.

We finally relaxed into conversation, and I relinquished my discomfort as he shared experiences of his life in the military. I tried to find humorous anecdotes from daily life in Levan. We had led very different lives for the past few years, but somehow I didn't feel alienated from him because of his experiences like I once had when I'd read his letters. I just wanted to know more, to understand him better.

We stopped for a late lunch in Moab but were on the road again within fifteen minutes, fast food between us. Samuel wanted to reach his grandmother's before we ran out of daylight, and we had a ways to go yet. The landscape had steadily grown more stark and dramatic. Huge plateaus and jutting mountains thrust upwards out of the flats, like enormous castles coated in thick red rock. I'd often wondered how the fleeing Mormons had felt when their leader had declared that the Salt Lake Valley was "the place." They had traveled so far and long, suffering terribly, only to wind up in a rather barren, treeless, waterless valley. How their hearts must have trembled within them and how despair must have threatened to overcome them. But they'd prospered. I wondered now how the ancient Indian tribes had existed and thrived in this desert landscape. However breathtaking and majestic it might be, it was completely inhospitable. I must have mused aloud, because Samuel leaned into the wheel and his eyes narrowed on the scenery around us as he began to talk.

"The Hopi actually have an interesting legend about how they came to be on this land."

"The Hopi?" I questioned blankly.

"The Hopi Indians occupy a section of land here in the four corners area, mostly in the high desert of northeast Arizona, surrounded on all sides by the Navajo Nation. The Hopi are pacifists—in fact, Hopi means 'the peaceful and wise people.' This story kind of illustrates that quality of humble acceptance that is traditionally Hopi. Anyway, the Hopi say that back when the first humans crawled up from the underworld into this world, mockingbird met them with several ears of corn in all different sizes and colors laid out before him. Mockingbird told them that each tribe or family must pick an ear of corn. The ear of corn would tell them their destiny—for instance, the Navajo were said to have picked the yellow corn which meant they would have great enjoyment but a short life."

Samuel stopped talking at this point and glanced at me ruefully. "I haven't necessarily had great enjoyment in my life, so I'm hoping the other half of the Navajo destiny won't apply either.

"So all the tribes started grabbing the corn. The Utes took the flint corn, and the Comanche took the red corn. The Hopi stood by and watched everyone grabbing and jostling for the best ear of corn, but they didn't take any. Finally, there was only the short blue corn left—the piece nobody else wanted. The short blue corn predicted a destiny of hard work and toil, but also predicted long, full lives. The Hopi leader picked up the blue corn and accepted this destiny for his people, and they wandered around looking for a place to live. Eventually, they came to the three mesas in the desert. The God of death, Masauwu, owned the land. He said they could stay. The Hopi looked around them and said life will be difficult here, but nobody else will want this land, so no one will try to take our land away."

I laughed out loud at that. "I guess that's looking at the bright side of things."

"Well, they had it mostly right. The Hopi were farmers and because they actually came up with successful methods to grow crops in this environment, they were constantly being raided by surrounding Ute, Apache and Navajo tribes who wanted their corn."

"So nobody wanted their land, but they wanted their crops?"

"Pretty much."

We drove in silence for many miles more, each of us lost in reflection.

"I like how you know not only your history, but the history of other tribes. You are like my own personal guide of all that is Native American."

"You'll find that most of the legends among Native Americans are variations of the same stories. We might tell them a little differently, or have our own slant on things, but they're all similar, especially among tribes that occupy the same geographic area. The Hopi share a lot of religious similarities with the Navajo. Each tribe is big on religious ceremonies. Both religions center around harmony, of things being in balance, and the importance of having a good heart, which mostly comes from being at peace with the people and circumstances in your life."

"*Hózhǫ*," I remembered aloud.

Samuel gaped at me and then nodded his head. "Yeah, *hózhǫ*. How did you know that word?"

"I remember talking about harmony with you a long time ago. I've thought about it many times since. I even wrote *hózhǫ* on my Wall of Words.

"Imagine that—a little girl from Levan, Utah with a Navajo word written on her wall."

"Imagine that," I agreed. "So Samuel?"

"Yeah?"

"Have you found it?"

"What?"

"Harmony, balance, *hózhǫ*…whatever you want to call it. Since you've been gone all these years, have you found it?'

Samuel looked at me for a moment and then returned his gaze to the road. "It's an ongoing thing, Josie. You don't just find it and keep it. Just like maintaining balance on a bike—one little thing can start you wobbling. But I learned that a big part of harmony for me is having a purpose. I also had to let go of a lot of anger and sadness. When I met you all those years ago, I was filled with anger. I started changing when my heart started to soften."

"What softened your heart?" I asked softly.

"Good music and a friend."

I felt my eyes burn a little and turned from him, blinking quickly to lap up the sting of tears. "Music has incredible power."

"So does friendship," he supplied frankly.

"You were every bit as good a friend to me," I responded quickly.

"No I wasn't. Not even close. But as nasty and mean as I often was, you never held a grudge. I could never figure you out. You just seemed to love me no matter what. I didn't understand that kind of love. Then I had an experience that taught me. You know I took my dad's scriptures with me when I left for the Marine corp. I'd read them a little. I'd flipped through them, reading this and that, starting and stopping. I don't think I ever told you about the experience I had. It might be in one of those letters I brought over.

"I was in the middle of Afghanistan in an area where we believed a large group of Taliban fighters had hunkered down. There was one guy in particular that we really wanted bad. Rumors of Osama himself were rampant. I'd been sent on ahead with another sniper—we're always sent out in pairs—to scout out an area thought to overlook a possible opening to a series of caves the terrorists were supposedly using as a hidey hole. I'd been battened down on my belly, looking through my scope for hours on end for three days. I was exhausted and irritable, and I wanted to blow up the whole Godforsaken country and just go home."

"It sounds terrible," I commiserated.

"It was," Samuel laughed without much humor and shook his head. "Before I'd been sent out on this little scouting trip, I'd been reading the parable about the prodigal son. It'd made me a little bit mad. I felt angry for the son who stuck around and was faithful and then got pushed aside by his dad. I thought I understood what Jesus was trying to teach with that parable. I thought it was all about that Jesus loves the sinner not the sin, and that he will forgive us if we will just return to him and allow him to heal us. And I knew all that was true, but I just kept thinking about how it wasn't right and it wasn't fair, and the 'good son' didn't deserve to be taken for granted. I was even thinking that Jesus' parable wasn't the best example of welcoming the sinner back into the fold—that he could have used a better story to illustrate his point.

"So here I am, tired, ticked-off, and I've got this story of the prodigal son running through my mind. Just about this time, I see what looks to be the target approaching this entrance with two other men. I get excited because I'm thinking—finally someone's going to get what they deserve. Can you imagine it? I'm critiquing the master teacher in my head, and I'm getting ready to blow another guy's head to kingdom come. I'm all excited, I've got the orders to shoot to kill, and suddenly my partner says—"It isn't him."

"It's him! I'm saying. It's him! It's a go! I'm insisting that I shoot even as I'm realizing it isn't our guy, but I don't stand down." Samuel's voice and body were tense as he retold the story, and he shook his head adamantly, transported back to the craggy overlook in a country far away.

"I'm actually getting ready to pull the trigger and suddenly, out of nowhere, a voice speaks to me, as clearly as if my buddy were talking directly into my ear."

Samuel paused, and all at once his face was drenched in emotion. "But it wasn't my partner. He's still whispering frantically—insisting it isn't our guy. The voice I heard wasn't audible to anyone but me. The voice said 'How much owest thou unto my Lord?'"

The silence in the cab was thick with something akin to anguish—and although I didn't quite understand what the question implied, I knew Samuel had understood, and waited for him to master his emotions enough to share his insight. He breathed deeply a few times and continued hoarsely, his voice cracking a little.

"The story of the prodigal son isn't just about the sins of the son that left and came back. It's about the sins of the faithful son as well." Samuel looked at me, and I stared back waiting for him to continue.

"That day, in a rocky corner of Afghanistan, I was so wrapped up in everyone getting what they deserved, that I almost killed a guy that I knew was not a target. He could have been looking for his lost goat for all I know. The thing is, what do any of us really deserve, Josie? What are we entitled to? The words that I heard that day were words from the very next parable Jesus teaches in the book of Luke about the unjust steward. I'd read it right after I'd read the parable of the prodigal son—but I'd been so wrapped up in what I had perceived as injustice in the one parable, that I hadn't really read the words in the next. 'How much owest thou unto my Lord?' How much? How much do I owe? The truth is I can't ever pay my debt. Ever. We ALL owe everything to God. There is no level of debtedness. I am no less in debt than that man who almost lost his life at my hand. The more faithful son is no less in debt that his prodigal brother. We all owe Jesus Christ everything. Yet at the end of the parable the father says lovingly to his angry son, 'Son, thou art ever with me, and all that I have is thine.' Now that is love. Two sons that were undeserving, both of them loved and embraced. That day, with a gentle reminder, a merciful father showed me how undeserving I was—and saved me in spite of it. That's the day I really started to understand."

I unhooked my seatbelt and slid over next to Samuel on the wide bench seat. I laid my head on his shoulder and wrapped his right hand in both of mine. We sat with tears in our eyes, hands clasped, beyond words for many miles.

We arrived in Dilcon just before sundown. It looked a lot like any other small town. The landscape was a little different, and its signs boasted Navajo rugs and jewelry—but it didn't seem that different from Levan, truth be told. We wound through the town and out again, traveling down roads without signs or markings, occasionally passing a herd of sheep or an occasional double wide trailer. I counted a few abandoned pick-up trucks. I saw a hogan standing forlornly in the middle of nothing and pointed it out to Samuel.

"When the owner of a hogan dies it is not lived in anymore. Do you remember *chįįdii?* How the bad spirit remains? Whether you believe in *chįįdii* or not, respect for tradition just dictates that the hogan be left uninhabited to return to Mother Earth. You'll see abandoned hogans here and there. Fewer and fewer Navajo live in hogans these days. It's just more comfortable to have running water and electricity and temperature controls. We've got some hold-outs, though. Grandma Yazzie is definitely one of them."

I didn't know how Samuel found his way, turning down this road and up another until finally he bounced his way over uneven earth to a lonely hogan with an old pick-up truck that looked like Old Brown's older brother parked out front. A huge corral made of juniper logs was knit together in seemingly haphazard fashion to the north of the hogan. At least a hundred sheep were confined within the enclosure. The hogan faced east. The door was open, and the deepening shadows of the setting sun created shade in the front where a little old woman sat combing what looked to be wool around a large wooden spool. She didn't move or rise as we slowed to a stop, and the truck heaved a grateful sigh of arrival as Samuel turned the key. We stepped stiffly out our respective doors, and I held back as Samuel strode forward and picked the little woman up off her stool holding her tightly in his arms. Her wool and spools fell unheeded to her feet as she clasped him to her, her small hands running up his arms and strong back, patting his cheeks and muttering something I could not understand.

Samuel eventually let her down and turned toward me, reaching back his hand, and with the Navajo language bouncing off his tongue introduced me to his beloved Shimasani Yazzie.

Grandma Yazzie was beautiful in the way old wood is beautiful. Warm and deep brown with a depth of wisdom that had me searching the lines in her face for the answers to life's biggest questions. Her hair was white and thick and pulled back and looped in the traditional Navajo bun. Her shirt was a faded purple, the sleeves long, and her skirt was full and layered and dusty blue. She wore ancient lace-up cowboy boots on her feet and large turquoise and silver rings on the ring finger of each wrinkled hand. She wasn't very tall, maybe five feet, but she was sturdy and compact—a stiff wind wouldn't blow her over; in fact, I had the distinct impression that very little would blow her over.

She nodded to me almost regally, and then turned her attention back to her grandson. She gestured toward her hogan and bid us come inside. The hogan was more spacious than I expected. A huge loom took up almost one whole side. A pallet lay against an adjacent wall with a small chest of drawers and a small wood burning stove.

A large table with two chairs made up what consisted of the kitchen area.

"Grandma is worried that you will be uncomfortable here," Samuel spoke softly to me. "I've told her you've never had anyone fuss over you, so she shouldn't fuss over you either. I told her you will only be uncomfortable if she is uncomfortable. I think that made her feel better."

I marveled briefly how well Samuel understood me.

We ate a simple meal of fry bread and mutton stew. I felt my eyes getting heavy as I sat outside on one of the chairs from the kitchen and listened to the gentle cadence of Samuel and his grandmother conversing. Grandmother Yazzie's hands were always busy. She had shown me, with Samuel interpreting, the rug she was working on at her loom. The rug had only the natural colors of the wool woven into the complex design. She said she mixed some of her own dye from different plants, but she would use no dyes on this rug. The red, brown, black and grey in the design were the colors of the wool taken from her sheep. I asked her if she planned the pattern beforehand. Samuel answered for her, before he even translated what I'd said.

"The pattern will emerge on its own. The wool lets you know what the pattern will be. There are traditional patterns—I forget what they all mean. But each pattern tells a story. Some stories are complicated and involve very intricate detailed patterns. Grandma says this is a ceremonial rug."

This made sense to me, and I mused aloud, "Weaving is kind of like writing music. The song almost writes itself. You just have to start playing."

Samuel immediately launched into Navajo, telling his grandmother what I had said and what he'd told me. She nodded her head as he spoke, agreeing with his explanation, smiling a little at me as he must have told her what I'd said about music.

That night, Samuel slept outside in his truck bed, and I slept in a bedroll in the hogan, with Samuel's grandmother lying silently beside me. That night I dreamed that I sat at the loom, weaving a rug patterned with ears of corn in red, yellow, blue, and white. A mockingbird sat at my shoulder and told me to choose my destiny. Every time I would reach for the yellow corn the mockingbird would peck my hand and chirp "not for you! Not for you!" in a squawky parrot voice.

We spent the following day on horseback, herding sheep down the canyon to grassier climes. Winter set in early in the higher elevations, and in another month the sheep would stay pastured near Grandma Yazzie's hogan. We'd gotten up before the sun, and I did my best to look pretty, even without much to work with. I knew my days with Samuel were numbered, and I wanted to make them count. I hadn't examined my feelings for him beyond the pleasure of having him back. I knew my avoidance of any deep contemplation on the subject was self-deception, but I just couldn't make myself consider what came next. It'd been a long time since I'd spent any real time in the saddle, and I knew I'd be feeling it the next day. I had never herded sheep before, and I knew Grandma Yazzie didn't necessarily need my help so I hung back, waiting for direction, and mostly just enjoying the quiet companionship of Samuel and his grandmother.

The chill of the morning eventually gave way to sunshine and blue skies, with an underlying reminder of fall in the smell of the wind. When we reached the valley where the sheep would spend several hours, we climbed off our horses, hobbled them by tying their back legs together, and enjoyed a little jerky and some fry bread left over from the night before. We then settled in for some quiet time while the sheep grazed.

I had started to doze a little, listening to Samuel talk to his grandmother, not understanding anything of course, not feeling the need to. I felt Samuel brush at my arm, and opened one eye blearily in question.

"You had a tick crawling on you. Grandma says they've been bad this year."

The thought of a tick burrowing its way into my arm was as effective as a cold-bucket of water on my sleepiness. I sat up, brushing down my arms and legs and running my fingers through my hair.

"You know why a wood tick is flat don't you?" Samuel sat where he'd been resting against a large rock. He didn't seem all that concerned with the idea of a wood ticks crawling around.

"I've never looked at one long enough to know they were flat," I admitted, still brushing off my jean clad legs.

"Another Navajo story…Grandma tells it better than I do….but the legend is that Coyote, the trickster, was out walking one day when he met an old woman. The old woman tells him there is a giant nearby and he should turn around and leave. Coyote says he's not afraid of anything, especially not a giant, and he keeps walking. He picks up a sharp stick though, just in case, thinking he might need it if he comes across the giant. Eventually, he comes to the mouth of this huge cave, and curious as most coyotes are, he walks in to explore. After walking a little ways, he sees a woman lying on the floor of the cave. He asks her what's wrong. She says she is so weak she cannot stand. Coyote asks her if she is sick. She says she is starving to death from being trapped inside the belly of the giant with nothing to eat. Coyote says 'What giant?' The woman laughs and tells him he is inside the giant's belly, too. The cave that he had walked into was the giant's mouth. 'It is easy to walk in,' the woman says, 'but no one ever gets out.'

"Not knowing what else he can do, Coyote keeps walking and exploring. Then he comes upon many more people, all weak and starving to death. Coyote says to them, 'If this is the belly of a giant, then the walls are made of muscle and fat, and we can cut into the walls and eat this meat.' So Coyote uses his sharp stick and his teeth and cuts meat from the walls of the giant's belly. He feeds all the people, and they are happy. They say, 'thank you for feeding us, but we still can't get out.' Coyote says to them, 'If this is the giant's belly, his heart can't be too far away. I will find his heart and stab him and kill him.' One of the people say, 'See that big pumping volcano over there? That is the giant's heart.'

"Coyote crawls up the volcano and stabs his stick into the heart of the giant. The giant yells out. 'Is that you, Coyote? Quit cutting me and stabbing me, and I will open up my mouth and let you out.'

"But Coyote doesn't just want to just save himself, he needs to save the others, too. Thick lava starts to spill out of the volcano that is the giant's heart. The giant starts to shake, and Coyote tells the people that the volcano is causing an earthquake and the giant will open his mouth, and the people can run out. As the giant is in his death throes, he roars in pain and the people trapped in his belly run out of his mouth. Coyote has saved them." Samuel finished his tale and sat looking at me, expectantly.

"That's a good story…but I'm not sure what it has to do with the wood tick." I raised my eyebrows in question.

"Oh yeah," Samuel smiled back. "See, the wood tick is the last to get out, and he is just crawling out when the giant dies and his jaws close. Coyote has to pull him out between the giant's teeth, and he gets flattened in the process."

"Ahhh, that makes perfect sense." I laughed out loud. "I like how Native American legends seem to be a mix of the very far-fetched and the very practical."

Samuel's grandmother had been sitting nearby, working with her wool again, and she looked up as I chuckled. She seemed to have followed our conversation, and I concluded that she must understand English better than she could speak it.

She spoke to me now, though I didn't understand. Her face was kind and her words soft.

"Grandma says that just like the stories in my Bible, the legends have hidden lessons if you look deep enough. It is the lesson behind the story that is the most important part." Samuel translated for me as he gazed at his grandmother, his expression matching hers.

"Like parables?"

Grandma Yazzie nodded her head, like she understood my question. She spoke to me again, this time in stilted English, and I listened attentively, knowing it was uncomfortable for her and knowing she tried for my sake.

"Coyote not know he trapped." She looked down at the wool she was carding, and didn't say more.

I looked at Samuel for further clarification, not really understanding what his grandmother was trying to communicate. Samuel was still for a moment, and then he leveled his gaze on mine, squinting a little against the sun that had infiltrated our limited shade.

"Coyote was inside the belly of the giant, and he didn't even know it. He was completely unaware that he was trapped. I think that's what grandma was trying to say."

"You could also argue that Coyote was the only one who wasn't trapped." I shrugged, knowing that Samuel's grandmother's interpretation of the legend had reminded him of me. My stomach twisted at the knowledge, and I was suddenly eager to turn the tables on him. "Coyote had no trouble getting out—but he knew he couldn't leave everyone else behind."

"Hmm. I should have known you'd see it that way." Samuel reached out and brushed his fingertips down my cheek. "I feel like I'm back on the bus, trying to keep up. You were always two steps ahead of me."

"Would it make you feel better if we arm wrestled?" I poked at him, "I'm sure I wouldn't stand a chance." I was relieved to turn the conversation in a different direction.

Samuel laughed out loud, and his grandmother looked up sharply, her eyes resting lovingly on his grinning countenance. Her gaze slid reluctantly from his face to mine, and her eyes were full of questions.

# 19. *Crescendo*

THERE ARE SUPPOSED to be links between math, music, and astronomy—some of the greatest composers have been avid star-watchers. The connections between math and music made sense—although there is more to the connection than timing, counting, and notes on a line. In fact, there is something neurological that occurs in the brain when certain types of music are played. That neurological change is said to positively affect our mathematical abilities. I'd been fascinated by what some researchers have called the Mozart Effect, and have used the study to convince more than one mother to keep her struggling child in piano lessons.

But the only connection I'd ever made between astronomy and music was in the way each made me feel. When I looked up into the firmament, I felt the same reverence that moved in me when I listened to the swell of great music. I'd never had anyone teach me about the stars like Samuel's grandmother had done for him. What I'd learned in school textbooks failed to inspire me, as if some vital piece was being omitted. The galaxy was a riddle that everyone pretended to know the answer to, but no one really did. At school, I'd often find myself growing impatient with facts and figures that seemed like paltry suggestions for something that was beyond words and explanations.

After dinner on our third day there, Samuel and I climbed a

rocky rise near his grandmother's hogan as the sun set. And as the purple dusk was overcome with black, we watched the stars blink and awaken above us. As the night deepened and the display became more dramatic, I felt that familiar, humble wonder that I always felt when I contemplated the heavens. My limbs were heavy and my belly was full, and I felt more content and relaxed than I could remember feeling in a very long time.

Samuel's grandmother had killed a goat in honor of his visit, and she'd spent the last two days cooking and preparing dishes. I was not especially squeamish, but when Samuel had told me that his grandmother used literally everything from the goat, I had been a little doubtful about my ability to take part in the feast being prepared. I'd even watched her make blood cakes, and amazingly enough, in spite of the gruesome name, they weren't bad. They were heavy and filling and when they were cooking they smelled delicious. Two of Grandma Yazzie's friends came and helped her with her preparations, and I was struck by how similar they were to the women in my church, laughing and giggling and working side by side. I marveled at the ingenuity and resourcefulness of these people. They even used ash from the juniper trees to leaven and thicken their bread.

The goat feast had been a lighthearted gathering of Grandma Yazzie's friends, all who seemed to know and hold affection for Samuel. His mother had come as well but seemed ill at ease and confrontational towards Grandma Yazzie. In some ways, she looked older than her mother, although she was probably only in her late forties. Deep lines and sunken eyes told a tale of a very sad woman. Samuel seemed glad to see her and embraced her warmly, but shrugged with acceptance when she left not long after she arrived.

Now, lying beside Samuel on the smooth surface of the sandstone rise, looking up into the endless expanse of the night sky, I asked him about the woman who was his mother.

"She still lives with my step-dad, although I haven't seen him since I left that last time my senior year in high school. My shimasani's hogan has been neutral ground for my mother and I to see each other over the years."

"She doesn't seem to like Grandma Yazzie very much," I said truthfully.

"She can't ever get a rise out of Grandma. I think she tries to provoke ill-treatment from her to justify her own bad feelings. But my Grandma just loves her and, from what I can see, offers peace whenever she comes around. Sadly, my mother has betrayed herself too many times, and she is turning into a bear."

"A bear?" I questioned, confused.

"Another legend. When I was little, my grandmother told me a story about a woman who was captured by the bear-clan. At night they were bears, but in the day, human. The woman marries the chief of the bear clan and eventually, after living with the bear clan for many years, she starts to grow fur and becomes a bear."

"And your mother is becoming like the bear she married?"

"Ahh, you catch on quick, Josie. Actually, in the legend, the bear is selfless and loving, and dies for his family in the end, but I was always struck by the idea that we become what we surround ourselves by," Samuel sighed. "Or maybe it's just easier to blame my step-dad for what my mother has become than to hold her accountable."

"I think the legend is truer than you even realize. Have you ever noticed how old married couples start to resemble each other after many years of marriage?" I giggled at the thought of some of the very old couples in Levan, and how they could almost be brother and sister they looked so much alike.

"So if you marry me, in fifty years my hair will start to curl and my eyes will be a brilliant blue?" Samuel teased softly, not turning toward me, his eyes trained on the stars above us.

My heart stuttered, and the image of growing old with Samuel suddenly played through my mind in moving pictures. I sat up abruptly, wrapping my arms around my knees, and struggled to think of something, anything, to say that would take the pictures from my head and the longing from my heart.

If Samuel perceived my discomfort, he didn't pursue it, and his voice was soft as he moved the conversation to less personal ground, but he stretched his hand out and ran his fingers gently through my curls as he spoke.

"I'll be at Camp Pendleton in San Diego for the next couple of years, Josie. I accepted an assignment at the base with the sniper division. I will be an instructor, training and working with Marines who are expert riflemen. I won't have to live on base, and I won't be considered active for deployment with my unit. I've been accepted to law school at San Diego State, and I can attend classes in the afternoon and evenings."

He had it all planned out. I guess he'd figured out what he'd wanted. When we'd stood in the kitchen the morning after our run, he'd claimed he hadn't decided what came next. It seemed he now knew. I was proud of him and frustrated all at the same time.

"How do you do it, Samuel?" I asked, and I was surprised at the confrontational edge to my voice, "How do you come here and see your grandma, see her growing older, knowing one day she'll be gone, not knowing if this time might be the last time you see her, and then leave again?"

"Do you think my shimasani needs me to stay, Josie?" Samuel sat up beside me, and the fingers that had been gently twined in my hair now slid to my chin, turning my face to his. "Do you really think she wants me to stay?"

I tried to jerk my face from his hand, but he leaned into me and answered his own question. "I accomplish nothing by staying here. My grandmother knows I love her, and she expects me to keep moving forward. Do you remember how, when I was born, my grandmother buried my umbilical cord in her hogan so that I would know I always have a home?"

I nodded a brief yes.

"This place is in my heart, but it can't be my home, not now, maybe not ever. Do you remember how Grandma knew it wasn't right, so she dug up the cord and put it on the gun rack?"

Again, I nodded.

"There are many kinds of warriors, Josie. I've been one kind, and you know the saying goes, once a Marine always a Marine, but now I need to be a different kind of warrior for the Navajo people. I want to get my law degree so I can help native people retain their lands, and not just the Navajo people. Our government doesn't need acres and acres of land. Do you know that the United States Government OWNS more than half of the land out west? As much as 60% of the land in some states. The government goes in and takes the land in the name of the people, but what it is doing is taking the land *from* the people. The founding fathers, as well as a few of the great chiefs, would be rolling in their graves if they knew about the land grab that has happened by our own government."

Samuel breathed out in frustration, dropping his hand from my face and running it through his hair. "Don't even get me started, Josie." He paused and then confronted me again. "So you think I should live here with my grandma in her hogan? Is that what you're saying, Josie? Live here and herd sheep? Do you think my grandma would think I loved her more if I did?"

I felt like the lowest of life forms, and I shook my head miserably. "No, Samuel, I don't. I'm sorry. I'm not really sure what I meant."

The silence around us was broken only by the occasional distant laughter floating up from the hogan below and an orchestra of happy crickets united in their evening song. Several long moments passed before Samuel supplied gently, "Maybe we aren't really talking about me, Josie."

Samuel waited patiently for an answer, but after significant time passed without a response, he silently rose to his feet. He reached his hand down, and I took it, letting him pull me up beside him.

"We've got an early morning tomorrow, Josie. Let's go back and see if they've saved us any goat gut ice cream."

"Ugh!" I cried out, totally falling for it.

"Just kidding, sweetheart. Goat eyeballs are actually quite tasty, though. They're considered a delicacy among my people."

"Samuel!"

His laughter eased the churning in my heart, and I followed him down the steep path back to the dim light of Grandma Yazzie's hogan.

There were no tears when Samuel and his grandmother said their goodbyes the next morning. The sun was just peeking its way over the eastern mountains as they spoke in low tones, their cheeks pressed together, Samuel's forehead resting on her shoulder, his back bowed to accommodate their embrace. I turned from them, embarrassed to find my own eyes were moist when theirs were not. I guess I just didn't like goodbyes.

I felt a gentle touch on my sleeve, and turned to see Grandma Yazzie standing close beside me. Her eyes searched mine, noting, I'm sure, the wet that was threatening to overcome them. She reached up and patted my cheek with her warm, rough palm. When she spoke, her English was almost perfect.

"Thank you for coming. Samuel loves you. You love Samuel. Go and be happy."

I put my hand over hers and held it for a moment. Then she stepped away from me, and my eyes overflowed. I turned from her quickly, stepping into the cab of the truck. Samuel must have heard what she'd said; he was only a few feet away. Our small bags and the two bedrolls were already stowed in the truck bed ready to go, so it was only a minute before he climbed in beside me and started the truck.

As we pulled away, I found myself gulping as I tried to stem the flow of tears that would not be calmed. I jabbed at the jockey box, seeking reinforcements, and grabbed a handful of brown Taco Bell napkins and scrubbed at my face, desperately trying to dam the stream of my unruly emotions.

"Oh Josie," Samuel sighed gently. "Your heart is too tender for your own good."

"I don't usually cry like this, Samuel. Geez, it's been *years* since I've cried like this. Since you've been back I can't seem to stop. It's like a cloud has burst inside me, and I'm caught in a constant downpour."

"Come here, Josie," Samuel said, and when I slid over next to him he kissed me gently on the forehead and smoothed my hair from my damp cheeks. "Well then, maybe you should go ahead and just let it rain for a while."

And so I did. I cried until I was all wrung out, and I didn't think I would cry again for a good many more years. Then I laid my head down on Samuel's right thigh and fell asleep with his hand in my hair and Conway Twitty singing "Don't Take it Away" on the radio.

We made good time on the way home. Apparently, all those tears I'd cried had been heavy, because I felt strangely weightless and empty for most of the drive. Samuel and I talked of this and that, but the conversation was light and roaming. We got caught in a downpour, of the natural variety this time, and when the rain cleared a huge rainbow traversed the sky. This prompted another Navajo legend about Changing Woman's sons trying to reach the Turquoise House of Sun-God across the Great Water. The story told how, when they reached the Great Water, they followed Spider Woman's directions and with songs and prayers, put their hands into the Great Waters and a huge Rainbow Bridge appeared to take them to the Sun-God. The story also involved the sons meeting a little red headed man who resembled a sand scorpion and spitting four times into their hands, but it was a good story regardless.

The peculiarities in the story made me wonder if many of the Native American legends had started out as truths long ago, and had gotten warped in the telling from one generation to the next, like that game children played at parties where everyone sits in a circle and one person whispers something in the ear of the person sitting next to them, and that person repeats what he heard to the person sitting next to him and so on, until it travels around the entire circle. If the circle is big enough the phrase at the end rarely even resembles the original phrase. I asked Samuel what he thought of my theory.

"Most likely some of that has happened," Samuel acquiesced. "There was no way to accurately record the stories because we didn't have a written language. Many of our legends and our history have been recorded now, however, and I guess you could say that is one bright spot in the assimilation of the Navajo children into American schools. We can speak and write in English and can preserve our culture in that way.

"I think many of the legends weren't ever truths to begin with, though. Not in the way you mean, at least. Many of the legends were stories the native people used to teach their children and to create a code of conduct in which to live by. They didn't have a Bible to teach their children about a loving Savior, His atonement, and a life after this one. I think many of our legends are an attempt to explain what they didn't understand—including where they came from and why they existed. They wanted to know what we all want to know. Who am I? Why am I here?"

I pondered what Samuel had said and wondered about my own desperate questions after Kasey had died. It hadn't been until he died that I really questioned God's plan for me. I hadn't really questioned who I was and why I was here until I could no longer look at my future with any kind of joy or anticipation, until I needed help finding a reason to continue. It was then that I had needed answers most of all, and the only answer I had found, my only reason for being, had become my father's need. Then Sonja had needed me, and I had found a measure of joy in service, and it had sustained me. Until now. Now I had questions again.

We rolled into Levan at about six-thirty that night. I felt haggard and filthy, but was loath to part with Samuel for any length of time. I suggested that we rendezvous back at my place for dinner in an hour, giving each of us a chance to freshen up after several days of showering with a bucket and a hand towel.

I greeted my happy dog with a hug and a kiss and stumbled into the bathroom avoiding the mirror entirely, deciding that what I didn't know couldn't hurt me. I scrubbed and lathered and moisturized and came out of the shower feeling almost new again. I threw all the clothes from the five day trip into the wash and pulled on a skirt, a light weight pink top, and enjoyed putting on make-up with a full mirror for the first time in days. My nose was a little sunburned and my cheeks had a few more freckles, but when I was done I looked refreshed, and my hair gleamed around my shoulders.

I started some pasta on the stove and defrosted some sausage in the microwave. I fried it up and poured some homemade tomato sauce over it that I had canned a few weeks previous and decided it would suffice for an easy meal. I ran out to my garden on a whim, craving fresh vegetables in a salad and was just straightening up with my basket full of produce when Samuel surprised me, walking around the corner of the house towards me. My heart performed a series of flips, and I caught my breath before it left me senseless. How, after only an hour apart, could I be so desperately happy to see him? His black hair shone, and his warm skin glowed as he shot me a smile that sent a jolt from my stomach to my now wobbly knees. I curled my bare feet in the cool dirt pushing up between my toes and smiled back at him, waiting for him to reach me.

He stopped in front of me, and without missing a beat, he took the basket from my hand, set it down beside my feet, and wrapped his arms around me. He smelled wonderful—like juniper trees, Ivory soap and temptation all mixed together. My eyelids fluttered closed as his lips found mine and didn't retreat for several long minutes.

"I missed you," he breathed, and there was a rueful expression on his face as my eyelids lifted heavily to meet his gaze. He dropped another kiss on my needy lips as he leaned down and picked up the basket of vegetables, looping his free arm around my waist as we made our way into the house.

We ate with Yazzie sleeping at our feet, and the sound of a distant lawn mower humming through the open kitchen window. Beethoven softly serenaded us from the living room stereo, and I had been lost in the music and the meal for quite some time when I realized that Samuel had stopped eating and was listening intently.

I watched him, waiting for him to tell me what was wrong.

"What is that called?"

"The piece?"

"No...not the name of the piece. The musical term. You explained it to me once. I just remembered it as I was listening to the music continually return to that one sound. What is it called?

"Do you mean the tonic note?" I asked, surprised.

"Yeah, I think that's what you called it."

"Your ear has become very sharp. You're hearing the tonic note, even when it isn't being played. It's more subtle in this piece than in some other works."

"Explain it to me again," he demanded, his expression one of deep concentration.

"Well...a tonic note is the first note of a scale, which serves as the home base around which all the other pitches revolve and to which they ultimately gravitate. If a song has a strong tonic base you can hum the tonic note throughout the song, and it will blend with every note and chord."

"That's right. I remember now." Samuel seemed to be pondering this bit of musical theory very seriously, and I kept stealing looks at his frowning countenance. I cleared the dishes, and we washed and dried side by side, Beethoven's 13th String Quartet winding down behind us. He walked in to the living room and switched it off as I put the last dish in the cupboard. He moved to the piano and lifted the lid over the keys.

"I haven't heard you play for so long, Josie. Will you play for me tonight?" His voice was wistful as his fingers ran over the piano keys.

"I don't know. You never did sing me the Irish Lament," I teased gently, reminding him of our agreement at Burraston's Pond.

"Hmm. That's true. We had a deal. Okay…I'll *tell* you the Irish Lament; I won't sing it. But you have to promise me something first."

I waited, looking at him.

"You have to promise you won't run away."

Samuel moved from the bench, tall and straight, and looked down at me. "I don't want the poem to make you feel uncomfortable. It's a poem about lovers. It might scare you and make you run away, or it might make you fall in love with me." I blushed and snorted as if his suggestion was ludicrous.

"So I can't run away but it's okay if I fall in love with you?"

"That depends," he retorted smoothly.

"On what?"

"On whether you run away."

"You're speaking in riddles."

He shrugged. "Do we have a deal?"

"Deal." I held out my hand, but my heart lurched a little in my chest.

Samuel closed his eyes for a minute, as if to pull the words from some recess in his mind, then he tilted his head toward me and began to recite softly:

*Oh, a wan cloud was drawn o'er the dim weeping dawn*
*As to Josie's side I returned at last,*
*And the heart in my breast for the girl I lov'd best*
*Was beating, ah, beating, how loud and fast!*
*While the doubts and the fears of the long aching years*
*Seem'd mingling their voices with the moaning flood:*
*Till full in my path, like a wild water wraith,*
*My true love's shadow lamenting stood.*

*But the sudden sun kiss'd the cold, cruel mist*
*Into dancing show'rs of diamond dew,*
*And the dark flowing stream laugh'd back to his beam,*
*And the lark soared aloft in the blue:*
*While no phantom of night but a form of delight*
*Ran with arms outspread to her darling boy,*
*And the girl I love best on my wild throbbing breast*
*Hid her thousand treasures with cry of joy.*

There was a giant lump in my throat, and we stared at each other. I breathed deeply, trying to halt the emotion rising over me. Samuel closed the final step between us.

"That's exactly how it happened, too. You suddenly came out of nowhere in the middle of a rainstorm. And then you were in my arms."

"Are you trying to seduce me, Samuel?" I'd meant to sound playful, but my voice came out in a low plea.

"No." Samuel's voice was warm and intense, and he shook his head as he spoke.

"Am I the 'girl you love best'?" Again my striving for lightness fell short, as I was unable to clothe the words in jest. I didn't want him to answer my question and quickly withdrew my gaze from his and walked to the piano. I slid onto the bench and launched into Chopin's "Fantasie Impromptu," my fingers flying dizzily over the keys, the music as frenzied and frantic as my racing heart. The second movement smoothed into the lovely melody and I played for several minutes with Samuel standing behind me, unmoving. When the piece resumed the flying pace of the opening movement, he moved behind me and placed his hands on my shoulders, and I struggled to finish the number.

"You ran away. You said you wouldn't," Samuel sighed behind me.

"I'm right here."

"Your fingers are flying, trying to escape."

I put my hands in my lap and bowed my head. Music was too revealing. Chopin had just told Samuel exactly what I was feeling, despite my attempts to avoid him.

One of Samuel's hands rose to my bowed head and he traced a loose curl that had been lying against the nape of my neck with his calloused fingers. I shivered.

"Will you play something else?"

"You can't touch me. I...I can't concentrate when you do." My voice was a whisper, and I cringed at the childlike breathiness.

Samuel's hands fell away from my shoulders, and he moved away without response and leaned against the living room door, where he could see my face as I played. That wasn't much better. I tried to close my eyes so I could concentrate. I knew what he wanted to hear. I knew what I wanted to play, but worried that once again, it would lay my heart open, revealing too much.

I let my fingers dance lightly across the keys, giving in to the vulnerability that I knew echoed in my very first composition. I hadn't written any music for a very long time. I had composed feverishly until I met Kasey, and then I'd let myself be seventeen. I'd been young and in love, and I hadn't felt the melancholy that induced my most creative moments, and I hadn't wanted to write. I'd wanted to be seventeen. I had enjoyed acting my age for once in my life. Of course, since he'd died, melancholy hadn't been a problem. But my gift had been strangely silent in the last five years.

Now "Samuel's Song" rose lovingly from the keys and wound

its way around us. I embellished as I played, remembering all the old feelings. A girl in love with someone she couldn't have. My heart ached in my chest, but I let it. I wasn't going to hide anymore. I kept my eyes closed, and my hands knew their way. The keys were cool against my fingertips, and I lost myself in the sweet agony of my song.

Suddenly, Samuel was next to me on the bench, his long body sliding next to mine, my hands falling discordantly from the keys as his arms wrapped around me and his lips captured mine anxiously. My arms rushed to embrace him, as my right hand rose to his face. My head was pressed into his shoulder, and he pulled me across his lap, his mouth moving feverishly over mine.

I heard myself say his name as he moved his lips from mine to rain kisses across my jaw and down the silky column of my throat. I shuddered deep down in my stomach, and my hand tightened on his face, pushing him from me to stare into his eyes. He looked down at me, and his breath was harsh, coming in pants like it never did when he ran. His eyes glittered and burned, and his lips were parted as he struggled to control his breathing.

"How am I going to keep my promise if you keep kissing me?" I whispered urgently.

"What promise?"

He hadn't released his hold on me, and I was still grasped tightly in his arms.

"Not to fall in love with you," I murmured emphatically. The heat from my belly defied gravity and rushed to my already flushed face.

He didn't respond, and I pulled myself from his arms. He let me go. I rose and stepped away from him.

He stood behind me, and I moved toward the door.

"Josie."

"Yes."

"You didn't let me answer your question."

"Which question was that?"

"You asked me if you were the girl I loved best."

Now I didn't respond.

"You're not the girl I love best, Josie." My shoulders tightened against rejection. "You're the only girl I've ever loved," he finished quietly. My breath caught, not quite believing what I was hearing. "I know I'm moving too fast. I just can't seem to help myself. I watch you and listen to you and all I want to do is hold you and kiss you, and I…I'm sorry if I am pushing you…" His voice faded off. I didn't know how to respond. My heart had resumed its gallop, and I laid a hand against my heart to ease its rhythm. His hands were gentle on my shoulders, and he turned me to face him. I looked up into his face and was lost in what I knew was coming.

"I want you to come with me to San Diego. I want you to marry me. Now, next week, next month, whenever you're ready. You can go to school—or just play the piano all day. I don't care as long as you're happy and you're with me." Samuel's hands framed my face and his eyes pled with mine.

"First you tell me not to fall in love with you and five minutes later you ask me to marry you!" I blurted out. I was reeling, euphoria threatening to bubble up and carry me away while the weight of my responsibilities clawed in my throat.

"Oh Josie! I'm making a mess of this, aren't I? Please try to understand," Samuel groaned out. "I do want you to love me, Josie, because I love *you* so much it makes me ache. But if you're going to run away, loving me will just make you unhappy."

"I'm not the one leaving, Samuel! Why can't you stay here? Why do you have to leave?" I cried, sounding to my own ears like a very young child.

"For the same reasons I can't live on the reservation. My future isn't here. I have commitments that I have to keep to the Marines, to myself, even to my people. This isn't where I'm needed."

"I need you!" Again the child in me made her appeal.

"Then come with me."

"I can't go. I can't leave. I'm needed here."

"I need you," Samuel implored softly, repeating my words. "I need you because I love you."

I felt strangely detached, as if I was watching this scene play out in a Jane Austen novel. I felt grief, but it was a sympathetic grief, the kind of grief I often feel for someone else's pain—almost the way I'd felt at my mom's funeral—like it wasn't real yet. I stepped back from Samuel.

"I can't go with you, Samuel. I'm sorry." My voice sounded funny, and it felt heavy on my lips, similar to those awful dreams where you try to speak but can't because your mouth is suddenly unable to form the words.

Samuel's face tightened briefly like he was angry with me, and then it softened as he gazed down at me. His black eyes lingered on me for a moment more.

"I was afraid of that. I realized something tonight when we were listening to Beethoven. You're like the tonic note. You're the note that all the other notes revolve around and gravitate to. You're home. Without you, the song just might not be a song, your family might not be a family. That's what you're afraid of, isn't it? Who will step in and be the home base, the tonic note, if you go?" Samuel's eyes were bleak as he continued, his voice husky and low. "That's what you've been for me ever since I met you. The note I could hear, even when it wasn't being played. The one I've gravitated toward all these years." He leaned into me and kissed the top of my head gently. His hand cupped my cheek briefly, and his thumb traced my trembling lower lip.

"I love you, Josie," he said. Then he turned and walked out of my house.

The following morning his truck was gone, just as it had been the day after Daisy's colt was born all those years ago.

# 20. The Leading Note

SAMUEL HAD BEEN gone for two weeks, and I kept myself as busy as I could. I did all my regular duties—I cut hair, I taught piano lessons, and I ran several miles a day. In addition, I harvested what was left in my garden. Then I canned until the early morning hours, bottles of beets and tomatoes and green beans and pickles. I made lasagnas and casseroles and stuck them in the freezer in single serving sizes. When there was nothing left to bottle or freeze I alphabetized and reorganized my food storage. Then I decided the house was in need of a deep clean. I scrubbed blinds and washed curtains and steamed carpets. Then I started in on the yard. In other words…I was a mess.

I made myself listen to the music I loved as I worked. I would not be a coward anymore. If I acted like a lunatic, so be it! In my mind I raged and I vowed that Samuel's leaving would not make me resort to musical holocaust. I was done with that nonsense! I played Grieg until my fingers were stiff, and I worked with the frenzy of Balakirev's "Islamey" pounding out of the loud speakers. My dad came inside during that one and turned around and walked right back out again.

On day fifteen, I made a chocolate cake worthy of the record books. It was disgustingly rich and fattening, teetering several stories high, weighing more than I did, laden with thick cream cheese frosting, and sprinkled liberally with chocolate shavings. I sat down to eat it with a big fork and no bib. I dug in with a gusto seen only at those highly competitive hotdog eating contests where the tiny Asian girl kicks all the fat boys' butts.

"JOSIE JO JENSEN!" Louise and Tara stood at the kitchen door, shock and revulsion and maybe just a little envy in their faces. Brahms "Rhapsodie No. 2 in G Minor" was making my little kitchen shake. Eating cake to Brahms was a new experience for me. I liked it. I dug back in, ignoring them.

"Well Mom," I heard Tara say, "what should we do?!"

My Aunt Louise was a very practical woman. "If you can't beat 'em, join 'em!" she quoted cheerfully.

Before I knew it, Tara and Louise both had forks, too. They didn't seem to need bibs either. We ate, increasing our tempo as the music intensified.

"ENOUGH!" My dad stood in the doorway. He was good and mad, too. His sun-browned face was as ruddy as my favorite high heels.

"I sent you two in for an intervention! What is this?! Eater's Anonymous Gone Wild?"

"Aww, Daddy. Get a fork," I replied, barely breaking rhythm.

My dad strode over, took the fork from my hand and threw it, tines first, right into the wall. It stuck there, embedded and twanging like a sword at a medieval tournament. He pulled out my chair and grabbed me under the arms, pushing me out of the kitchen. I tried to take one last swipe at my cake, but he let out this in-human roar, and I abandoned all hope of making myself well and truly sick.

"Tara! Aunt Louise!" I shouted frantically. "I want you gone!! That's my cake! You can't have any more without me!"

My dad pushed me through the front door and out onto the porch, the screen banging behind him. I sunk to the porch swing, sullenly wiping chocolate crumbs from my mouth. My dad stomped back inside the house and suddenly the music pouring from every nook and cranny stopped abruptly. I heard him tell Louise he would call her later, and then the kitchen door banged, indicating my aunt's and Tara's departure. Good. They would have eaten that whole cake. I saw the way they were shoveling it in.

My dad lumbered out the front door and sank into the swing beside me. We rocked in silence for a while, my feet tucked under me, his feet in his old boots pushing back and forth, back and forth. There was a briskness to the night air that hadn't been there a week ago. The fall was in full thrust now, the leaves brilliant in their death throes. I felt the winter coming on. What had Samuel told me about Changing Woman and spring being a time of rebirth? Changing Woman ushered in the seasons, brought new life. This season wouldn't be ushering in a new life. My life would remain the same.

I suddenly felt very old and tired...and full. Shame and fatigue crashed over me, and I reached for my dad's hand. His palms were chapped and worn, and they were almost as brown as Samuel's. How I loved my father's hands! How I loved him. I had made my dad worry about me. I looked up into his face and saw the emotions I was feeling mirrored in his eyes. I brought his hand to my cheek and leaned my face into his palm. He cupped my face in that big palm, and his eyes filled with sadness.

"Josie Jo. What am I going to do without you?" His voice was gruff and tired.

"I'm not going anywhere, Dad," I said softly, my voice cracking a little as I thought of Samuel.

"Yes honey, you are." Emotion shook in his voice. "You are going to go. I won't let you stay here anymore."

I felt the bottom drop out of my chest and my heart plummet, crashing in tiny pieces at my feet. My hand, still holding onto his, fell to my lap.

"Don't you want me to stay with you, Dad?" My voice quavered, and I bit down on my bottom lip.

"Honey, it isn't about what I want anymore. I've let you take care of me and your brothers since you were nine years old! I just can't, in good conscience, let you do it anymore."

"Dad!" I cried out in denial. "You've taken care of all of us! I just did my part!"

"You did more than your part, Josie. You never were a child—not after your mother died. You always had this wisdom and maturity that made me feel like maybe it was okay to let you have your head. But your heart rules your head, Josie. You would stay here forever just to take care of me and stay true to a love that will never be returned. Not in this life. Kasey's gone, baby. He isn't coming back."

"I know that Dad, believe me, I do….I just don't know how to say goodbye this time. It isn't the same as it was with mom. I knew it was coming, even as young as I was. I knew she was going to die. I knew she was going to have to leave me. And I knew she expected me to go on living and loving and learning. I just don't know how to say goodbye this time," I repeated, and bit back a sob. My dad pulled me into his lap, just like he'd done over four years ago when he had found me in my mother's wedding dress.

He rocked me, rubbing my back, and smoothing my hair as I wept into his shirt. I thought I was done with tears. I didn't want to cry for Kasey anymore. But I knew I wasn't crying for him. I think I was crying out of self-pity, and that was even worse. I rubbed angrily at my cheeks and pressed my fists into my eyes, willing myself to stop.

"I'm in love with Samuel, Dad."

My dad's feet stuttered a little in their rhythm and then, with barely a hitch, resumed rocking.

"I thought maybe you might be. You've been acting so strange lately." He lifted me up off his chest so he could stare into my face. "But honey….isn't it a little too soon to know? He was only in town about a month."

I laughed out loud, the sound harsh and humorless. "I've loved Samuel since I was thirteen years old, Dad," I responded, staring back into his eyes, smiling at his shock. I patted his cheek, reassuring him. "Don't worry, Dad. It wasn't like that." I leaned back against him as I told him our love story. For that is what it was.

"Samuel and I met on the school bus. We were assigned to the same seat. For eight months we rode that bus back and forth from Nephi, and we slowly became friends. We fell in love to Beethoven and Shakespeare. We argued about books and bias and principles and passion. Our friendship was truly unique." I paused, gathering my thoughts. "I didn't know how special he was until he was gone. I didn't realize I was in love with him; I just wanted my friend back. And he was gone so long. He was gone long enough for me to believe he was never coming back—gone long enough for me to fall in love again. The second time, with Kasey, I was old enough to recognize it for what it was. I was smart enough to hold on tight, and that made losing Kasey even harder. I had been in love before, and I knew how it felt to lose it."

"I never knew anything about Samuel, Josie." My dad's voice was disbelieving.

"Nobody did, Dad. I didn't know how to share him. I thought if I talked about him it might make you nervous. He was eighteen years old, and half Navajo Indian to boot, which would have made you even more uncomfortable because you didn't know anything about him or where he came from. I was your thirteen-year-old daughter. Do you see the dilemma?"

"Yeah. Not an easy sell, huh?" my dad muttered and chuckled sympathetically at my long ago plight.

We rocked in silence once more.

"So what now, Josie?" my dad said slowly. "Where is he?"

My heart contracted fiercely. "I told him I couldn't marry him, Dad. This is my home. He's a Marine, and he has responsibilities. He can't stay, I can't go. That's all there is to it." My voice carried a bravado that was all pretend.

"Is it because of what you said before, Josie?" my dad asked gently.

"What do you mean?" I asked hesitantly, not following.

"When you said you didn't know how to say goodbye this time. Why can't you say goodbye? You just said yourself you loved Samuel even before you loved Kasey. Why would you give Samuel up when Kasey is lost to you, anyway?"

"I've never been the one to leave, Dad." I didn't know how to put any of this into words. My dad looked at me somberly, waiting. "Everyone has left *me*....Mom, Samuel, Kasey, even Sonja. *They* left. *I* stayed. I don't know how to leave. It just feels wrong. It feels wrong to leave Sonja, wrong to leave you, and it feels like a betrayal to let Kasey go."

"Don't you think he'd want you to?"

"I honestly don't know, Dad. Being left behind is horrible."

"Ah honey, you're not thinking straight." He was quiet for a moment, and I could tell he was struggling to say what came next. "And don't think I didn't know that some of your dilemma is leaving me. I won't have it, Josie. I am your father, and you are not going to stay here your whole life out of loyalty to me. Growing up and moving out is not the same thing as leaving, and you can't think of it like that." His voice was stern, and I decided not to argue with him.

"Do you think Kasey loved you, Josie?" my dad asked after a moment or two.

"I know he did, Dad," I answered, and felt myself getting choked up all over again.

"I know he did too, honey. But I don't know that you woulda been as happy as you coulda been if you'd married him."

I was stunned. "What are you talking about?" My dad had never expressed any misgivings to me about Kasey.

"Kasey was a good boy. He was everything a man wants for his daughter. He would have been loyal and hardworking. He would have been loving and faithful and committed to you all your life."

"But...?" There was a 'but' in this equation, and I couldn't even guess at what it might be.

"But you woulda been lonely deep down. You woulda been fightin' it all your life."

"I wasn't lonely with Kasey ever!" I argued sincerely.

"You woulda been, honey. You have this hunger for...for things that are a mystery to me. You've got music in your blood. You see beauty in things other people just take for granted. You need understanding, and, and...deep conversation, and someone who can keep up with that mind of yours! When you were just a little kid you would ask me the strangest things about God and the universe...things that would blow me away. One time, you were playing with this puzzle on the floor, and you couldn't have been more than five or six. You stopped and looked at the puzzle for a long time. Finally, you asked me, 'Dad, do you think this puzzle could ever put itself together if I shook it just right?' and I said, 'No honey, I don't think there's any chance of that.' Do you remember what you said then?"

I shook my head in soggy bewilderment.

"You said, 'Well, then I guess there's no way the world just happened by itself. Someone had to put it together.' I thought about that for two weeks! Hell, Josie...I don't understand half of what you say when you talk...and I know for dang sure poor Kasey Judd didn't have a clue most the time either."

I didn't know what to say. I just sat there with my mouth agape.

"You said you and Samuel fell in love to Beethoven and Shakespeare. That tells me somethin' right there." My dad leaned forward resting his hands on his knees, looking off into the moonlit sky. When he spoke again his voice was hoarse with emotion.

"What does Samuel do when you talk to him, Josie? What does he say? Does he hear you, the way none of us can?" My father gazed at me then, and there were tears in his eyes.

I brought my hands to my dad's face, deeply moved by his understanding. An understanding I had never given him credit for. Tears trickled down my cheeks and ran along my jaw, spilling down my neck.

"The way I see it Josie, is God knows your heart." My dad's eyes never left mine, and we both wept unabashedly. "He took Kasey away for a reason. Kasey was not for you. You would never have seen that on your own. I know you've thought God turned his back on you. But He's looked out for you, Josie. He's prepared someone for you who can love every part of you. I don't want you holdin' back all your life, sharing yourself in doses that people will accept. If Samuel is man enough to take it all, every last drop...then I hope you know where Samuel is...because I expect you to find him."

My dad stood up, walking toward the front door, the emotion of the evening getting to be too much for him. He needed his horses like I needed "Ode to Joy." His hand rested on the handle of the door, and he turned toward me again. "You have somethin' written on that wall in your room. I remember reading it....it's been there forever. It's scripture, I think...but you changed it a little. Somethin' about what true love is. If what you and Kasey had was true love Josie, he wouldn't want you to stay."

He sighed. He'd said what he'd needed to say and was eager for a cessation of conversation. "I love you, Josie. Don't stay out here too long. You've gotta do somethin' with that cake mess in there." He smiled at me and was gone, trudging through the house and out the back door, escaping to the solace of his equine friends.

"And true love suffereth long, and is kind; true love envieth not; true love vaunteth not itself, is not puffed up, doth not behave itself unseemly, seeketh not her own, is not easily provoked, thinketh no evil. True love rejoiceth not in iniquity, but rejoiceth in the truth; true love beareth all things, believeth all things, hopeth all things, endureth all things. True love never faileth..." I whispered the words to myself, and finally found a way to say goodbye.

Dear Samuel,

When two complimentary notes are sung or played in perfect pitch, a phenomenon occurs. The related frequencies actually split, like light through a prism, and overtones can be heard. It almost sounds like angel voices singing along in perfect harmony. They can be difficult to hear, they glimmer in and out like faulty radio reception, but they are there, a little miracle waiting to be discovered. The first time I heard them I thought of you and wanted to tell you that I'd finally heard it, a strain of God's music. When I'm with you a similar phenomenon occurs. I hear music.

Wherever you go, I'll follow. I just want to be with you. Will you marry me?

I love you,

Josie.

# Postlude

I MARRIED SAMUEL Yates a month later, the day after Thanksgiving, in the beautiful chapel in Levan. Samuel had a friend, a fellow Marine, who played the piano by ear. He was stateside for our wedding, and after listening to "Samuel's Song" a few times, was able to play it flawlessly as I walked down the aisle. Sonja was unable to attend, but she was there in that song. I remembered her words to me when I'd poured my heart and soul into it so long ago. *"If I didn't know better, Josie, I'd think you were in love."*

Samuel was breathtaking in his dress blues. Both of his grandmothers and his mother sat together and wept as a trio. My dad and Don Yates were equally overcome. The chapel was full of family and friends. Even Kasey's parents came. I like to think maybe he and my mother were able to attend, to step into our realm for a brief moment.

I wore my mother's dress and swept my hair up under the long white veil I'd wrapped myself in years ago on our front swing, mourning the bride I thought I'd never be.

Tara was my only bridesmaid, and she wore yellow and gleefully tossed pink rose petals as she pranced down the aisle. When it was time, I walked with measured steps toward Samuel, and his face reflected the joy that sang in my soul. He reached out for me, accepting my hand as my father gave me away and then slid into the pew next to Aunt Louise, letting her hold his hand while he cried, unashamed.

Samuel and I exchanged the simple vows of countless generations, but he surprised me by reciting the verses written on my Wall of Words from 1st Corinthians, Chapter 13. As he spoke the words with such heartfelt devotion, I marveled that God had brought me to this day and to this man.

When the words were spoken and we were pronounced man and wife, Samuel slid a ring on my finger, a stone to represent each of the four sacred mountains of the Navajo Nation embedded in the silver band. It had been his mother's ring, given to her by Samuel's father.

Then I kissed my husband for the first time. He whispered something in my ear, and I looked into his face as he repeated the word softly.

"It is my Navajo name."

I touched his face reverently.

"You are my wife, and the closest person to me. You should know my name because it is yours now as well."

My heart was so full I couldn't speak.

"I have a Navajo name for you too, Josie. I gave it to you long ago. My *Chitasie*," Samuel murmured.

"What does it mean?"

"Teacher."

# Author's Note

LIKE THE MAIN character in my book, I grew up in Levan, Utah. My family moved there when I was just shy of six years old. We didn't have any family in Levan, and it was a series of strange coincidence that brought us there. Levan is a great little place, full of wonderful people, and it holds a special place in my heart. There really is a beautiful old church there, built early in the 1900's. There really was a 'country mall' and Pete's bar. There actually was a Shepherd's Mercantile and an old school. The Levan Cemetery does sit about a half mile north of Tuckaway Hill—and many of the descriptions are very accurate.

Every author has to write about what they know, and though I used many of the last names that you'll still find in Levan, I tried very hard to get the feel of the people and the place without using actual people or their names for my story. Any similarities are simply coincidence and were not intended to personify any real living person or persons. The events and people described in this book are completely fictitious.

The stories and legends of the Navajo and Native American people are retold with the utmost respect and no copyright infringement was intended. The song used in the book is not an actual Navajo song, though I tried to contain the sentiment of many of their ancient songs. I have been fascinated by the Native American culture for many years. As a second grade teacher I spent an entire quarter on Native American studies, and my students and I fell in love.

A wise person once told me that if we don't know each other's stories, how can we learn to respect and love one another? I have found this to be true—the more I understand a culture or a people, the more I grow to love them. Any mistakes in the retelling of the stories are my own, and any possible misrepresentations about the people or the culture were not intended. I did my absolute best to simply educate my readers about a fascinating portion of our combined American Heritage that is mostly unknown. There really were Navajo Code Talkers. Their story is incredible. My hope is that I inspire an interest in the Navajo people that will engender respect and further study. There are many websites and books out there that are worthy of the topic.

To the United States Marine Corp: Words aren't enough! Thank you for who you are and what you do. I believe there are many lives you save, not just in the fields of battle, but within your own ranks. In my book, the Marine Corp gave Samuel a home and something to believe in. In the USMC he found his purpose. I know that is the case with many young men. And again, any mistakes or mischaracterizations about the Marine Corp or its procedures and history are my own and were unintended.

Finally, the music Josie loved to play and listen to does indeed exist. I love so many of the great composers and sought to bring them and their music to life in my book. I highly recommend the book '*Spiritual Lives of the Great Composers*' by Patrick Kavanaugh, and encourage you to check it out. Try listening to some of the music mentioned in my story as well. I believe many of these compositions are life altering.

I hope you enjoyed reading *Running Barefoot* as much as I loved writing it.

Amy Harmon.

# About the Author

AMY HARMON KNEW at an early age that writing was something she wanted to do–and she divided her time between writing songs and stories as she grew. Having grown up in the middle of wheat fields without a television, with only her books and her siblings to entertain her, she developed a strong sense of what made a good story. Amy Harmon has been a motivational speaker, a grade school teacher, a junior high teacher, a home school mom, and a member of the Grammy Award winning Saints Unified Voices Choir, directed by Gladys Knight. She released a Christian Blues CD in 2007 called "What I Know"–also available on Amazon and wherever digital music is sold. Her first two books, "Running Barefoot" and "Slow Dance in Purgatory" are rich with humor, heart, and fast paced story telling.

For more information about Amy and her books, visit:

http://www.authoramyharmon.com/
https://www.facebook.com/authoramyharmon
http://www.goodreads.com/author/show/5829056.Amy_Harmon
https://twitter.com/aharmon_author

Made in United States
Troutdale, OR
11/30/2024